ALSO BY ELISA A. BONNIN

DAUNTLESS

STOLEN CITY

STOLEN CITY

ELISA A. BONNIN

Swoon
READS

SWOON READS

NEW YORK

A FEIWEL AND FRIENDS BOOK
An imprint of Feiwel and Friends and Macmillan Publishing Group, LLC
120 Broadway, New York, NY 10271 • fiercereads.com
Copyright © 2022 by Elisa A. Bonnin. All rights reserved.

Our books may be purchased in bulk for promotional, educational, or business
use. Please contact your local bookseller or the Macmillan Corporate and
Premium Sales Department at (800) 221-7945 ext. 5442 or by email at
MacmillanSpecialMarkets@macmillan.com.

Library of Congress Cataloging-in-Publication Data

Names: Bonnin, Elisa A., author.
Title: Stolen city / Elisa A. Bonnin.
Description: First edition. | New York : Swoon Reads, 2022. | Audience:
    Ages 14–18. | Audience: Grades 10–12. | Summary: When twin thieves,
    Arian and Cavar, attempt to pull off a daring heist, they find themselves
    embroiled in court politics and family secrets, making their mission more
    than just another artifact theft.
Identifiers: LCCN 2022010080 | ISBN 9781250795632 (hardcover)
Subjects: CYAC: Twins—Fiction. | Brothers and sisters—Fiction. |
    Stealing—Fiction | Fantasy. | LCGFT: Fantasy fiction.
Classification: LCC PZ7.1.B6665 St 2022 | DDC [Fic]—dc23
LC record available at https://lccn.loc.gov/2022010080

First edition, 2022
Book design by Mallory Grigg
Feiwel and Friends logo designed by Filomena Tuosto
Printed in the United States of America by Lakeside Book Company,
Harrisonburg, Virginia

ISBN 9781250795632 (hardcover)

10 9 8 7 6 5 4 3 2 1

To Tweety, for all our daydreams.

PART ONE

KINESIS

CHAPTER 1

CAVAR

THE HUMMINGBIRD CAFÉ WAS ONE OF THOSE FEW LEITHONIAN establishments that boasted a long tenure, aided mostly by the fact that they had surrendered to Aelrian rule almost the very day it had been declared. As an outsider, Cavar didn't feel qualified to judge their behavior, but the shop had flourished since the occupation, becoming a favorite of the citizens of the Imperial Quarter. And the coffee was quite good. It was worth the glare his companion shot him as he stood underneath an awning just outside the shop, sipping at the paper cup he'd bought to go.

Outside, dusk was falling over the city, the thin sliver of sky visible through the gaps in the rooftops painted with orange and violet and gold. At street level, the shadows were deep enough that the lamps had been lit, dappling the narrow streets in alternating swaths of light and shadow. An island city-state, Leithon hadn't had much room to expand outward, not without trampling over what little farmland they had. So, over the centuries, the city had expanded *up*. It became a maze of looming buildings and narrow streets, divided by two large thoroughfares. The Road of Law, which led from the docks at the southern end of the city to the Bastion, the enormous stone complex at the north of the city that was the seat of government and military power, and the Road of Shadows, the east-west thoroughfare that led from the land gate to what was left of the Spire. Outside of those roads, whether poor area or Imperial Quarter, the view from the street was mostly the same. Tall buildings of varying degrees of finery, stretching up and up until only the faintest gleam of sky could be seen from between them, rooftops crisscrossed by rickety-looking bridges that only the very brave or the very foolish used and everyone else avoided.

In Leithon, even before the occupation, it was a generally held truth that respectable business only occurred close to the ground.

But Cavar wasn't interested in respectable business. And he'd had a tip from a reliable source that if he kept his eyes turned skyward, he might find something worth seeing.

"I don't understand why we're here," his companion remarked, leaning against the wall beside him and folding her arms across her chest. Linna had declined to buy anything inside the shop, which Cavar thought was poor camouflage on her part. Like him, she was dressed like a merchant, silk shirt and fine trousers and embroidered coat pulled close around her to protect herself from the damp chill of a Leithonian night. Her long, dark hair was pinned up in a severe bun, and her dark eyes glittered from behind the fake glasses she wore to make herself seem more respectable. She was an even worse fit for the Imperial Quarter than Cavar, with his black hair and light brown skin, but the city's Aelrian rulers looked favorably on well-dressed foreigners.

They certainly counted.

To a casual eye, they blended in perfectly with the evening scenery. Only their shoes—soft, well-worn leather boots—and the knives concealed inside the sleeves of their coats and hidden pockets of their clothing suggested that they were anything other than what they claimed to be. That they had any other motive for being here tonight.

"I thought I'd see the city," Cavar said with a smile, swirling the coffee around in his cup before taking another sip. "Get a feel for the place before we begin."

Linna snorted. "For a Weaver, you're a bad liar. Tell me what this has to do with finding the Star."

Possibly everything, Cavar thought, remembering what his

mother had told him before he left the Wastes. Since taking on the position of the First Weaver, Reiva eth'Nivear had become a harder and harder person to read, but she'd been his mother again when she pulled him aside the night he left and told him who he should find in Leithon. She'd called it a favor for a friend, a personal request separate from his mission, but Cavar had a feeling that if things went well, he could kill two birds with one stone.

"We're going to need help if we're going to reclaim the Star," he told Linna. He had to tell her *something*, but the details of his plan were best saved until he had confirmation. Until he knew that they were really what he was looking for. "I thought we could hire on some local color."

Linna did not look impressed. "The underground, in this city?" she asked, her nose wrinkling in derision. "It's a shadow of its former self, except for the Resistance. And you're out of your mind if you think the Resistance would let you walk away from here with an artifact like the Star."

"I wasn't talking about the Resistance," Cavar murmured, turning his eyes back up to the rooftops. Above, the sky was darkening, shadows replacing orange and gold. The first stars would come out soon. He rolled his stiff shoulders, taking another sip from his cup.

Any minute now.

There was a sudden blur of motion. Two figures darted across the wooden planks that spanned the roof, so quickly that no one would have been able to see them unless they were looking up just as Cavar and Linna were. From this distance, it was impossible to pick out any details, only that there were two of them, moving quickly, heading west over the roofs.

"What was that?" Linna asked, puzzled. "I thought the rooftop paths in the Imperial Quarter were closed. They're too well guarded."

Cavar grinned. Maybe it was the coffee, or maybe it was the

sudden charge in the air, but he couldn't help the thrill of excitement that ran through him then. His informant had been right. He crushed the empty cup in his hand, tossing it into a nearby wastebasket.

"Apparently nobody told them that."

A clamor rose from the east, a discordant alarm. The people in the streets looked up, but of course there was nothing more to see. Cavar slipped his hands into his pockets and started to walk, thinking. The Imperials would be out in force. A theft in the maximum-security vault of the First Aelrian Bank wasn't something they could overlook. He had to catch them first.

If they were heading west, they would have to get down off the rooftops to cross the Road of Law. That would be where their pursuers would try to catch them, and if Cavar was lucky, that was where he would meet them too.

Linna hurried to catch up with him, a shadow at his side. Together, they cut through Leithon's evening crowds, its Imperial citizens stopping to murmur at each other in wonder and confusion at the rising alarms. She didn't try to stop him, but he could hear the impatience in her voice when she spoke up.

"You can't tell me you mean to go after them. We'll walk right into an Imperial patrol."

"Aren't you curious how they'll get out of that?" Cavar asked, grinning.

"I'm more concerned with keeping us *out* of an Imperial prison."

"It's a little too late for that, isn't it? After all, we're here to take their most prized artifact."

Linna rolled her eyes. "And *those* are the thieves you want to hire to help us do it? Do you even know a thing about them?"

He knew a few things, thanks to his mother. But he couldn't blame Linna for her skepticism.

The Athensor twins, the last children of eth'Akari.

He felt a shiver run down his spine, a flutter of excitement in his belly.

It was said that the Weavers were the agents of the world's fate, weaving its loose threads together to keep them from getting tangled. But in that moment, Cavar felt as if he had been woven into the tapestry, by some hand other than his own. As if fate had gotten tired of their hubris and had decided to show the world that she could make even a Weaver dance on her strings.

It was an utterly exhilarating feeling, and Cavar couldn't wait to see what would happen next.

CHAPTER 2

ARIAN

ARIAN RACED ACROSS THE ROOFTOP PATHS, HER HEART POUND-
ing with the thrill of the chase. Alarms rose up around her, the
entire Imperial Quarter working itself into a frenzy. She knew that
she should have been upset about that, should have been upset
that they had tripped the bank's security at all, but the sound of the
alarms made her lips curl back into a grin.

It had been a long time since she had been able to stretch her
muscles like this. A long time since she had been able to properly *run*.

She let her hand drop to the pouch at her waist, where their cargo
rested. Breathless, she looked over her shoulder at her brother.

"You *had* to go back for that, didn't you?"

Liam was out of breath, sweat plastering his dark hair to his
forehead. Even after three years, he still had trouble keeping up
with her. His pace probably wasn't helped by the piece of stone he'd
hung around his neck, its carved face peeking out from where he
was using one hand to press it firmly against his chest.

"Mena's Amulet"—he gasped, speaking the words between
puffs of air "—is an immensely—valuable artifact—"

"You say that about all of them." A gap between rooftops
appeared ahead, narrow enough to jump over. She stopped talking
to focus, kicking off the ground and clearing the gap easily. Liam
stumbled as he landed on the other side. His form, which had never
been all that great to begin with, was not helped by the fact that he
still hadn't let go of the damn amulet.

"Put it in your pocket," Arian said as Liam pushed himself up off
the ground and started running again.

"Then it's useless!"

"It's useless *now!*" she said, but she knew better than to argue. Liam treated magical artifacts like they were children. Arian, on the other hand, had a slightly more tempered view. They were valuable pieces of cargo, but not worth their hides. And if they had survived centuries, surely they could handle being shoved into a pocket.

At the edge of the rooftop, she drew up short, catching her breath. The wind whipped strands of pale, sweat-soaked hair out of her face, cooling her overheated skin. Beside her, Liam drew to a grateful stop, chest pumping like a bellows as he rested his hands on his knees.

"Why are we—stopping?" he asked between breaths. Behind them, the alarm was still ringing. Stopping was a risk, especially in the Imperial Quarter, where the rooftop paths had fallen out of the underground's control and no one knew exactly which routes the Imperials had compromised, but Arian had a feeling that pursuit on the rooftops wasn't their biggest problem. The Imperials didn't have to catch them right away; they only had to make sure that they couldn't leave the Quarter.

And if Arian were a lazy, greedy little Imperial, she wouldn't bother chasing them on the roofs. Instead, she'd wait for them where the rooftop paths were nonexistent.

The Road of Law.

The open sky above the Road of Law taunted her, wide enough that there was no way of crossing it unless one could fly. Bridges never lasted very long when they were made above the Roads of Law and Shadows. The thoroughfares were too easy to patrol, and even before occupation, Leithon's police had been quick to cut down any they could find.

If Arian were an Imperial, she would head them off at the road.

She grinned, letting her hand fall again on the pouch at her waist, on the little ink-filled vial that was going to buy them enough food and supplies to last the rest of the year. She didn't much care about magic, but it was still a valuable artifact. A valuable artifact they had snatched out of the vaults of the Aelrian bank, right underneath the Imperials' noses.

Arian would be damned if she let them catch her and take it back.

"We're gonna run into a problem," she told her brother, inclining her head toward that empty space.

Liam straightened up, finally releasing his hold on that damn amulet. It better have been worth it, Arian thought, because if that thing was going to get them killed—

"You ever figure out how to make people fly?" Arian asked.

"You know that's impossible," Liam said. "Come on, even *you* were there for those lessons. I don't have the power to move that much air. Now, the two of us together . . ."

He trailed off, which Arian was grateful for. She didn't want to hear him talk about how much her potential was wasted, how she should have stuck with her magical training instead of dropping out and running away from home. None of that mattered anymore.

"We don't need to fly to trick Imperials," she said, walking to the edge of the rooftop. She could see Imperial guards running in the street below, and took a step back out of view in case one of them got smart enough to look up. This particular gap was wide enough that they needed a bridge, and unless the Imperials had gotten to this route, there should be a temporary one stashed in a small hidey-hole in one of the attics around them.

She smiled.

"We just need to be smarter than them."

GETTING ON AND OFF THE ROOFTOP PATHS MEANT USING ONE OF a number of access points, hidden staircases and ladders in varying degrees of repair and equally varying levels of terror. The ladder that Arian found hadn't been in good shape before the occupation, and after the occupation it was more rust than steel. But it was in a less-populated section of the Quarter, one that the Imperials hadn't yet fully expanded into, and because of that, it had been left alone.

By the time she reached the ground, her heart was pounding again, the rush of adrenaline making her feel sharp and alive. Above, the buildings of Leithon still pressed in on her, but she wasn't far from the Road of Law, and she knew that as soon as she burst onto the main throughfare, the Imperials would be on her.

Good. It was time to give them a show.

Arian pulled up the hood of her coat, tugging it over her pale blond hair. And then she took off at a run, bursting out of the narrow alley and into the orange light of fading day. The sky yawned open overhead, the paved road filled with end-of-day traffic in Leithon. Carts and carriages, streams of people walking home or to nights out or pausing to buy dinner at the food stalls that lined both sides of the road, two deep in some places. And patrols, of course.

Arian felt another jolt in her heart as first of the patrols spotted her, although she wasn't trying very hard to stay hidden. She heard one of them shout, a voice ringing in the square before they all took off running, heading toward her. Arian ran into the road, ducking out of the way of a carriage, then changed direction and plunged, heart in her throat, into a procession of white-robed penitents walking the Road of Law as part of their evening prayer. There were shouts of alarm as she tore through the group, shoving aside Imperial and Leithonian alike and making some drop their candles and prayer beads, but the diversion had the intended effect. The Imperials pursuing her hesitated, letting her burst through the group and into the nest of alleys on the other side of the road.

A handful still pursued her. She could hear their footsteps behind her as she darted through darkened alleyways. It took her eyes a moment to adjust to the change, heading from bright sunlight into darkness, but Arian knew this city like she knew her name. She could be blindfolded, and she would still know where to run.

Her Imperial pursuers didn't have that advantage. And that was why Arian was able to dart into an alley so narrow that she was practically wedged in, breathing in the foul, stagnant air while her pursuers ran right on, screaming at her to stop.

They didn't see her at all, and she was dizzy and breathless with relief, bright flashes gathering in her field of vision until she closed her eyes and gulped down huge breaths of air.

Her hand dropped to the pouch at her side, feeling for the vial. It was still intact. It had been a gamble taking it with her, but one that had paid off.

Now, if Liam made it out alive, they could count this as another win for the family business.

Arian waited until the sounds of pursuit dwindled down to nothing, then waited thirty slow counts more. When she was certain she wouldn't be followed, she slipped out of the alley, grimacing as she pulled some of the grime on the walls away with her.

She'd done her job. Now it was time to go find her brother.

CHAPTER 3

LIAM

ALL THINGS CONSIDERED, LIAM HAD THE EASY JOB.

It was Arian who had to lead on the Imperial patrols, pulling death-defying stunts to get across the Road of Law with her life and their cargo intact.

Liam just had to pull off a little bit of smoke and mirrors to get himself safely across while Arian kept the guards busy. Well, himself and his ill-gotten gains.

He ran his thumb over the smooth surface of the amulet, feeling a flash of guilt for having gone back for it. It hadn't been their target. They didn't have a buyer for it, and in Arian's mind, it was just going to take up space in their hideout until they could find someone willing to buy it or Liam could put it to good use. Arian didn't always see the potential such things had for research. But if Liam was right about what it was, about what it could do, it would only be an asset to them moving forward.

The problem, of course, was that the amulet wasn't much use to him *now*. And an artifact that might or might not be able to nullify magic wasn't going to help him cross a road.

For that, he needed his sister's help.

While Arian ran off to distract the guards, Liam waited in the shadows just at the edge of the Road of Law. And when she dashed across the street, drawing every eye along with her, he focused his mind on a pinpoint on the other side of the city, a single copper coin. He had dropped it through a gap in the boarded-up windows of a shack that hugged the stone buildings on the other side of the Road from him. Before the occupation, it had been a bakery, one that Liam still remembered fondly.

Now it was a flammable relic, another piece of the city to burn.

He'd expended a bit of his will into the coin, a preplanned distraction in case anything went wrong and they needed to divert Imperial attention. He'd hoped that he wouldn't have to use it. The Empire's ban on the practice of magic in Leithon meant that every public use of magic risked his and Arian's discovery, and he really didn't want to destroy more of the past than he had to.

But . . . well. He touched the amulet again, the stone cool and heavy against his chest.

He'd gotten greedy. Arian would be the first to tell him to take responsibility.

Liam poured his will into the coin, letting out a shuddering breath as he felt his body go cold, all the warmth washing out of him like water through a sieve. His breath puffed in the air, even though the night wasn't that cold. Magic always had a cost, even the most minor use of it. He clenched his jaw tight against his chattering teeth as, on the other side of the street, a building went up in flames.

People screamed. The old bakery wasn't on the Road itself, but it was close enough that a fire sent the nearest stall owners into a frenzy. They rushed to get out of the way in case their wooden stalls were next. The people on the street ran to the other side of the road, clogging traffic. And the other half of the Imperial patrol, the one that had been scouting the area for Liam, ran in that direction shouting about fire.

It was a risk, but a calculated one. The patrol probably already knew that mages were involved. After all, ordinary thieves didn't simply break into the colony's most secure bank. They'd be on the alert for any sign. And indeed, as they ran across the street to the source of the fire, Liam saw that one of the patrol members wore silver trim on their uniform. An Imperial magebreaker.

He repressed a shudder as the magebreaker passed by, his mind, as always, threatening to take him back to the day of the occupation, the day of blood and pain. If he let himself be caught here, that day wouldn't just be a memory. So as the patrol swept past, shoving people out of the way and clearing a perimeter around the burning building, Liam fought to keep from showing any evidence of discomfort as he stepped out into the street. He joined the flow of panicked citizens, the boundaries between Leithonian and Imperial broken in the face of an indiscriminate threat, and let the crowd conceal him as he edged his way subtly toward the other side. He was helped by the fact that, unlike Arian, who had inherited their father's pale blond hair and unplaceable features, Liam resembled their mother. Dark hair and glittering dark eyes, features that were as Leithonian as the Spire was—as the Spire had been. Nobody would look at him twice in this city.

He stepped into the narrow paths on the other side of the street and made sure to look like he was in a hurry to get away from the fire, maintaining a worried expression and a quick pace until he had gone a few blocks and was certain that no one was chasing him. Only then did he allow himself to slow down, although he couldn't relax. There was a tight knot of anxiety in his stomach, a sour taste in his mouth. He remembered the magebreaker, and his heartbeat quickened.

Close. Too close. If they'd found Arian—

—but Arian hadn't used magic in years. Even if she had the potential, it had been long enough that not even a magebreaker would be able to sense it on her. Liam hoped.

Well, prayed. Or he might have, if he thought that there was anything left to pray to.

With each step, he tried to shake off his nerves. He would never be used to this, the rush of fear after each job that left him jittery and uncertain. He'd never be like Arian, who reveled in danger and fear.

He found a hidden stairwell and made the long climb up to their meeting place, his heart sinking when he emerged on the twilit rooftop and didn't see Arian there. But then she stepped out of the shadow of a building and Liam felt a deep relief. He swallowed hard to keep it out of his face and voice, because he knew that Arian didn't like it when he got sentimental.

"They sent out a magebreaker," he blurted instead as she walked up to him.

Arian stopped walking, arching her brow. "We robbed *the bank*. What did you think they were going to do?"

"I—"

Liam hesitated, opening his mouth and then shutting it again. Arian was right. He should have known when they triggered the alarm what that would mean. If he said anything now, he'd only be proving one of her many points. That he wasn't committed, that he thought this was a game, that he did things without understanding the consequences. He'd heard it all before.

"Should we go back to the hideout?" he asked instead. "Security's going to get tighter tonight."

"That's the most sensible thing you've said all day," said Arian.

She began to walk away. Liam followed, but froze when Arian stopped suddenly, every muscle in her body going tense. With a flick of her wrists, gleaming knives fell into both her hands.

Something moved up ahead. A young man approached them from around an old tower, a foreign merchant from the looks of him, although no foreign merchant would ever find their way up here with such ease. He had his hands upraised to show that he meant no harm, an easy smile on his face. A stern-looking woman followed along behind him, her eyes narrowing in a glare as she eyed the two of them.

Arian sank deeper into her stance, raising her knives. "Who the hell are you?"

The young man cocked his head to the side like a curious bird, his eyes roving over Arian and then Liam behind her. Liam felt those eyes rest a few seconds too long on the amulet that hung over his chest, and he resisted the urge to cover it with his hand, his mind scrambling to piece together a counterspell in case he attacked. But the stranger's bright smile didn't fade as he looked back at Arian.

"You're the twins of eth'Akari, aren't you? The children of Rinu eth'Akari and Catherina Athensor? I'm Cavar eth'Nivear. A Weaver. I have a job for you."

CHAPTER 4

ARIAN

UNDER THE CIRCUMSTANCES, THEY HAD LITTLE CHOICE BUT TO take the Weavers to the ossuary, a fact that chafed at Arian as she and Liam led them through damp, narrow passageways away from the city above and into the maze of catacombs lurking beneath.

The ossuary was a safehouse that Liam and Arian had constructed in the early days of their operation, hidden underneath the city. Its name wasn't purely aesthetic. It had, in the far reaches of the city's past, once served as a boneyard, a final resting place for the elite. But that had been centuries ago, and the place was forgotten now. Their section of it was protected by a handful of magical wards of Liam's own invention. It was their safest stronghold, but that didn't make it a pleasant place to be.

They'd done what they could to make it habitable. Between Liam's magic and Arian's more practical skills, they had carved out spaces of their own from the old monks' living area, bedrooms, a pantry, a storage room where some of their more valuable contraband rested, and a living and dining area complete with a fireplace.

It would almost have been comfortable. If not for the dead.

The four of them sat around a wooden table in the living area, mugs of steaming tea on the tabletop between them. Arian ignored her own drink, leaning back in her seat and studying their guests. Linna, like Arian, hadn't touched her mug. She looked distinctly unimpressed with their accommodations, glaring daggers at them from the other side of the table. Cavar, however, held his mug cradled in both hands, looking down at it as if he could find the words he wanted in the steam that curled over the surface of the drink.

"I'm not sure how much you know about the Weavers—"

"We know enough," said Arian.

"Right," Cavar said, with a faint smile. "Rinu would have told you."

Arian and Liam's father, Rinu eth'Akari, hadn't told them anything, but Arian wasn't going to tell Cavar that. The mention of his name set off a wave of uncomfortable emotions inside her, emotions she immediately squashed. The last time they had seen him, they had been fourteen. It had been only four months before the occupation, but they hadn't known *that* at the time.

One big happy family. His visit had even convinced her to come home.

She wanted to laugh, thinking back to it. Because four months later, their whole world had changed, and Rinu eth'Akari had vanished.

She was grateful when Liam spoke up, because it meant that she didn't have to. She gulped down a sip of too-hot tea, scalding the roof of her mouth while Liam answered.

"We know the relevant information," he said. The Weavers were an organization that meddled endlessly with world politics, magic, and gods only knew what else. They lived out in the wilderness, between Paran and Arvuan, and if rumors were to be believed, they had their fingers in every shady deal in the world. They'd been credited with the assassinations of kings and queens, the toppling of nations, and once, the crippling of an entire region's copper industry. Arian didn't know how much of that was true. She *did* know that the Weavers couldn't be hired. They worked only for themselves and served their own agendas.

And they hadn't saved Leithon from the Empire, so they were basically worthless.

Cavar sipped at his tea. "Well, that should make this easier, at least. I'm looking for an artifact, one of great significance to the First Weaver."

"You believe the artifact is somewhere in this city?" Liam asked.

"I do," said Cavar.

"What makes you think that?"

Arian raised her mug to her mouth, watching Cavar as she waited for his answer.

"Because prior to Imperial occupation, the artifact was last known to be in the possession of the Speaker of the Arcanum," Cavar said. He hesitated, and then added, "Your mother. Catherina Athensor."

Arian lowered her cup without taking a sip. She set it on the table, pushing it away from her. Beside her, Liam's expression darkened, his eyes breaking away from Cavar's face. He was tense. She would have bet anything that his hands were clenched under the table. She reached out with her foot, nudging him lightly in the leg. Liam didn't jerk at the touch, but he did look up again.

"Kuthil's Star."

"You know it?" Cavar asked.

Liam nodded. "Of course," he said. "It's a magical repository. In the right hands, it can be used to gradually store a portion of a mage's power, giving them a source of power that they can tap into in an emergency. In the wrong hands . . ." He trailed off.

Cavar gave him an apologetic smile. "It's the wrong hands our society is mostly concerned with."

"Yes," Liam said. "That would make sense."

"Care to clue me in?" Arian asked. She tried to appear uninterested, but she couldn't quite keep the tremor out of her voice.

"It steals souls," Cavar said, ignoring the look of disapproval that Linna shot him. "Just as it can take some of a mage's power and store it for a later time, it can rip the life force out of living flesh, using that as a source of power."

"That's what happened to the man who tried to steal it from the Weavers, isn't it?" Liam asked. "Kesi eth'Akari."

Cavar nodded. "Kesi stole the Star from us and brought it here. His goal, as far as we are aware, was to use the Star to absorb a portion of the power from the Arcanum, where the world's magic naturally gathers. But your mother turned it against him, using the Star to capture *his* soul. I think that's actually how your parents met."

"I've heard a portion of this story," Liam said. "You want us to steal the Star back for you?"

"We'll help, of course," said Cavar. "Reclaiming the Star was originally our mission. But magical artifacts are your area of expertise, and we don't have as strong of a foothold in occupied Leithon as we would like. We'd like to hire you on to assist us."

Linna's expression could have soured milk. It told Arian exactly whose idea enlisting them was, and made her wonder if Cavar had asked her to let him do the talking.

Liam frowned, thinking it through. "It won't be easy. The Star will be in the vaults at the heart of the Bastion. No one's ever broken into it."

"Then find a way," Linna said, acid in her voice. "Or can't you even handle that?"

Arian was sorely tempted to kick her in the shins. She refrained, in part because Liam had insisted they be *professional* about this.

"We're talking about the damned *Bastion* here," Arian said. "It's not exactly a walk in the park. It's as old as the Spire—"

"Which has, demonstrably, been broken." Linna pushed her chair away from the table and began to get up. "Cavar, this is wasting our time. We should go—"

Cavar reached out, grabbing Linna by the arm and holding her there. "A moment more, please, Linna. I know it will be difficult. We aren't completely without resources. We would be happy to help. And of course, you'll be rewarded. Will you take this job?"

Arian glanced at her brother. A look passed between them, laced with meaning.

Liam nodded. "We'll do it. I'm not sure how yet, but we'll find a way. I think our first step should be to gather information. Arian, can you—?"

"Yeah," said Arian, not waiting for him to finish. She had already gotten to her feet. "Lyndon will be wanting to know about the bank job anyway. I'll take him with me." She gestured at Cavar with her thumb. "You can babysit the nasty one."

"Lyndon?" Cavar asked.

"Unofficial head of Leithon's Resistance." Arian shrugged. "If there's any business going on in this town, he knows about it. And if someone's come up with a way to get into the Bastion, he'll know about it too." She turned to Linna. "It looks like we'll be working together for a little bit. If you want to stay down here, you can pick out any of the empty rooms to bunk in." She grinned. "Unless your kind prefers coffins? Because that can be arranged."

"Arian," Liam said. "Be *nice*."

"I *am* being nice," said Arian, but she relented. She needed to go outside anyway. All this talk about her parents made the room feel entirely too close, the weight of the air crushing. She nodded at Cavar. "Come with me. I'm putting you to work."

ARIAN'S BAD MOOD LASTED THE ENTIRETY OF THE WALK OUT OF the ossuary, and it was all she could do to keep her hands to herself and her hood up, eyes lowered to the street below. In the old days she could have taken her temper out on a few sandwich boards, could have ranted about whatever was bothering her to any street vendor who would listen. But she couldn't do that anymore, because doing that would attract attention, and *attention*, in Empire-occupied Leithon, was deadly.

The ossuary's one weakness as a safehouse was that it was just off the Road of Shadows, which meant that the closest accessway to the rooftop paths was several blocks away. That meant dodging Imperial patrols, which was an easier task on some days than on others. *Technically*, they weren't doing anything illegal, just walking through the streets. But there had been a bank robbery in the Imperial Quarter today, and the guards would be angry. They took that anger out on Leithonian hides, and this wasn't an area where anyone too important to bother would live.

So, she kept her head down and shoulders slumped as they moved past a group of violet-uniformed Imperials, the fall of her coat hiding her knives from view. Out of the corner of her eye, she saw Cavar doing the same, looking appropriately humble until the patrol had passed. Arian had just started to feel relieved when a second patrol rounded the corner, heading straight for them.

She stopped walking, clenching her jaw. No rest for the wicked.

"How are you at acting?" she asked, drawing up beside Cavar.

"It's been a while, but I can take on a role fairly well," Cavar said. "Why?"

She jerked her chin toward the approaching patrol. "Better brush off the rust. We have company."

CHAPTER 5

CAVAR

CAVAR EYED THE IMPERIAL SOLDIERS AS THEY APPROACHED, drawing in a slow breath through his teeth. There were three of them, all young men, none particularly high-ranked. They looked like trouble.

Beside him, Arian tensed. She stepped back, her hand finding his and gripping it tightly.

"Act like we're courting," she said, bowing her head and turning her face away from the men.

Cavar squeezed Arian's hand to show that he understood, tilting his face up toward the nearest soldier with some defiance.

The soldier's eyes narrowed, his mouth pulling into a sneer.

"What's the matter, foreigner?" he asked. "You lost?"

Cavar was prepared to show deference by lowering his gaze, to bow and scrape until the soldiers let them through. But the look in the soldier's eye stopped him, a look of malice and rage. The theft at the bank today had the entire Imperial contingent up in arms. There were probably more than a few guards out there in bad moods. But this one was dangerous.

He was out for blood, and he wasn't going to rest until he had it. Cavar had to make it not worth their while.

Instead of bowing his head, he drew himself up straighter, narrowing his eyes.

"Not at all," he said. "I know exactly where I'm going. Unfortunately, you seem to be in my way."

Behind him, he heard Arian suck in a breath. Cavar tightened his grip on her hand as the soldier stepped forward, scowling and meeting his eyes.

It was a calculated gamble. There weren't many people who would speak with that sort of confidence in Imperial-occupied Leithon, not many people whose voices carried markers of affluence and significance outside of the Imperial Quarter. But for the Empire to hold on to Leithon, it couldn't afford to alienate its high-class visitors, and its soldiers would know not to mess with anyone who looked like they had money and power.

He hoped.

"What did you say, bastard?"

Cavar did not look away. "You heard what I said." He stared down the bridge of his nose at the soldier, his voice cold enough to freeze fire. "Move. Or I will move you."

"Where do you get off—?" the soldier asked, clenching his hand into a fist. For a second, Cavar thought he had miscalculated. His hand twitched toward one of his concealed knives—would killing an Imperial officer hurt their cause, or should he just take the beating? He couldn't look at Arian to check. There was no time.

The soldier raised his hand. Cavar's breath caught. He reached for the knife.

One of the other soldiers stepped forward, grabbing his companion's arm before he could swing.

"Jem, wait!" he said, pulling him back. He looked at Cavar, his gaze wary and calculating. "Er—um . . . who exactly are you . . . sir?"

Cavar's free hand fell back to his side. If it wasn't so important that he keep up the persona, he would have sighed in relief.

"Who I *am* is none of your business. And if this is how the Empire treats its guests, I assure you, I will take *my* business elsewhere." He glanced back at the first soldier, who had now gone pale. "Jem, was it? I wonder how your superior officer will react when he finds out how you've treated me today. I'm sure he's looking for someone to blame, after that disgrace at the bank."

Jem stumbled back at once, bowing his head. Cavar realized that he had gambled correctly. The two of them probably thought he was from Paran, Leithon's nearest neighbor to the south. His father was Parani, after all, and Cavar resembled him. Paran wasn't allied with the Empire, but at the moment, it wasn't an enemy either, and its lords often traveled past the Empire's borders, both as honored guests of the state and incognito in search of more *exotic* pleasures.

He wasn't wearing formal attire and wasn't in a portion of the city that a guest of state would willingly enter. But the way that he spoke and his vice grip on Arian's hand marked him as nothing less than an incognito lord.

Jem removed his hat, nervously wiping at his forehead as Cavar stared him down.

"Didn't mean any trouble, uh—sir," he said. "If you could see your way clear to—forgetting this incident—"

Cavar made a disgusted noise in the back of his throat. "You seem to be under the impression that you're worthy of memory. Get out of my sight." He looked back at Arian, jerking her arm roughly toward him as he started walking away. "Come."

Arian stumbled in surprise, but quickly kept pace behind him as he stalked off down the street. Cavar kept walking, not looking back. He didn't release Arian until he was sure that the soldiers were gone.

When he did, she jerked her arm away from him, rubbing at her hand like she had been burned.

"I told you to act like we were *courting*," she said. "Not like you just bought me at a gods-damned *auction*."

Cavar shook his head. "It wouldn't have worked. They weren't afraid of me, or of you." Arian scowled at him, and Cavar remembered the moment the guard had approached, the hatred in his eyes as he raised his fist. "Would you rather I killed them?"

He was surprised to find the question wasn't entirely hypothetical. Cavar watched her, waiting.

"No," she said, sounding like the word pained her. "We can't explain away a dead guard."

She stepped away from him, walked forward a few paces, and then spun, slamming the flat of her foot into the nearest wall.

"I hate this," she snarled. "I hate this fucking city."

He waited a few moments for her to calm down. When the flush had faded from her cheeks and some of the wildness had left her eyes, he spoke. "Is it always like this around here?"

Arian glared at him. "If you're going to say I shouldn't go out by myself, *don't*. I'm not some lost little girl. I can handle myself."

"I don't doubt that," Cavar said. "I don't doubt that you could have taken care of all three of them, if you were in a position to do so."

"Yeah, well, there's the fun part," said Arian, rolling her eyes. "I'm never in a position to do so." She let out a puff of air, folding her arms. "No. It's not always like that. The dogs are better trained in the good parts of town, and when I'm in the bad parts, I try not to stay on the street."

Her eyes tracked upward, toward the rooftop paths.

"Is the entrance close?" Cavar asked.

Arian shrugged. "Close enough. But thanks to your little show, we should take the long way around. Just in case any of them are following. Follow me and…walk behind me for a minute. Nothing personal, I just need a little—" She made a vague gesture. It might have been "space" or "time," but it really didn't matter. Both were in short supply. He nodded anyway.

"I'm right behind you," he told her, stepping back. "You won't know I'm here."

Arian's snort told him exactly what she thought of that.

CHAPTER 6

LIAM

THE OSSUARY WAS SILENT AFTER ARIAN'S DEPARTURE, ITS SHAD-ows darker and its echoes colder. Arian had a tendency to do that, to bring life and color into a room and then take that same life with her when she was gone. Liam doubted she had any idea of the effect she had, but that was so typical of her. Arian had no idea just what she left in her wake, and it was always Liam's job to hang around and pick up the pieces.

One of those pieces was sitting at the kitchen table, pointedly *not* drinking her tea. Inwardly, Liam sighed.

Babysit the nasty one indeed.

He put a smile on his face, the same warm, relaxed smile that he had practiced for ages in front of the mirror as a child, until the outside reflected what he felt on the inside. He'd never dreamed back then that all his work at making himself look natural would be useful now, now that the world had fallen apart and he could never truly portray what he felt on the inside. But Arian was right. Out of the two of them, he was better at putting people at ease. And no matter what else Linna was, she was a client.

"I can show you around if you like. Although there isn't that much to see."

Silence. It was like talking to a stone. Liam let the last echoes of his voice drag on just past the point of awkwardness before he tried again, feeling increasingly out of place. "Um . . . I can show you to your room?"

Instead of answering, Linna narrowed her eyes at him and said, "You don't resemble him at all."

Right. His father. Rinu eth'Akari. Liam felt a touch of self-consciousness, acutely aware that Linna probably knew more about his father than he did.

"I've been told," Liam said. "Out of the two of us, I look more like my mother."

Linna held his gaze, the sustained eye contact making him squirm. He broke first, so that he was looking at the gap between her eyebrows when she let out the breath she was holding, her shoulders slumping in . . . resignation? Defeat? He wasn't sure.

"I wouldn't mind the tour," she said. "I don't suppose we have anything better to do."

Liam nodded, grateful for the truce. "It's more an orientation than a tour. If you're going to stay here, you need to be aware of a few things. There are . . . some dangers."

Linna perked up, her gaze sharpening in interest. "Traps?"

"Not exactly." Liam ran a hand through his hair, wondering how best to explain it. The ossuary had been a pet project of his before the occupation, when he'd had time to study something as simple as the history of the city. Magic flowed through the world in currents, and through some quirk of fate, Leithon had been one of those places where the currents converged. That was why the Arcanum had been founded here, why this had once been the foremost place in the world to train new mages. But before the Arcanum, the use of magic in Leithon had very few rules. Various organizations had sprung up, trying to decide what magic was and what it should be used for.

The ossuary was a holdover of that more chaotic time. And unfortunately, some relics remained.

"You'd call it dark magic, probably," Liam said. "The old monks here used to practice it. There are still some unstable pockets of it in the crypts, so as a general rule, don't go there. The living area should be safe, though. I cleared out most of the enchantments from this space and added a few to increase insulation and airflow. It isn't a luxury hotel, but you should be comfortable."

Linna started to nod but stopped, frowning at him as if she had only just remembered something.

"*You* cleared it out?" she asked.

"That's right."

"You were of the Arcanum?"

"*Am,*" Liam corrected her. "Magic doesn't fade away simply because someone wills it gone. The talent doesn't work like that, no matter what the Empire thinks."

"Then you weren't there when—" Linna broke off abruptly, as if she had only just realized that what she had been about to say was better left unsaid. Liam was grateful for that, but she'd said enough already. Enough to make him remember the smoke thick in his throat, the smell of blood in the air. He reached up to touch the amulet that still hung around his neck, his thumb brushing against the cool stone. The feel of its carved ridges and whorls was soothing.

He said, "I was lucky," and tried to believe that he meant it.

Linna, thankfully, didn't press. Her reservations about hiring them apparently didn't extend to intentionally causing them pain. She gave him an appraising look and said, "You must have been . . . what fourteen, fifteen when the Arcanum fell? That's young to be a full member."

"I graduated at thirteen." The memory was laced with enough pride and grief to make his skin crawl. His greatest accomplishment. Once. "I'd . . . really rather not talk about this right now."

Linna nodded. "Of course."

Liam couldn't help but wonder what she saw when she looked at him. Liam Athensor, the Speaker's son. The *gifted* one.

He clenched his free hand into a fist, hard enough to feel the imprint of his nails on his palm. Hard enough to hurt a little, the pain bringing him back to the present, where the city was occupied and the Arcanum was a smoldering ruin of its former self. Where Catherina Athensor lay dead with her blood on an executioner's blade, and Liam's glittering future had gone up in flames with everything that was left of his city. Where the only thing he could do was playact at rebellion, keeping little dribs and drabs of power out of the hands of an Empire that already had too much.

In a way, he was glad that Cavar and Linna had come here, glad that they had asked them to reclaim the Star. It gave him the chance to set things right. To pay for that moment when the world had fallen apart around him and all he could do was hide so that they wouldn't kill him too.

His throat was thick with grief and longing. He swallowed and thought that under the circumstances he could be forgiven for not offering Linna another smile. "I'll show you what you need to avoid. There's my workshop, where we keep our collection of artifacts. Normally, I'd tell you to please not go poking around in there, but, well . . . you're a Weaver; you probably wouldn't listen. So I'll ask it as a professional courtesy and also warn you that those vaults are warded."

He conjured flames in his hand, a shiver running down his spine as the warmth bled out of him. It was unnecessary—they had plenty of lamps—but it felt good. Magic had always been an outlet for him, a way to take the feelings that had built up inside him and let them burn. The flames sat in his cupped palm, warm but not hot enough to hurt. He curled his fingers around them and started to walk, but he hadn't gotten very far before Linna spoke up again.

"We have stories about that sort of magic too. Death magic, dark magic, whatever you want to call it. It's dangerous, but powerful."

Powerful enough to take down an Empire.

The words hung in the air between them. He was grateful that his back was to her because it gave him the opportunity to control his expression, so that he could look back over his shoulder and give her a smile that did not reach his eyes at all.

"It's forbidden for a reason," he said. "And nothing's worth bringing something like that into the world."

But just as with half of the words Liam said these days, it was hard to get himself to believe them.

CHAPTER 7

CAVAR

CAVAR HAD BEEN IN LEITHON LONG ENOUGH TO SEE THE EFFECT of Imperial invasion on its inhabitants. While he had never visited before its occupation, he didn't doubt that if he had, the city would have been different in all ways from the Leithon he saw now. He understood that the invasion had been a terrible thing for its citizens, that it had destroyed their way of life and left no one in the city unscathed, although those who could shield themselves with wealth and power had been protected from the worst of it.

That understanding, however, had always been at a remove. He had no personal attachment to Leithon and was enough a student of history to know that nations rose and fell all the time, that if the Empire maintained its hold on the city, this event would become a footnote in the city's history.

He understood what the loss of the Arcanum meant, and that was an entirely different thing, but the Arcanum, in one form or another, would come back. Leithon was still a convergence zone for magical power. Magic didn't die.

When it came to Leithon's occupation, Arian didn't have the luxury of distance. The city was writ into her bones, her soul. She knew what it had been before and was attached enough to the idea of *before* to be hurt by *after*. Cavar understood that, and so, when she asked him to walk behind her as they made their way through the city streets, he did. He kept his distance from her as they climbed up onto the rooftop paths, accessing them from a ladder that someone had placed in an inconspicuous alley. Once on the roof and away from the Imperial eye, Arian relaxed. She let out a slow breath, her arms hanging loose at her sides.

"Technically, you're not supposed to be up here," she said as she walked across a wooden plank without any apparent concern for the sheer drop to either side of her. "The underground doesn't know you, and they used to kill people for trespassing. But we're spread thin, and I think Lyndon will forgive us when he hears what you have to say."

She led him across rooftops, around towers, and along increasingly precarious bridges until he spotted their destination: a small two-story structure that had somehow been built on top of an existing residential building. Nestled in the shadow of Leithon's spires and crenellations, it would have been impossible to see from street level, impossible to find unless one was used to walking the rooftop paths, and unless one already knew that it was there. The sign above the door called it the Spinning Wheel. Cavar couldn't help but smile. So it wasn't only the Weavers who thought they held the threads of fate.

Inside, the air was laced with the smell of smoke and spirits. A low murmur of conversation spread throughout the room, punctuated here and there by laughs and curses. Arian, still walking a few feet ahead of him, became even more relaxed.

Cavar allowed himself to release some of the tension that had been building up inside him during their walk but didn't let his guard down fully. He could see people eyeing him with suspicious glares, glares they avoided giving Arian. He kept his hands well away from anything that might have been a weapon and closed the gap between himself and Arian, making it clear that he had come in with her.

A lean man with dark red hair broke away from a group of dice players, making his way over to them. He had an easy grin on his face, his posture the sort of relaxed that told Cavar he wasn't simply pretending. He seemed genuinely happy to see Arian, and Arian smiled to see him in turn, although it was the sort of exasperated smile that someone might give a precocious child or a particularly spirited puppy.

"Haven't seen you around here in a while," he said. "We've got room for one or two more at the table if you're interested."

"I'm not here to play dice, Reid," Arian said. "I've got business." She nodded at Cavar. "Is Lyndon around?"

Reid frowned, looking over his shoulder at the crowd. Most people, Cavar noted, avoided his eye. A few braver ones jerked their heads toward a door in the far wall of the room. He turned to Arian. "He might be out back. Want me to check?"

"Please," said Arian, nodding at a balcony that overlooked the main floor. "We'll be upstairs."

"Be back in a second then," said Reid, taking off. He picked his way carefully through the crowd, heading for the door.

Arian inclined her head toward the stairs. Cavar followed her up.

The upper level was much quieter than the lower. Hardly anyone waited for them there, aside from a pair of burly guards seated at the table nearest the stairs. Cavar followed Arian as she picked a seat at a corner table by the rail. The moment he sat down, the guards stood up, disappearing down the steps. A glance at Arian told him she wasn't alarmed by any of this.

"This is the business floor," Arian said, resting her arms on the scarred tabletop between them. "They've probably gone to tell someone we're here. If Lyndon didn't already know we were around, he will soon."

"What is this place?" Cavar asked.

Arian stretched out further, half slumping against the table as she waved one hand at their surroundings. "It's neutral territory. It was useful back in the day when everyone ran in different crews— good place to meet and chat without worrying that someone was going to stab you in the back. Of course, it's all different now, but this is still *the* place to get anything done in this city."

"The occupation centralized the city's underground, then?"

Arian shrugged. "We're not all buddy-buddy or anything, but it's kind of hard to keep up territory wars when the whole city is one giant occupied territory. Nowadays, you're basically either in the Resistance or just trying to survive."

"And you?" Cavar asked. "Which side are you on?"

"Haven't figured that out yet."

At Cavar's arched eyebrow, she rolled her eyes, folding her arms on the tabletop and resting her chin on them. "Look, I'm not a freedom fighter or anything. I'm just trying to get by."

"But you *are* helping the cause. You and your brother both. You're taking magical artifacts out of the hands of Imperials."

Arian raised one hand, making a vague gesture. "It's good money. And sticking it to the Empire's a bonus, sure. But I'm not in this to be a hero."

"Then what are you in it for?" Cavar asked. "Just money? Because if that's all it is, you could easily take your skills elsewhere. It would be safer for your brother too. If they find him, they'll kill him."

Arian didn't answer. She pulled a small butterfly knife out of her pocket, flicking the blade open and gouging slivers of wood out of the tabletop. From the looks of it, that was a common enough diversion here. At length, she said, "You're a client, Nivear. Not my friend. It's none of your damn business why I do what I do."

Which meant, likely, that she didn't know the answer herself.

"Right, of course," Cavar said. "I'm sorry."

Arian looked like she might have said more, but stopped as a man walked onto the upper floor. Cavar placed him somewhere in his early thirties, but it was difficult to tell. His hair was mostly dark, with the occasional fleck of gray, and he approached the table with a smirk on his face and a relaxed gait that suggested he was much more competent than he seemed. Cavar kept a hand close to his weapon.

"Anyone else would be lying low after the job today," the man said. "You never did learn caution, Arian."

Arian grinned. "Caution's for people who get caught."

The man's smile told Cavar exactly what he thought of that. Arian pushed her chair away from the table and stood up, gesturing between the two of them.

"Cavar, Lyndon," she said. "Lyndon, Cavar. You two sit and chat. I'm going to go get drinks."

CHAPTER 8

ARIAN

THE MAIN FLOOR OF THE SPINNING WHEEL WAS CRAMPED AND crowded, thieves, smugglers, and degenerates from every part of the city packing the place from wall to wall. Arian picked her way through the crowd with practiced ease, her arms held loosely at her sides and her eyes fixed straight ahead of her. People moved out of her way, clearing a path between her and the bar. They did it because they recognized her, because she was known here. Because she was one of them.

It should have felt like home, but it didn't. Even at the height of her career in Lyndon's crew, when she had been living in the attic room over his headquarters and coming here almost every night, it hadn't felt *comfortable*. It felt like Arian the thief was a garment that she was putting on, one that was familiar because she wore it so often but that chafed and itched nonetheless.

But everything in her life itched that way. If the roles she took on could be compared to clothing, "Arian the thief" was the least uncomfortable piece in her wardrobe. She would gladly wear it, compared to everything else she owned.

Reid sidled up to her in the middle of her walk to the bar, once again abandoning his dice game. She wondered if he knew that his inattention was costing him but decided against pointing it out. Reid had always been a bit of a paradox—if he hadn't risen so high in Lyndon's ranks, she might have actually considered him naive.

"You're getting fleeced," she said, inclining her head toward the game. Reid looked back over his shoulder with a quizzical frown, then shrugged, looking back at her with a grin.

"Nothing I can't afford to lose. Did you see Lyndon?"

"Yeah," said Arian. "He's upstairs. Just getting drinks. Things good with you guys?"

"Pretty great," said Reid, still grinning.

"Aila hasn't kicked you out of the house yet?"

"Not yet, but she's probably thinking about it." He slipped his hands into the pockets of his trousers, shooting Arian a knowing smile. "Interesting client you've got there."

"Yeah. He's a Parani collector."

"Sure," Reid chirped, "and I'm the emperor."

Arian rolled her eyes. "You know I can't talk about it."

"Oh, come on, Arian. We're all on the same side here."

"Are we?" Arian asked as they reached the bar. She waved off his reply, turning to the bartender. "Three pints."

The bartender grabbed three tankards off a drying rack, beginning to fill them with ale. Reid gave the man a meaningful glance, then looked back at Arian. "You gonna need help carrying all that upstairs?"

Arian let out an exasperated sigh, rolling her eyes. "Are you trying to tell me you want in on this?"

Reid's silence was answer enough. Arian felt a headache building up behind her eyes and decided it wasn't worth the effort of arguing. She pinched the bridge of her nose, then looked back up at the bartender.

"Make that four."

REID HELPED HER CARRY THE DRINKS BACK UP TO THE SECOND floor, each of them carrying two full tankards. Cavar and Lyndon watched them approach with raised brows. Arian was pleased to see that neither of them had tried to kill the other yet. She set drinks in front of herself and Cavar as Reid pulled up a chair.

"The court jester over here is Reid," Arian said. "Feel free to ignore him. Reid, Cavar."

"Pleased to meet you," said Reid. "Cavar isn't a Parani name."

Cavar smiled as he picked up his mug. "I'm only Parani on my mother's side."

Reid smirked. "I bet you are."

Lyndon reached for his own mug, glancing at Arian. "As entertaining as this is . . . Business?"

"Right, yeah." Arian took another long sip to steady herself, wiping at the froth that had gathered on her upper lip. "Business. I need to get into the Bastion."

Lyndon's and Reid's expressions were almost worth cutting both of them in. A hush fell over them before Lyndon cleared his throat. "Sorry. I thought you said you wanted to get into the Bastion?"

Arian smirked. "I did. And you can't blame me for this one. This one's all on the client."

She inclined her head toward Cavar, who had the grace to look slightly abashed.

Lyndon set his drink down, scowling as if it had gone sour. He leaned back in his seat, folding his arms, and was silent for a few moments. "It will be difficult."

"I notice you said 'difficult,'" said Arian. "Not 'impossible.'"

"Nothing's impossible." Lyndon grinned. "But this might be as close as you get." He exchanged a look with Reid, one that Arian didn't miss.

"You've been working on a way to get into the Bastion," she said.

"Wouldn't be much of a resistance if we weren't," Lyndon said. "But we're not there yet. We have some ideas, but . . ." He shrugged one shoulder.

"It's the Bastion."

"Pretty much. Not built to be easy to get into. Why do you need to get in?"

Arian gestured at Cavar, silently giving him the floor.

Cavar set his drink down slowly. "I want an artifact back."

"Obviously, or you wouldn't be here with her," Lyndon said. "What artifact?"

"It's called Kuthil's Star. It once belonged to the Speaker."

Silence fell. Reid's and Lyndon's eyes slid toward her. Arian scowled, looking away.

"It's valuable?" Lyndon asked.

"Exceedingly," said Cavar. "But more importantly, it's dangerous."

"It steals souls," said Arian. "Turns them into fuel for magic. That's as far as I understood it, though. Liam'll probably talk your ear off about it if you ask. All I know is it's not something we want to leave with the Empire."

"No." Lyndon's face was grim. "Definitely not. But what are you going to do with it?"

"Take it back to its keepers, who will lock it away until someone worthy of it returns. We don't," Cavar added, at Lyndon's look of distrust, "intend to use it."

"And who's we?"

Cavar shrugged. "The Weavers in the Wastes."

That quieted Lyndon again. He watched Cavar closely, deep in thought, his eyes occasionally flicking from Cavar to Arian in a way that made her uncomfortable. Finally, he nodded, unfolding his arms and sitting up again.

"We'll help you get into the Bastion," he said. "On one condition."

There was always a condition. Arian sighed, leaning back in her chair.

"Which is?"

"We want your brother."

"No accounting for taste," said Arian, without missing a beat.

"I'm serious," Lyndon said. "We're planning something. I can't fill you in on the details yet, but we could use a good mage, especially one who we know won't talk. You tell Liam we'll help you get into the Bastion if he gives us a hand in return."

Arian frowned. She leaned forward on the table, clasping her hands tightly together on its surface. "You'll turn him into a revolutionary. And when the Imperials catch him doing magic, they'll kill him."

"If he wants to fight for Leithon, don't you think that should be his call?"

Arian stared at her hands, fighting down her rising unease. She'd seen the look in Liam's eye whenever he talked about the Empire. He would jump at the chance to do something. She knew that Lyndon knew that too.

She hadn't lied earlier. Arian wasn't in this for a revolution. She just wanted to keep her brother alive. Was that too much to ask for? To keep *one person* alive?

Ever since the occupation, it had felt like she was trying to hold water in her bare hands. She hated it. But she knew that Liam would never believe her if she told him that Lyndon had nothing to offer. He'd come down here himself to negotiate. She also knew that he would never give up on the Star, not when he had a chance to get it back. It was too personal for him. For them.

She breathed out and said, "We need to know that your help is worth it before we make any promises. Let's meet another time. I'll talk to him. See if he's interested. In the meantime, you come up with what you can do for us on your end. If it's worth it . . ." Arian shrugged.

Lyndon grinned at her.

"Deal."

CHAPTER 9

LIAM

"YOU DID *WHAT*?" LIAM ASKED, STARING AT ARIAN FROM ACROSS the dining table.

"Sold you out to the Resistance," Arian said casually. She had tipped the seat back so that it was balancing on its hind legs, one wrong move from sending her crashing to the ground. "Or at least, I told them you'd think about it."

On any other person, her apparent callousness might have worked, but Arian was the one person who Liam could consistently read. He knew her well enough to know that she was faking it.

"What do they want me to do?" he asked.

"They'll come up with a plan for us to break into the Bastion," Arian said. She paused, tilting her head up toward the ceiling as she frowned in thought. "Might be that they already have something in the works. But they aren't going to share unless you agree to work with them. They've got some kind of job . . . I don't know. Some revolutionary nonsense, probably going to get them all killed . . ." Her voice faltered on the last word, her gaze still fixed on the ceiling.

Liam frowned, his eyes moving from Arian to Cavar, standing as still as a statue behind her, and then to Linna, sitting in front of their firepit with her back to them, ostensibly making dinner over the smokeless blue flame that Liam had conjured up. She was definitely listening to every word. On the table in front of him was his project of the day, one of Arian's daggers that he was trying to copy the amulet's nullification powers onto. He'd abandoned it as soon as Arian and Cavar returned, and he couldn't bring himself to think about it right now.

The possibility of death frightened him, of course, but his mind had caught on another word in that sentence.

Revolutionary.

He inhaled, and in his mind he was hiding in the Arcanum again, on the day of the occupation. The day that everything changed.

"They need me for this job?" he asked.

Arian shrugged, still not looking at him. "They said they needed a mage, a good one. Arcanum-trained mages are kind of in short supply these days. So I guess you'll do."

"What are the chances that we'll get into the Bastion on our own?" Cavar asked.

"I hate to say anything's impossible," Arian said. "But the Bastion's a walled compound, and its walls are loaded with ancient magic—like, 'before the Arcanum' ancient magic. It's impossible to climb over them. Even if they could be climbed, they're patrolled around the clock, and you'd probably get shot before you were half-way up. And even if you did make it through, you'd still only be in the outer keep. The *inner keep*, where anything of value would be, is guarded by its own walls, and those are even higher. There's only one set of gates into the compound, and those are also guarded around the clock. No one goes in and out unless they're properly vetted—papers, invitations, the works."

"Sewers?" Cavar asked.

Arian shook her head. "The compound's waste flows out into the bay. Just about everyone who's tried to head in that way doesn't come out again. Either they get caught by the guards, or they die of starvation trying to find their way through the tunnels. One guy made it back out, but he said he never reached the Bastion, just spent his time crawling through shit and piss in a maze that never got anywhere until he almost lost his mind. He was lucky to find the exit again." She rocked forward, her chair slamming onto the floor with a loud crack as she rested her elbows on the table and examined her nails. "Rather not go that route, if it's all the same to you."

"Then who goes in legitimately?" Cavar asked. "People have to go in and out. What do we need to get through the front door?"

"Servants, Imperial military, government officials," said Arian, ticking them off on her fingers. "Leithonian servants live inside the compound. They go out for errands, and they have passes that say who they are. But the Empire's not hiring, and anyway, even if they were, none of us would pass a background check. We'd have to come up with an entirely new identity from scratch, on the off chance that the Empire decides they need a new laundry maid or boot shiner or whatever. And everyone else is Imperial, with citizenship and papers and everything. There aren't enough Imperials in Leithon that we could just *pretend* to be one. In the old days, people used to go in and out all the time, for parties or visits to the royals or whatever, but now . . ."

She paused, looking across the table at Liam. He flushed, realizing that his inattention must be obvious. He avoided her eyes, pretending to be engrossed in studying the tabletop. Arian's dagger still lay there, reflecting lamplight. It was easier to look at that than it was to look at her.

"What?" Arian asked. "You've thought of something."

"I . . ." He hesitated, because the thought he'd had was probably not very useful. It was less of a thought than a correction. A technicality. And he knew that Arian hated it when he got bogged down in technicalities, but he thought that this one might be relevant. Even though just thinking about it made him feel cold, made him feel like pressure was rising somewhere unquantifiable inside him and making his skin feel too tight for his body.

Now was not the time for hesitation. He swallowed.

"Technically . . . that's not true. About the military. Being all Imperial. There's the Leithonian contingent."

Arian's expression darkened. It was amazing how quickly it happened, like a shroud had been dropped over her face. One moment, she was thoughtful and contemplative, the next she was hard. Almost merciless.

"No," she said.

"What about the Leithonian contingent?" Cavar asked.

"Fucking traitors," said Arian. "They were on duty the day the Empire came calling. They disobeyed the king and threw open the gates. Got the royals executed but got to keep their jobs, except their jobs now consist of licking Imperial boots and keeping the rest of us in line. And they're led by the biggest traitor of them all." She glared at Liam as she said that, fire in her eyes, and he felt something unpleasant in his stomach squirm.

"It can't hurt to go talk to her," he said.

"You think she's going to listen to you?" Arian asked. "You tell her what you're planning, and she's going to throw you in a cell. She's as Imperial as the rest of them."

"No," Liam said. "Zephyr's different."

"She's not your little girlfriend anymore," Arian said. "When are you going to wake up and face the world? We're not kids playing pretend here. You could *die*."

"I *know this isn't a game!*" said Liam. He was surprised to find that he had raised his voice and winced at the sound of the echo against the ossuary's stone walls, sharp and keening. "But we need to find a way into the Bastion. If *anyone* knows a path, it would be her."

Arian glared at him. This time, he held her gaze, waiting, focusing on his heartbeats. He wouldn't back down. After a long moment, she was the one who broke eye contact. She rolled her eyes, getting to her feet.

"Your funeral. But don't say you weren't warned."

She started walking away, heading toward the exit.

"Where are you going?" Liam asked.

"Back to the Wheel," said Arian over her shoulder. "Need to send a message to Lyndon saying we agree to a meeting. I might stay for a few drinks, so don't wait up."

She slipped into the tunnels, barely giving the ossuary a second glance.

CHAPTER 10

ARIAN

THE HIDEOUT WAS QUIET BY THE TIME ARIAN RETURNED THAT night, her lantern hooded to let only the faintest sliver of light through. She paused to listen in the ossuary's hallway, but there was no sound coming from her brother's room, no light shining from beneath the curtain that hung in the door frame. Her nerves were still singing from their earlier conversation, and the drinks she'd shared with the others at the Wheel had done very little to numb them.

A meeting had been set, for the next night. She knew that she should head straight to bed, but her thoughts crowded each other out for space, and if she was being honest, she had never been able to sleep well in this place anyway.

It might have been safe from Imperial patrols, but they were still surrounded by the dead.

She ran a hand through her hair in frustration as she made her way through the hall, pausing only when she reached the opening that led to the living area.

Cavar was awake. The Weaver was sitting in front of the remnants of their fire, looking like he was waiting for someone. Waiting for her, probably. Arian hesitated in the mouth of the hallway, torn between moving forward and stepping back into the shadows.

As she moved, he lifted his head, meeting her eyes. That made her decision for her. She drew a deep breath and stepped out into the dim firelight.

"You didn't have to wait up for me," she said.

He smiled. "I wasn't. I can't sleep."

Cavar shifted, giving her space to sit beside the fire. Arian dropped down beside him, keeping her eyes on the flames. She could feel exhaustion creeping at the edges of her vision—it had been a *very* long day—but she knew she'd spend the night tossing and turning if she tried to sleep now.

"Did you have fun?" he asked.

Arian snorted. "I don't think I've had fun in years."

"Unless you're on a job?"

She frowned at him. "How could you possibly know that?"

"I saw you earlier today. Running from the Imperials. You looked like you were having the time of your life."

Arian bit her lip, looking away from him. She fixed her gaze on the smoldering embers of the fire. He wasn't wrong. Earlier that day, when they were running from the guards, she'd felt . . . alive. Triumphant. But those feelings didn't last. She was barely able to enjoy her victory before it all came crashing down again.

Reality.

The reality was that her mother was dead, her father was nowhere, and her brother was the only one she had left in this world. She was trapped on this island, a twisted mockery of home, and she couldn't shake the feeling that it was her fault somehow. As if she, a scrawny fourteen-year-old, could have held off the force of an entire empire by—what, staying at home, eating her vegetables, and not talking back to her mother?

If she'd been at home when the soldiers came, she probably would have died. She knew that in her head, but that didn't stop it from eating at her in the middle of the night, when there was no adrenaline rush to keep the thoughts at bay.

She wrapped her arms tight around her legs. "What the hell? Don't watch me that closely. Creep."

"Sorry," Cavar said. "It's a force of habit. Observation, I mean. It's sort of what we do." He paused, and then said, "I know of your father. He's . . . apparently an acquaintance of my mother's."

Arian looked up at him, surprised. And—although she hated to admit it—hungry. She wanted to say that she didn't care what her father was doing, didn't care if she never heard from him again. But in the dark of the night, she couldn't fight the eagerness, the longing, and she hated it. She'd told Liam to grow up, but she was still a child. A child who still believed her father would come and take her home.

"You've met him?"

"Once," Cavar said. "Maybe twice. But we hardly exchanged any words. He was there to meet my mother."

"Your mother?"

"Reiva eth'Nivear. The First Weaver. So, you aren't the only one who's had to deal with high expectations." He smiled, but his fingers curled in the blankets that had pooled around his waist, as if he were drawing warmth from them. The motion was surprisingly human, and it made Arian realize how little she knew about Cavar. "She's dealt with your father more often. But from what I gather, they don't exactly get along."

"They don't?"

"He hasn't talked about this?" Cavar asked.

Arian shook her head, her eyes on the flames. "He barely spoke about the Weavers at all. I don't know anything about what it's like over there in the Wastes."

"I see," said Cavar. "Well, Mother's a traditionalist, and your father . . . he's known to be a bit of a wild card."

Arian snorted softly. "That sounds like him."

"I can see the family resemblance, to be honest. It's just . . . until my mother told me, I never knew that Rinu eth'Akari had any children."

Arian looked away, self-conscious. She hugged her knees closer to herself.

"I'm not surprised you didn't," she said. "He probably doesn't talk about us."

"He might," Cavar said, "if he had someone to talk to. But I don't think he talks to anyone about anything. He really hasn't tried to contact you, since . . . ?"

He let the sentence hang in the air, not finishing it, but Arian knew what he meant. Since the occupation, since Leithon's fall, since those Imperial bastards executed their mother. She opened her mouth to answer, but too many words threatened to spill out—too many "nos" and "not even a messages" and "it's not like we haven't tried to contact him." She closed it again. "I'm sure he cares," Cavar began.

"Don't try."

Cavar didn't speak. The silence stretched on between them, broken only by the crackling flames. Arian wished that she could get up, that she could just go to sleep, but at the same time, she found herself unwilling to move. It hurt. It really hurt, sitting here with him and talking about these things.

But it was almost a sweet pain.

She drew in a breath. "He came to visit four years ago, in midsummer. The midsummer before the Arcanum fell. I don't even know if he's . . ."

Alive. The word froze in her throat. Cavar's hand rose from where it rested in the blankets and then, as if he thought better of it, sank back down.

"He's alive," Cavar said instead. "I saw him, not long before I left. He came to speak to my mother."

Arian exhaled, trying to sort out her tangled feelings. She was relieved that he wasn't dead. And . . . betrayed. Betrayed that he hadn't come to see them.

"I always kind of hoped that he'd . . ."

That he'd what? Come to see her? Send a message? Why? Because she was *special* to him? Because when she ran away from home, when she ran off with Lyndon and the others to steal and bribe and play the politics of Leithon's underworld, it wasn't just because she wanted to be rebellious but because she wanted to be like him? A Weaver, someone who pulled strings and influenced fate. It sounded so ridiculous now.

She was a petty thief and he knew it. Everyone she loved knew it.

Liam the prodigy, Arian the disappointment.

It had been that way from the day they were born.

"I think he came to talk to my mother about the Star," Cavar said, his voice hushed like he wasn't certain he should be talking about this at all. "I think that's part of the reason why she sent me to Leithon to retrieve it. Why she specifically told me to find you."

Cavar's words sank into her like lead, weighing her down. She hated him for bringing it up.

"Why are you telling me this?"

"He cares. In your place, I'd want to know."

Arian shook her head, a knot forming in her throat. She curled herself tight over her knees, making herself small. "You're not helping."

"I'm sorry. I'm trying."

"I know." The words sounded too strained to her ears, too close to the edge. She got up, turning her face away from him. "I'm going to bed."

He didn't turn as she left, keeping his face toward the fire.

"Good night."

The words were whispered so softly that she almost didn't hear them. She bit her lip and kept walking, not looking back.

CHAPTER 11

ZEPHYR

LIEUTENANT ZEPHYR VENARI OF THE LEITHONIAN CONTINGENT stood in the inner courtyard of the Bastion, a practice sword in her hand and a shield strapped to her arm as she faced off against four members of her company.

Mat's sword came in at a sharp angle, thrusting straight at her face. Zephyr raised her shield to block it, the blunt practice blade skittering against the shield's black surface. She didn't stop to look, didn't stop to think. She shifted her weight and thrust out from below the shield, her own dull blade smearing red chalk across Mat's padded vest. He made a choked sound as the strike slid home, and she thrust her shield at him, knocking him back.

As Mat stumbled, she spun, her sword knocking Orrin's out of his line of attack. Her brown braid, soaked with sweat, swung out behind her like a counterweight as she stepped inside his reach, collapsing her arm and thrusting the hilt of her sword at his chin. He jerked his head back, gasping in surprise, drops of sweat running down his face.

The air was colored with the first touches of summer, the late spring sunshine bearing down on them as they trained in the Bastion's courtyard. Her padded vest made practice stifling, but she wasn't done. She knocked Orrin out of the round with a slash to the chest, then turned to regard her last two opponents, shield raised.

Her breath came fast, her heart pounding, but despite the heat of the day and the thrill of battle, her mind was elsewhere. She was thinking about the message she had received on her walk here, a folded piece of paper that had been slipped into her hand by a hooded passerby whose face she hadn't seen.

There's something we need to talk about.
I'll come by tonight.

It hadn't been signed, but it hardly needed to be. She would have recognized that handwriting anywhere.

The second she read the message, it crumbled into dust, falling from her fingertips like ash. She kept walking, resisting the temptation to turn and look back.

Now her opponents circled her warily, but her thoughts were still on the message, on Liam. It had been months since she had last seen him. Years, maybe. They hadn't spoken much since the occupation, but she had an idea of what he was up to these days. Stealing artifacts for the Resistance, a crime punishable by death. She didn't have any evidence, but she knew in her heart that yesterday's break-in at the Imperial Bank had been him.

And now he wanted to talk to her. Now. When the whole Bastion was abuzz with preparations for the new governor's arrival.

She didn't know what he was planning, but she could guess enough to worry her. She wouldn't turn him in, *couldn't*, but if he got himself caught, what could she do? She couldn't protect him, not with her family in Imperial custody, not under the scrutiny of Commander Selwald and the rest of the guard. It made her heart sick.

She managed, barely, to block Cressida's attack, to use her sword to knock Harlan's away as he rushed in. The blows brought her back to reality, and she shifted her weight, pushing her shield against Cressida's sword and knocking the other fighter back. She slipped her blade out from its lock with Harlan's and spun, interposing her shield between herself and Harlan's sword while Cressida was still distracted. Cressida tried to raise her shield as Zephyr slashed at her midsection, but she moved too slowly, the practice blade sliding across both of her arms.

As Harlan pushed back against her, Zephyr sprang away, holding her shield up and pointing her sword at him.

The two of them were the only ones left, and Harlan was wary. He had his own shield up, his gaze fixed on hers from behind it. They circled each other, tracing the boundaries of the sparring circle as the rest of her contingent watched. Zephyr locked eyes with him from over their shields, maintaining the distance between them.

Then she stopped, waiting.

Harlan stopped at the same time as she did, and she could see the calculation in his eyes. She didn't move. She waited, breathing slow and deep, letting air fill her lungs as she fixed her gaze on him.

He broke first, rushing at her with his sword raised high and his shield in front of him.

It was a feint, one that Zephyr saw instantly. Instead of blocking his slash with her shield the way he expected, she moved past him, stepping out of the way entirely. Her sword hissed through the air, slamming into his back hard enough to send him sprawling onto the ground.

It was over.

Zephyr breathed hard in the aftermath, looking at the people who surrounded the sparring circle. Most wore the gray uniforms of the Leithon contingent, but a handful wore Imperial violet.

There was no applause. Once, there might have been. But now the circle was silent. Each of those people in gray had trained for the Royal Guard with her, before the occupation. To continue their service—to keep their lives—they had gone back on their oaths to Leithon and sworn fealty to the Empire. There was not a single person in her contingent who hadn't betrayed their city in some way, but her betrayal had been the worst of all.

She was their commander and they respected her. But they would never love her.

She stretched out a hand toward Harlan.

"Sorry," she said. "I didn't mean to hit so hard. Battle got the better of me."

Harlan wheezed out a breath as he propped himself up, facing her. "Happens to the best of us." He offered her a grin, but there was no warmth in it as he took her hand, letting her pull him to his feet. "Good fight, Lieutenant."

"And you," Zephyr said. She released his hand, making her way out of the circle. The crowd parted for her as she walked into the shade, numbed fingers working at the buckles of her padded vest. The sweat-soaked garment slid to the ground. Discipline demanded that she pick it up and set it aside, so she did, propping it up against a wall. She set her shield and practice blade down near it, and only then did she go looking for water.

A blond Imperial soldier was waiting for her at the tap, leaning against the wall in his violet uniform. He offered her a smile as she bent to fill her canteen.

"Might I compliment you on your performance, Lieutenant Venari?" he said. "That was well fought."

"Your compliments are graciously accepted, Lieutenant Albrent," Zephyr said, which was both the safest thing she could say and the last thing she wanted to.

"Please. Call me Leon. After all, we're equals here."

Zephyr *highly* doubted that. They might have been the same rank, but Leon Albrent's violet uniform and her gray one told a different story.

"I'd prefer to keep things professional. If it's all the same to you."

Albrent offered her a condescending smile. "As you will."

Zephyr took a long drink of water, considering her next words, but Leon's attention had moved away from her. His gaze was fixed now on Cressida, who was being helped out of her vest by another member of the contingent. "It never ceases to amaze me. In Aelria, women don't generally join the guard." His tone implied that there were a lot of things Aelrian women didn't do.

"Leithonian women are made of stronger stuff."

"Oh, no doubt," said Albrent. "On that note, how is your sister doing lately?"

Zephyr took another drink. It was the only thing she could do to stop herself from saying something reckless. "Fine. The healing halls say that she's making excellent progress with her training."

"So, she's still hiding behind her books." Albrent sighed with regret. "That's a pity. Do you think she'll be around for the lord governor's arrival? She would enjoy the dances."

Zephyr had it on good authority that Lyssa would not enjoy any dances at all, but she refrained from saying so. Instead, she said, "I'll see what her schedule is like."

"It wouldn't do you any harm to attend some of the festivities yourself," Albrent noted. "If you like, I could escort you to one of the balls."

"I believe my services will be required for most of His Lordship's stay, but thank you for your invitation."

"You really do work yourself too hard, you know?"

The alternative, Zephyr thought, was significantly worse. And since there was nothing she could reasonably or politely say to that, she didn't try. Instead, she made some comment about wanting to clean up before the start of her next shift and walked off to the baths, making her way through the horde of servants, guards, and Bastion staff who had come out to make the place ready for the new governor.

As she passed a pair of maids carrying fresh laundry for one of the guest rooms, she caught sight of Commander Selwald watching from an upstairs window. The commander of the Imperial Guard was standing with his hands clasped behind his back, his gaze fixed disapprovingly in the distance. It was well known that the commander wasn't looking forward to the new governor's arrival, and tensions were running high. The Bastion had become a powder keg, an explosion waiting to happen.

And Liam wanted to meet with her. For all she knew, he would be walking right into that inferno, and she wouldn't be able to protect him.

CHAPTER 12

LIAM

THE DAY OF THE IMPERIAL OCCUPATION HAD BROUGHT WITH IT A general winnowing of Liam's social circle, in part because a significant portion of his acquaintances were now dead or in exile. Most of his connections in the city were closed to him, for their safety and his. In theory, Lieutenant Zephyr Venari of the Imperial Guard, Leithon contingent, was one of those closed connections.

In practice, things were a little more complicated.

He knocked on the door of her apartment in the Imperial Quarter, one she had rented after her father had cast her out of her family home. It was just after sunset, and the flickering light of the oil lamps turned the building's hallway a warm orange. For a second, he thought that she wouldn't respond. And then the door opened and Zephyr poked her head out into the hallway, looking both ways before taking him by the forearm and dragging him inside. She slammed the door shut behind him.

Zephyr still wore her uniform. She was leaner, in expression and in body, than she had been the last time he had seen her. Her green eyes were furtive, darting from one direction to another, as if she thought an Imperial spy might be hiding under his jacket.

"You shouldn't *be* here," she said. "If they catch you—"

"I'm just another face in the crowd," said Liam, which was true. It was easy enough to make people overlook him. All he had to do was change his clothes and his posture, and no one gave him a second glance. Unlike Arian, he carried himself with an aura of respectability. He never made people think that he might be trouble.

The touch of her hand on his arm brought back memories of

more pleasant times. He pulled away and said, "I liked your old uniform better."

Zephyr dropped her gaze. Her face was flushed, but he didn't know if that meant she was ashamed. He didn't let his gaze linger too long. It was easier to look at any other part of her than her face.

"Dwelling on the past doesn't help anybody."

Liam swallowed a retort as she stepped away from him. The Leithon contingent didn't wear the same violet uniforms as the Imperial Guard did. They didn't adorn their shields with the Imperial seal or with any seal at all. Instead, they wore gray, drab versions of the Imperial army's violet. Every day, for the contingent, was a reminder that they didn't matter. Not to the Empire they had chosen to serve, and not to the Leithonians they had betrayed.

He couldn't help feeling sympathy for her, but his stomach churned whenever he thought about what she'd done.

Zephyr didn't pretend that he was just here to visit, that things between them were as they had always been. She didn't offer him a seat, didn't even let him move out of the entryway. Her hands opened and closed at her sides, grasping at air, and her mouth worked for a bit before she said, "How are you, Liam? How are you doing?"

He wanted to laugh. He felt it burning in the back of his throat, something bitter and cruel and not quite his. He forced it back. "As well as I can be. How is your father? Your family?"

"He's—fine," Zephyr said, although he didn't miss the pause there. "He's not . . . not happy with the current situation, of course. But he's alive."

Zephyr's father, Kallan Venari, had been the previous commander of the Royal Guard, a staunch loyalist and a prime target for execution. He was alive because of what his daughter had done. Zephyr had opened the gates for the Empire and, in doing so, had saved her family's lives, won a promotion to lieutenant, and taken command of what was left of the Royal Guard. That choice had cost her most of her friends, her reputation, and the comfort of her home.

Arian called her a traitor. Most Leithonian loyalists—and Arian *was* a loyalist, no matter what she said to the contrary—called her a traitor. Liam wanted to. But he could never shake the feeling that if it had been his mother's life on the line, or Arian's, he might have done the same thing. It had been four years, and they'd been so much younger back then.

But they'd murdered his mother in front of him and let her life's work burn.

Liam couldn't quite forgive Zephyr. No matter how much he understood what she had done.

"I didn't come here for a social call," he said. "I need your help, Zeph."

She blanched at his words, looking pained. Most of him felt guilty; he never wanted to cause her pain. A small fraction of him, that vindictive part that had been born out of the destruction of the Arcanum, wanted to cause more. He pushed that part of himself away.

"Help?" Zephyr repeated, sounding on the edge of panic. "*How?* I can't be seen with you, Liam. My family—"

He held up a hand to stop her. He'd heard it all before. "You wouldn't have to be seen with me. If all goes well, you won't even have to see me again. I just need to know something, and I'm *trusting* that you won't turn me in just for asking. Will you?"

"You know I won't. But, Liam—"

"Is there a way to get into the Bastion?"

A series of emotions crossed Zephyr's face—disbelief, then suspicion, then alarm—before her expression settled into a quiet dread.

"Why do you want to know?"

"You don't want me to answer that."

"No, Liam, I do," said Zephyr, shaking her head. "I can't discuss this with you. I can't talk about—"

"It has to do with Mother."

The words were soft, but in the room's silence, they carried. Zephyr fell silent, her expression helpless.

"It's one job," Liam said. "One job, and then I'll never come here again. I wouldn't have asked you if it wasn't important. But I need to do this, Zeph, and I can't do it alone. I need you. Please."

I need you to show me that you still care. That the Empire doesn't own you. Please.

Zephyr drew in a shuddering breath, wrapping one arm tight around her middle. She looked away.

"There's no way to get into the Bastion besides the main gates," she said. "If there was a way in, we would have used it to get the royal family *out*."

That was that, then. Liam waited a few moments more, but when she refused to speak, he breathed slow and deep, trying to hide his disappointment. He didn't know why he had expected anything better.

"Thank you for your time, Lieutenant," he said, inclining his head toward her. "Have a good evening."

Zephyr bit her lip, her fingers tightening on her arm. She turned away as if she were shielding herself from a physical blow. Liam turned to face the door.

She spoke up just as his hand touched the handle.

"Liam."

He looked back.

"It's a myth."

"I don't care. Anything you can tell me is useful."

She took a deep breath, keeping her eyes on the ground. "There are . . . legends that talk about an ancient passage, leading into and out of the Bastion. The passage supposedly leads from the heart of the fortress to Halfstone Bay. We've never found it. If the passage exists, it hasn't been used for centuries. But . . . I honestly don't know if it can be used anymore."

"Why's that?"

"Because of the legend," said Zephyr. "It says—and I don't know if this is true—that the passage will open only to the Speaker. The Speaker of the Arcanum."

He stood there, stunned. She looked up then, meeting his eyes.

"Liam," she said, "the last person who could have opened that passage was your mother."

⬇⬇⬇

THE ARCANUM HAD ONCE BEEN LEITHON'S CROWNING JEWEL, equal to the Bastion in grandeur and splendor. It stood apart from the city at the end of the Road of Shadows, hugging the coastline of Halfstone Bay. Some of his earliest memories were of this place, of passing beneath the watchful gaze of the carved eye at the top of the gates, of spending all his free time in the library. Learning to control the power that was woven into air and water, earth and lightning and fire. Breathing that power in and letting it fill him, growing and swelling until he and the magic were one and the same. Seeing the pride in his mother's eyes as she watched him grow, as he rose through the ranks and people started to know about him, started to whisper when they thought he couldn't hear.

The Speaker's son. So bright, so talented.

Maybe someday, he would be just like her.

The gates were broken now, torn from the walls. They lay flat on the ground, their protective spells gone, testament to the power of the Empire's magebreakers. Rust and the elements had already started to reclaim them. The eye of the Arcanum stood out amid the wreckage, watching him go past like a relic from a bygone age.

On the other side of the walls, the inner courtyard was silent, the only sound coming from the wind moving through the ruins. The broken cobbles were stained with blood.

He tugged the hood of his cloak down and kept walking.

It was technically forbidden to enter the ruins of the Arcanum, but Liam found that that rule was seldom enforced. Anything obviously magical or of value had been removed by the Empire the day that they raided the place, and looters had picked clean whatever they left behind. Now it served as a reminder of the Empire's might, a reminder that they *wanted* people to see. Still, Liam made sure to keep his face hidden, made sure to go when it was dark and no one would see.

He wouldn't have come here at all if it wasn't for Zephyr's words, if she hadn't talked about a door that invoked the power of the Speaker. Because there *was* a door that only the Speaker could open, and before he returned to the ossuary, there was something that he needed to know.

Entering through the main doors brought with it a rush of memory. He had never, in his whole time here, known the Great Hall to be quiet. It was always full of life, of conversation, of laughter.

It was quiet now. There was nothing but dust and the faint smell of rot.

At the center of the building, there was a spiral staircase. Here, the stairs led both above and below. Above would be the rooms of the masters, with the Speaker's study at the top. Below . . .

Below was what he was looking for.

He took the stairs that led down into the dark. As he moved farther downward, he held out his hand, forming fire in it to light his way. His steps echoed off the stone, shadows stretching high above him as he moved deeper and deeper into the earth.

There were two places in the Arcanum that were the sole domain of the Speaker. The study on the upper floor where his mother had spent most of her time was what most people thought of as the Speaker's domain. But being head of the Arcanum was only part of the Speaker's role. It wasn't the whole of it.

The Speaker had duties beyond a single organization or even a nation. They had duties that predated the Arcanum and possibly even the practice of magic as they knew it. The nature of those duties was a tightly guarded secret. By necessity, they were passed on only to the Candidate, the mage who would become Speaker when the current Speaker died.

Catherina Athensor, Liam's mother, had risen from Candidate to Speaker at the age of nineteen, years before the twins were born. And despite her serving as Speaker for nearly twenty years, a Candidate had never been found.

There was a door at the bottom of the stairs, in the deepest part of the Arcanum where the dust refused to settle and the air was cold enough for him to see his breath. It was a simple stone door, unadorned. There was no doorknob, no latch, but none was needed.

The door would open only for the Speaker or the Candidate. It was how the Candidate was chosen. Their position was entirely contingent on their ability to open this door.

It was the heart of the Arcanum. Whatever was behind this door was the only reason there could *be* an Arcanum. It was the purest sort of magic, the oldest, most ancient sorcery. It *chose* the Speakers, chose those who would become its voice.

It had not chosen him.

He approached it slowly, his free hand hovering just over its surface. The memory of his last attempt filled him, the shock that had run through his body as the door rejected him as Candidate. He wasn't supposed to have been down here. No one was supposed to come here, except when the Candidate was selected. But he hadn't been able to keep himself away.

He had come down in the middle of the night when everyone

else was asleep, when his father was in town and his mother was home and there was no chance of her ever finding out what he had done. But she had found out anyway. Somehow, the second he touched the door, she knew, and she had come to find him. She had given him the scolding of his life, and part of him still burned to remember it.

She wasn't there to catch him now. No one was.

There was no one left of the Arcanum but him.

He drew in a breath and pressed his palm flat against the door.

There was a moment when nothing happened, a moment when Liam dared to hope. Then a shock raced through his veins like a thunderclap, hurling him bodily away from the door. He struck the stone steps hard enough to bruise, his world spinning as the impact knocked the wind out of him.

It was a while before the ringing in his ears subsided enough for him to raise his head and face the door. It stood there, stubbornly shut, accusation and judgment all wrapped up in one package. Anger and pain rose inside him, clawing at him from the inside.

There's no one left, he wanted to scream. *There's no one left, so open, damn you! Open for me!*

The door remained shut. He sat there for a few moments longer, his vision blurring with tears, but the door did not move.

He didn't remember picking himself up off the ground, but he must have, because somehow he began the long climb home.

CHAPTER 13

CAVAR

THE SPINNING WHEEL WAS CROWDED THAT NIGHT, OCCASIONAL bursts of rowdy laughter rising up from the floor below. It softened by the time it reached the upper floor, a low hum of background noise at the perfect level to ensure that they wouldn't be overheard. The floor was empty except for the four of them.

They sat at a table in the center of the space—Cavar, Arian, Liam, and Reid, who had been appointed as Lyndon's representative for the evening. Linna stood guard by the stairs, leaning back against the wall. Her eyes were fixed on nothing in particular, but Cavar knew that she was ready to act the instant anyone from below came a little too close. A bit paranoid, maybe. Arian and Reid both seemed sure that no one would violate the Spinning Wheel's rules.

But when treason was being discussed, it never hurt to be cautious.

"Lord Eismor's coming," Reid said. He grinned at them, leaning back in his seat. The self-satisfied look on his face evaporated when no one reacted.

"Uh, sorry," Arian said, from where she was half draped across the table. "*Who?*"

"Oh, come on," Reid said. "Niall Eismor? Imperial lord? Close friend of the Emperor? *Really not ringing any bells?* He's going to be the governor of Leithon."

At the last sentence, Arian perked up, lifting her head.

"They're appointing a governor? I thought that bastard Selwald was going to stay in charge forever."

"Can't keep him in charge, can they?" Reid said, shrugging. "He's a military officer, not a nobleman. It would *look bad*." He said the last two words in an exaggerated, airy tone, drawing his hand through the air.

Cavar understood. As far as the rest of the world was concerned, the Aelrian Empire's *activities* in Leithon were distasteful, but nothing new. The Empire would continue to swallow up small nations while everyone else, those nations that were older and more established, looked the other way and hoped the Empire would never come for *them*.

They were probably safe. Aelria had a vested interest in not scaring the other powers. It still relied on them for trade and imports and wanted to appear friendly.

The sooner Aelria brought its new city under "proper" rule, the sooner the rest of the world could pretend that the occupation of Leithon hadn't happened. He thought back to his study of the Aelrian Houses, trying to dredge up anything he knew about House Eismor. The name *sounded* familiar—possibly one of the Houses close to the Imperial throne—but he'd never been assigned a mission in Aelria proper. He hadn't studied as much as he should have, something he would have to remedy.

"This is final?" he asked Reid.

"About as final as it can be," said Reid. "There's no papers or anything like that. Officially, Lord Eismor's just coming to check the place out, see how Selwald is running things. But everyone knows he'll be taking over as soon as he can."

"Selwald isn't going to be happy about that," Arian said. "But I don't see how that helps us."

Reid's grin stretched from ear to ear. He leaned back in his seat, casually folding his arms. "Been a while since the Bastion's had a proper noble in it. They'll have to dust off the old ballroom."

Liam leaned forward, suddenly excited. "They're going to have guests?"

"They'll be drowning in guests, probably," said Reid. "The vultures are already circling—if you go down to the port, you'll find it full of shiny flagships. All the blue bloods in the area are rushing to pay tribute—you know, in case the Imperial wolves go after *them* next."

Cavar considered. Up until now, Leithon had been closed off from the world, with most people afraid to go near it until the dust had settled. But a lord of the Imperial Court would have an entourage. Retainers, servants, followers, minor lords trying to curry favor. And like Reid said, foreign dignitaries would be coming out of the woodwork.

"The Bastion's going to be full of foreigners," Cavar said. "This could be our chance to get in."

"Exactly," said Reid. "Boss has been thinking about getting someone on the inside for a long time now. The problem is, we're all Leithonian as the Spire, and nothing we do is gonna change that. But word on the street is that *you* caused quite a stir the other day, Mr. Incognito Lord."

He turned his grin onto Cavar. Beside him, Arian's face flushed red.

Cavar frowned, thinking.

"It could work," he said. "I can pass myself off as Parani easily. And Parani titles can be bought, so they have more . . . variety in their nobility. It's hard to keep track of all their lords. I know what an official title looks like. If you can introduce us to a decent forger, we could make something happen."

"Could you do it?" asked Liam. "Imitate a Parani lord?"

"I've done it before," said Cavar, thinking back to one of his first official missions as a Weaver. An infiltration of a Parani lord's estate—the Weavers had heard that he was dabbling in human trafficking. He'd played a convincing young lord and had managed to set things up so that it looked like the local authorities had discovered the other lord's misdeeds.

"I'd also need to get word out to our contacts outside the city," he said. "We need resources to make it more convincing. So, I'll need a decent smuggler."

"Can we help you with anything else while you're at it?" Reid said. "Maybe you need a crown? Seven golden horses?"

"No, thanks," said Cavar, with a quick smile. "But I *will* need an entourage of my own. Nothing too big, of course. I don't want to make too much of a splash. Maybe a servant and a bodyguard."

He looked meaningfully at Arian and knew that she understood when she sat up in her seat, chewing thoughtfully on her thumbnail.

"I can play servant if it gets us inside," she finally said.

"And we can get you that forger and that smuggler," Reid said. "So that just leaves your end of the bargain." He smiled at Liam.

"What would I need to do?" Liam asked.

"We need you to help some of our people," said Reid. "The less everyone knows about the details, the better, but chances are they'll die if we don't help them, and we could use some magic. If you're interested, the boss'll contact you later on."

"Your people?"

"Resistance members. They got into trouble doing work for us. If we manage to help them out, it'll be *really* embarrassing for Selwald. What do you say?"

Cavar didn't miss the way that Arian watched Liam, the tension in her body as they all waited for his response.

Liam nodded. "I'm interested. Help us get Cavar and Arian into the Bastion, and I'll help you."

"Fair enough," said Reid. "We've got two weeks until Lord Eismor gets here. That's not a lot of time, but if we hurry, we can put something together. If you want to send a letter to your friends, you'd better start writing."

"That's fine," Cavar said, already thinking about how he was going to explain the massive withdrawal he was going to make from one of the Weavers' bank accounts. His mother would be furious, probably. He should not have been as excited about that as he was. "Can I have some paper and a pen?"

CHAPTER 14

CAVAR

"LOOK, ARIAN, I'M NOT GONNA TELL YOU HOW TO DO YOUR JOB," said Reid. "But I don't think palace servants *normally* look like they've just sucked on lemons."

Arian whirled on him with her fists clenched, her face turning bright red. "Don't you have pockets to pick or something?" she asked. "Why are you hanging around here?"

"Uh . . . it's my place?" Reid asked, pillowing his arm behind his head. He was draped over the small workshop's couch, a lazy grin on his face. "And anyway, I am doing something. I'm your identity coach."

The apartment, which also served as a shopfront for Reid's partner, Aila, took up half the third floor of an old narrow building. It was in the heart of Old Leithon, where buildings clustered tightly together like plants in an overgrown garden, and so although it was only late afternoon, very little sunlight filtered in through the workshop's glass windows. It gave the room an air of gray shadows, chased away by the lamp that Aila had placed on the end table next to her so that she could see her work.

Her work, at the moment, consisted mainly of sticking Cavar with pins. He tried to hold still as she held a half-cape in the Imperial style up to his shoulders, muttering to herself under her breath. She had a particularly long pin in her hand, gleaming in the lamplight, and he felt a touch of nerves.

It had been seven days since they had first gotten the word that Lord Eismor was coming, and Aila had barely slept since then. He knew that she was doing her best to put together enough outfits for him and Arian to play their roles convincingly, but her accuracy had dropped noticeably over the last few days. And while Cavar had tried to tell her that she could just alter the clothes he had brought with him, Aila was insistent that he have at least two new outfits.

"A lord has to look presentable," she'd said. "Everyone knows that. You can buy more clothes once you're in, but you can't show up at the Bastion looking like a *merchant*."

He supposed she would know. Before the occupation, Aila had been an assistant for a well-known tailor. She spent her days helping her mistress design clothes for Leithonian dignitaries and nobility. After the occupation, her mistress had been imprisoned for loyalist ties. Aila and those who had managed to escape had fled into the city, some of them setting up shop elsewhere and many of them doing work for the Resistance on the side.

Cavar didn't argue. New clothes in the latest fashions would only serve to cement his position, and if his letter had gotten through to the mainland, he would soon have the funds to pay her back. So he resigned himself to long days of fitting, being poked and prodded, while Arian tried on various servant dresses and tried to affect an air of quiet humility, with mixed results.

Right now, she folded her arms over her chest, a decidedly unhumble scowl of frustration on her face.

"My identity isn't important anyway," she said, pointing at Cavar. "It's *his* you should be helping with. I just have to bow and scrape, but if he can't play a convincing lord, we're all out on our asses."

"I'm Lord Nasirri Rezavi," Cavar said calmly. "A second-generation Parani lord. My father is a wealthy merchant who bought our titles, and I'm desperate to prove myself as one of the elite. My father prefers to run his business and not become involved in politics, but I'm here to show the new governor that our family is just as political as the rest of them."

It was a story they had been working on in the evenings, when they were all gathered in the ossuary. He and Arian had spent most of that time tossing ideas back and forth about the finer points of Nasirri's identity. Liam and Linna joined in on occasion, but they were both busy with their other jobs: Liam with assembling all the useful magical artifacts he could think of and transferring their complicated spellwork onto less obvious items so that Cavar and Arian could have as much arcane help as possible while they were in the Bastion, and Linna with piecing together the weapons and tools she would need to take on her own identity as Nasirri's bodyguard.

"What about his personality?" Arian asked. "What's he like? How does he talk to people?"

"Nasirri is reserved," Cavar answered. "Careful. He was a child when his father bought their titles, and he's ambitious enough to want more, to play the games of court and try to get a higher position for himself. He's hungry to prove himself and he doesn't think much of people who were born into their power, but he'll toe the line and be respectful to his peers. He doesn't engage much with the older and more established families."

Arian rolled her eyes. "You want to play the dark, brooding lordling, be my guest. Some Aelrian lady might even fall for him."

Cavar shrugged, earning him a glare from Aila and a prick of pain as she accidentally jabbed him in the arm. He winced but said, "That's not my intent."

"You don't sound like you'd mind," retorted Arian, scowling.

Reid sat up, his smile growing wider. "You know, Arian," he said. "If *Riana's* going to be the lone servant of someone like that, people are gonna start thinking that Lord Nasirri isn't available, if you know what I mean." He waggled his eyebrows suggestively.

Arian's glare was unamused. "Aila, I'm sorry, but I'm going to have to kill him."

"Take it outside, please," Aila mumbled around a mouthful of pins. "It's hard to get blood out of the floorboards."

"Riana's not gonna take any of that shit anyway," Arian said.

"She's fiery. She does what Nasirri says because she has to, but she's not happy about it. She's not gonna embarrass him in public or whatever—she knows how to keep her head down and stay out of trouble. But she doesn't like him, and she doesn't like nobles, and she doesn't like this whole thing."

The room went silent, the last echoes of Arian's voice fading away. Cavar cocked his head to the side, watching her, and Aila paused in her work. Arian scowled at them.

"Uh . . . ," said Reid. "I thought you were supposed to be playing a character."

"Yeah," Arian said. "She's me. So what? Simple lies are the easiest."

"It might not be the best idea . . . ," Cavar began, choosing his words carefully, "to play a character so close to home."

Arian folded her arms, seeming to collapse into herself. Cavar caught sight of that look on her face, the bone-deep weariness that he saw in her sometimes when she thought about the city.

"What's it matter?" Arian asked. "Maybe I'm tired of pretending to be someone else. Maybe I just want to be myself for a change."

"Arian—"

Arian shrugged, tugging at the servant's dress she was wearing. She picked up the bundle she had made of her own clothes. "Sorry to do this, Aila, but I'm gonna get changed. Can you take care of him?"

"Where are you going?" Cavar asked.

"Out," Arian said in reply. "I've got a week before I need to play your nursemaid. Might as well make the most of it."

CHAPTER 15

ARIAN

ARIAN STOOD ON THE ROOFTOP PATHS, HER FAVORITE PLACE IN the world. It was the only place in Leithon, aside from the open roads and the residential areas that ringed the city, where the sun always shone. She knew she was being ridiculous, acting like a child, but she couldn't stand to be in that workshop any longer. To be reminded of the fact that she was about to lose her freedom, and for what? For the pocket change that Cavar and the Weavers were going to pay her to retrieve the Star? They could have been paying her a king's ransom, and it still wouldn't have been enough.

The money wasn't worth it, and she was silly for doing this at all.

Except it had never been about the money.

The city gleamed in the sunlight, which dappled the rooftops in gold and shone into the narrow streets. From her perch, she could breathe in the sea breeze, close her eyes, and pretend that things were as they had always been. That she was still only a small-time thief working her way through Leithon's black market, that her brother was still one of the Arcanum's rising stars, that when she returned to her small attic room, her mother would have sent her another message, asking her to return to their family home.

But that would be a mistake. Because when she opened her eyes, she would see the broken Spire of the Arcanum and remember that her mother was dead, that there was nothing more Arian could do for her but clean up her loose ends.

Arian clenched her fists tight against the tide of memory. She should have been there when the tower fell. Maybe in another life, she would have been.

"Arian."

Someone stepped onto the rooftop behind her. Arian didn't need to look to see who it was. Reid knew that this was where she went when she needed to think, to be somewhere where she could taste the air. A smarter person would have left Arian alone rather than risk getting hit with the brunt of her temper, but Reid had never been all that smart.

She expected it from him and was too tired to be angry.

"I'm not going back," she said, looking over her shoulder. The sight of him gave her pause. Reid's eyes were wide, his face pale. He looked *scared*. But she had only been gone an hour. What could have happened?

She felt a flash of guilt and terror. Had something gone wrong? Had they been found out by the Imperials?

Were they already dead or in prison because Arian had run away again?

"What?" she asked. "What's going on?"

Reid shook his head, gasping for breath. Arian resisted the urge to smack him, her other hand closing around his shoulder and turning him to face her.

"*Reid!* Talk to me!"

He shook his head again, wetting bloodless lips with his tongue. "It's Lord Eismor," he said. "He's here—now. He's arriving *now*."

The hand that was holding on to his shoulder went slack, falling back to her side.

"What do you mean he's arriving *now*?" Arian asked.

"His boat's pulling into the harbor," Reid said. "He's already here."

Arian stared at him in disbelief. When his words sank in, she took off running.

⚓⚓⚓

THE OSSUARY WAS IN DISARRAY. CAVAR, EVIDENTLY, HAD RUSHED back as soon as he heard the news. He was standing in the middle of the living area, talking with Linna in urgent tones. Linna was sweaty and out of breath, like she had just run a mile. Their conversation broke off as Arian approached, the two of them whirling to face her.

"What the hell just happened?" she asked, rounding on Cavar. "I thought we had a week!"

"We *had* a week," Cavar said, expression grim. "Apparently, the timeline's moved up."

"I just came from the docks," Linna said. "A ship is coming in, flying House Eismor's flag. If we're going to get into the Bastion, we need to go now."

"How's that *possible*?" Arian asked. "You'd have to fly to get here from Aeldoran in less than two weeks."

Cavar and Linna exchanged a glance, and Arian had the worrying sensation, once again, that things were happening that she didn't understand. At length, Linna pursed her lips and said, "It appears that Lord Eismor won't be coming himself. He's sending his eldest son, Lord Kaolin Eismor. And Lord Kaolin had a much shorter distance to travel than his father. He was administrating some of Lord Eismor's holdings on the Imperial coast."

Arian cursed Aelrian nobility with every bone in her body. If they could be counted on to follow through on what they said they were going to do, the plan would have gone off without a hitch.

"What do we do now?" she asked Cavar. "Do we have everything we need?"

Cavar glanced at Linna, whose expression was tight-lipped.

"We have enough. The funds came through, and thanks to Aila and her friends, I have a few good outfits. It won't be a glorious entrance, but maybe staying unnoticed is for the best. We'll just have to make do with what we have."

Making do with what they had. Like they were baking a cake,

not breaking into the most secure fortress in Leithon, something that, if they were caught, would get them executed. And if word got out that they were after the Star, if they got caught trying to *steal* it—

Well, Arian didn't think their deaths would be pretty.

But she remembered the Star, remembered it hanging around her mother's neck in a setting of silver, a blue gem that glowed with its own inner light. It was her mother's, and it was Leithon's, and if they abandoned the plan now, they were never going to get it back.

Arian sucked in a breath, looking back up at Cavar. "Fine. What's the plan?"

"We'll enter the Bastion tomorrow," said Cavar. "I'm going to write a letter of introduction, using Lord Nasirri's seal. You'll have to go to the Bastion to deliver it, as Riana. Give the message to the gate guards. They'll know what to do."

"Message delivered to the Bastion," Arian said, her stomach churning with nerves at the prospect. "Done. What next?"

"Next, come straight back here. This development has thrown off some of our plans. We'll need to do what we can to fix them before we enter the Bastion. And tomorrow, as soon as it's reasonable, the three of us will call on Lord Kaolin."

Arian nodded. "Seems easy enough. I'll get dressed. Should give you enough time to write your message."

Cavar nodded, stepping aside as Arian moved to her chambers in the back of the ossuary, where the clothes that she would be wearing as Riana waited. As she passed him, he turned to watch her.

"Wind in your veins," he muttered, his voice almost too soft to hear.

Arian stopped walking, looking over her shoulder at him. She didn't miss the look that Linna was giving him, one of intense disapproval. "What was that?"

Cavar smiled, but it was a tense smile. It didn't reach his eyes. "It's a Weaver blessing. It means luck in the face of danger."

Luck in the face of danger. Arian could get behind that. She had a feeling they would need it.

CHAPTER 16

LIAM

THE WAVE OF EXCITEMENT AND FEAR THAT THE ARRIVAL OF LORD
Kaolin's ship sent through the city was almost palpable, a ripple through the air. When Liam arrived on the roof of the old custom-house, the last stop on the rooftop paths, he found Lyndon already there, a few other members of the Resistance crouched in the shadows of the ancient guard tower.

Lyndon's expression was dark. This section of the paths was the least secure, but Imperial patrols rarely came up this far. Footing here was unstable, and after a few injuries, including one guardsman who died from a fall, the old buildings around the dock had been closed off. The underground, with their knowledge of the paths, usually managed to get through safely. Liam only managed to pick his way across the crumbling ruin because one of Lyndon's officials had spotted him coming and escorted him to where the others were waiting.

Still, the fear of discovery meant that these paths were seldom used. The fact that there were this many Resistance members here told Liam that the rumors were true before he even saw the ship.

The *Osprey* bobbed up and down in the waves of Leithon's harbor, a sleek, well-tended Aelrian vessel. A group of people were gathered expectantly around the pier. Lyndon moved aside as Liam approached, wordlessly giving him space to watch. Liam did so, mimicking the way the Resistance members concealed themselves behind the rooftop's crenellations so that if anyone looked up at the roof, it would be difficult to pick them out amid the shadows and ruins.

"That's him," Lyndon muttered, nodding at a figure in dark

clothing who had appeared on the deck of the ship. He stood alone. "Lord Kaolin Eismor."

Someone passed Liam a spyglass. He raised it to his eye. The lord was younger than Liam had expected, a slender youth in his late teens or early twenties with dark hair grown slightly long in the Aelrian fashion. Why Lord Eismor had sent this boy instead of coming to Leithon himself was anyone's guess. Maybe he feared assassination at Commander Selwald's hand—not unreasonable, from what people were saying. Or maybe this had been his plan all along. Maybe he had wanted to make a gift of Leithon to Lord Kaolin from the start.

Whatever the case, Liam thought this would still work. The young lord would gather the same sort of attention his father would, but he would be more pliable. It would be easier for Cavar and Arian to get close to a young heir around their age than it would be for the two of them to escape the notice of a lord who had survived the machinations of Imperial Court for half a century.

The timing, however . . .

Liam didn't like irregularity.

Magic was a precise art. The slightest mistake could result in disaster. In his studies as a mage, he'd developed a love for order, for straight lines and predictable results. This work—thief work, Resistance work—this was the opposite of that.

It made him nervous.

He bit down on the inside of his cheek, thinking. The timing was unfortunate. He didn't know if Cavar had everything he needed to convincingly play Lord Nasirri. But Cavar had already been seen in the city. He would have to go in as soon as possible, or it would look like Lord Nasirri was being deliberately disrespectful, not calling on a peer immediately.

And then there was Arian. His sister, going to the Bastion by herself. Where he couldn't follow. Where anything could happen.

She would be all right, he told himself. Arian wasn't like him. She was strong, she was resourceful, and she thrived on irregularity.

And this could be good for them. Lord Kaolin wouldn't be as dangerous as his father.

"If I were you, I'd get out of here," Lyndon said. "Security's going to tighten up any minute now. And we can't lose our mage before our job."

"You're not leaving," Liam pointed out, but he turned the spyglass onto the gathered crowd, picking out a number of Imperial uniforms. There were guards, but no magebreakers. No one who could sense magic being used by another. He spread his awareness out around them just in case, as faint and fragile a net as he was able. It was a variation on the technique Imperial magebreakers used to catch someone in the act of magic, and Liam had used it a few times to avoid them whenever they moved through the city. He was a bit proud of it. It was subtler than the techniques magebreakers used, and it helped him find them before they could find him.

He didn't expect to detect anything. He'd cast it out as a reflex, a thing that he did every now and then whenever he was out in the streets. But something pulsed in his net.

It wasn't the forceful touch of someone drawing in power, nor was it the tentative nudge of someone feeling out the boundaries, trying to trace it to the person who had cast it. Instead, it felt as if Liam had cast the net into a current. It was the nonchalant touch of someone using magic unintentionally, someone too untrained in the art to control themselves, or—more likely—someone so powerful that they *couldn't* control themselves. It wasn't something he had felt in a long time, not since the fall of the Arcanum. He froze, searching for the source of it.

"Are you listening to me, kid?" Lyndon asked. "I'm telling you, you should get back—"

Liam ignored him. His head jerked from left to right, scanning the crowd around Lord Kaolin.

Magic had a signature, an aura. It left a trace that was unique to the mage who cast it. And Liam knew this mage. The last time he had felt this aura, the Arcanum had been burning down around him.

His eyes landed on a man standing right behind Lord Kaolin, his hair dark and his eyes the blue of winter. He was dressed in Aelrian court fashion, different from the last time Liam had seen him, but the aura that surrounded him remained the same. He wore a sword belted to his waist, a silver blade that made Liam's gorge rise, a high-pitched ringing noise in his ears drowning out all sound.

The last time he had seen that blade, it had been slicing through his mother's neck. The last time he had seen that man, he had been wielding it.

"Hey. Liam!"

Lyndon snapped his fingers next to Liam's ear. The sound shocked him and he winced, coming back to himself. He hissed when he realized that the spyglass was hot to the touch, the brass around his fingers melted and warped. He'd started using fire without even meaning to, leaving impressions where he'd gripped too tightly. His hands were shaking. He took a step away from the edge.

"I'm sorry—" he said, the words coming out too fast. It felt like he wasn't getting enough air. "I—I don't—I'll replace the spyglass."

"Damn right you will," Lyndon said, but there was no heat in the words as he took the spyglass from Liam, glancing from him to the docks. "What did you see?"

Liam thought about answering him, thought about telling him the truth, but the words wouldn't leave his mouth. He swallowed, trying to remember how words worked so that he could put the syllables together. But he could feel the panic rising, could feel it like a fog in his brain, a constant clanging noise that stopped sounds from making sense and made speech impossible.

He shook his head.

Lyndon raised the dented spyglass to his own eye, looking out at the docks. What he saw—*who* he saw—made his expression even grimmer. He lowered the spyglass, clicking his tongue at the assembled thieves to get their attention.

"We're done. Let's get out of here."

Someone took Liam by the elbow to help him back across the roof. He went, but even in the warmth of full sunshine, he felt cold. He was still trembling sometime later, when they parted from him on the paths that led to the Road of Shadows, letting him head back to the ossuary.

CHAPTER 17

ARIAN

CAVAR WAS STILL WRITING WHEN ARIAN STEPPED OUT OF HER room, wearing a plain, undyed dress belted at the waist with a head-scarf wrapped around her pale blond hair. She hadn't done any-thing to alter her features. Riana would be living at the Bastion for weeks, in the company of other servants and under the scrutiny of an entire Imperial court. If she had to apply dye or makeup each time she went out in public, she would increase her chances of get-ting caught significantly. The simplest disguises were the easiest, and luckily, none of the Imperials would know her by sight.

Still, having her real face looking out from behind Riana's made her feel exposed. She wondered if Cavar was right. If she was play-ing this too close to home.

It was too late for regrets. She waited for Cavar to finish, mar-veling at the way Nasirri's handwriting, so different from his own, flowed onto the page. If he hadn't been a Weaver, he could have made a killing working as a forger.

"It's the same handwriting I used on that assignment I told you about," Cavar said, when she commented on it. "The one in Paran. High-class Parani children are all taught the same style of penmanship."

"Is there anything you *don't* know how to do?"

Cavar laughed, signing Lord Nasirri's name onto the bottom corner of the page with a flourish. "You should ask my mother. Or Linna. I'm sure they'd have an answer for you."

Arian grimaced. Linna always looked at her like she had just drunk sour milk. "Somehow I don't think Linna and I have much to talk about."

The smile dropped from Cavar's face. He rolled the letter into a scroll, Paran's favored mode of communication, and tied it shut with a strip of silk, then laid the scroll flat on the table. Taking the seal they had designed for Lord Nasirri, he dripped wax onto the silk binding, carefully pressing the seal down onto it. She watched his hands because it was easier than watching his face.

"Give it time," he said. "Linna doesn't take well to outsiders. But she doesn't mean any harm."

Arian privately thought that it would take either a miracle or an apocalypse to get her and Linna to see eye to eye—and in the case of the latter, she wasn't fully convinced that she wouldn't just leave the Weaver in the fire and sort it out later. But she didn't say that. Instead, she took the scroll and tucked it into the carrying case she had tied around her waist.

She'd been hoping to slip away before Linna could return, but unfortunately, she ran into the other Weaver in the tunnels on the way out. Linna had already changed into an unfamiliar grayish robe that seemed to be made of smoke itself. She wore her weapons openly now, her hair tied back in an elaborate knot. She looked good, which didn't help Arian's mood. Linna got to stride into the Bastion looking like a warrior queen, while Arian had to dress like a scullery maid.

As if reading her thoughts, Linna turned, fixing dark eyes on Arian.

"Is Cavar inside?" Linna asked, inclining her head in the direction of the ossuary.

"Find out for yourself," Arian said. "You have eyes."

Linna paused, looking back at Arian. "You really are Rinu eth'Akari's daughter, aren't you?"

Arian scowled. The last thing she wanted to do today was talk about her father. "If you have something against my dad, take it up with him. I've got somewhere else to be."

Linna made no move to stop Arian as she shouldered past her, although she did turn her head to watch her go, her mouth pressed tight in disapproval.

"You're heading to the Bastion?"

Arian stopped walking, wondering which god she had insulted badly enough to punish her with this conversation. "Obviously."

Linna's brows arched, but she said simply, "Good luck."

Arian frowned at her, unable to tell if Linna was being sarcastic or not. She left Linna alone in the tunnels, walking away.

CHAPTER 18

LIAM

THE SECOND FLOOR OF THE SPINNING WHEEL WAS AS PACKED AS Liam had ever seen it, the floor's round tables clustered as close together as possible to allow those in attendance to speak quietly and still be heard. The bar downstairs was closed and eerily silent, the room lit only by the flickering light of a single lantern. In a way, although the Wheel was as high in the air as it was possible to be in Leithon's city proper, and it was made of wood and not stone, it reminded Liam of the depths of the ossuary, the catacombs with the dead.

He repressed a shiver, thumbing at the patch of skin that peeked out between the long-sleeved shirt he was wearing and his glove. The motion, a steady back and forth, soothed him, grounding him in this very unsettling moment. He fought back the sense that he really wasn't supposed to be here at all.

This was his first time in the Spinning Wheel without Arian, and his mind was still full of what he had seen yesterday. *Who* he had seen. Emeric Roth, the Aelrian Empire's senior magebreaker. The person who had been sent to deal with the Arcanum. With the Speaker herself.

"Hey," Reid whispered from beside him, "are you okay?"

Liam jumped. He pressed down hard on the skin of his wrist, feeling the pulse point beneath his thumb, and forced himself back to reality. His role here was important. While Arian and Cavar scrambled to prepare for their entrance into the Bastion tomorrow, he had to handle *this*. Acting as liaison between his sister and the Leithonian Resistance.

He looked up at Reid. He had to look up, because while he was seated in a chair facing Lyndon in the center of the room, Reid was perched on the table behind him, his legs hanging over the edge. He had the same casual ease that Arian had whenever they were out in the city or in the Spinning Wheel. Like he belonged here. Liam, on the other hand, had felt like there were ants crawling all over his skin since he'd left the safety of the ossuary.

"I'm fine," he whispered in response, which, even though it wasn't the whole truth, was true enough. He looked back at Lyndon, who was currently deep in discussion about what sounded like food and medical supplies. How much had his attention wandered? He breathed deep and resolved to pay closer attention from here on out.

Lyndon wrapped up his discussion and looked up from the center of the room, his eyes fixing Liam in his seat. On the best of days, Liam found eye contact an unnecessary formality, but today Lyndon's gaze was like a hammer blow. He felt like Lyndon could see right into his soul.

He held his gaze for a moment and then, as if he could sense how Liam's heartbeat was picking up and his breathing quickening, he looked away.

"How are our infiltrators, Liam?" Lyndon asked, his voice loud in the room's sudden silence. "Are they ready?"

Liam cleared his throat. This was what he had come here to do, and although he would never ask, he had the feeling that Lyndon had waited for him to come back to himself, that this was what he actually wanted to talk about. It was embarrassing, to have to be accommodated like this, and he wouldn't let it happen again.

"They're working on final preparations right now. They're planning to present themselves soon. In the morning. I think the sudden change of plans unsettled them, but they'd already been working overtime to get into character. We'll just have to see what happens."

"Will they be able to communicate with us?"

"Aila's already dealt with that," Reid said, stepping into the conversation before Liam could answer. "She's worked out a system with some of her friends. When Arian goes out to market or does Nasirri's errands in the city, she can drop off letters with them."

"She might have people watching her, though," Liam added. "She'll need to be careful."

Lyndon shrugged. "Arian can lose a tail. I'm not worried about that. But if she gets in, she'll be the closest thing we have to a contact on the inside. Will she be willing to share information with us about what's going on in there?"

"I'm sure she would," Liam said, although privately he wasn't as sure as he would have liked. Arian's relationship to the Resistance was . . . complicated. He still remembered how she had looked when she was telling him what they wanted.

To borrow a mage.

He hadn't forgotten why he was here. The Resistance needed a mage. And he had a feeling he was about to find out exactly what he was in for.

"Excellent," Lyndon said. "Then we should leave the Bastion to our enterprising young friends and move on to the next issue on our list. Ah, but I've forgotten to introduce you. Friends, this is Liam. He's an Arcanum-trained mage and, if we all play our cards right, our way into Blackstone Deep."

Heads turned in their seats, swiveling to focus on him. Liam swallowed, uncomfortable with the scrutiny. His mind was already working. As soon as Reid hinted that they needed Liam to help Resistance members who had gotten into trouble, he'd suspected their destination. Blackstone Deep had been Leithon's prison prior to the invasion, and the Aelrian Empire was notorious for co-opting existing structures in its conquered territories. It was still being used as a prison now, with Imperial guards instead of Leithonian ones.

The problem was that the Deep had, like the Bastion and all other Leithonian institutions, magical protections. With Leithon's reputation as the center for magical learning, and the Deep's location—woven into the cliffs of Halfstone Bay, not exactly close to the Arcanum, but closer than most other institutions in the city—its magical protections had been . . . thorough. Various Speakers had held different views on crime and punishment, but most thought that any prison from which escapees had a chance of running onto Arcanum grounds needed to be especially well guarded. There was also the possibility—one that had come to fruition several times over the centuries—that one of the Arcanum's own would be found guilty of a crime and need to be imprisoned.

And so, the result was that Blackstone Deep was more secure than most prisons of its kind, equipped with doors that opened only if registered persons touched the doorknobs, passages that would change direction seemingly of their own accord, and magehold cells, which had been built specifically to detain mages and suppress their magic. He had a feeling that the simple nullification spell cast on the amulet that he had taken from the Imperial Bank had been derived, in part, from those that guarded magehold cells.

It was not a place where one went lightly. And while it didn't have the Bastion's reputation for being totally unbreachable, breaking in was not an easy thing to consider.

But if Lyndon thought Liam's help was worth their assistance, then he already knew that. Because the Imperial Bank, which had once been the Bank of Leithon, was also one of those buildings that had magical protections. And he and Arian had been able to slip past those.

It was a simple equation in the end. In every case but the Bastion's, whose wards had been put into place by the First Speaker and responded to some magic that only the Arcanum's Speakers and Candidates could parse, the wards were locks, and the Arcanum had the keys. And Liam was the last member of the Arcanum alive and working in Leithon.

They were all watching him. He could feel their scrutiny. It was the same, and yet different from, the way people had looked at him when he had been younger. An expectant look, like they were all waiting to see something amazing.

It would be harder to get into Blackstone Deep than it had been to slip into the Imperial Bank. It was entirely possible that the same sort of wards that protected the Deep also protected the Bastion, that those spells would be just as impossible to break without the power of the Speaker behind him. He doubted they were on the same level—the Deep wasn't as old as the Bastion, and the First Speaker hadn't been involved in its construction—but it was always possible that it was beyond him.

Beyond him like the Speaker's door was beyond him.

He looked around the room. No one had looked at him like that in a very long time.

He swallowed past his nerves and said, "I'm sure I can find a way."

CHAPTER 19

ZEPHYR

ZEPHYR STRODE ACROSS THE BASTION GROUNDS, A PAIR OF guard members in Leithonian gray trailing along behind her. They were wearing their dress uniforms, fresh from the assembly that had welcomed Lord Kaolin Eismor to the Bastion. The young lord had seemed bemused to see them there, but he made no comment, even offering her a slight smile as she passed. The smile had held the same patronizing edge as those of Leon Albrent and the other Leithonian soldiers. She didn't appreciate it, but the Venaris had held the Royal Guard for generations, and not for lack of discipline. She had remained at attention, holding her salute as Lord Kaolin passed. Her composure had nearly broken when she saw the mage who was traveling with him, but she had managed to keep herself together until the lord and his entourage had disappeared into the main keep.

Now that Lord Kaolin was ensconced safely in the Bastion, the rush that had dominated the keep before his arrival had settled down, bringing with it a hush that was crypt-like in comparison. It was that time between afternoon and evening when the world slowed for a breath, and aside from the soldiers making their rounds and the servants tending to Lord Kaolin's cargo, the Bastion grounds were still.

The smell of cooking hung in the air as the welcoming feast neared, and Zephyr's mouth watered. But while the Imperial officers would likely be asked to dine with the young lord, Zephyr wasn't holding her breath for any such invitation. She would eat later, in what had once been the Royal Guard's mess hall. If she could even eat at all. Her stomach was twisted in knots, and it was all because Liam had sent her another message. It had found its way to her on her morning walk to the Bastion, the same way as the last.

Say nothing. Please.

She didn't know what she was supposed to say nothing about, but she remembered their meeting and felt a distinct sense of unease. She had told Liam about the door only because it was impossible, a fairy tale that would never open again. She'd thought that would have been enough to keep him safe, to keep him out of danger.

But she should have known better. She should have known that he would keep trying, and now she didn't know what he would do.

There was too much work to be done to think about it for long. Zephyr left her Imperial counterparts to fuss over Lord Kaolin and went to relieve her soldiers currently on patrol out in the city.

She was passing by the servants' gate, her mind still wrapped up in thoughts of riots and the patrol routes that would be most efficient at stopping them, when she caught sight of someone out of the corner of her eye. A young woman standing at the gate, handing a scroll to a guard. Her head was bowed, but Zephyr recognized her. She froze.

Arian?

The girl nodded at something the guard said, lifting her head so Zephyr could see her clearly. There was no mistaking it. What was Arian doing here? And why was she dressed like a maid?

Her mind flashed back to her meeting with Liam. She felt a touch of cold. She'd warned him off, but did Liam mean to enter the Bastion anyway?

Arian walked away, fading back into the crowd. Behind Zephyr, the soldiers stopped, noticing her fixation.

"Lieutenant Venari?"

She held up a hand for silence, thinking hard. If Arian was masquerading as a servant, that could mean nothing good. Dread coiled in her stomach, for Arian and Liam both.

Zephyr motioned for the soldiers to wait, walking over to the gate guard. The guard, dressed in Imperial violet, looked her over as she approached. His eyes rested on the lieutenant's insignia on her collar. His lip curled, but he raised his hand in salute.

"Lieutenant. Can I help you with something?"

"Just curious," Zephyr said. "What did that girl want? The one who was here a moment ago?"

"Ah, her? She works for some Parani lord. Has a message for Lord Kaolin."

"I see." Zephyr kept her face smooth, showing no hint of the dread bubbling up inside her. "Coming to call on the lord, is he?"

"That'd be my guess, but you won't hear me gossiping about it," the guard said. His tone implied very strongly that Zephyr shouldn't either. "Was there anything else, Lieutenant?"

"No," said Zephyr, nodding at him. "Thank you."

He saluted at her and she returned it, walking away.

"Venari!"

Zephyr had gone about two steps before a sharp voice rang out across the courtyard. She drew up short, snapping to attention. Out of the corner of her eye, she could see the two soldiers accompanying her doing the same.

Commander Selwald was striding across the grass. His Imperial uniform was pressed to perfection, the embellishments that marked his rank shining in the late-afternoon sunlight. His hair had been combed, his shoes shined. He did not look happy. The lord commander of the Imperial Guard rarely did, but Zephyr thought he looked angrier than usual. She even thought she knew why, but it would be suicide to say as much to his face.

She drew herself up straighter, facing him.

"Commander."

Selwald stopped in front of her. He didn't return her salute. She didn't relax, staying at attention as his eyes moved over her, no doubt looking for something to take fault in. They took in her uniform, the shine on her shoes and the length of her nails, the long brown hair tied in a neat knot at the back of her head. She bore the scrutiny with as much grace as she could muster, and eventually he motioned for her to be at ease, scowling. She relaxed but kept her posture straight, hands resting loosely at her sides.

"Any idea why Lord Kaolin wants to see you?" he asked.

That surprised her. She wasn't able to keep it from showing on her face.

"No, sir."

Selwald looked over her again, as if trying to find any hint of deceit. When he could find none, his eyes snapped back to hers. His gaze was intense, but she forced herself not to look away.

"Well, he does. He's waiting for you in the solar. I trust there's no need to remind you to be on your best behavior."

"No, sir," Zephyr said.

"Go," said Selwald, inclining his head toward the Bastion. "Don't dawdle."

"Sir!" Zephyr snapped off another quick salute, then sent her soldiers off to assist with the patrols. They left without looking back, glad for any excuse to leave Commander Selwald's company. Zephyr stayed just long enough to watch them go before moving quickly toward the Bastion.

"Venari," Selwald said, stopping her.

She paused, looking back over her shoulder. The commander's gaze was on her again, his eyes narrowed in warning.

"Remember whose side you're on."

There was little chance of her forgetting, Zephyr thought, fighting to keep her face smooth. Inwardly, her stomach lurched. Lord Kaolin wanted to see her? She hadn't done anything to merit suspicion, unless—unless they knew about Liam. About her meeting with him.

"Yes, sir."

Selwald scowled, but waved at her to get going. She saluted and turned, heading toward the Bastion, where the young lord waited.

CHAPTER 20

ZEPHYR

IT WAS ALWAYS DIFFICULT TO LEAVE THE OUTER KEEP BEHIND, TO walk away from the barracks and training grounds and offices and make her way into the Bastion's heart. The Bastion's outer keep had been changed so much by Imperial occupation that it was practically unrecognizable, and the pain those changes brought her had been sharp and sudden, a wound that had healed over time. The Bastion's heart wasn't like that. It ached.

The inner keep of the Bastion had housed the royal family of Leithon for centuries. She couldn't walk through its halls and not remember how proud she had been the first time she had ever come through here, how it had felt to see her father guard the king at his throne. Those days were dead and gone, the king and queen slain in the occupation and their children carted off to Aeldoran to be turned into Imperial courtiers. Most of the time, Zephyr felt like she was making peace with that.

But it was hard to find peace walking through the inner keep, making her way across lengths of tiled floors and decorated hallways along paths that had been walked by countless generations of Leithonian royals. Harder still to quiet the little voice in the back of her mind that told her it would still be walked by Leithonian royalty today if it hadn't been for her.

The keep had changed little in the days since the invasion. The Aelrian Empire had seen no need to alter what were essentially luxury apartments in a well-appointed mansion. Even the Leithonian emblems that had been worked into stained glass windows or mosaics were allowed to remain where most other such symbols had been destroyed, markers of the city's once-independent history.

It was like walking back through time. Faces of long-dead kings and queens watched her from portraits on the wall, their stares accusing. She kept her eyes on the ground and walked fast, not daring to meet their gaze. Her father would say that it served her right, that she *should* feel ashamed to face them. She couldn't disagree, but she was relieved when she reached the door to the solar, guarded by two men in Imperial violet. The sight of them reminded her of the occupation and its consequences, and it hurt, but this was a familiar pain. They straightened as she approached, and she was half expecting them to give her a hard time, but evidently, Lord Kaolin had informed them that she was welcome. They saluted and pulled open the door.

The inside of the solar was guarded by four soldiers, none of them, Zephyr noted, wearing Imperial colors. They were dressed in black and gold, House Eismor colors. Each of them eyed her with a look of cold competency, and all were armed. She supposed this must be Lord Kaolin's personal guard and wondered what it said about him that the young lord didn't trust Commander Selwald's soldiers to guard his life.

Likely, it meant that he was smart.

The lord himself was seated on one of the couches in the solar, a book in his hand. As she entered, he closed it, turning to face her. He smiled.

Zephyr stood at attention, saluting.

"You wanted to see me, my lord?"

"At ease, Lieutenant," Lord Kaolin said, handing the book to one of his guards. He gestured at the chairs in front of him. "Have a seat."

Zephyr stepped forward. Almost immediately, the nearest guard moved in front of her, blocking her path. He held his hand out, his expression stern. She unbuckled her sword, passing it to him. When he didn't pull away, she handed him her pocketknife as well, then took the offered seat. Her eyes tracked the guard as he walked away, but he only moved to place her weapons on the far side of the room before returning to his post by the door.

She looked back at Lord Kaolin, who watched her with that smile still on his face. "So you're the one who opened the gates."

Zephyr clenched her hand into a fist at her side to keep from showing what she felt on her face. Seated in front of him, she felt as if she were back in that moment again, when she was fourteen and a knight only in name, a child chasing her father's coattails. When the Imperial army was at the gates and her father was going to fight them and Zephyr knew, just knew, that he would die, the same way Liam's mother had.

She forced herself to nod. She had done that. She wouldn't turn away from it. "Yes, my lord."

"I've heard of you," said Kaolin. "They gave you your own contingent, did they?"

"Yes."

"An interesting idea, I have to say. I'm not sure if you're aware of this, Lieutenant, but there are some in the Imperial Court who dislike the idea of Leithonians being given any sort of power in this city."

"I had not heard that, my lord." She had, of course.

"Are you attending the welcome feast, Lieutenant Venari?" Lord Kaolin asked.

Zephyr stared at him, unsure how to respond. What would be the polite response in this situation? "No, my lord," she ventured, uncertain. "I . . . didn't think I was invited."

Kaolin cocked his head to the side. "All the officers are invited. Were you not informed?"

Zephyr very much doubted that Selwald had any intention of relaying Kaolin's invitation to her. But it would be inappropriate at best and suicidal at worst to say as much. "No, my lord."

Kaolin's frown suggested that he understood more than he let on. "I see. Well then, allow me to extend the invitation personally. I hope to see you there."

Zephyr privately thought that she would rather cut off her own arm than sit at an Imperial dining table with the likes of Leon Albrent and Commander Selwald, but she bowed her head. "If that's what my lord wishes."

Kaolin gave her a knowing smile. "It is. I have no doubt that you'll be instrumental in the process of uniting this city, Lieutenant Venari. And it must be united, if we are ever to put that unpleasantness behind us and move forward together."

That unpleasantness. It was such a polite way to refer to the invasion of her homeland, the death of the royal family, the destruction of the Arcanum and the restructure of everything she had ever known. But it was also so very Aelrian of him. Zephyr found that she couldn't even hate him for it, like she hadn't expected anything else.

She drew in a breath. "I'm not entirely sure how much I can aid you, my lord."

"You can start by answering a question. What do you think of Commander Selwald?"

Zephyr paused, remembering the commander's words. A chill crept down her spine, the sense of impending doom.

"The commander is a capable man."

"No doubt," said Kaolin, holding Zephyr's gaze. "But that is not what I asked. Does he command your loyalty, Lieutenant Venari?"

His eyes bored into hers. She could feel the snare tightening around her and couldn't help looking to the left and right, as if Commander Selwald were hiding in the shadows. "He is my commanding officer."

"Perhaps I am not making myself clear," said Lord Kaolin. "And I've never been one for the games of court, so allow me to be frank.

When you leave this room, will you report the details of this conversation to Commander Selwald, or can I trust you to keep this conversation secret from him?"

The snare snapped shut, tightening around her neck. Zephyr looked helplessly at Lord Kaolin, her hands gripping her knees. A thought came to her, a frantic thought, that she couldn't divide her loyalties any further. If she turned her cloak a second time, she would have no colors left.

What came out of her mouth came unbidden, before she could think about the words. When she did speak them, she wished that she could take them back. "He has my family."

Lord Kaolin's eyes hardened. He didn't look like a boy anymore, Zephyr thought. He looked like what he was, the heir of an Imperial lord.

"I see. Well, I *was* going to ask you if you felt that I was safe here, but I believe you've already answered my question. You're dismissed, Lieutenant. I'll see you at the welcome feast."

He waved his hand distractedly, reaching for his book again. Zephyr rose, feeling as if her knees wouldn't bear her weight. She walked shakily toward the door, where the guard presented her with her sword and pocketknife. Her fingers moved automatically, slipping them back into their places with the ease of long familiarity.

It was when she had replaced her knife that she couldn't bear it any longer. She looked up.

"My lord."

Kaolin lowered his book, looking over his shoulder at her. "Lieutenant?"

"It's good that you have your personal guard," Zephyr said. Her heart pounded as the words escaped. What was she doing? She was going to get herself and her family killed. "I would keep them around you for as long as possible."

Kaolin grasped her meaning instantly. He nodded.

"Thank you for your recommendation, Lieutenant. I will keep that in mind. I hope that, if it comes to it, the Leithonian contingent may also be counted on to guard me."

She nodded numbly, not trusting herself to speak. Before she could dig herself a deeper hole, she gave Lord Kaolin a quick bow, leaving the room. Zephyr walked back down the hallways of the Bastion, heart pounding as she considered that meeting and its implications, considered the rat's nest that the keep was becoming.

If she was right, Arian would be here soon. And wherever Arian was, Liam wasn't far behind.

Divided loyalties. She was running out of colors to wear, cloaks to turn.

She would only end up betraying them all.

CHAPTER 21

ARIAN

ARIAN LEAPED INTO THE AIR, PULLING HER LIMBS CLOSE AS SHE whirled to dodge an imaginary blow. She bent her knees upon landing and unfolded her limbs, the point of her dagger cutting through the space where her opponent would have stood. Sweat beaded on her skin as she jerked back, snapping her head out of the way of a punch.

Her skin was flushed and warm in the cool morning air, her lungs burning.

Something moved out of the corner of her eye.

Arian whirled, a knife flying out of her hand before she could even think about it. Cavar knocked it aside with the back of his hand, a movement so smooth that it looked casual. The knife bounced off one of the ossuary's stone pillars, skittering onto the floor.

His brows rose. Arian stared at him, reality asserting itself. She breathed deep, wrapping her arms tight around her middle and trying to keep her shame from showing on her face.

It was the morning of their infiltration into the Bastion. In a few hours, Lord Nasirri Rezavi of Paran would be presenting himself to Lord Kaolin Eismor of Aelria, accompanied by Riana Barton and an attendant from the Order of Smoke and Mist, elite Parani mercenaries who specialized in bodyguard work.

"Linna gave me this response from Lord Kaolin," Cavar said, holding up an ornate envelope in one hand. "He would be happy to receive Lord Nasirri and is looking forward to their meeting."

"Great," Arian said. "I'm sure Lord Nasirri is *thrilled*."

"I'm sure he is," said Cavar. The Weaver stepped forward, nudging her fallen knife aside with his foot. The knife made a scraping sound across the stones, and Cavar looked from it to her. Arian's face burned.

"Do you want to talk about it?" Cavar asked.

"There's nothing to talk about. You snuck up on me, that's all. It's a practice knife. It wouldn't have hurt you that much."

"I'm not talking about the knife."

"I'm fine. I'm not a rookie on my first heist. I'll deal with it."

"You don't want to do this."

Arian shrugged, deliberately not looking at him. "It's a good plan."

"But you don't like it."

She exhaled in frustration. "What do you want from me? It's a good plan. It doesn't matter if I like it or not; I'll make it work."

"Arian."

Arian drew in a breath, determined to rage at him, to scream him down until she could shake loose this knot of unease that had lodged itself in her chest. She opened her mouth, raising her eyes to his, and paused.

Because he had gotten closer. Much closer than she expected.

Cavar was standing in front of her, eyes on hers. His dark eyes gleamed like steel. He wasn't dressed in Lord Nasirri's clothes, not yet. Like this, he was still himself, still Cavar eth'Nivear. His expression was solemn, his eyes shadowed where they met hers. He had something in his hand, and it took Arian a moment to realize that it was her knife, offered to her hilt first.

She took it, slipping it back into its sheath. Her fingertips brushed the back of his hand as she did, sending a spark through her that bothered her on more levels than one. Arian let her hand fall to her side, looking away.

"Arian," Cavar said, his voice soft.

"I'm scared."

The words slipped out of her mouth, spoken so softly that even Arian wasn't sure she had said them out loud. She knew what Cavar would think: that she was just a girl playing at thievery, that she wasn't up to the danger. It was exactly what Lyndon or Reid would have thought if she had said those words to either of them.

But that wasn't it. This mission didn't scare her because of the danger.

Arian was—she liked to think—the best thief in this entire damned city. She lived for the danger, the excitement, the thrill of being one second away from disaster. She lived for the feeling of freedom she got when she walked the rooftop paths, the rush she felt when she executed the perfect scheme.

Danger had never scared her. At least, not like this. She would be lying if she said she wasn't afraid of death, but death had always been a risk of her job. It was a risk that she accepted.

This mission didn't scare her because she was afraid to die. It scared her for a reason more fundamental than that. It scared her because of who she had to *be*. She had spent the past four years in hiding, pretending to be weak so that the Empire would leave her alone. And now she was going to walk into the Bastion, under their very noses, and pretend to be weak. To be afraid of them. The Empire, their power.

What if one day she stopped pretending? What if one day that became the truth?

That scared her more than death, more than danger. But Cavar wouldn't know that, and she didn't have the words to explain it to him.

She kept her head bowed, waiting for judgment, but it never came. Instead a hand landed on her shoulder, the touch tentative at first. She sucked in a breath at the warmth of it, a jolt running through her body at the contact. Arian froze, unsure whether she wanted to push him away or to lean closer.

"You're strong," Cavar said. "It will be okay."

Arian gritted her teeth at the words, reaching up and covering his hand with her own. She pulled it off. "I don't need your pity."

"I'm not saying it out of pity." The hand that she was holding moved, fingers closing around her own. "You're strong. You have a strength that no one can take from you. Remember that, and nothing in that place can harm you. Keep that close to you, and the Imperials won't know what hit them."

Arian stared at their joined hands, and for a second, she couldn't muster the control, the composure she needed to pull her hand away. But the memory came back to her all at once, of who she was and of what she was about to do. She slipped her hand out of his slowly, lowering it back to her side.

"We've got a job to do. No sense standing around here talking. Let's get it done."

CHAPTER 22

LIAM

ARIAN, CAVAR, AND LINNA LEFT THE OSSUARY EARLY THAT DAY.
Liam stood at the entrance into the tunnels to see them off, watching as they turned a corner and vanished into the twisting maze of the underground. He reflected on the fact that this might be the last time in a long while that he would see his sister.

Then, when the last echoes of their footsteps had faded away, he stepped back, retreating into the ossuary.

Liam drew his hand through the air as he walked, summoning an orb of blue flame to hover over his shoulder and light his path. He moved through their small living area, past their contraband and supplies, past the ancient storage rooms that they used for food and water, deeper and deeper into the catacombs themselves.

There were several reasons why the two of them had chosen the ossuary as their headquarters. It was defensible, it was well hidden, it was just eerie enough to dissuade all but the most serious of pursuers.

But it was also haunted.

Not by ghosts. Liam wasn't sure that ghosts, at least in the way that they were commonly understood, existed. But by magic, and by memories.

He moved past rows of graves, their markers worn smooth by the passage of years, as he made his way into the heart of the boneyard. It was a long walk, and as he walked, his mind treated him to images from the past, rosy memories that belonged to someone else. Studying magic with his mother, meeting a girl with brown hair and green eyes, desperately working up the courage to hold her hand.

And then the flames. He'd stood in the wreckage hidden from

his pursuers beneath the last veil that his mother had ever conjured as that man bore down on her, silver sword flashing.

Emeric Roth, Senior Chancellor of the Aelrian Order of Magisters and Magebreakers. Liam had learned his name after the fact. He never thought he would see him in Leithon again, but Roth's presence here meant something.

He even thought he knew what.

The Arcanum, the purest source of magic in the known world. Magic didn't just gather in Leithon, it *erupted* from it. It was in the ground and the air and the water and the stones, and magic was power. The Empire had destroyed the Arcanum because it couldn't bear the idea of a neutral party having that much power. But that didn't mean they were going to ignore it forever.

Roth was here, which meant that the Empire had come to claim its prize. To stand up against that, Liam needed *power*.

All magic needed power. Liam and most of the mages of the Arcanum drew theirs out of the natural world, manifestations of the elements like fire, water, earth, and air. The artificers, the reclusive mages who created magical artifacts, drew on power from within, from their own life energy. To prevent injury, they could draw only a little at a time, taking years to perfect their delicate works, but they were limited only by their imagination. The Speaker and Candidate had access to the purest forms of magic—they could bend light and shadow and turn the very bones of Leithon to their will. But the old magic, the magic of the ossuary . . .

That used a different source of power.

He told himself that it wasn't just about Roth. That the secrets that lay in the ossuary would also help him with his work for the Resistance. He could use the spells here to break into Blackstone Deep, whose protective wards had probably not been created to withstand this type of magic. He could *help* the Resistance. Help them take Leithon back.

With Arian and her cynicism gone, Liam finally had the space to consider how much he wanted that.

His footsteps echoed in the darkness, his summoned fire lighting his way. At length, he reached a space where the graves simply ended, where there was only another wrought-iron gate at the end of a passageway. Liam shouldered his way through that gate, careful of the rust and wear on its edges, and stepped into a small, closed chamber.

There was nothing here but a blank wall in front of him and a staff propped up in the corner. Liam took it in one hand, testing its heft and weight. Unlike his mage's staff, hidden under his bed in his chamber, this was made of steel, cold to the touch. It was tall, nearly his height, and slender, runes carved into its surface.

It was the first artifact that he had ever reclaimed alone, the only one that Arian did not know about.

Liam breathed deep and waved his hand, extinguishing the fire. At once, he was plunged into complete darkness. He channeled power into the staff, and the runes etched along its side began to glow, shining with a cold white light.

A chill washed over him as he held tight to the staff, a fell breeze stirring the air. Whispers sounded on the breeze, endless whispers, puffs of air like fingertips dragging across the side of his face. He gritted his teeth against the cold and reached out, touching the end of the staff to the stone wall in front of him.

A sigil traced itself onto the wall, shining in the same cold white light.

There was a click followed by the sound of grinding stone, and then the wall began to open, two halves sliding apart. Inside was another chamber, only slightly larger than the one he was standing in. It was dark and full of dust and terribly, bitterly cold.

In his and Arian's career, they had acquired a vast quantity of magical weapons, most of which they sold and some of which they kept for themselves, should they be needed.

In Liam's opinion, this chamber contained the most valuable weapon of all.

Knowledge.

The walls were etched with symbols and words, each stone panel a chapter out of an ancient grimoire. Liam held up the staff, letting its cold light wash over them as he moved forward, peering closer at the nearest passage.

This was dark magic, sealed away by the Arcanum eons ago, written and recorded by the monks who had worked here. The keepers of the dead. It was the magic of life and death, making and unmaking, the tools to create a wight or shade by binding a stray soul to the mortal plane or the tools to destroy one utterly. It took power from life, not just the practitioner's own life, but also the lives of others.

This wasn't about Roth. It wasn't *only* about Roth, but still . . .

Liam knew that Emeric Roth would not be brought down by common spells, not with the weight of the Imperial magebreakers behind him. The Arcanum had tried to fight him once before. The Arcanum had failed.

It was time to use weapons the Arcanum didn't have. Weapons that Roth would not be expecting.

He leaned closer to one of the panels as he started to read, lips moving soundlessly as they felt out the shape of the spell.

PART TWO

CATALYSIS

CHAPTER 23

CAVAR

A SMALL GROUP OF LORD KAOLIN'S PERSONAL GUARD MET CAVAR, Arian, and Linna at the entrance to the Bastion, forming ranks around the three of them as they were escorted inside. Cavar, wearing the court clothes and regal bearing of Lord Nasirri Rezavi, walked at the head of the group, studying the Bastion grounds. Beside him, Linna, in the grayish-black armor of the Order of Smoke and Mist, looked appropriately wary. She kept her hands a respectful distance from her weaponry, but her eyes moved left and right, looking for threats to her lord. And behind them both, Arian kept her head down and did her best to remain unnoticed.

Cavar took note of the banners on the Bastion grounds, House Eismor's black-and-gold banner standing side by side with the Aelrian military's violet and gold. Soldiers in bright violet uniforms swarmed the outer keep, a few of them watching the procession. He supposed that word of Lord Nasirri's arrival had spread, and if the Imperial military was anything like the Parani one, the tale of three hapless guards encountering the incognito lord had been passed around so many times that it would be unrecognizable by now.

He saw some of the soldiers eyeing Arian and worried about how she would fare. But it would be unseemly for Lord Nasirri to show too much concern for his servant in a procession like this, so he trusted Arian to handle herself, keeping his attention fixed on the path ahead. They passed through the walls that separated the inner keep from the outer keep, making their way into the heart of the Bastion.

Here, the military presence was lighter, and those soldiers who had been permitted entrance into the inner Bastion were better behaved. He noticed a variety of uniform colors here, not just the black and gold of House Eismor and the violet of the Imperial military, but uniforms in the colors of other noble Houses. The Leithonian contingent, of course, wore gray. They bowed politely as Cavar and his company passed them, entering the castle.

Inside, in a magnificently appointed foyer, a group of maids dressed in identical uniforms bowed to Cavar and offered to direct the other members of his party to their suite. Without blinking, Linna looked over her shoulder at Arian.

"See to the rooms."

Arian nodded and gave Cavar a proper—if somewhat stiff—bow. He watched out of the corner of his eye as the maids whisked her away, trailed by the footmen they had hired to carry their things. Once they were gone, the honor guard marched them forward, toward a man standing at the foot of the foyer's grand staircase— Lord Kaolin Eismor.

Cavar offered the young lord a gracious bow.

"My lord," he said. "Might I compliment you on acquiring so fine an estate?"

Kaolin smiled at him, returning the bow. "Your compliments are appreciated, Lord Nasirri. Although they are perhaps premature. Rulership of Leithon has not yet been transferred to me."

Cavar smiled. "Ah, but your answer only confirms the rumors. I assume such proceedings are in the works?"

There was an amused gleam in Lord Kaolin's eye as he returned the smile, inclining his head like a fencer acknowledging a touch. "Who can say? It's an interesting time for the Aelrian Court."

"Doubtless. Even in distant Paran, we hear of the Empire's conquests. One might wonder what new avenues for commerce might be opened by so . . . earnest an expansion."

"Yes," Kaolin said. "One might, although I'm afraid I was never much for commerce. Lord Nasirri, if you would follow me, I would introduce you to some of the other peers who have accompanied me from Aelria. Perhaps there, you might find those more learned in the arts of trade than myself."

It was as smooth a transition to introducing the other members of his court as Cavar could have expected, and he wondered how much of Lord Kaolin's claims to deficiency were true. So far, the young lord seemed like the sort of person Lord Nasirri would love as a friend and hate as an enemy.

"Of course, my lord. Nothing would make me happier."

He motioned for Linna to follow as Lord Kaolin led them up the stairs. The lord's personal guard trailed them, wary, although it seemed to Cavar that their wariness was not directed toward him, instead focused on the Imperial soldiers behind them.

An interesting time for the Aelrian Court indeed.

BY THE TIME CAVAR RETREATED TO HIS ROOMS TO DRESS FOR dinner, it was almost evening, the sun casting long shadows against the halls of the inner keep. The maid who saw him and Linna to his suite was appropriately deferential, but Cavar wondered whether she might have been sent to keep an eye on him. Conscious of that, he kept conversation with Linna to a minimum, saying very little to her as he stepped through the door into his sitting room. As soon as the door closed behind him, Linna went to scour the room for traps and hidden passages, and Cavar moved past her, entering the large, richly appointed bedroom.

Arian was already there, putting away his clothes. Her scowl told him she would rather be doing almost anything else. At his approach, she tensed but did not look up, continuing her work.

"Is your business concluded, my lord?" she asked.

It was a code phrase the two of them had decided on, to indicate whether it was safe to break character. Cavar closed the door behind him. "It is."

Arian let out a sigh of relief, nearly dropping the shirt she was folding. "Thank the gods." She flopped backward onto the large bed and spread her arms out to either side of her. "I thought I was going to die if I had to play the maid for any longer."

Cavar smiled, unbuttoning his collar. "Surely it can't have been that bad."

Arian groaned, throwing an arm over her eyes. "Worse."

"You must have learned something, at least. Castle maids are prone to gossip."

"Oh, there's gossip, all right. Apparently someone named Lady Liliana is sleeping with a Lord Reichart, despite being betrothed to some lord up in Aelria." Arian snorted. "Real useful stuff."

Cavar shrugged. "Court gossip can be useful." He took a seat at the edge of the bed beside her, half expecting Arian to move away. She didn't, keeping her arm over her eyes.

"Yeah, right," she drawled.

He took the opportunity to study the room. "Are we being watched?"

Arian held up two fingers. "Two listening spells. One in the sitting room, one in the bedroom. Found them using one of Liam's tricks. No peepholes or anything like that. The spells were mostly inactive too. They were pathways to listening in, but no one was using them. They're not exactly falling all over themselves to spy on us, are they?"

"Lord Nasirri is hardly a threat under the circumstances," Cavar said. "They'll watch him for protocol's sake, but Kaolin must know that any true threat to his rule will come from inside Aelria. Given that we're having this conversation, I take it you disabled the spells?"

"First thing I did." Arian removed the arm from over her eyes, pointing at a coin she had left on top of the dresser. "It's a trick coin. Apprentice artificers used to make them, back in the days of the Arcanum, to help them sneak around after lights-out at the dorms. It plays recorded noise. If anyone listens in right now, they're just going to hear some bags getting unpacked, maybe some indistinct conversation. I'll fix it so they hear a different set of sounds every day, in case they listen in more than once."

"Impressive," Cavar said.

"You hired the best," Arian said, stretching her arms out over her head. "You got the best. What about you? You learn anything interesting?"

Cavar frowned, recalling everything he had taken note of while walking with Lord Kaolin. "Things are tense between the young lord and the military. He seems to think Commander Selwald can have him killed at any time. Nothing that gets us closer to the Star, though."

Arian grunted, closing her eyes again. Cavar looked over the room one more time, frowning as he caught sight of the open door on the room's other side. It led into a spacious dressing room where, from this angle, he could see the edge of Arian's own trunk of belongings. He nudged her with an arm and her eyes snapped open.

"The dressing room?" he asked.

Arian's eyes widened, a flush spreading over her face. She rolled onto her side, turning her back to him. "They set up a cot for me in the dressing room. In case you . . . have need of me. The maids seem to think that—well, they seem to think that—they think that we—" She broke off.

"Huh. Well that's convenient."

"Convenient, my ass!" Arian growled, flipping over and punching him in the thigh. Her face was still red. Cavar lifted a placating hand.

"I didn't mean it that way. If they think that you and I have a . . . less than proper relationship, it could excuse a lot of things.

Including the two of us being found in places where we shouldn't be. And if you're nearby at night, it makes planning our next move much simpler."

Arian didn't respond, but Cavar got the sense that she wasn't fully convinced. She rolled away from him, getting to her feet.

"Well," she said, her back to him as she walked toward the dressing room. "You need to get to dinner, and I'm tired, so find your own clothes."

The dressing room door closed with a crack and didn't open again while Cavar was there.

CHAPTER 24

ARIAN

OVER THE NEXT COUPLE OF WEEKS, THEY FELL INTO A ROUTINE.
Cavar continued to act as Lord Nasirri, attending parties and social engagements and doing whatever else the upper crust of Aelrian society did with their time. Linna shadowed him and pried information out of the soldiers who guarded the other nobles. While the two of them did come back with information about Aelrian politics and the major players in the area, they were more a distraction than anything else. Their positions were far too visible for them to spend their time skulking around the Bastion, which meant they couldn't *actively* search for the Star.

That was where Arian came in.

Being a maid was humiliating, but it came with one advantage. She was invisible. Nobody looked twice when they saw a Leithonian servant wandering around, particularly when said servant was openly dressed in the livery of a visiting lord. Once or twice, she had to dodge the attentions of some amorous Imperial soldiers, but that was nothing new, and Lord Nasirri's rumored attention helped her more than she wanted to admit. Most soldiers left her alone.

Her status as a servant meant that she was far more mobile than either Cavar or Linna. She had even managed to walk past the treasury once, or at least the hallway that led down into it. It was under the keep, at the end of a long narrow corridor guarded on both ends. She was willing to bet that there were magical safeguards built into the corridor too, to stop anyone from getting in by magical means.

Once or twice a week, she went out into the city on Lord Nasirri's errands. She couldn't meet with Liam or any of the

Resistance directly, in case she was being watched, but every now and then, she dropped in at a tailor's shop to check on a new coat or other piece of frippery that Nasirri had ordered. The tailor was one of Aila's friends, and they exchanged letters folded into clothes or hidden with payment. It was a slow way of getting information across, and they didn't write too much for fear of discovery, but it allowed Arian to share what she was learning with the Resistance. And it allowed her to keep in touch with her brother.

Unfortunately, she hadn't learned much that would be of use. And when she explained the situation with the treasury, Liam agreed that the direct approach should be a last resort. None of them knew what spells had been worked into the stone, and unless they could turn themselves invisible, they weren't going to get past the guards.

So entering the treasury directly was out. Not that Arian had honestly expected that would be an option.

It was on the second week since their arrival at the Bastion that Arian found her first lead. She was walking down one of the servants' corridors, a basket of Lord Nasirri's laundry tucked under her arm, when she caught sight of someone moving down the hallway that intersected with hers, his bearing imperious and his steps quick. Arian froze, clutching the laundry basket tighter as she pulled her scarf down over her head.

The man who passed by was not anyone she had been expecting.

Long dark hair pulled back into a tail behind his head. A pale face. Eyes of winter blue.

Emeric Roth.

Arian kept her eyes on the ground, holding her breath as Roth strode past her. She felt the weight of his gaze as he glanced in her direction, but a serving girl carrying a basket of laundry didn't warrant his attention, and Arian resembled her father more than she did her mother. He kept walking.

Roth. Roth was here, with Lord Kaolin. She wondered if Liam

knew, and decided that if he didn't, she wasn't going to be the one to tell him. He was already in enough danger, with Lyndon filling his mind with revolution. If he knew that Roth was in town, it would break him, and she'd already seen him broken once. She hadn't seen what he'd seen on the day of the occupation, and even then, seeing Roth made rage coil in her gut. But she was stronger than her brother, and she wouldn't see him break again.

She could handle this on her own.

Feelings aside, Roth was a curiosity. And, like Lord Kaolin himself, an opportunity. There was no way that a man like him could come to Leithon without becoming interested in the magical artifacts the Bastion held. And Kuthil's Star was the most prized artifact of all. If Roth took the Star out of the treasury for his own purposes, it would save them the trouble of having to get in.

He was walking alone, carrying a lantern, down a darkened corridor that was rarely used by anyone except for servants. That was even more interesting. She smirked as she crept forward, peering down the hallway.

Making her decision, Arian tightened her grip on the basket, one of her hands slipping beneath the first layer of laundry. There, hidden inside the folds of cloth, was a slender dagger—the same one that Liam had transferred his amulet's protections onto. It should be resistant to magic now. She shifted it closer to the edge of the basket, where she could reach for it more easily, then moved to follow Roth.

There were ways that mages could use to detect people around them, but they operated on small scales. Magic worked on a different plane from the rest of the physical senses, a different layer of reality. A mage might be able to detect magic being cast from miles away, but even the most powerful mages couldn't detect ordinary human beings for more than a handful of yards, and her enchanted dagger wouldn't be detectable until she tried to use it.

Her feet moved whisper quiet on the stones as she trailed Emeric Roth from afar. She followed him as he walked down narrow corridors, using the play of light and shadow to her advantage to duck out of sight whenever he looked back.

He didn't see her. He could detect magic, but this wasn't that. It was simple human skill. Her heart pounded as she followed him, skin flushed with the thrill of the chase. He led her deeper into the castle, into the bowels of the Bastion.

Then he stopped.

Arian stopped several yards behind him, hiding herself in a shadowed alcove in the stone wall. He looked around again, but his eyes skipped over her without seeing her. He was carrying a light, and that made him blind to anything outside his circle of illumination. She blended into the shadows and held her breath as Roth looked back at the wall, stretching out his hand.

He passed through it, lantern and all.

Arian blinked in surprise, staring at the darkened space where he had been standing. When he didn't reemerge, she reached out, tapping the stone wall beside her. It was solid. But that hadn't mattered to Roth. He'd passed straight through the wall, like a ghost.

It was a use of magic that she hadn't considered before. She didn't even know if it was possible.

Arian lifted one of her hands from the laundry basket, staring at the wall. Maybe there was something she could do, if she focused.

Maybe . . .

A hand grabbed her arm, drawing her out of her thoughts. Arian dropped the basket and whirled, the dagger in her hand aimed squarely at the intruder's throat. Her captor knocked her knife aside with a mailed fist, grabbing at her shoulder with her other arm. Arian's eyes narrowed as she recognized the girl in front of her. She lowered the knife.

"Skulking around in the dark, Zeph?" she asked. "How the mighty have fallen."

"Don't give me that, Arian," Zephyr said, her eyes narrowed in challenge. "What are you *doing* here?"

"Sure you want to know?" Arian's lips parted in a feral grin. "Your new boss might not like it."

"Do you even understand how dangerous this is? Gods, Arian! You're in the Bastion with—with some Parani stranger! Do you know what could happen to you if you're caught? What could happen to Liam?"

At the mention of Liam's name, Arian's smile faded. She reached for Zephyr's hand, pulling it off her shoulder. "Leave my brother out of this."

"I will *not*. I can't let you do this, Arian. You have no idea what you're dealing with."

"Report me, then. Go ahead. Do it. Call your Imperial masters. I'm waiting."

"I'm not going to do that." Zephyr wrenched her hand out of Arian's grip with enough force that Arian felt a twinge in her shoulder, stepping back. "But *you* should know better. You both should. You're playing with fire, Arian. Sooner or later, you're going to get burned."

"You think we don't know that?" Arian asked, taking a step forward. "Let me tell you the difference between us and you, since you don't seem to be getting it." She stepped closer still, closing the distance between her and Zephyr so that she could look her in the eye. "We'd rather die in the fire than live without facing it at all."

Zephyr shrank back as if struck, eyes widening. Before she could recover, Arian gathered up the basket of laundry and the dagger, walking away. She felt angrier than she had in a long while, but there was power in her rage.

"You think I'm not facing the fire?" Zephyr asked from behind her, her voice strained. "You think I don't know the consequences of what I did?"

Arian didn't look back at Zephyr. She was afraid that if she did, she might do something drastic. Instead, she clenched her fists and said, very quietly, "You look really cushy from down here. Go tell my mother how hard your life's been."

Zephyr tried to get her attention once more after that, speaking her name softly into the darkness.

Arian raised one hand, making a rude gesture in the air. She walked on.

CHAPTER 25

CAVAR

KAOLIN'S HORSE PUT ON A SUDDEN BURST OF SPEED, SEPARAT-ing him from the pack of nobles and propelling him to the other end of the promenade. As the others gasped, Cavar spurred his own mount forward with a nudge at its sides, closing the distance between him and Kaolin. He pulled up swiftly as he reached the young lord.

Kaolin looked over at him from his own saddle, flashing him an unguarded grin. "You ride well, Nasirri."

How would Lord Nasirri react to such a compliment? With pride, certainly. Nasirri would take pride in outdoing members of the nobility whose families were more established. And perhaps with some unguardedness of his own.

"I'm Parani, my lord," Cavar said. "We are born in the saddle."

"You may be," Kaolin said. "But House Eismor breeds the best horses in the world."

"Perhaps that's what they say in Aeldoran. But the Empire does not own the world yet."

"I believe that sounds like a challenge." Kaolin looked back at the parade of nobles and their mounts, struggling to catch up. "Race you to the end of the path?"

"It would give your friends a show. Although perhaps you do not want to embarrass yourself in front of them."

"Oh, I think I can handle a little embarrassment." Kaolin's smile told Cavar he had no intention of losing. "Besides, we'll be far enough ahead that they likely won't see. On three?"

"On three," Cavar agreed.

They counted backward from three. On the third count, Cavar spurred his horse forward at the same time as Kaolin did. His heart leaped at the sudden burst of speed, and he had to bite back a grin. The gasps from behind them faded, lost to the wind. Cavar pulled back as they reached the end of the path, startled servants leaping apart as Cavar's mount beat Kaolin's by a hair.

When they came to a stop, Kaolin was laughing. He extended a hand toward Cavar from horseback, flushed and grinning. "I think you went on 'two.'"

"My lord," Cavar said, his voice a mockery of outrage. "Are you accusing me of cheating?"

"If the shoe fits, Nasirri," Kaolin said, but he smiled as he looked back at the other courtiers, now leagues away. The smile faded as he reached down, stroking his horse's neck absentmindedly. "Most of them have never seen battle. Nominally, they're the commanders of armies, or will be, but this is the closest they've ever come to a battlefield."

Cavar's brows rose. "And you've seen battle, my lord?"

Kaolin's expression darkened. "My father believes in a more . . . practical education. I've seen a lot of things. But it's because I've seen these things that my father believes me fit to rule Leithon."

The way he said the words, careful and clipped, implied that his father had designs on ruling more than just Leithon. Cavar filed that away for the future, but it was a nuance that Nasirri wouldn't notice, and so Cavar pretended not to notice either.

"You may very well be suited to governing this place," Cavar said instead. "Certainly you're less frivolous than some of these others."

Kaolin chuckled. "There is that. But enough politics. It's going to take a while yet for them to catch up. Drink with me?"

Nasirri would not refuse an opportunity to be alone with Lord Kaolin. So when Kaolin slid from the back of his horse, handing the reins to a stable hand, Cavar did the same. "I'd be honored, my lord. Perhaps we'll see if it's true what they say, about Aelrians and their liquor."

"And perhaps we'll see if it's true what they say about Parani," Kaolin said, smiling in return as he led Cavar away. "I have a vintage here that will satisfy even your tastes, I'm sure . . ."

↓↓↓

THE DOOR TO THE DRESSING ROOM WAS OPEN WHEN CAVAR returned. Arian was sitting cross-legged on her cot, a whetstone in her hand and her dagger lying on the thin mattress in front of her. She leaped to her feet as he entered the room.

Cavar leaned against one of his bedposts, attempting to take off his boots. The world spun alarmingly, and before he knew it, Arian was standing in front of him, her brow furrowed and her lips pulled into a frown.

"You're drunk," she said.

"And you," Cavar said, "forgot to say the pass phrase."

"Are we being watched?" Arian asked, looking skeptically at the door as if expecting an Imperial to burst through it at any moment.

"No. But consistency is the key to any operation." Cavar let one of his boots fall to the ground and flopped back onto the bed without bothering to remove the other. Arian made an impatient noise in the back of her throat. He made a half-hearted attempt to raise his other leg, wiggling it at her. "Could you help me with my shoe?"

"Like hell."

She braced herself against one of the bedposts, glaring down at him. Arian looked very nice hovering over him. So nice that he almost missed her next question. "How much did you drink?"

"Enough." The rest of him, the part that was still thinking with his brain, managed to pull together enough of his fractured thoughts to come up with a proper assessment of the situation. "Enough to play my part convincingly."

"What part?" Arian asked. "Nasirri's a drunkard now?"

"He enjoys the privileges of high society."

"Which means?"

"He likes to drink." Cavar grinned at her. He couldn't help himself. "It was *very* good wine."

"I'm sure it was," Arian said, sounding unamused. Cavar's grin faded somewhat as he met her eyes.

"Is something wrong?" he asked.

"Oh, nothing," said Arian, pulling away from the post. "Just that while you were riding horses and getting drunk on high-society wine, *I* was getting work done."

Something in her voice nagged at him, and he slid his hands out to either side of him, pushing himself up so that he was sitting on the edge of the bed. It took longer than he would have liked, and his head swam, which was a bad sign. It told Cavar that perhaps he *had* been a little overindulgent with the wine. "You've found something? What is it?"

Arian ran a hand through her hair, shooting him an impatient glance. "I'll tell you when you're sober. I'm not explaining this twice."

"I'm listening," Cavar said, which was true. He was too well trained to let a little wine impair his ability to function, at least where the mission was concerned. Arian, however, pressed her lips together, looking doubtful. He offered her a reassuring smile. "Try me, Arian."

Arian sighed. "Fine. I think Emeric Roth is up to something. I caught him sneaking around corridors earlier today. He walked through a wall and I lost track of him. Now I just need a good map of the Bastion, and—what?"

"What?" Cavar repeated.

"You're smiling," Arian said.

Cavar touched the side of his mouth and found that it was true. He schooled his face into a more composed expression, but a glance at Arian told him that he wasn't fooling anyone. It gave him the strangest urge to break out in giggles, and the smile broke onto his face again.

"Are you going to tell me what the hell is so funny?" Arian asked.

"You're very pretty, Arian."

"Oh, for the love of—" Arian pressed her palm to her face. "You're clearly not listening to any of this. I'm going to bed. Wake me up when you're sober, lover boy."

"I *was* listening!" Cavar protested. "Emeric Roth, Senior of the Order of Magisters. Sneaking around, walking through walls." His eyes widened as her words finally hit him. "Wait, did you just say he walked through *a wall*?"

Arian rolled her eyes. "Good *night*, Cavar," she said, beginning to walk away.

The world kept spinning. Cavar closed his eyes, bowing his head. "I might have had a little too much wine."

"You think?" An arm rested on his back, supporting him, and Cavar blinked his eyes open. "Come on," Arian murmured, her face suddenly, undeniably close to his. "Lie down. Nice and easy."

"Okay . . . ," Cavar muttered under his breath, in a way that he had to admit was kind of pathetic. But he couldn't help it. At that moment, if Arian had asked him to do a flying backflip out the window, he would have done his best—and suffered the disastrous consequences. She lowered him back onto the mattress, and her arm lingered there for half a moment before she pulled away.

"Linna can help you find a map," he mumbled, partly because he wanted to show her that he was still thinking about the mission, but also partly because it was hard to look at her.

"Get some sleep," she said, straightening up. "We'll talk about it in the morning."

"I meant what I said," Cavar said, to no one in particular. "You really are very pretty."

Arian hesitated in the doorway to the dressing room, one hand on the frame. She looked back over at him, and there was something on her face that he couldn't quite read. Shock? Sadness? Some mixture of the two? It frustrated him, because he was telling the truth, and why wouldn't she believe it? And why was it so important to him, just then, that she believed it?

She looked him in the eye. "Go to sleep."

Because she asked it of him, he closed his eyes. And before he knew it, he was asleep.

CHAPTER 26

LIAM

THE STAFF WAS COLD IN HIS HAND, THE CHILL BITING INTO HIM even through his heavy gloves. Water condensed on its surface from the thick fog that surrounded them, and Liam tightened his grip to keep it from slipping. Through the fog, he could see the lights of Blackstone Deep, or at least, the lights of the gatehouse that guarded the entrance into the prison tunnels.

He blinked stars out of his vision, sucking in a breath of clammy, wet air. Conjuring up the fog had not been simple, and he had worked hard to make it look natural. The proximity of the ocean had helped, giving him a source of water that he could draw on, and the air here was used to carrying both fog and magic—it had been pliable. But water was a tricky element, and he breathed deep and slow, trying to regain some of his energy for what lay ahead. The staff in his hand quivered with anticipation, but Liam wasn't going to give it what it wanted. Not yet.

"Are you sure this is going to work?" Lyndon asked him, voice laced with skepticism. Liam drew in another fog-laced breath before he answered.

"It should. You can leave the magical protections to me. As long as your people can deal with the guards."

Lyndon snorted. "Guards are the least of our problems," he said, but he added, "My people will do what they can."

They waited, eyes on the orange light of the guards' lanterns. Lyndon had chosen a small crew for this assignment, seven of the Resistance's best. To Liam, who was used to working with Arian and Arian alone, it still seemed like a lot, too many to hide but too few to mount an invasion.

It didn't matter. They were supposed to break into the prison. Get in and then out. They weren't here to tear the whole thing down.

His grip slipped on the staff, just a little. Liam tightened his shaking hold. This had to work. He wasn't the Speaker or the Candidate. He couldn't alter the fabric of their spells, couldn't change whatever they had set into motion to guard the prison. But at the very least, he could take them all down.

There was a scuffle at the gates. The guards' lanterns flickered, but between the thickness of the fog and the distance, he couldn't see or hear anything else. Liam held his breath. A moment later, one of the lights blinked on and off three times. The signal.

"Let's move," Lyndon said to Liam and the other three waiting with them. Liam walked forward with the rest of them, moving across the thin grasses and rocky ground that covered this side of the island, between Leithon and the Arcanum. The air was laced with the smell of salt, the grass slippery beneath their feet until they neared the prison, and then the grass gave way to loose rock and gravel, as if even grass didn't want to grow anywhere near this place.

The prison's stone walls hummed with energy Liam could feel from here. As they neared, Liam could see what had happened at the gate.

Reid and another member of Lyndon's group stood on either side of the gate, holding the lanterns. At their feet were two unconscious soldiers, both dressed in Imperial violet. At Lyndon's signal, two of the others accompanying them moved to tie up the guards, while a third took the lantern from Reid, who walked over to them, wiping his gloved hands on his trousers.

"Any trouble?" Lyndon asked Reid.

Reid shook his head, keeping his voice low. "None. They went down nice and quietly. But that was the easy part, wasn't it? Next patrol is coming by in five minutes." He looked at Liam as he spoke, and Liam felt his mouth go dry with the weight of responsibility.

One of the things he had learned about people was that they rarely said what they meant. Sometimes requests were hidden, ensconced within seemingly innocuous statements. His ability to parse the meaning of those statements varied, but he understood this one perfectly.

Five minutes until the next patrol.

Five minutes to get through the Deep's magical wards, or they were all dead.

It wasn't a lot of time. He had known, going in, that he wouldn't have a lot of time to do what he needed to do, which was why he had chosen this course of action. In theory, it was simple. Foolproof. But Liam had learned enough by now to know that reality seldom complied with theory.

Still, he had brought them all out here with his assurances that he could do this. Even if he wanted to, there was no going back now.

"Stand back, please," he heard himself say as he shouldered his way past Lyndon and Reid to face the prison gate.

The gate's heavy wooden doors were shut and locked, but the lock wasn't the problem. Either of the unconscious guards would have the key. The problem was the buzzing sensation that started up in Liam's mind as he stepped toward the doors, a feeling like insects were swarming just underneath his skin. The wards here were woven so tightly together that it was impossible to see the original threads, as if a cloth of magic had been laid over the gate and the walls. They had been laid by not just one mage but several, over the centuries of Leithon's existence, each new Speaker adding their own touch to the spells that guarded the Deep.

The last hand to touch these spells had been his mother's.

Liam could feel her, that magical signature that he recognized from somewhere deeper than his mind, from something in the very heart of him. He wanted to breathe it in, to close his eyes and imagine that she was right there in front of him, that when he opened his eyes, the world would be back to the way it had been. But he didn't have the time.

He raised the staff in his hand, infusing it with power. Cold blue light danced over the staff's surface, the metal coming to life with a hum and a quiver beneath his grip. He'd taken this staff because it was a particularly good conductor—it was hungry for magic and power. It had once been built to force the potential out of a mage, to allow them to push themselves past their body's safe limits and use more of their life force than they would have been able to otherwise. For emergencies or grand workings or desperation, Liam wasn't sure, but that wasn't what he used it for now.

The writings in the ossuary had taught him the basic principles of dark magic, how to take power from another instead of using one's own. And while turning those principles on a living thing was certainly forbidden, what he was planning to do was a bit more of a . . . gray area.

Both dark magic and ordinary magic fed on life. And the spells that protected the Deep were a sort of life, the life force of all the practitioners who had placed them.

He touched the tip of the staff to the gate and focused his will, altering the flow of power through the staff so that it drew from the wards rather than from him.

It began to warm in his hands, first gently, and then so hot that he could barely hold on. He clenched his jaw, choking back a scream as power rushed through him, the staff trembling in his grip. Steam rose from its surface where the fog touched it, cold blue light shifting and becoming red like fire. The life force of centuries flooded into the staff, and into him.

He couldn't hold it. It was more than he expected. He had to do something with the power. He had to—

Liam let out a choked gasp, flinging the power as far away from him—and from them—as he could. The air was suddenly filled with the smell of ozone. There was a deafening boom and, in the distance, a streak of blue lightning crashed down from the sky, tearing through the fog as it struck the ground. Liam dropped to his knees, spent. Spots floated in his vision, and his mouth tasted coppery and stale. His teeth were chattering suddenly. He felt so cold.

"I'm sorry," he said when Lyndon dropped to a knee beside him. "I didn't mean to—didn't mean to give us away—"

"Are the wards down?" Lyndon asked.

Liam reached out with his mind, but where he had once felt the wards, he felt only nothingness. A void where they had been. He nodded.

"Yes—I think so—"

Lyndon's grin was frightening. "Then you didn't give us away. It was just a bit of lightning on a stormy day." Already, people were moving behind him. Liam heard the click of the lock falling open, saw Reid shouldering his way through the wooden door. He could feel no hint of recognition, nothing activating from within the Deep. It had worked.

But it wasn't good enough.

He'd barely been able to disable those spells. He was certain that the spells that protected the Bastion, the treasury, would be stronger still. If he wanted to break through them, he needed to become stronger too.

Lyndon's gloved hand appeared in front of his face, making him jump. Liam hadn't even noticed the Resistance leader had stood up.

"They'll be coming to check it out soon," he said. "And there might be more wards inside. Are you ready to move?"

Liam still felt dazed, but now that the gate was open, he could see Lyndon's people slipping past the courtyard, heading into the prison tunnels. Still, there were no alarms. He had done that. He had taken down the Empire's protections, had opened the way. He hadn't been able to help during the occupation, but now—

—people could go *free* because of him. Leithonians. His people.

He reached out and grabbed Lyndon's hand, letting the man haul him to his feet.

CHAPTER 27

ARIAN

MORNING BROUGHT WITH IT A SENSE OF CLARITY. IT HAD RAINED in the night, a summer thunderstorm that had scoured the Bastion grounds with its fury, and the light that shone in through the small, high window of Nasirri's dressing room was pure and refined, the life force of creation distilled into a sunbeam.

It was also shining directly into Arian's eyes, so of course, she hated it.

Arian groaned, throwing a pillow over her face to shut out the light as she tried to hold on to the last few fleeting details of her dreams. There had been a warmth in them that she wanted back, but reality refused, as always, to give in to her desires. She sighed, running a hand through her hair as she pushed herself up to her feet.

Cavar was in the sitting room, his head propped up in his hand and cup of steaming coffee raised to his lips—compliments, according to the note that lay beside the coffee pot, of Lord Kaolin Eismor. He looked miserable.

"...never drinking again," Arian heard Cavar mumble as she crept up behind him. "I don't care what Lord Kaolin says. Nasirri is going to take vows. He'll become an ascetic."

Linna stood in front of him, already dressed in her armor. She looked up as Arian approached, their eyes meeting. A look passed between them, one of exasperation and commiseration.

As quietly as possible, Arian picked up the lacquered tray that she used to fetch Lord Nasirri's breakfast, slipping out of the room. To her surprise, Linna followed her out, closing the door behind her. Arian bit back a comment. Outside their rooms, she wasn't

Arian Athensor. She was only Riana Barton. Her eyes darted left to right to make sure that they weren't being watched before she spoke.

"What is it?"

Linna's reply came in barely more than a whisper. "You're searching for a map. I'd try the Royal Library."

So Cavar *had* been listening last night. Good for him.

She nodded at Linna, looking away. "I'll be back with breakfast. And then I'll take care of it."

Linna nodded. She touched two fingers to her lips in the Weaver gesture of farewell and turned, slipping back into the room.

ARIAN HAD BARELY TAKEN TWO STEPS OUT OF LORD NASIRRI'S suite before she realized that *something* was wrong in the Bastion. The hallways were emptier than usual, and the few people she saw in the servants' passages hurried along without stopping to chat, heads bowed and eyes darting from left to right. In the kitchens, she risked asking one of the cooks what had happened, pausing for a chat while she waited for them to prepare Nasirri's breakfast. All the cooks knew was that something had happened in the city last night, and the Imperial military was a kicked beehive, violet-uniformed soldiers swarming in the courtyard and heading out into the city in droves. Rumors were already spreading, everything from the Leithonian Resistance burning down the Imperial Quarter to a gang of pirates waiting to raid the harbor. Whatever had happened, Arian wouldn't be able to learn the truth from here, but at the words *Leithonian Resistance*, she felt her heart seize up. She hoped to any gods that were listening that Liam hadn't gotten himself killed.

By the time Cavar had finished picking at his breakfast, though, she relaxed. She'd heard nothing about mages being captured in the night, and neither had Linna when Arian asked her, grudgingly, to check. From what Linna had found, hanging around the guards' barracks on the pretense of borrowing a whetstone, there had been a prison break at Blackstone Deep. No one had been caught, so if Liam was involved, he had gotten away.

She could worry about him another day. In the meantime, she needed to find her map, which meant a trip to the library.

The Royal Library was on one of the Bastion's upper floors, and it took up most of the floor it was situated on. It was, to hear Liam talk, one of the greatest libraries in the world, rivaled only by the collection that had once been housed in the Arcanum. It wasn't the sort of place that a serving girl like Riana would normally go, at least not without a master to follow, and "Lord Nasirri" was presently too indisposed to feel up to intellectual pursuits. But Arian had a plan.

In Cavar's dressing room, she put on a wig and a livery dress she had filched from the laundry room. A few careful applications of makeup and Riana Barton was gone, replaced by a nameless serving girl in Lady Liliana's colors. That done, Arian slipped out the window under Linna's supervision and made her way back through the halls with no one the wiser.

The library was almost empty, aside from a few maids dusting the shelves. The situation in the city had driven the nobility into their quarters. Although anyone important enough to be allowed rooms in the Bastion was, of course, above suspicion, very few people felt confident enough to be out at leisure when soldiers were underfoot.

It was a good time for clandestine encounters, though, which was why it had been almost embarrassingly easy to get the maids to leave. All Arian had to do was claim that Lady Liliana needed the library clear for personal reasons, and they believed her. The whole Bastion was still talking about her affair with Lord Reichart. Arian prayed that the two of them had the good sense to stay in their rooms as she made her way to the reference section.

There were very few maps of the Bastion available outside the Bastion walls, and for good reason, but there was no reason why such information needed to be kept secret within the Bastion itself. Arian found what she was looking for in a packed alcove filled with hastily filed floor plans of most of Leithon's major government buildings.

The map she found wasn't complete. The most secure parts of the Bastion—the barracks, the treasury, and the royal apartments—had been left out of the floor plans, with nothing more than a note to show their general location, but the mapmaker had not seen any need to redact the servants' passageways. She traced her path yesterday with a finger until she arrived at the spot where she had lost sight of Emeric Roth the day before.

And there she paused, lips pursed as she considered the map.

On the other side of that wall was a blank space labeled *Treasury*.

Roth had entered the treasury the other day. She could only think that he had gone to see the artifacts housed there, those that had been taken when the magebreakers raided the Arcanum. Whether he had gone after the Star specifically was something that Arian did not know. To find out, she would need to get into his rooms. Into the rooms of the most powerful mage in the Empire, the man who would happily execute her if he found her, the one person in this keep Arian needed to avoid at all costs.

No pressure.

CHAPTER 28

LIAM

"YOU LOOK PALE. BEEN SICK LATELY?"

Liam turned at the sound of the voice, looking up at the speaker from over his tankard of ale. He'd hardly touched it since entering. As attractive as drinking to forget sounded, he didn't care for the taste, and ever since ordering it, he found that he didn't want to wipe what he had seen at Blackstone Deep from his mind. Not the emaciated prisoners huddled in their cells, begging to be set free, and not the scars and trembling limbs of the people the Resistance had actually freed, bringing them out of the dark.

Traitors to the Empire. People just like Lyndon and his crew. People the Empire had broken.

The nightmares had kept him up half the night, and the backlash from the magic he had used—the fever and nausea and shaking—had plagued him for the rest of yesterday. But there was no point in telling Lyndon that. If the Resistance was anything like Arian, then he wasn't supposed to admit that he felt sick. He was supposed to pretend that everything was fine. It was a lie they all told themselves.

"I just haven't gotten much sun," he said instead. "It hasn't exactly been a good climate for daytime wandering."

He gestured down at the lower floor of the tavern to make his point. It was early enough in the day that the Wheel was practically deserted, but it never closed. Like any good meeting place, it was always open for those who needed it, Imperial presence or civil unrest be damned. And the Imperial presence in the city had only increased. The break-in at the Deep wasn't widely reported, but he had noticed a doubling of Imperial guards. There was a startling amount of civil unrest too, which confused him. Post-occupation Leithon had always been a tense place, but lately it felt as if the city was winding itself tighter, preparing to come undone at any moment.

Lyndon followed his gaze, frown deepening in understanding.

"True enough. That for me?" he asked, inclining his head toward the second tankard waiting on the table.

Liam waved at it distractedly and Lyndon picked it up. He downed about half of it in one sitting, which made Liam wince, imagining the taste.

"Good stuff," Lyndon said, plunking the half-empty tankard back down onto the table.

He looked over at Liam, and while he was still smiling, Liam caught the gleam in his eye. The sight put him instantly on his guard. It was easy to forget that had the Empire not invaded Leithon, Lyndon would have been well on his way to conquering its underground. Now, thanks to the Empire, the point was moot. There were only two types of criminals in Leithon these days: those who worked with Lyndon against the Empire, and small, fractured groups that worked alone.

He and his sister were nominally the second type. But his mind was still full of the Deep, hollow haunted eyes that had made him drag himself out of bed as soon as he was well and come here.

But for what? Liam didn't really understand. It wasn't absolution, even though the feeling in his chest was a lot like guilt. He knew he hadn't done anything wrong. Commiseration? Somehow, he didn't think Lyndon was going to be a shoulder to cry on, even if he could figure out exactly what was bothering him.

He knew only that he felt restless, that he had felt driven to come to the Wheel, and that it was going to bother him all day until he figured out why.

"Your sister seems like she's been getting some sun," Lyndon said, making Liam look up.

"You've seen her?" he asked, careful to keep his tone somewhere in the realm of polite interest. From the look Lyndon gave him, he wasn't fooling anyone.

"Just the other day," Lyndon said, taking another long swig of his ale. Liam eyed the small amount left in the bottom of the other man's mug and readied himself to signal for another. "Met her at one of Aila's girls' stores. She asked to meet in one of her letters."

He was eyeing Liam carefully, trying to see how much he already knew. Liam kept his face smooth, although the truth was that he had no idea what Lyndon was talking about. He hadn't heard from Arian since she'd asked for advice about the treasury.

"What did she want to talk about?" Liam asked, aware that he might be tipping his hand and not particularly caring just then.

Lyndon shrugged. "She asked if I had any tips for undoing magical locks. I told her that was more her area of expertise."

Liam was glad he hadn't touched his ale, because if he had, he might have choked on it. "She's not planning to go for the Star, is she?" he asked. "*Now?*"

Arian was reckless, but the idea that she would make plans to break into the treasury without informing him was difficult to believe. He let out a relieved sigh when Lyndon shook his head.

"I was worried about that too, but Arian swears it's something else," Lyndon said. "A . . . side project. She really didn't tell you anything?"

"Nothing," Liam said, without thinking. When his brain caught up to his mouth, he wished he could take the words back. The Imperial occupation had made a thief and a smuggler out of him, but he had never had much of a talent for intrigue. He felt his face start to flush and hid it by taking a sip of his ale.

"Well, that's odd," said Lyndon. He shot Liam another grin. "Downright unfriendly, I'd say. I thought for sure she'd have gone to you first."

That was what Liam would have thought. He felt cold. If Arian wasn't going into the treasury, then there was only one other reason he could think of for her wanting to bypass magical protections, only one other mage in the Bastion.

She had to know by now, *had* to, that Emeric Roth was here. There was no way that she could be in the Bastion, breathing the same air as him, and *not* know. But she hadn't said anything to him about it in her reports, and she hadn't asked him for help. That meant that she didn't want him to know Roth was here. That she was trying to *protect* him, the same way she had always done.

Lyndon propped his elbows up on the table, leaning in closer to Liam.

"So," he said. "You're not here to talk about Arian. You have no clue what she was doing here, wouldn't've known a thing about it if I hadn't told you. That sort of begs the question, kid. Why *are* you here?"

Why was he here? He didn't know. To give himself more time to think, he raised his tankard to his lips, choking down a sip of bitter ale. The taste was a shock to his system, but when he lowered it, he felt a little closer to the root of what was bothering him.

"Are the . . . are the prisoners okay? The ones we freed, I mean."

Lyndon's brow furrowed. "They're shook up, but they're safe," he said. "They're with our people in the city. I can't tell you where. Is that all you came here for? Your work is done. You've paid your dues. We'll take care of them from here."

Liam stared down at his drink, studying the patterns in the froth. There was something at the back of his mind, a shape that he had only just glimpsed in the depths of that prison cell. In the way that it had felt to tear through ancient spells, to hold that much power in his hands, to know that he was doing *something*. Helping, somehow. Fighting back.

He didn't like danger. He didn't light up the same way Arian did when she defied death, the odds, and everything. But this . . .

This was better than hiding in the dark.

He felt like he was approaching a point of no return. But no, he thought as he stared down at the amber liquid in the glass. The point of no return had been four years ago, when Roth and his magebreakers had invaded the Arcanum, when Roth had killed his mother. When the Empire had swarmed his city and its people and had killed anyone who resisted them. Or worse, he thought, his mind still on the haggard looks of the people in the prison.

Everything after that was only a natural progression. As natural as water flowing downhill.

"Are you sure there isn't something else I can do?" he asked, his words heavy in the air. He knew that Arian would disapprove, but he didn't care because for once, the words that came out of his mouth felt *right*. "For you . . . or them?"

Lyndon was silent for a long time.

"If I didn't know any better," he finally said, "I'd think you were asking to join the Resistance."

It was easier not to look at people when he was talking to them. Especially when he was saying things like this, words that felt dredged up from the very heart of him. "It can be another trade. I'll help you, if you help me with something."

"Interesting," Lyndon said, a smirk touching the corner of his lips. He drew his hands back. "We already lent you a ship, helped your Weaver friend smuggle weapons and money in from Paran, and we already carry messages between you and your sister. I don't know what more we can do for you to help you find the Star. But this has nothing to do with the Star, does it?"

"No," Liam said. "It doesn't."

Lyndon met his eyes. "What do you want to do?"

Liam pushed his drink away and laid his hands flat on the table-top, leaning toward Lyndon. He was sure that Lyndon already knew what he wanted to say. Lyndon would accept, of course. He couldn't refuse. Lyndon was a businessman at his heart, and this idea would benefit them both.

"I want to kill Emeric Roth," he said. "And I want the Resistance to show me how."

CHAPTER 29

ZEPHYR

ZEPHYR WALKED DOWN THE LONG HALLWAY AS QUIETLY AND unobtrusively as she could, keeping her head down to avoid being recognized. She told herself repeatedly that she wasn't doing anything wrong, that she was only responding to a summons from her lord, but the shadow of Commander Selwald loomed over her. Lord Kaolin had requested that she come after dark, in plain clothes, and the clandestine nature of his request did nothing to put her at ease.

At least no one was watching her—a Leithonian girl in a plain blue dress, moving through the inner keep. The Bastion was so secure that most people assumed anyone in the inner keep had a reason to be there. Still, she missed her sword at her side, her shield at her back. The arms might have made her more visible, but they also made her safer. Lieutenant Venari might have been many things, but she was still a soldier, still someone worthy of respect.

Out of her uniform, she was just another girl swept up in the tide of Empire-occupied Leithon.

She kept to the lesser-used routes as she made her way to the royal apartments, dodging Imperial soldiers and courtiers as well as she was able. Her heart pounded with every step that she took. She didn't relax until she found herself standing in front of the doors that led into the royal apartments. Zephyr didn't bother to knock on the door in the empty hallway outside, not wanting to risk being recognized. Instead, she opened the door and stepped inside, closing it behind her.

Her heart started pounding for a different reason, and it wasn't because the guards on the inside of the door spun toward her and drew steel. It was because now that she was inside, now that she had made it, the gravity of what she was doing came back to her again.

No more coats to turn, Zephyr reminded herself. No more colors to wear.

She drew in a shaky breath and straightened up, squaring her shoulders. One of the guards, recognizing her, drew back and sheathed his sword.

"Lieutenant Venari."

He nodded at her. Zephyr nodded back.

The other guard stepped back, his blade rasping as he slid it into the scabbard. Zephyr glanced at him. "More oil, guardsman. Your sword shouldn't make that sound when drawing or sheathing."

The guard tensed, but he didn't glare at her as a regular Imperial soldier might have. Kaolin's guard, it seemed, were better mannered and better trained.

"Yes, Lieutenant."

She nodded and handed the knife in her boot to the first guard before he could even ask for weapons. Then she lowered the scarf from her head, letting it drape over her shoulders instead. The guards didn't challenge her as she moved into the apartments.

Lord Kaolin waited for her in the sitting room. It had once been the private sitting room of the Leithonian royals, and yet he looked quite at home in it. He sat on the couch, leg crossed over his knee, reading again. He looked more tired than he had the last time Zephyr had seen him. His face was paler, dark circles stark beneath his eyes. She wondered if he was ill, but his gaze was as sharp as ever as he looked up to face her. He set his book facedown on the table, keeping it open to mark his place as he rose to welcome her.

"Lieutenant," he said.

"My lord." A lady would have curtsied, but a soldier bowed.

Zephyr bowed, and didn't rise until Lord Kaolin indicated that she could.

"I was hoping we could speak casually." Kaolin admitted. His tone seemed tighter and more clipped than it had been during their last conversation, harsher. "I find that the trappings of rank are often cumbersome in these situations. Please, call me Kaolin."

"If that's what my lord wishes," she said, her tone measured and neutral.

"It is," Kaolin said. "And for yourself? Would you prefer Lieutenant Venari or Zephyr?"

"Zephyr. Please."

"Very well." Kaolin nodded. He turned away from her, his expression growing almost sheepish. "I must admit to reading your file, Zephyr."

"My file, my l—?" She caught herself just in time. "Kaolin?"

"Yes," Kaolin said. "After our conversation last time, I was curious. Your father, Kallan Venari, was once the commander of the Royal Guard. Commander Selwald has him under house arrest. You have a younger sister training in the healing halls, and a younger brother, still a child. Your mother, despite not being under the same strictures as your father, rarely leaves your estate. You no longer reside there but have a private apartment in the city. You seldom visit."

She felt a chill run down her back at his words, said so matter-of-factly. When she didn't respond immediately, he looked up, taking note of her expression.

"You weren't aware that all of this was being recorded. Your private visits, and your mother's movements, among other things."

She lowered her gaze. "I . . . suspected."

"But it's quite different hearing it said so frankly," said Kaolin. "I understand." He turned away, facing the window. "Tell me, Zephyr.

When you think about your siblings, are you concerned for their futures?"

What was she supposed to say to that? The answer was so obvious that it was almost a non-question. "Of course I am."

Kaolin clasped his hands behind his back. "By all accounts, they're very bright. Your sister, particularly, is rising through the ranks at her apprentice hall."

"If you'll forgive my frankness." She paused, waiting for him to gesture that he would. "Brightness isn't exactly a valued trait among Leithonians."

"And certainly not from a family that's already being watched," Kaolin said, acknowledging the point with a nod. "Is that what you're trying to say, Zephyr?"

"You know it is."

Kaolin turned to look out of the sitting room's large window. "Commander Selwald rules through fear. That's how he keeps you and the rest of the Leithonian contingent in line, how he keeps your mother confined to the estate, how he keeps people like your siblings too scared to show their gifts to the world. The only people willing to fight him are those who have spent their lives defying the law, but even those are too few to cause any meaningful change. But that will not last.

"Selwald understands that when people are pushed far enough, anger replaces fear. He knows this system is not sustainable. So, what is he going to do when the city grows restless, when people like your parents or those on the street decide they are done with fear? Will he allow the people to revolt so that he can crush them again? He knows that the cycle will never end—that Leithon will never be satisfied with Imperial rule until Leithonians and Imperials are treated the same. Will he concede and give them these rewards after their revolution? No, it would only make him look weak. He wants to rule this city, to keep it for his own. So, what would he do then?"

Kaolin looked back, meeting Zephyr's eyes solemnly. "What would a man like Commander Selwald do, with a rival in town and a city on the brink of revolution?"

Zephyr's eyes widened. "He would start that revolution himself."

"Exactly," said Kaolin. "He'll take that anger and direct it against his rival. Against me."

She could practically hear the rhetoric already: *Everything hurting you is a result of this man, this symbol of Imperial aristocracy and dominance. I'm just like you, a cog in the Imperial machine. We should rise up together. Overthrow this lord, and I will work to create a new Leithon. A Leithon free of aristocratic interference. A Leithon that belongs to the people.*

Except it would be a lie. Because it was Selwald who represented the very worst of the Empire. Selwald who had broken their city. Some would see that, but most wouldn't. Most would just be happy to be given someone to blame.

They would overthrow Kaolin, and at the end Selwald would sweep in, quell the revolution, and grant the Leithonians citizen status in the Empire. And he would be a hero. But that wouldn't last.

Kaolin was grim. "There are Imperial soldiers moving through the city, Zephyr. They slip out at night, and not to patrol. Not to go out drinking or gambling. No one knows what they are going out to do. If you want to help this city, help me *find them*. If you believe in me more than you believe in Selwald, help me keep this city."

Once again, Zephyr felt the pressure of choice on her shoulders. Two paths, diverging in front of her. One led to death, destruction, and the slim chance of glory; one led to a slow, painful smothering, the destruction of her identity, her integrity, her morals, everything she was and everything she believed in.

Once, when faced with that same choice, Zephyr had chosen life, had chosen what she considered the lesser evil. It had smothered her, and she had let it.

Now . . .

Now, she wasn't only choosing for herself and her family. She was choosing for the entire city, for all their futures.

She wanted to fight for something again. To be a *knight* again.

Zephyr looked up at Kaolin.

"I'll do it."

CHAPTER 30

ARIAN

"ALL RIGHT," ARIAN SAID, CHECKING HER GEAR FOR THE THOU-
sandth time. "Let's go over the plan again."

Across the room from her, Cavar was dressed in Lord Nasirri's
finest, his hair swept back and jeweled ornaments decorating his
suit. He stood with his hands clasped behind his back, the picture
of an arrogant young lord. She barely recognized him. Linna waited
beside the bedroom door. She wore a more formal version of her
dark gray armor, partially hidden beneath a silk shirt and trousers,
her garments emblazoned with the insignia of House Rezavi.

Cavar glanced at Arian and said, "Linna and I will head down to
the ball. We'll signal you with these—" He held up his hand, revealing a slender silver chain that encircled his wrist. "—once either of
us sees Roth at the ball. Three long presses if either of us sees him,
and three short presses when he leaves."

Arian and Linna wore identical chains. They were minor artifacts, taken from the instructor quarters of the Arcanum after the
occupation. The chains were what Liam called intrinsically linked—
each carried pieces of the same ingot of silver, and so were magically
attuned to each other. They transmitted sensations and had once
been used by the Arcanum's instructors to signal each other in the
event of an emergency. What one chain registered, the other chains
would convey. Arian would feel their signals, and vice versa.

"If I have to give up but everything's fine otherwise, I'll pull on
mine once," Arian said. She demonstrated by pinching the chain on
her wrist between two fingers and pulling, hard enough to pinch a
little. "Two pulls means I need help. Three means we all need to run.
We'll meet at the ossuary if that happens."

It was one of the few things her father had taught her: Always have a plan for failure.

A chime sounded from the room's clock, marking the fifteenth minute past the hour. The ball had started fifteen minutes ago. In the Bastion's ballroom, a handful of guests would already be congregating, mostly military officers who were famous for their punctuality and lowborn guests who could not afford the discourtesy of being late. The lords, like Lord Nasirri, would be late without fail.

"You should go," Arian said.

Cavar nodded, motioning for Linna to follow him. Arian watched as the two of them left the room, then retreated to her cot in the dressing room. She closed the door behind her and withdrew something from her pocket, a device that looked like a windup key inserted into a small bronze stub. Arian climbed into bed and pulled the sheets over her shoulders, taking on the role of the sick maid, then wound up the artifact, placing it on the nightstand beside her. She closed her eyes and counted the seconds, waiting.

↓↓↓

HALF AN HOUR LATER, SHE WAS MOVING THROUGH THE BASTION, dressed as Lady Liliana's maidservant. The key still rested on her bedside table. It had recorded an impression of her lying in bed and would display that to anyone who looked into the room, whether their methods were magical or mundane. It wouldn't hold up against a closer inspection, but the chain she wore was warm against her skin, and she had hopes that Cavar or Linna would warn her if anyone was about to come knocking. Roth's quarters were on the other side of the keep from Lord Nasirri's, not so close to Lord Kaolin's rooms that the young lord would be accused of favoring him, but not so far away as to insult the mage either. Like Nasirri's, they were a suite with a sitting room and a separate bedroom. According to palace gossip, Roth was unusually picky about who he allowed into his quarters. Only his personal staff were allowed inside to clean, and rumor had it that a terrible fate awaited anyone foolish enough to try to sneak in.

Arian didn't doubt that there was truth to the rumors, but she wasn't afraid. Roth didn't scare her. If anything, she welcomed the challenge, the chance to put one over on him. It was her own personal revenge for what had happened to her mother.

As she reached Roth's door, she stopped, because anger was only going to get her killed. She drew in a breath and sank into a state of calm, the sort of peace she felt only when she was on a job. She ran her fingers through the air just over Roth's door, breathing deep, feeling for the telltale prickle of magic.

There was magic here. The entire door was ensorcelled, a thin webbing of power coating the wood. The spells around the lock were thicker, a tight knot that made Arian's hair stand on end. It told her that if she tried to force her way in the old-fashioned way, there would be blood, and most would be her own. But she wasn't an amateur, and this wasn't her first time breaking into a room protected by magic.

Liam liked to think that Arian hadn't used magic since their days in the novice classes. Most days, Arian also wanted to believe that that was true. But she would be the first to admit that those early lessons had been useful, and in her time since the Academy, Arian had developed a few tricks of her own.

She touched a finger to the doorknob and breathed deep, bracing herself for the cold touch of magic at work. It was a little like picking a physical lock, slipping a thread of power—nothing more than a thread—through the web and burrowing deep. Nothing that could be detected. Nothing that would reveal who—or what—she was.

The air around the doorknob began to shimmer. Wards lifted themselves off the metal surface and into the air, a fragile network of gleaming lights.

The spells weren't broken. Roth would be able to sense if they were. They had merely been moved, encouraged to think that the doorknob was somewhere else.

When the spells had been safely moved, she reached for her physical tools, beginning to pick the lock. Arian held her breath, waiting for an alarm to activate, but nothing happened.

Something clicked beneath her hand and she smirked, pushing the door open.

Now, she thought. *Let's see what you're hiding.*

CHAPTER 31

ZEPHYR

THE BALLROOM WAS FILLED WITH IMPERIALS, DECORATED SOL-diers in violet uniforms, courtiers in fashionable dresses and formal attire, and honored merchants in their most expensive clothes trying not to look out of place next to the noble lords they wanted to be. There were foreign dignitaries there, Lord Nasirri among them, but the only other Leithonians around her were servants. She felt drab and dull in her gray dress uniform and saw how the people around watched her with obvious pity and distaste.

Zephyr tried not to show that their reactions bothered her. It had been her choice to wear her uniform, her choice to show the Imperials that she wasn't cowed by what they made of her. In some ways, she was more comfortable in this uniform than she would have felt in a dress.

It reminded her what she was here for.

She moved through the crowd with ease, making small talk with those Imperials who would deign to speak with her, but her attention was fixed on Lord Kaolin. The lord had made her task at this ball clear. She was to watch for any outside interference from Selwald or anyone else. At the moment, Kaolin was speaking with a trio of Imperial ladies in multicolored dresses, his personal guard arrayed protectively around him. Zephyr did not let her guard down. Commander Selwald was present at the ball, and while Zephyr didn't think the commander bold enough to try something in front of so many witnesses, he had surprised her before.

Lord Kaolin moved off into the crowd to greet guests, and Zephyr lost sight of him. She tried to follow, but bumped into a passing guest hard enough to startle them both. Zephyr stumbled back and quickly righted herself. Where had he come from? She had been careful not to brush against anyone as she moved through the crowd, but she hadn't even seen him approach. Her eyes tracked up to his face and quickly widened.

Lord Nasirri. Arian's Parani lord.

He watched her, surprise and disbelief written across his expression. Beside him, his bodyguard stepped forward, one hand drifting casually toward her weapon. Zephyr assessed the situation quickly. She had her doubts that Nasirri was who he said he was—Arian wouldn't be caught dead in the company of a real lord—but even if he wasn't a nobleman, he was good at pretending to be one. And it would be foolish to act as though he wasn't a lord. Nasirri had more standing in this court than she did.

Zephyr held up her hands to show that she was unarmed.

"My apologies, my lord," she said. "I wasn't looking where I was going."

She lowered her eyes in deference, but in the back of her mind, she was panicking, trying to catch a glimpse of Kaolin. Where had he gone?

Nasirri waved his bodyguard down. She could feel his gaze on her and forced herself to stay still, wondering if Arian had told him anything about her at all.

"You are Lieutenant Zephyr Venari of the Leithonian contingent?" he asked. He spoke their language like every Parani she had ever met. His accent was perfect. Under any other circumstance, she would have believed his story of being a Parani lord without question.

Who exactly was Arian dealing with?

"Yes, my lord," she said, daring to meet his eyes. Nasirri held her gaze for a long moment, and she searched his eyes for any indication that he wasn't who he said he was, any cracks in the mask he wore.

She found none. He gave her a curt nod.

"Don't let it happen again," he said, moving past her.

Zephyr stood still as he left, feeling the weight of his gaze lift from her. The tension stayed with her long after he was gone.

Lord Nasirri—whoever he was—was dangerous.

But he wasn't the danger she needed to be concerned with now.

She put Arian and Lord Nasirri out of her mind and let her gaze sweep the room, looking for any sign of dark hair or House Eismor colors. Her heart nearly stopped when she saw Kaolin kneeling on the ground, his drink spilled on the carpet beneath him.

Zephyr took a step toward him, right hand reaching for a sword that wasn't there, but relaxed when she saw that he had only fallen. Emeric Roth was helping him to his feet, and while Zephyr couldn't stand the sight of the man, she didn't think that he meant Lord Kaolin any harm. He was a friend of Lord Eismor and had no particular connection to Commander Selwald.

Roth clasped Kaolin's hand and said something to him that made the young lord laugh, shaking his head and brushing the dust off his knees. A servant was already moving to pick up the fallen goblet.

All was well. Nothing out of the ordinary had happened. So why did she feel so uneasy?

She started walking, moving toward the two of them. She would feel better once she spoke to Lord Kaolin, she decided. Once she made sure for herself that things were all right.

She was halfway there when a man in a violet uniform blocked her path, making her stop short.

Lieutenant Leon Albrent. He leered at her, a glass of wine in his hand. "Where are you going in such a hurry, Lieutenant?"

"I—" Zephyr's eyes moved past him, to where Kaolin had accepted a dance from a pretty young noblewoman, his guards staying a respectful distance behind him. She looked back at Leon. "Nowhere."

"Really?" Leon asked, leaning closer toward her. She could smell the alcohol on his breath. "You could have fooled me."

"I was just going to get another drink," Zephyr said stiffly. "So if you'll excuse me, Lieutenant Albrent."

She made to walk around him. Leon took a step to the side, blocking her again. "What's the hurry? I've been meaning to talk to you."

"You can talk to me anytime. I'm on the practice grounds every morning."

"Now's as good a time as any. If you wanted a drink, come have one with me." He smiled, but there was an edge to his smile as he reached for her arm, grasping it by the elbow. Zephyr sucked in a breath through her teeth, resisting the urge to elbow him in the ribs.

"Lieutenant Albrent," she said, her voice cold as steel. "I'd appreciate it if you let go of my arm."

Leon held her gaze, challenging, but Zephyr didn't back down. Something in her eyes must have had an effect on him, because he took a step back, holding his hands up. The smile vanished from his face, his expression becoming something darker and more menacing. When the smile returned, it was somehow worse than if he hadn't been smiling at all.

"Fine," he said. "I'll get to the point. Is it true that you and Lord Kaolin are *involved*?"

Zephyr fixed him with her most level gaze. "No."

"Because that's what people are saying," Leon said, as if he hadn't heard. "They said you've been making *special* visits to Lord Kaolin's quarters. Out of uniform."

Rumors were inevitable. She and Kaolin had met twice over the past several days, once to discuss Commander Selwald's possible revolution, and again to come up with a counterstrategy. That last meeting had been pointless. While there were rumors of soldiers heading into the city to meet with unknown people, no one in the Leithonian contingent knew who they were, and none of the Imperials would talk to her. Nobody seemed particularly worried. Most people seemed to think they were just buying drugs or indulging some vice or another. Everyone seemed more concerned about catching the Resistance members who had broken into Blackstone Deep than they were about stray soldiers.

But that was beside the point. "There is nothing improper happening between me and Lord Kaolin," she said.

"Hmm," said Leon. "Well, that's interesting. Because if there's *nothing* going on, then why are you visiting his chambers? If someone didn't know any better, they'd think you were planning something."

Zephyr bit back her retort—that it was hardly illegal to speak to someone who was meant to be the city's governor. She knew as well as he did that Commander Selwald wouldn't see it that way. And when she didn't respond, Leon's smirk told her that she was right.

He walked past her, clapping her on the shoulder as he did. The touch lingered long enough to make Zephyr wish for a bath.

"I'd be careful, Lieutenant," he said. "Your position is precarious as it is. I'd hate to see your pretty little head spiked on the gates. Although," he added, as he vanished into the crowd, "if this really is just a sordid affair, I'm offended you didn't come to *me*."

CHAPTER 32

ARIAN

ROTH'S CHAMBERS WERE SURPRISINGLY PLAIN ON THE INSIDE, not what she would have expected from a lord's right-hand mage. There was a quiet, almost scholarly air to the room that reminded her of Liam, even though she knew that her brother would never appreciate the comparison. The sitting room was as decadent as any room in the palace, but other than a collection of books that could fill a library on their own, there wasn't much of the place that spoke to Roth's sensibilities.

Of course, that was just what she could see at face value. A man like Roth would have secrets upon secrets, and it was her job to uncover them.

She moved slowly through the sitting room, feeling for any other protective spells. There were a few layered on the walls and in patches on the floor, but nothing that she couldn't avoid. Being able to sense magic wouldn't help her if she triggered a physical trap, but Arian felt more confident about her ability to get around those. They would be subtler, for a room in the Bastion. A trick lock on a desk drawer that would release a poisoned needle, or paint her skin and clothes in indelible ink. Standard enough.

She looked around the room, wondering where to start. The writing desk was obvious, but if Roth had taken anything from the treasury that night, if he had taken *the Star*, he wouldn't keep it in an obvious place. The desk probably held all sorts of juicy political secrets, but Arian didn't care about politics.

Where did Roth keep his *real* secrets? The ones he didn't want even his employers to know about?

The bookshelf was tempting. Almost every mage she had known

was unhealthily attached to their books. But she had a feeling Roth was the sort of man who knew he had secrets that people wanted. He wouldn't keep his secrets somewhere so . . . visible.

Something personal, then. Something that he could carry with him whenever he traveled without eliciting suspicion. Arian's eyes swept over the sitting room, but nothing fit the bill. She made her way into the bedroom.

The layout of the room was the same as Cavar's chambers, although the dressing room where a servant might sleep was used purely for storage. A pile of books had migrated from the sitting room to the table beside the bed, and the sight reminded her so much of Liam that it startled her. Another comparison her brother wouldn't appreciate. She moved on.

The room was buzzing with protection spells, but nothing that looked like a place where Roth would keep his secrets. It was still too open, too obvious. She was searching for something small, something out of place.

Arian found what she was looking for in the dressing room, hidden among clothes, books, and scrolls.

It was a leather pouch, about the size of a small book. Compared to all the fine objects in the room, it was worn down and completely unremarkable. That was what made it stand out. The damage to the leather wasn't cosmetic; it had gotten this way from years of wear. It was also *dripping* with protective spells, so thick that she had to spend several heart-stopping minutes untangling them. Whatever was in here, Roth clearly felt it was important enough to take with him everywhere, and also important enough to keep hidden.

Holding back the protective spells with one hand, Arian teased the clasp open, holding her breath.

What she found wasn't the Star.

Instead, the pouch contained a round slab of stone, its surface weathered by time. Arian drew it out with one hand, squinting down at it in the dim light. The stone was white and flat, engraved with a complicated knot. She didn't feel any magic, but there was something about the stone that gave her pause, something about the pattern. It was . . . familiar.

She remembered being a child, sitting on the floor of the living room in the rare times when her father was home, grabbing at the symbol engraved on his belt. The same symbol.

It was a Weaver symbol. A clan sigil.

The sigil of eth'Akari.

The chain around her wrist jerked to life, pressing into her skin three times.

The stone slipped from her fingertips, nearly tumbling to the ground. She caught it between two fingers, cursing as she lost her grip on the protective spells. Arian pulled them back, managing somehow to slide the stone into the pouch and replace the clasp. She put it back where it had come from and released her hold on the protective spells, letting them settle into place.

There was no way of knowing if she had messed up—if that one lapse of attention was enough to trigger an alarm. She couldn't feel any active magic, nothing that told her she was in danger, but if Roth learned she was here, if Roth learned *who* she was—

Arian fled the room, heart pounding.

CHAPTER 33

CAVAR

IT WAS A MARK OF HIS TRAINING THAT HE'D MANAGED TO STAY AT the ball for as long as he had after Roth left, when every fiber of his being wanted to run back to his quarters to make sure that Arian had made it out alive. The entire time he spent socializing, he was expecting the other shoe to drop, expecting Roth to send soldiers back into the ballroom to arrest them. But no one came, and the chain around his wrist remained still. Whatever had happened, Arian must have been able to get away.

That didn't stop him from walking a little quicker when he finally excused himself from the ball. He headed back to his quarters and did not breathe until Arian walked out of the dressing room to greet him.

"What happened?" she asked as he closed the door behind him.

"Roth left the ball," Cavar said. "You made it out all right?"

"Obviously. Roth left in a hurry?"

"He stopped to talk to some people on the way out. I don't think he was tipped off. He looked like he was dying to leave. He hardly talked to anyone the whole time he was there. The only time I saw him interact with someone was when he knocked Kaolin over by accident."

Arian nodded, some of the tension going out of her. She exhaled, leaning against the wall. Her eyes drifted to the ground, and Cavar got the sense that she was building up to something, trying to find the words.

"Did you find anything?" he asked.

Arian didn't answer immediately, although she did raise her eyes from the floor. She turned her head to the side, staring at the ornate patterns on the far wall before she looked back at him. "What do you know about eth'Akari?"

Cavar blinked at her. "It's your clan. Your father never told you about it?"

"My father called himself a clanless bastard. When he bothered to talk to us about the Weavers at all. He said they were all wiped out, except for him." This time, he knew he wasn't imagining the bitterness in her voice. "I don't even know what it means to be part of a Weaver clan."

"Your clan is sort of . . . your family," Cavar said. "It's the people you're raised around, the people you travel with. But in some ways, each clan is like its own nation. They have their own rules, their own cultures. Weavers are sort of . . ." He paused, thinking. "Weavers are a clan unto themselves. When we're chosen as children, we leave our families and begin our training. But we retain our clan names, and most of the children of Weavers become Weavers themselves."

"So what happened to eth'Akari?" Arian asked.

Cavar frowned. "You realize everything that happened to eth'Akari was before my time."

"You still know more than me. And I want to know."

Her gaze never wavered. His eyes drifted from her to the bed between them. "Do you want to sit down?" he asked.

"I'll stand, thanks."

"It's a long story."

"I'm listening."

Cavar nodded, trying to decide where to begin. "All I know about eth'Akari is hearsay. Some of it I learned from my mother, but everyone has a different version of the story. Your father probably doesn't even know the whole truth."

"Stop stalling, Cavar," Arian said. "I'm a big girl. I can take it."

It was the use of his name that did it, his actual name and not any of the hundred other nicknames that Arian had given him. He nodded again, launching into the story.

"The Wastes are vast, and when you're out in them, most of the time, you're with your eth, your clan. We meet twice a year for major feasts, but we can go months without seeing another eth. Weavers travel among the clans frequently, but not every resident of the Wastes becomes a Weaver. Some of us only live with other clans when we marry into them; others might never visit another clan's territory. So nobody is completely sure what happened to eth'Akari. All we know is this—roughly thirty-five years ago, when your father was still a child, representatives from eth'Akari arrived at the traditional meeting grounds for the Midwinter Feast. Sometime between midwinter and midsummer, the clan vanished. There were nearly five hundred of them at the time, including the children. And not a single one came to the next feast."

"Vanished?" Arian asked. "How?"

Cavar shrugged. "No one knows. Like I said, our society keeps all but a handful of us isolated. But whatever happened, only five members of eth'Akari survived. One of them was your father, who had run away from home at midwinter and was living with eth'Nivear. Before you ask"—he added as Arian opened her mouth—"I don't know *why* he ran away from home, or why he chose to travel to my clan."

Arian shut her mouth, but Cavar could tell that she wasn't happy with it. She gestured for him to go on.

"At any rate," he said, "your father survived. And there was one other survivor, a boy from eth'Akari. He was found wandering the Wastes, dehydrated and delirious. According to him, he had no memory of the event."

Arian snorted. "Convenient, that."

"Very."

"So this guy was, what, a relative of my dad?"

"A distant cousin, probably. I'm not entirely sure. While all clan members share a common ancestor, not all clan members are directly related." He smiled wryly. "We *have* actually tried not to keep ourselves inbred."

"By bringing in fresh blood from all over the world so that you can have Weavers who look like anyone it might be convenient to impersonate," she said, waving a hand dismissively. "*That* I know."

"Right," said Cavar. "Anyway, this boy—the survivor, eventually recovered, and while he never got his memories back, he, your father, and my mother trained as novices together. They were inducted to the Weavers at about the same time. From what my mother tells me, they were like siblings. His name was Kesi eth'Akari."

"The one who stole the Star," Arian said. "How did that happen anyway?"

Cavar's expression hardened. He didn't answer immediately. Arian caught the hesitation and raised her eyes to meet his.

"Cavar?"

"I'm not entirely sure of the details. But he betrayed the Weavers. He stole the Star and fled to Leithon, where my mother and your father hunted him down."

"That was when my father met my mother." Arian's voice was soft. She lowered her arms to her sides, fingertips brushing against the wall behind her.

Cavar nodded. "It must have been."

"And Kesi?"

"As far as I know, he put up a fight. So they killed him." He frowned, searching her eyes. "Your parents never told you any of this?"

"Not much," said Arian, "They told me about Kesi stealing the Star, and how they hit it off from there." She shook her head, resting her hands on her hips and turning away.

"What brought this on?" he asked, when the silence between them became unbearable.

Arian shrugged. "Something I found in Roth's bedroom."

"Was it the Star?"

"If I found the Star, do you really think we'd still be *here*, and not halfway to the mainland?" Arian asked, rolling her eyes. She hesitated. "It was a stone. One engraved with eth'Akari's sigil. He kept it in a pouch in his wardrobe. Cavar, could—could Roth be from the Wastes?"

He heard the question that Arian was avoiding.

Could Roth be related to me?

"It's . . . possible. Not likely, but possible." There was no shared set of physical characteristics that defined the people who lived in the Wastes. They had been born of all nations, all cultures, and in the case of those clans that historically produced Weavers, they tried very hard to keep it that way.

He drew in a breath. "It's possible he could be someone like you. Someone who belongs to eth'Akari by blood, but who hasn't lived in the Wastes. That might be how he survived."

Arian nodded slowly, reluctantly. "Maybe. But would that mean anything?"

"I don't know." They still knew too little about Roth, about his motives and goals, to draw any conclusions. "It's useful information, at least." Cavar paused, noting the way she folded her arms tightly against herself. "Are you going to be okay?"

"I'm always okay," said Arian. "I just need a minute. Sorry."

She stepped back into her room, closing the door behind her.

CHAPTER 34

ZEPHYR

BY THE TIME SHE MANAGED TO GET TO LORD KAOLIN, EMERIC Roth was heading for the door. Zephyr kept the mage in her periphery, but he was in no hurry to leave, stopping to chat with acquaintances on the way out. His demeanor was calm and personable—or at least as personable as Roth ever was—and he didn't seem worried or concerned. He looked like a man who had reached the limits of his sociability, and not like a man who had done anything worth running from.

Kaolin looked unharmed as well. He had just finished his dance with a young noblewoman whose name Zephyr did not know, and had stepped aside to accept refreshments from one of the servants. He was as cautious as ever—she caught him discreetly handing the drink to one of his guards to taste before taking a sip.

She stopped a few feet away from him, close enough to catch the attention of his guard, far enough away that she wouldn't be perceived as a threat. Zephyr accepted a drink from a servant and picked up a small plate of food, attempting to disguise her proximity as casual. Despite that, she thought she could *feel* Leon's eyes on her. She took a sip of champagne to calm her nerves, watching out of the corner of her eye as Kaolin came to join her at the refreshment table.

"Are you enjoying the party, Lieutenant?" he asked.

"Yes, my lord."

"Is that so? You've hardly danced at all."

"I'm afraid I'm not much of a dancer," Zephyr said. Kaolin offered her a gracious smile, and with a sudden sinking feeling in her stomach, Zephyr knew where this was going.

He offered her his hand. "I have difficulty believing that. May I have this dance?"

↓↓↓

ZEPHYR HAD TO LOOK RIDICULOUS, DANCING IN HER UNIFORM

with Lord Kaolin in all his finery. She tried not to show that it bothered her, keeping her face smooth and her back straight as she followed Kaolin through the movements like this was one of her practice drills. She could feel eyes on her as Kaolin led her around the room, and her face burned with embarrassment. But the dance had given her and Kaolin the privacy to speak.

"You noticed the fall?" he asked, lowering his voice to a murmur as he led her through the steps of a waltz.

"I did. You asked me to keep an eye out for anything strange."

"Yes, well—" He paused to turn her. "—I'm a little embarrassed about that. I slipped on the polished floors. No harm done, although I'm hardly the picture of poise right now."

Zephyr nodded, looking into Kaolin's eye as they moved in a slow circle on the dance floor. The young lord looked the same as he ever had. So why couldn't Zephyr shake the feeling that something was different about him? That something was wrong?

"Is there a problem?" Kaolin asked, tilting his head to the side. Zephyr looked away.

"No. I was only thinking that it was a good thing that it was Roth who was there to catch you, rather than someone who would harm you."

Something changed in Kaolin's expression at the mention of Roth. It was a subtle change, a sharpening of his features, but it was enough to give her pause as the music swelled, the pace of their dance picking up to match it. The expression faded as soon as it had come, retreating behind the blue of his eyes, but she couldn't shake the chill that it had given her.

She didn't know who the person who had looked at her then was, but it wasn't Kaolin.

Kaolin smiled, and suddenly he was young Kaolin Eismor again, and they were only dancing together at the welcome ball. She could almost dismiss the way his grip on her tightened. A figment of her imagination. "Yes. He's one of my father's most trusted advisors. I'm glad it was him."

Zephyr followed his lead as they moved across the dance floor and didn't say anything more. They danced to another song, and then Zephyr took her leave, offering Kaolin a quick bow before heading back to the sidelines. She stayed until the ball was over and Kaolin was back in the safety of his own rooms, but there were no other incidents. Nothing except Leon Albrent watching her with increasing suspicion and dislike, and the nagging sensation that she was missing half the story, that there were things happening she didn't understand.

🌱🌱🌱

THAT NIGHT, SHE COULDN'T SLEEP. SHE COULDN'T SHAKE THE feeling that something had changed, that something was deeply, terribly wrong.

It had to be her imagination. She was already predisposed to dislike Roth, but he would have no reason to harm Kaolin. He didn't have any ties to Commander Selwald, and his association with Kaolin's father had been mutually beneficial to both of them.

Unless—

A thought nagged at her, and Zephyr rolled over onto her side, chasing it.

—unless it wasn't Selwald that Roth was supporting. She'd been thinking of this as a game between two players, House Eismor and Commander Selwald, but if Roth wasn't one of their pieces, if he was a player all on his own—

That would be different. That would change things. She knew from looking at him that Roth was ambitious, but assumed he was vying for power in his homeland. But what if it wasn't the Empire that Roth wanted?

What if it was Leithon? What if it was the Arcanum?

Unable to stop herself, Zephyr sat up in bed, shoving the blankets off. There was only one person who would be able to tell her for sure if what she was thinking of was even possible, only one person she knew who had magical expertise and who she could trust.

The question was, would he be willing to help her with *this*?

Zephyr dug around in her desk until she found it, her fingers closing around cool metal. It was a steel figurine in the shape of a bird, something that Liam had made for her once. He had given it to her while he was studying artifice, a gift so that they would never truly be apart.

She gripped the little bird tightly in one hand, then walked over to her window. Zephyr opened it a crack, just wide enough to let the bird through. There was no telling who could be watching her right now. She had to be swift.

Breathing deep, Zephyr opened her hand, imbuing the bird with her will the way Liam had taught her. For a second, the bird was still, as if the spell hadn't taken. But then it stirred in the palm of her hand, shaking out its wings like it was flicking water off its feathers. It raised its head, cocked it to the side, then spread its wings and flew out into the moonlight.

She knew she should sleep. It would take Liam a while to get back to her, if he even responded at all. She needed to be wide awake tomorrow, needed to be alert, but sleep wouldn't come. Zephyr dozed on the edge of wakefulness until she heard the sound, a steady *tap tap tap* on her windowpane. She climbed out of bed and threw the window open. The bird hopped onto her windowsill, a scrap of paper clutched in its beak.

The paper burst into flames as soon as she read it, but she had been able to take in the words.

A place, a date, and a time.

CHAPTER 35

LIAM

"YOU LOOK EXHAUSTED," REID SAID, DROPPING INTO THE SEAT beside his. "Lyndon giving you a hard time?"

Liam jumped—he'd been so lost in thought that he had almost forgotten where he was and what they were doing. It took him a moment to process what Reid had said to him, a moment longer to remember what it meant. When he did, he let his lips curl into a weary smile.

"Ah," he said, "yeah. I'm still not used to the training, I think."

"Hmm." Reid pursed his lips in thought, propping his head up in his hand. "I know the boss is trying to help you with this Roth thing, but I think he's wasting his time teaching you to fight. You just need some kind of trick, like a ring that spits out poison. Ooh, you could send him a box of treats, but hide a spider in with them. Make it look like an accident."

Liam frowned. For a moment he wondered if he had misheard, but no, he'd heard him clearly enough. He tried for politeness. "Have . . . have you ever assassinated anyone, Reid?"

"Who, me?" Reid looked affronted. "Of course not. But you know, I've read up on the theory."

"What he means is he's read the tabloids," a feminine voice said from behind Reid. "And those books they sell at the news shop for kids—what is it, *Burty Barton and His Amazing Adventures*?"

"It's *Bartholomew Bartley*, thank you very much," Reid said, shooting the speaker a glare. And then all in one breath, he added, "*andHisAmazingAdventures.*"

Liam looked up to see a dark-haired woman dropping into one

of the table's empty seats. She was trailed by several others, a few of them the mean-looking sort that Liam wouldn't ordinarily want to meet, but others more innocuous looking, the sort of people he wouldn't look at twice at on the street. They were taking seats at the tables on the second floor of the Spinning Wheel, which once again had been set up for a meeting.

He recognized some. They had cleaned up since the prison break and were dressed in better clothes, but they still wore the same haunted looks they'd had when he'd found them in their cells. They sat together at a table near the center of the room, three men and one woman, and their faces were all ice and steel as they waited for the meeting to begin.

He felt a touch of shame. Here they were getting ready to plan their next steps, to figure out how to take Leithon back, and he was still thinking about the message he had received last night, the meeting he had planned with Zephyr. After so long, the prospect shouldn't have made his heart flutter the way it did. He knew if any of them learned about his plans, they would call him an Imperial sympathizer and throw him out of the room. And if Zephyr found out how he was spending his time, she would do worse.

He had to stay focused. He had promised that he would be here, that he would help however he could. He pushed thoughts of Zephyr out of his mind. *This* was more important now.

He faced the center of the room as Lyndon approached and did his best to look like he knew what he was doing. It was the exact same approach he had used during his magical training, when he'd pretended that he was focused in class and actually listening to his instructors. In a way, he supposed that he hadn't grown up that much at all.

But then he looked at the former prisoners, the ones who were tracking Lyndon's progress with their eyes. If it wasn't for him and the other Resistance members, they would *still* be languishing in their cells, in the heart of Blackstone Deep.

I did that, he told himself, and the swell of pride he felt at the thought wasn't a lie or an affectation.

He'd helped them. He'd done *something* to hurt the Empire. And if he could do that, then surely he could do so much more.

Lyndon reached the center of the room and cleared his throat, calling the meeting to order. Conversation died down, all eyes turning to him. He let his gaze sweep the room, lingering on each one of them before he said, "Well, the news is out. We made it into Blackstone Deep."

A few chuckles erupted from the crowd. Rumors of the prison break had been spreading through the city for the past few days, despite the best efforts of the Imperial soldiers to quash them. The soldiers insisted that the Deep was as secure as it had always been and that the rumors were baseless, but no one in the city had failed to notice an increase in their presence, a tension in the guards who patrolled the streets. Unprovoked assaults on Leithonian citizens had increased in the past few days, and security in most Imperial buildings had tightened. It had gotten so bad that Lyndon had advised a general pause on all their usual activity, since the Imperials would be out for blood.

Liam almost couldn't blame them. First the bank, and now the prison. With a new lord in the Bastion and everything else going on, it probably wasn't an easy time to be an Imperial soldier.

But they were taking it out on the city population, and that he couldn't forgive.

He steeled himself, his eyes on Lyndon as he waited to hear what the Resistance would do next.

"Some of you may have met Liam," Lyndon said, looking directly at him. He felt a twinge of anxiety as heads turned to face him again, but this wasn't the first time he had been on display. He kept his expression neutral. "Our resident mage. He helped us out in the Deep, and I'm sorry to say we've thoroughly corrupted him. I'm sure we can count on his aid in the future."

There was a smattering of applause, a few hoots and shouts of excitement. Lyndon raised his hand to restore order, but he was stopped by an outburst from one of the prisoners. It was the man at the front, the scarred one who had helped lead the others out of the prison. The one whose eyes still haunted Liam's dreams.

"When are we going to start the revolution?" he asked, loud enough to cut through the noise. "That's why you broke us out, isn't it? When are we going to fight?"

Lyndon frowned, facing the man. Liam could see from his expression that he wasn't used to this, to being interrupted on his own stage. "Everyone here wants those Imperial bastards out. But we need to weaken their hold first. Soon, we'll—"

"That's not what they're saying out on the streets," the man said. "They're saying the Resistance is getting ready. Stockpiling weapons. Aren't we going to *fight*? Isn't that why *we're here*?"

Lyndon stared at him, stunned into silence. As the seconds dragged by without an answer, Liam felt something shift in the room, an undercurrent of uncertainty. It was difficult to describe, but it felt the same as if he were working on a spell and starting to lose control of it, its energies unraveling at his fingertips. It felt like that moment just before he lost control.

And then Lyndon gathered himself. When he spoke next, his voice was soft, but edged with steel.

"Where did you hear that?"

"Everywhere. It's all they can talk about at the docks." The man looked at the others who were with him for confirmation, and although they nodded, Liam saw the confidence began to slip from his face. "I thought . . . wasn't that why you broke us out, boss?"

"We broke you out because you're our people," Lyndon said. "And we're going to hit the Empire where it hurts, don't get me wrong. But tell me, Thad . . ." He leaned closer, frowning down at the man. "Who's out there talking about revolution? Because if there's one brewing, it's not ours. Not yet."

The man, Thad, shrank into his seat. Liam heard sharp intakes of breath from around the room. In the silence, Thad's voice was clear as a bell.

"We—we heard the rumor down at the docks, like I said," said Thad. "Around the safehouse. The—the dockworkers all say that the Resistance is about to break into the Bastion. That they're planning . . ."

"That we're planning?" Lyndon prompted, when Thad went silent.

"That you're planning to kill the young lord," said Thad, at last. "To take the city back. And that they've got friends in the Imperial military who are going to help them do it."

Lyndon's expression was dark. Liam knew, seeing his face, that that couldn't be true. Arian had always said that Lyndon would put his head in a noose himself before he bent the knee to any Imperial. But Liam wondered, hearing the murmurs that rose in the room around him, how many of the others knew that.

It didn't matter. Even if no one in this room believed the rumors, other people would. *Imperials* would, and if they were out for blood now, Liam only imagined how they would get once they heard rumors of rebellion.

"Well," Lyndon said, his voice so soft that it would have been impossible to hear if the room hadn't quieted down as soon as he raised his head. "Well, folks, it looks like our plans have changed."

CHAPTER 36

ARIAN

CAVAR WAS IN THE SITTING ROOM WHEN ARIAN RETURNED FROM the kitchens. He was seated on one of the plush armchairs with a book in hand, feet resting on a footstool. Even relaxed, he looked so much like Nasirri that Arian almost forgot who he really was. She wondered if he would be able to return after this, or if he would stay Lord Nasirri forever.

"Is your business concluded, my lord?" she asked, shutting the door behind her.

He looked up at her from over the top of his book, and for a moment, she saw only Nasirri. Then something shifted behind his eyes and Cavar came back, slowly, like a curtain being pulled away from a window.

"It is."

Arian sighed and walked to the chair opposite him, flopping down into it. She kept her attention on the door in case anyone walked in—it wouldn't do to have someone see Riana sitting with her master like an equal—but half the Bastion thought she was jumping into bed with him anyway. Any indiscretion on her part probably wouldn't matter.

"I thought you were hanging out with Lord Kaolin today," she said.

Cavar's lip curled—she recognized that as a Nasirri expression. "Our young lord has other dinner arrangements."

"Ooh, scandalous," said Arian. She leaned back into her seat, propping her feet up on the footstool beside his. Cavar moved to give her room. "Anyone we know?"

"Actually, yes." Cavar glanced at her sidelong. "Your friend Lieutenant Venari."

Arian blinked. What was Zephyr doing getting cozy with Lord Kaolin?

"You're sure?"

"Fairly certain," said Cavar, which, coming from a Weaver, was just a nice way of saying *of course I'm sure, who the hell do you think I am?* Arian tilted her head back and stared up at the ceiling, thinking.

"How do you know her?" Cavar asked, after she was silent for a while.

"My mother was friends with her father. She hung around a lot. She and Liam were a thing for a little bit, but we were never really close. Her dad never liked mine, and I was always . . ." She ended with a vague gesture.

". . . your father's daughter."

Arian shrugged. "Sure. To hear my father talk about it, Lord Venari carried a torch for my mother for a while. Kind of broke his heart that she chose some ruffian from the Wastes instead of him."

"So the lieutenant and Liam . . ."

She made a face. "Insufferably sweet. Couldn't sit in the same room as them without gagging."

"Sounds terrible," Cavar said, although his smile made it clear that he was being sarcastic. And possibly mocking her. Arian wasn't sure, but she kicked his leg lightly for good measure.

"Awful," she said. She glanced away from Cavar again as her mind began to wander, going to memories she would rather forget. "She was good for him, you know. Brought him out of his shell a bit. I kind of wanted them to stay together."

"And then the occupation happened," Cavar said.

"And Zeph decided to turn traitor," Arian said, feeling like something was stuck in her throat. "And that . . . did something to my brother."

"It broke him?"

"A lot of things broke him. Zeph was just the icing on a really shitty cake." She shook her head. "But we're not here to talk about history. Go back to what you said a moment ago. Zeph's meeting with Lord Kaolin? In private?"

Cavar nodded. "There are rumors among the soldiers that they're . . . involved. I was hoping you could tell me if that's reasonable. I only met her at the ball for a few minutes, and I got the impression then that she was self-possessed and driven, but that tells me nothing about any potential romantic entanglements."

"Four years ago, I'd say no," said Arian. "But everyone's changed nowadays. Who knows? Why is this so important?"

Cavar smiled at her. "Think it through."

She rolled her eyes, resisting the urge to lean over and smack him. *That* would be really hard to explain if someone happened to walk through the door. She folded her arms, thinking. "If Zeph's meeting with our lordling for a little bit of fun, that's one thing. If they're not involved, it's another thing entirely."

"More secrets," Cavar said.

"Yeah," said Arian. "Did I ever mention that I fucking hate politics?"

He gave her a wry smile. "Would you believe it if I said I did too?"

"I'd say you were just playing a different kind of politics." Arian flashed him a quick grin. "And sorry, lover boy, I'm not that easy to woo."

Cavar returned her grin with a smirk, and the two of them lapsed into a comfortable silence. Arian leaned back and enjoyed the moment of rest, her thoughts spinning around in her head.

"I think we might be in the clear as far as Roth is concerned," she said. "He's been holed up in his rooms since the ball. Haven't heard a peep. Still, just in case, probably better that we don't break into his room again."

"Our next steps, then?" Cavar asked.

"We should move on, I think. Start thinking of ways to get into the treasury and get this over with."

He put his book aside, frowning. "I think I might have something on that score."

Arian sat up straighter, intrigued. "Yeah?"

"It's not much. But I know who has access to the treasury. An Imperial bursar by the name of Nathaniel Hosner. I'm having dinner with him next week."

"Why?"

"On paper? Because Lord Nasirri wants to propose a business venture. But if I happen to find out how to unlock the treasury along the way, well . . ." He waved his hand through the air dismissively.

Arian smirked. "I see. You said this dinner is next week?"

"I did. Why do you ask?"

"No reason. I'm just curious to see if I can figure out how to get into the treasury before you can."

"Interesting," Cavar said. "Is that a wager?"

"That depends."

"On what?"

"On what I get if I win."

Interest sparked in Cavar's eyes. Arian watched him, crossing her legs and carefully smoothing Riana's skirt over them. A part of her wondered what she was doing, playing around like this. It certainly wasn't conducive to the mission . . . but she would be lying if she said that she wasn't having fun. She wondered if Cavar was thinking along the same lines. If she was reading the look in his eye correctly.

The intrigued look vanished from his face as he lifted the book back up. He almost managed to look *bored*. If she didn't know him, she might even have believed it.

"Prize to be decided later?" Cavar asked. "How does that sound?"

"Hmm . . . it sounds like you're going to find a way to weasel out of this one *when* I win, Nivear."

"I wouldn't. Weaver's honor. But you sound so certain. It almost makes me wonder if you know something I don't."

"No prior knowledge," Arian said, grinning. "But then again, there's never been a door I couldn't open."

Cavar smiled. "Challenge accepted."

CHAPTER 37

CAVAR

ONE OF THE ANNOYING THINGS ABOUT LIVING TWO LIVES, CAVAR mused, was how difficult it was to find a moment alone. If he wasn't with Lord Kaolin and being forced to entertain courtiers, he was with Arian and Linna, going over their plans. They were the only ones who saw him as Cavar eth'Nivear and not Lord Nasirri, and while that arrangement normally worked well, it made it hard for him to discuss Weaver history without Arian listening in.

His opportunity came when Arian left early the day after their wager was made. Ostensibly, she was going to start her chores, but if she wasn't working on whatever scheme she had for breaking into the treasury, Cavar was going to resign.

He wasn't *too* worried about his own stake in the game. He had the advantage of being the only one to have a connection to the Imperial bursar, and besides, he didn't care if he lost. One way or another, he was going to get the Star, and if Arian was as creative as he thought she was, losing might be just as fun as winning.

He realized, as he waited for Arian to leave, that he was smiling. It surprised him. His work was important, but he couldn't remember the last time he had *enjoyed* it like this. There was something about Arian that made him do things like set up wagers, that made each day feel like an adventure. Something about her that he envied and felt drawn to in equal measure, but he couldn't give it a name.

He was, however, still on the job. And he couldn't ignore what Arian had told him about Roth and what she found in his rooms.

So when Arian left to roam the Bastion, Cavar went to find Linna.

The other Weaver was sitting in her chamber, tending to her weapons. It was early in the day, but she was already dressed in her armor.

She didn't even look up as he stepped into her small room and shut the door.

"Are you sure your lady love will like this? You coming to see other girls?"

"You didn't give me the pass phrase," Cavar said.

Linna rolled her eyes. "As if Lord Nasirri would have any reason to visit his bodyguard in her own chambers." She glanced at Cavar out of the corner of her eye, and her gaze was piercing. Cavar took a deep breath.

"Arian and I aren't involved," he said, leaning back against the door.

Linna rolled her eyes. "Please. As if I wouldn't notice the constant flirting happening in this suite. If you don't see the way things are heading, you're denser than I thought."

Cavar shrugged, although inwardly he felt a pang of guilt. Linna was right; he knew where things were going and he shouldn't have allowed himself to get so distracted. But Arian was . . . fascinating. She made him want to follow this thread to the end, if only to see where it would lead, even knowing that it would probably be heartbreak.

"It was bound to happen someday," Linna said. "But someone from the cursed tribe, Cavar? Really?"

"Eth'Akari isn't *cursed*. You're a Weaver, Linna. Don't be so superstitious."

Linna shrugged. "You have to admit, there is something strange about them. That entire bloodline . . ."

"Arian isn't officially eth'Akari."

"Semantics. And may I remind you that you're the one who finds the need to treat her like a Weaver when it's convenient and forget that when it isn't. But forgive me, *my lord*, we're not here to discuss your dalliances. What did you need?"

"I can't catch a break with you, can I?"

"It *is* my job to keep you humble," Linna said, but the corner of her lip quirked up in a smile. "Now what is this meeting *really* about?"

"Honestly, eth'Akari," Cavar said. "According to Arian, Emeric Roth had one of their markers in his wardrobe."

Linna frowned, pursing her lips. "Another lost son? Or something else?"

"What are the chances that Emeric Roth is related to eth'Akari, like Arian?"

"Given our range?" Linna asked. "Nonzero. As Rinu eth'Akari continually reminds us, Weavers are people too. But unlikely . . . we've hardly sent anyone to Aelria in years."

"Don't you find that a little strange?" Cavar asked, frowning. "For all we claim to weave the threads of fate, we haven't intervened in the Aelrian expansion yet? That's not normal."

Linna gave him the oddest look. Concern and curiosity and suspicion all blended into one. "Sympathizing with Leithon now? We're supposed to remain neutral, Cavar."

"I just think it's strange, that's all," Cavar said, ignoring the pang, somewhere deep in his chest, that warned him he really might be beginning to lose his neutrality. "If any other Empire did this, we would be on them like flies. Observing, at the very least, if not 'guiding' their progress. So why aren't we doing the same with Aelria?"

"Why do we do *anything*, Cavar? I can't read the First Weaver's mind. You'd probably have a better shot at that."

Cavar frowned, but he didn't say anything more. He couldn't tell her that he had stopped understanding his mother years ago, when she first pulled him from the children's classes at eth'Nivear so that she could personally oversee his training. It would sound too much like whining, and no matter how he felt about his job these days, Weavers did not *whine*.

"Back to the subject," he said instead. "Roth's ancestry. There's no way of proving whether he's related to them or not. Not with most of eth'Akari gone."

"No," said Linna. "No, there wouldn't be. But proving it isn't the issue. The real question is, what would it mean if it were true?"

"It would mean that Roth is descended from a clan of the Wastes, but so is Arian, so is Liam, so are many people. If he were descended from eth'Akari, it would be interesting, but if he was raised outside of the Wastes, I can't see how that would be much of a concern. But if he's *not* related to eth'Akari by blood . . ."

"That's trickier, isn't it?" asked Linna.

Cavar nodded. If Roth was just another lost son of eth'Akari, it made sense. Of course he would have a clan marker; of course he would keep it close. But if he *wasn't* descended from eth'Akari, then his possession of one of the clan markers was intriguing and more than a little unsettling. If it had been a large clan, like eth'Maranis or eth'Vaira, it might not have meant anything. But eth'Akari was a small clan whose only claim to fame was that they had disappeared, and that one of their only survivors had become one of the Weavers' greatest traitors.

Cavar didn't know how a powerful mage like Emeric Roth was connected to a doomed clan that had vanished under mysterious conditions, but none of the few scenarios he *could* envision were good. He shook his head, taking a deep breath.

"We'll need to look into this more."

"Eventually," Linna agreed. "Right now, however, Roth is not our concern until he *becomes* our concern. Our mission is to retrieve the Star. Don't forget that, Cavar."

"I know what our mission is."

"Really?" Linna asked, arching an eyebrow. "Because sometimes

I'm not sure that you do. Don't get distracted now. That's the last thing we need."

Linna's words stung, but he had not become a Weaver by willfully ignoring important truths. He nodded. "I'm working on the Star. I won't get . . . distracted."

She nodded, going back to her work. It was a clear dismissal, and Cavar slipped from the room, closing the door behind him.

ARIAN WAS IN THE SITTING ROOM WHEN HE LEFT LINNA'S ROOM, dusting the furniture. She looked up as he closed the door behind him, frowning. Cavar gave her his best smile and hoped that he didn't look too guilty.

"Do I want to know?" Arian asked, indicating the door behind him.

"Nope, probably not," Cavar said.

Arian rested a hand on her hip and cocked her head to the side, not looking amused at all. At length, she sighed. "Fine. Don't tell me. It's not like it matters."

"Doesn't it?"

Arian looked back over her shoulder, meeting his gaze. Her eyes burned their way into his, and he felt it again, that nebulous connection between them. It tugged at him like a taut string, and the rush that went through him was tempered only by Linna's warning. Arian looked away, breaking their gaze, but the connection was still there. He cleared his throat.

"I had to ask her a question."

She started dusting again, apparently satisfied. "Got an answer?"

"Not the one I was looking for. But an answer enough." The distance between them nagged at him, a few feet feeling like an ocean. He took a step closer in spite of himself, and then another, until he was standing beside her, leaning against the bookshelf she was working on. Later, he would lie awake and worry about this need to be close to her. To tease and prod and joke until he finally coerced her to smile.

Maybe Linna was right—maybe he was getting distracted. He should have cared about that more than he did, but when he was around Arian these days, it was very difficult to care about anything else.

"I had to ask her about Weaver business."

"My dad?" Arian asked. "Or about what I found in Roth's office?"

"Both," Cavar admitted. "But I'm afraid Linna doesn't know much more than we do."

Arian shrugged. "You all don't seem to know nearly as much as you pretend to."

Cavar wondered if she was right. The thought disturbed him, because if he thought about how little the Weavers actually knew, if he thought about things like why they had left Aelria alone for so long, why Rinu eth'Akari had not come back to Leithon since the occupation, and why he felt like his mother was growing more distant every day, he began to think something that he couldn't bring himself to admit. Something he thought he had crushed and buried so deep inside him that it would never see the light of day again. The thought that maybe—maybe he didn't want to be a Weaver after all.

CHAPTER 38

LIAM

THERE WEREN'T TOO MANY PLACES LEFT IN THE CITY WHERE AN illegal mage and the head of the Leithonian contingent could go to talk in private, but the dilapidated ruin of the apartment where Liam had spent most of his life did the job. There was a reason that he and Arian hardly used it, though. It wasn't secure, and it came with memories as thick as the dust, for both of them.

Pacing the living room and waiting for Zephyr to arrive, Liam tried to reconcile this broken, rotting chamber with the home that he had always known, the home that he still saw in his dreams sometimes. It was like the two were different places. The room was smaller than he remembered—he had hit his growth spurt after the occupation—and the memories he had here were of a warm place. A place of learning and safety.

A golden place.

He ran his fingers through the thick layer of dust on top of one of the bookshelves and wondered whether his memories had ever really been true, or if they were only a marker of the child he had been. A child who would believe anything.

A knock came at the door, startling him back to the present. Liam tensed, the air between his fingers buzzing with electricity, but Zephyr called out a second later, and the sparks died down, magic sinking back into his skin.

"It's me," she said, and he said, "Come in," like they weren't the people they had become, like this wasn't some gross parody of a different, better time that might or might not have existed.

She stepped into the apartment quickly, and he found himself relieved at the sight of her. Relieved, and immediately guilty at the force of his relief. Because now was not the time to feel happy about seeing Zephyr. Not now, with the Resistance's plans buzzing inside his head, with the weight of revolution heavy in the air. A revolution that—if Lyndon was to be believed—was a ploy, a power grab by the very people that Zephyr worked for.

The problem, Liam thought, was knowledge. This was hard for him because he had too much of it. He understood why some Leithonians had buried their heads in the sand, closed their eyes to the Empire. His life would be so much easier, he thought, if he wasn't filled with the constant need to *know things*, and then to put that knowledge to use.

If he had no conscience at all, he might have been able to live like her.

But there was no point in rehashing old hurts. Zephyr had asked to meet him. She'd said she needed help. So he smiled a little, and pretended not to notice the way her eyes took in the ruin of his childhood home, pretended not to see the guilt and distress on her face even though it was so obvious that even he could read it.

"You wanted to meet, Zeph?" he asked.

She said, "I had a question about magic. You don't have to answer it."

She was giving him an out, a chance to refuse her, but he was already here. Against his better judgment, he'd set up this meeting at her request, and he already knew that he would help her if he could.

They were both still bound by the past. Even if they both knew better, they kept reaching for each other.

"Fire away."

"Is it possible to use magic to alter someone's mind?"

A dozen different thoughts ran through his head. The scholarly side of him was worried only about the answer, running through everything he knew on the subject, but the other parts wanted more information. They wanted to know why Zephyr needed to know this, wanted to know what had happened in the Bastion or what she suspected.

He turned those other parts away, focusing on the scholar, but he could sense them there in the back of his mind. Waiting.

"When you say 'alter,'" he said, "what do you mean?"

"I mean, is there a spell that can turn someone into a different person?" Zephyr asked. "Or put someone under their control?"

"It's possible. Difficult, but possible. The human mind is a complex thing—it has shields and safeguards put into place to protect against exactly that. A sufficiently skilled mage could break through them and assert control, but it wouldn't be complete. Of course, research on the subject is limited, because mental manipulation is against the fundamental principles of magic."

Zephyr nodded, absorbing this. "It's dark magic."

"Very," said Liam. He could feel a shiver running underneath his skin, a reminder of the magic he had been practicing recently. He wondered if he should say more, and decided that Zephyr deserved it of him. For old times' sake if nothing else. "If I were wanting to control someone, I wouldn't go for direct control. Too messy, too obvious. I'd instead offer *suggestions* to the person's consciousness, make them think that they were coming to these decisions on their own."

"Is there a way to tell if that sort of thing is happening?" Zephyr asked.

"If you were a mage, you'd be able to sense it," Liam said. "But only if you were in the room when the suggestions were being given. It's easy to sense magic at work in the outside world, but it's very hard to sense it at work inside a person themselves. Like I said, the mind acts as a shield to protect against that sort of invasion of privacy."

Zephyr raised her eyes to meet his, and all the uncertainty in her face was gone. All that was left was the soldier. "And if you weren't a mage?"

"If you weren't a mage . . . you would have to look for signs in the behavior of the person being controlled. Things that don't add up. You can also watch the mage who you suspect is controlling them. That sort of magic wears on the caster eventually. They'd be more tired than usual. Moodier."

There was only one mage she could be thinking of, only one mage she would suspect. *He* was capable of that sort of magic—Liam was sure of it—but he wondered what had happened at the Bastion to make Zephyr suspect Roth of mind control. "Why do you ask?"

Zephyr's breath hitched. "No reason."

Liam frowned at her. "I have a right to know what my information is going to be used for, don't I?" His expression softened as he watched her, uncertainty growing. "Zephyr?"

Zephyr sucked in a breath. "I think that someone might be controlling Lord Kaolin."

Lord Kaolin. Kaolin Eismor.

The air in the room felt close, smothering. It was hard to breathe. When he opened his mouth to speak, he felt detached from himself. He hadn't expected the anger to take him so suddenly, but he could hear it in his voice when he spoke, just beneath the surface.

"Why do you care about Lord Kaolin?"

Zephyr didn't answer. The anger grew, a rising clamor on the inside of his chest, under his skin.

"Zeph . . ."

"It isn't what you think, Liam."

"What do I think?" Liam asked. "You don't even know what I'm thinking right now."

He wasn't sure what he was thinking right now. All he knew was that he was seeing the Arcanum burn again, seeing his mother die again, seeing Zephyr open the gates again. Zephyr glanced at his eyes, and whatever she saw there must have frightened her—she looked away.

"I'm working with him. I'm not involved with Lord Kaolin."

"I don't care about that!" Liam said, which wasn't true. He did care about that, very much, but it wasn't what they were talking about now. "Zephyr, he's an Imperial!"

"And in case you haven't noticed, *Liam*," Zephyr said, an edge coming into her voice, "I'm working for the Empire. I should at least get the choice as to *which part* of the Empire I'm working for."

"You're working for the man who wants to take over this city! The man working with the *monster* who killed my mother."

"And that's your problem, Liam," Zephyr said. "That's *all you know*. Ever since the occupation, all you've thought about is the past. It's consumed you. You can't even think about *moving forward—*"

"*Moving forward?*" He was aware that he was shouting now, but couldn't bring himself to care. "You want to *move forward*? You want to hand this city over to them all over again?"

"They'll take it anyway! It's better than drowning the whole city in blood because of your ideals."

"I'm fighting for this city—!"

"You're not fighting for this city!" Zephyr stomped her foot on the wooden floor, the sound sharp and cutting. It echoed in his mind. "You're fighting for *yourself*! Ever since the invasion, you've done nothing *but* fight for yourself!"

"And what have you been fighting for? Because it isn't for your people, Zephyr. It's never been."

He'd hurt her. He could see that. She flinched away from the words as if they were a blow, but blood was rushing in his ears. All the words he'd been holding back were threatening to spill out of him, to take all they could out of him until he was a shaking, raving husk of himself. He couldn't stop them. He might have had better luck bottling lightning.

"You talk about drowning the city in blood? *You're* the ones doing that! There's people out there now talking about revolution, and they're not getting those ideas from *me*. It's you and your people—"

"What are you talking about?" Zephyr said suddenly, her voice as cold as ice.

"Don't act like you don't know," Liam said, because he saw on her face that she knew *exactly* what he was talking about. He saw it in that instant before she withdrew, drawing deep into her shell until the only thing he could see looking out at him was Lieutenant Venari. They stared at each other for a long moment, two strangers in the hollowed-out remains of a life.

"Thank you for your advice," she finally said. "I'm leaving now."

She slammed the door on the way out. It closed with a crack, dislodging a layer of dust and forcing him to close his hands into tighter fists to maintain control.

As a child, when he was overwhelmed, he would fly into rages—meltdowns. The world stopped making sense, and he would scream and cry and rage until the feelings passed and he collapsed in exhaustion. As he grew older, he learned how to manage them—some—and being able to use magic helped. But he could feel the world closing in around him, the breathing coming fast in his throat, the familiar sensation that he was at the end of his rope, that he was about to lose control.

And he couldn't. It would be *dangerous*.

He had to wait. Until he was safely in the ossuary, until he was alone and no one would hear him except the dead. So instead, he bit his lip so hard that he could taste blood and gathered it up inside him, that anger and rage and *feeling* that was just too much for him to hold, and threw it out of him all at once.

Cold air rushed outward from him in an instant, blanketing the apartment with ice. He collapsed to his knees, his vision blackening from the sudden force of the magic, his body shaking with violent shivers.

He was safe. It was summer. The ice would melt by morning. An Imperial patrol would never find it—they rarely came all the way out here.

He took in a few more shaky breaths and then slowly got to his feet. He no longer felt the urge to scream. But in that moment of clarity that he had bought for himself, he understood something.

Zephyr had confirmed—if he was reading her right—that the Imperial military was spreading these revolution rumors. Which meant the Resistance needed to know, immediately. Armed with that purpose, Liam left the building, heading not for the safety of the ossuary but toward the rooftop paths and the Spinning Wheel.

If Zephyr wanted him to become a revolutionary, then he *would* become a revolutionary. It was time *someone* fought for this city.

CHAPTER 39

ZEPHYR

ZEPHYR WASN'T FULLY AWARE OF WHERE SHE WAS AFTER LEAV-
ing the Athensor apartment. Her thoughts were a swirling mass
on the inside of her head. She wanted to turn back and apologize,
wanted to turn back and scream, wanted to keep walking and never
look back. She couldn't believe that it had come to this between
them, this frenzy that tore at her from underneath her skin.

That conversation had driven home one point. Somehow, on
the day of the occupation, she and Liam had become different people. And they were never going to be the same again.

Something hot and wet stung at her eyes, and Zephyr clenched
her fists in frustration, because now she wanted to *cry*. But she
couldn't afford tears. She'd made her choice. She was going to find
out what was happening in the Bastion, and she was going to do it
for the sake of her city.

She kept walking and didn't look up until she realized where
her feet had taken her, realized that she was standing outside the
gates of House Venari's ancestral home. The gates were locked, as
they always were, and watched, as they always were. She had no
doubt that her presence here had already been noted, cataloged
into whatever dossier the Empire had on her and her family.

Once, a long time ago, those gates were never closed. Once,
she could walk through those doors and find the solution to every
problem, could sit at her mother's knee, unload all her worries and
let her soothe them away. Could go riding with her father and forget her cares. Could simply *be*.

She couldn't do that anymore. She knew what would be waiting
for her if she walked through those doors. Her mother's concern

and disappointment; her father's disapproving gaze. Her siblings' anger.

She didn't want to face that, so Zephyr took the coward's path. She walked away.

As she walked, she realized one thing was true. There *was* tension in the city.

In the dress she was wearing, she wasn't a soldier, wasn't a representative of Imperial authority. She was just another citizen walking the streets, and the people who might have quieted themselves in her presence when she was in uniform barely noticed her now. She could hear their murmurs of dissent, could practically feel the sparks of rage in the air.

Kaolin was right. Something was happening. After speaking with Liam, she had no doubt that Selwald was to blame for this. But what could she do to stop him?

Her apartment seemed so much colder than her childhood home, so much emptier. It wasn't that there was anything *wrong* with her apartment. By all measures, it was perfectly serviceable. It might even have been considered nice. It was a two-room affair in a decent part of town, with enough room for her uniform and weapons, and with the second room converted into a practice space large enough for her to work on her forms. Her neighborhood was pleasant, her neighbors polite, and the morning sun through her living room windows made the apartment glow.

But there was no real warmth in it.

And it was so very lonely.

Zephyr closed the door behind her. She paused in the middle of pulling her shoes off, her eyes drifting down to the floor just in front of her door. A pair of letters had been shoved under the gap, one after another. One was in the sterile, official style of Imperial communications. The other was different, warmer and more personal.

Technically, she was off duty. She could ignore the letters, could say that she hadn't seen them until later. She could hardly be faulted for being away from her apartment in her personal time, and if she was being honest, she wanted nothing more than to collapse on the couch, close her eyes, and sleep until that disastrous conversation with Liam was nothing more than a memory.

But she didn't have that luxury.

Zephyr sighed, picking the letters up off the ground. The way she felt didn't change who she was, and she had a job to do.

She opened the official letter first. It was a missive from the desk of Commander Selwald, although, she noted, not from the man himself. It had been signed by the commander, but the words were written in the neat hand of his secretary. The missive's orders were clear—she was to report to the commander's office as soon as her shift began the next day.

She had a feeling she knew what this was about. Leon Albrent was a petty person. There was no way he would have let her get away with practically confirming that she was tied to Lord Kaolin, and she had met with Kaolin again after the ball. The letter worried her. If Commander Selwald had enough evidence to accuse her of sedition, it wouldn't take him long to make use of that one item of leverage he had over her—her family.

Would Kaolin protect them if it came to that? Technically, she wasn't doing anything wrong by choosing to serve the city's lord over its military commander. Seen from that light, one could argue that it was Commander Selwald who was committing treason.

But even if he was inclined to help her, Kaolin wasn't the city's lord yet. The commander had years of experience over him, and that was even assuming that Kaolin was still his own person, not some puppet on Roth's strings.

The second letter wasn't as dire as the first, but if anything, it was even more concerning. It was a personal note, written in the style that one Imperial nobleman would use to write to another.

The note was placed in an envelope stamped with Lord Kaolin's seal, and it was handwritten, bearing his signature.

It was an invitation to dinner. But it was warm, personal. Not a business letter. It was written like it came from a suitor.

She knew that it was fake. That it was all part of the game they were playing, the camouflage that allowed them to meet in private, uninterrupted. But the letter was warm in a way that her apartment wasn't, and she felt her heart give a traitorous little flutter. It was followed immediately by dread. She wiped at her eyes, even though her tears had long since dried.

She couldn't let herself feel things like that. That was the one thing, the *one thing*, she couldn't allow herself to do.

But Kaolin had to know about Selwald. He had to know what she'd discovered.

Zephyr took in a breath and held it for a moment. Then she picked up a pen and wrote an answer.

Yes.

CHAPTER 40

LIAM

LIAM HAD BEEN HALFWAY TO THE SPINNING WHEEL WHEN A MES-senger intercepted him, a child who pressed a piece of paper into his hand and ran off across the rooftop paths without looking back. It was night, and Liam had only the light of the lantern he was carrying to go by, but he stood with his back to a crumbling wall and lifted the lantern up so he could read the message.

It was from Lyndon, a reply to Liam's note that he was coming. He had sent word ahead once he had gotten his breath back, still uncomfortable with the idea of walking into the Spinning Wheel and just asking to see their leader. It seemed like that was a good thing, though, because in the letter, Lyndon warned him *not* to come to the Wheel, and instead gave him directions to another meeting place.

The directions led to a section of the rooftop paths that Liam had never been in before. This area was dangerously close to derelict, and as Liam crossed over a makeshift bridge between rooftops, little more than a plank of wood laid down to span the narrow gap, he held his breath. His knees were shaking terribly when he reached the other side. It was almost too much, but he was determined to continue, so he adopted the shuffling, sliding gait he had first used when Arian took him up to the paths.

Thankfully, he didn't have much farther to go. He had barely taken a few steps when Lyndon slid out of the shadows in the hollow of what had once been an attic room. He carried no light and looked pointedly at the lantern Liam had brought with him until Liam extinguished it.

At first, the darkness took his breath away. But slowly, his eyes began to adjust, picking up the light of the moon and stars above, mixed with the faint gleam of streetlights from the city far below.

"Sorry for the theatrics," Lyndon said. "I don't want any more rumors right now, if we can help it."

Liam nodded. He'd had a feeling, when Lyndon had asked him to come *here* instead of to the Wheel. He felt a touch of guilt at that. He hadn't expected that asking to meet with Lyndon would cause this much trouble. But he couldn't trust Zephyr's information to a letter.

"I understand. But I needed to talk to you as soon as possible. I have some information that might be relevant."

Lyndon nodded, waiting expectantly. In the dim light, he was nothing more than a silhouette, a darkened figure with no facial expressions, no eyes to search him out and pierce deep into his soul. Maybe that was why it felt easier to open his mouth, to share everything that had happened that night. It was like he was alone in the ossuary, speaking to the air, confessing all his secrets into the dark.

When he was done, Lyndon was silent for a while. After a moment, he said, "You shouldn't have done that thing with the ice."

Liam nodded quickly, ashamed. He had been thinking the same thing since he left the apartment. It had been pointless and ridiculous and he didn't know how to explain that, at the time, it had been the only thing he could have done, that he would have exploded if he hadn't done *something*.

To Liam's relief, Lyndon didn't ask him to explain. He simply sighed and said, "Well, we work with what we have. This Venari won't report you, will she?"

"I don't think so," Liam said. "She's the one who asked to meet. If she reported me, she would have to explain what she was doing there, and it wouldn't look good for her."

"So there is something in that head of yours, besides magic and sentimentality." The words were harsh, but they didn't sound like an insult. Lyndon said it so matter-of-factly, like he was checking items off a list, taking stock of what he had to work with.

"I know it's not much to go on," Liam said, "but—"

Lyndon raised a hand. "It's enough. She wasn't surprised. Means there's probably been talk over in the Bastion about this too. And you said she seemed oddly concerned about Kaolin Eismor?"

Liam nodded, embarrassed. With time and distance, his anger was cooling, and he realized he may have overreacted. Certainly, it had been a long time. He didn't have the right to be jealous . . . if jealousy was what that emotion had been. Lyndon walked a few paces, moving closer toward the edge of the roof where he could look out over the city.

"I've heard rumors that the two of them might be . . . allied," Lyndon said. "But I don't think he's behind this. He doesn't stand to gain anything—if the city goes up in flames, Aeldoran will just whisk him home. Probably tell him he's not 'ready for the responsibility' or some other horseshit. If anything, this smells like Selwald."

"Trying to keep power," Liam said. "I was thinking the same thing."

Lyndon was quiet for a moment, and then he cursed out loud, the words sharp and guttural. "We'll have to lie low for a bit. Stay quiet until the heat dies down. We can try and keep the city calm, stop them from fanning the flames. It's gonna be hard enough to do with our youngbloods half ready to pick up swords and charge the Bastion tomorrow."

"Is there anything I can do?" Liam asked.

"You? You can try to stay out of an Imperial cell. No more of this meeting with ex-girlfriends who also happen to work with the Imperial military. And keep the magic to a minimum."

Liam nodded, disappointed but unsurprised. He was grounded, again, now that things were happening in the city, now that he had finally convinced himself that he could *help*. His whole life, people had showered him with praises when things were good, but he had never been called on to solve problems. In a crisis, he was usually asked to stand aside and let other people work.

The day of the occupation had been no different. He'd spent the day hiding in the Arcanum, unable to do anything but watch as the Imperial magebreakers tore through the place, while Arian had raced back and forth across the rooftop paths ahead of the troops in the city, warning anyone she could find to hide before the Imperials rounded them up and made examples of them.

He had a head stuffed full of books, but when it came down to it, it was always Arian who was *useful*.

So he was a little surprised when Lyndon spoke, because he was already thinking about how he could excuse himself, and whether now would be an acceptable time to walk away.

"Actually, there is one thing," Lyndon said. "Our would-be revolutionaries are apparently stockpiling weapons. If we can find them, we could keep them out of their hands, and in *ours*. And if they're obviously Imperial made, we can convince more people that this is a setup. I've already got my people searching, but once they find the place, we'll need a crew."

He turned to face Liam, and although it was impossible to tell for sure in the darkness, Liam thought he was smiling.

"You've handled yourself pretty well on previous jobs. So, you in?"

CHAPTER 41

ZEPHYR

ENTERING COMMANDER SELWALD'S OFFICE WAS A TRIAL.

The Imperial commander had chosen to retain the structure of Leithon's military, which meant that his headquarters were the same as those that had once been held by the Royal Guard. His office was her father's office, changed beyond recognition. Where the walls had once been decorated with scenes from the history of Leithon, they now sported stark Aelrian landscapes and propaganda slogans. Her father's books had been replaced with Aelrian military texts.

Zephyr thought the commander knew the effect this room had on her. That was why he insisted on calling her here every time he wanted to meet with her. Most days she could stand it, could choke down the feelings this room evoked in her, but after her meeting with Liam, her nerves were frayed.

Selwald had taken the city from them. And now he was working to destroy it.

Zephyr came to Selwald's desk and stood at attention. He didn't immediately acknowledge her, although there was no possible way that he could have missed her arrival. It was a common enough experience that she didn't flinch, settling into her stance and waiting. The commander busied himself for several long moments, arranging papers on his desk and signing memos with excessive slowness before he finally looked up at her. Even then, he didn't speak, holding her gaze. Zephyr met his glare with a level look of her own.

"Lieutenant Venari," he said at last, "it seems that you've made some unwise decisions."

"How so, sir?" Zephyr asked, keeping her tone neutral.

Commander Selwald's brow furrowed. "Did I not warn you to be discreet in your dealings with Lord Kaolin Eismor?"

"You did. Although not in as many words, sir."

"I believe my meaning was very heavily implied, Lieutenant." Selwald pulled a sheet of paper from the top of the pile on his desk, signed it, and set it aside. "I was under the impression that we had an understanding. You're a competent soldier. I shouldn't have to spell things out for you."

"I understood your meaning perfectly," Zephyr replied, her voice tight. "Sir."

"Is that so? If it is, then tell me why the leader of my Leithonian contingent is following Lord Kaolin around like some lovesick little twit. I took a *chance* on you, Venari. Most Imperial commanders would never consider treating you like a soldier, but I did. I expected better of you."

"With all due respect, Commander," Zephyr said, doing her best to keep her voice steady. "What I do off duty is irrelevant to my work."

"Not when your dalliances directly threaten our goals."

"Our goals?" Zephyr asked. "Do we have *goals*, Commander?"

"For gods' sake, hold your tongue!" Selwald snapped. Zephyr's mouth closed, her spine instantly straightening. It was more of a reflex than anything—long years of training had taught her to respond to the tone of command. Selwald eyed her for several tense moments, daring her to speak. When she said nothing, he picked up the sheaf of papers in front of him and started straightening them out, not looking at her.

When he spoke again, his voice was almost level. "I want you to understand something very clearly, Lieutenant. I. Am. Your. *Ally*. I have allowed you, your family, and your entire cohort to retain their lives. I have *given you command*. You think that Lord Kaolin will do the same? I am trying to help this city, so I would appreciate it if you would stop trying to make a monster out of me."

Zephyr's mouth opened to argue, but at a warning glance from Selwald, she shut it. The anger welled up inside her, a beast trapped in a cage. How dare he sit there and tell her that he cared about this city? From that chair, where her father had once sat?

The worst part was, she *wanted* to believe him.

She breathed deep and managed, barely, to hold her tongue.

"My actions as a private citizen still have no bearing on my work, sir."

Selwald held her gaze for several long moments, and she could see the threat in his eyes. She held her breath, waiting for the other shoe to fall, waiting for Selwald to threaten her family and everything she held dear.

"When at all possible, keep your interactions with Lord Kaolin to your private time," he said instead. "Dismissed."

Zephyr saluted. "Commander."

She turned, ignoring the disapproving glare Selwald's secretary, a prim Imperial woman, shot her on the way out. Selwald *was* plotting something. The number of people calling for rebellion in the city had increased, and if Liam was right, they weren't getting their ideas from the Resistance. Kaolin said that Imperial soldiers were spreading the word, convincing people that if they made a move against him, the Imperial military would be on their side, but Zephyr had lived with the Imperial military long enough to know how much of a lie that was.

Selwald had to be behind it. No one else had the ability to alter the mood of the entire island so thoroughly, or the motive to do so. It wasn't a question of whether Selwald was trying to wrest control from Kaolin; it was only a question of how or when.

She'd have to speak with Kaolin about this at dinner. It would be a good time to look out for any of the signs Liam had mentioned, the warning signs that Kaolin wasn't his own person.

She told herself that was the only reason she was looking forward to it.

CHAPTER 42

ZEPHYR

LATER THAT NIGHT, ZEPHYR HEADED TO HER DINNER WITH KAOLIN to find a table waiting in the center of his study, laid out with the sort of formality that she had come to expect from the young lord. She felt a touch of nerves, her meeting with Liam still fresh in her mind. Her eyes swept the room, looking for Kaolin.

He was standing near the head of the table, dressed in a suit less formal than the one he had worn to the ball, but only just. He offered her a quick smile in welcome, one of his hands resting on the back of his chair.

"I hope you'll forgive the theater. It was brought to my attention that rumors were starting to spread about us. I thought it might be best to play along. It gives us a reason to meet as frequently as we do."

Zephyr searched his face, looking for any trace of the otherness that she had noticed at the ball, but the man in front of her was the same Kaolin he had always been. Could she have been mistaken?

No. She couldn't relax just yet. She had to remain on her guard. This was still Kaolin Eismor, the man who wanted to take her city away. She could never let down her guard while she was with him.

"That doesn't bother me, my lord," she said, "as long as it doesn't bother you."

"Kaolin, please," he said, smiling. "And I'm glad to hear that. I'd heard you were spoken for." He walked around the table to pull out her chair.

Zephyr hesitated before taking her seat. A part of her wondered who had told Lord Kaolin that she was "spoken for," but the rest of her wondered why he was treating her like this when there was no one else of import in the room. She tried to relax as she took her seat, placing her napkin on her lap.

"I'm not spoken for anymore," Zephyr said. "Whoever told you that was misinformed, or else they had old information."

"I see," Kaolin said, taking his own seat. "Then I'm sorry to hear things didn't work out. I know this isn't the best for your reputation . . ."

"My reputation is dirt anyway," said Zephyr. "If it allows us to stay in communication, an affair is better than the idea that I'm plotting sedition. Unless *you* happen to be spoken for . . ." She hesitated, but she was still Lieutenant Venari and not some shrinking violet. She could say a damn name. ". . . Kaolin."

Kaolin smiled. "Not at the moment, no. My father would like to change that, and there *are* talks, but that's all they are. Talks. And so, as we are both free and unattached, wine?"

He held up his glass questioningly. It would be rude to refuse, but Zephyr wanted to keep her mind clear. She needed to make sure that this was truly Kaolin. Needed to know what she would do if he wasn't, and what she would do if he was.

"A little," she said. "I'm assuming we have business to discuss tonight. I have information for you."

"That's good to hear," Kaolin said, his expression growing sober as he beckoned a servant closer. The servant, also wearing House Eismor's colors, poured them both a glass of wine before backing away. "But let's eat first, and then move on to business. We do need to play a little at being involved if this is going to be convincing." He gave her a smile, one so unguarded that Zephyr almost forgot her suspicions. Almost. "It would be helpful if I knew more about you."

"There isn't much to know," Zephyr said. She felt out of her depth and tried not to compare this encounter to evenings spent with Liam. "You could learn everything there is to know about me from reading my file."

"I highly doubt that," said Kaolin as the servants brought out the first course. "Tell me about yourself. Your past, your family? I can tell you about mine if it will make you more comfortable."

Zephyr watched him carefully as she settled back into her seat, but Kaolin looked nothing if not sincere. She nodded, taking a small sip of wine.

"There isn't much to say," she said. "I started training for the Guard when I was seven."

Kaolin's brows rose. "So young?"

"As the firstborn of House Venari, that was my birthright and my responsibility. My family have been the protectors of Leithon for generations. It was always assumed that I'd take over the Guard after my father retired . . ." She hesitated, looking down at her wine. In a sense, she had done exactly that, taking command of the remainder of Leithon's military. But the fates were cruel to make her come into her inheritance that way.

"I see," said Kaolin, noticing her silence. "It's hard to picture a city this small having much in the way of nobility."

"There are a handful of families," Zephyr said. "Mostly connected to the royal family in some way. House Venari is special."

"How so?"

She almost told him. Almost. But there were trusts that went deeper than alliances, secrets buried so deep inside her that no amount of coat-turning could ever shake them loose. She shook her head.

"Family affair, then?" Kaolin asked. "I won't pry. My family has its fair share of secrets as well."

"House Eismor?" Zephyr asked, realizing that she knew very little about the House that Kaolin was from. "You're the only son, aren't you?"

Kaolin grimaced, but nodded. "Yes. I am the sole heir. I'm sure that thought keeps my father up at night."

"The two of you don't get along?"

"That would be an understatement. I often think that the number of military campaigns he's sent me on are his way of keeping me out of his way. But those campaigns have given me experience that most of my peers lack, so I suppose I should be grateful."

"I never knew," Zephyr said, looking at Kaolin with renewed sympathy. She knew exactly what it was like, to have a father who considered you an inconvenience.

"It isn't publicly discussed," Kaolin said, offering her a tight smile. "But, there. You've heard one of House Eismor's secrets. I believe that puts us back on even ground, Zephyr."

"Maybe it does," said Zephyr. She picked up her spoon, starting on the soup course. As she raised the spoon to her lips, she paused, looking back at Kaolin over the table. "Was there anything else you wanted to know?"

Kaolin frowned. "I'll admit to being curious, but please don't feel obliged to answer. The person you were attached to . . . ?"

Zephyr took a spoonful of soup with deliberate care, willing her hand not to shake. Kaolin was watching her intently. She met his gaze, her mind on Liam, on everything they had shared, on all her memories.

"A childhood friend," she said. "From before the occupation. It doesn't matter now."

"Doesn't it?"

Zephyr looked at him from across the table. He was smiling, the light gleaming in his eyes. She realized something that stopped her cold.

Kaolin was dangerous.

It wasn't just about Roth controlling him. She had been watching him the entire time, and she hadn't noticed anything off, anything different. But he was still dangerous.

He was an Imperial lord and an enemy of her people. He was

not her friend. And she couldn't allow herself to think of him in any other way. But the more she spoke with him like this, the more meetings they had, the less she could bring herself to see him as Lord Kaolin Eismor, an extension of the empire, and the more she saw him as just Kaolin, a human being like herself.

And he wasn't without his charms. There was a light in his eyes when he spoke of something he was truly passionate about that reminded her of the way Liam had been. Once. Before. She'd been thinking of herself as a soldier and a traitor for so long that she'd almost forgotten to think of herself as a girl. It was nice, in a hypothetical sort of way, to think that someone like her could attract the attention of someone like Kaolin.

But it was wrong.

Deliberately, she put her spoon down, meeting his eyes.

"There's something you should know," she said. "I think you're right about Commander Selwald. I've heard from a ... reliable source that the Leithonian Resistance isn't involved in the current unrest. They're just as confused as we are, and they think the Imperial military is behind it."

Kaolin's face grew hard, the warmth in it fleeing as her words sank in. He was Lord Kaolin Eismor again, extension of the Empire, and Zephyr knew that no matter what she might feel, there would be no more friendly conversation tonight.

CHAPTER 43

LIAM

LINES OF BLINDING LIGHT TRACED THEMSELVES ACROSS THE ossuary floor, wisps of smoke rising from them and filtering into the boneyard's chill air. Frost formed on the surface of the staff in his hand, the metal freezing to the touch even through the thick leather of his gloves. Liam watched carefully as the circle formed, runes inscribing themselves in bluish-white light around its edge. He raised his hands, the staff vibrating in his grip. Sweat beaded on his brow and he felt himself start to shiver, the magic leeching the warmth from his body and soul.

The line of light spread, wrapping once around the circle. And then the circle was complete.

The lines came together with a bright flash of light, and Liam felt the completion as a jolt in his bones, a sudden flash of warmth before it was gone, leaving him more spent and drained than before. He propped himself up on the staff to stop from crashing to the ground, the metal making a clanging sound against the stone that was much, much louder than it should have been. The sound echoed in the high chamber, ringing like a bell.

He stood at the edge of the circle for long moments, breathing in the stale air, before he lifted his head, studying his handiwork. The circle glowed with cold fire, tracing wards of containment and protection. The air was hazy just above it, shimmering with light that gathered at three of the circle's points, where Liam had placed the foci that would center the spell.

He leaned his weight on the staff and straightened up, wiping the sweat from his brow.

Then he reached for the bowl that stood on the table in front of him.

In one swift movement, Liam snatched the bowl from the table-top, tossing it into the circle. The bowl was made of stone, one of the relics that he and Arian had found while cleaning the ossuary. It wasn't particularly special, but it *was* old. It had survived hundreds of years underground, in this place of magic and death. Barring any outside interference, it would likely have lasted another several hundred years, gathering dust and age and memories.

The bowl flipped end over end in the air, past the boundary of the circle. He saw the moment it crossed that gleaming line, heading toward the circle's center.

The circle crackled sharply, white light tracing itself across the bowl's exterior. There was a flash, and then the bowl crumbled to dust, motes so fine that by the time they floated down to the floor, there was hardly any trace of them at all.

The circle shimmered and quieted, the runes that marked it pulsing as the light died. The bowl's energy revealed itself as liquid light, pooling in a depression in the middle of the circle. It was a pale, feeble light, barely a sip of energy. The bowl was an inanimate object. It didn't have life of its own. It didn't have much power of its own, only what it had absorbed over its centuries of existence. But if it did have life, that light would be brighter.

Bright enough to help him, maybe. Bright enough to make him stronger.

The thought revolted him. It was one thing to channel power from old spells, another thing entirely to take it from living creatures. This circle of unmaking went against everything he had been taught. Magic stemmed from life, and this circle had no purpose but to deal death.

But it would give him power.

And if he was going to stand against the Empire, if he was going to kill Emeric Roth, to avenge his mother and the Arcanum, he was going to need it.

Roth used dark magic too. He looked at the darker disciplines not as something to be feared but as something to be grasped, as something to be controlled. That was the only reason why he had been able to win against Liam's mother that day in the Arcanum.

His mother had been chosen by the very powers of creation, had touched the threads that bound the universe together. The only way that Roth *could* have defeated her, even distracted as she was by protecting Liam, was if he had reached for powers greater still.

Liam wouldn't make the mistake of underestimating him. He wouldn't be afraid of power.

He watched the circle shimmer for a moment more, then solemnly set the staff aside, propping it up against a table so that he could tug off his right glove. Beneath it, his hand was bandaged, white cloth wrapped tightly around his thumb. Liam unwound the cloth and checked the wound, frowning. It hadn't yet closed, and still oozed blood.

The circle was tied to his blood. He had used blood to create it, and blood would break it.

He knelt down beside its border and pressed his bleeding thumb to the line that marked the circle. White light turned red as his blood touched it and the circle began to peel away, the light fading as runes untraced themselves. When the red light reached the pool at its center, that energy flowed into him. Liam shivered as he felt power run through him, that meager amount of power.

He knew what his mother would say if she saw this circle, what his teachers would say. They would call it evil, an abomination. But they weren't here. He was. They had done the right thing up to the very end and look what had happened to them.

This was an age for abominations.

CHAPTER 44

ARIAN

IT HADN'T BEEN EASY GETTING INTO NATHANIEL HOSNER'S OFFICE, but it had been significantly easier than breaking into Emeric Roth's quarters. For one, she could do it during the day. For another, she even had a legitimate reason to be here. The office needed to be cleaned. If the maid assigned to the task had *mysteriously* acquired a nasty stomach bug and Arian had *coincidentally* happened to be in the room when the head maid asked for someone to cover poor Selna's tasks, well, that was just a happy accident.

Really, it was a good thing Riana was so diligent. Or else this never would have worked.

Of course, since it was the middle of the day, the office wasn't empty. Hosner himself worked at the large desk set to one side of the room, but he barely noticed her. She dusted her way through the rows of shelves that lined the office, glancing at him occasionally to take his measure.

He was a quiet, mouse-like man, practically drowning in his formal uniform, and he had the ink-stained fingers and perpetually distressed manner of the career bureaucrat. Arian would have bet anything that he had some scandalous vice, something that would seem totally out of character to anyone who knew him.

Always the quiet ones.

Now, where would a man like Hosner hide a treasury key?

Somewhere secure, traditional, and boring. He wasn't Roth. He didn't look like the type whose mind ran in dangerous, twisted circles. He was the type to head home, lock his door, and think he was safe because he had paid good money for his safety. Security wasn't his concern; protocol was.

A locked desk drawer, then, or even a hidden safe. Both things that Arian had worked with before. All she had to do was find her way back here at night, and she could be in and out without anyone the wiser.

She was still trying to work out when she could do that when the door opened and another maid walked in.

Arian stopped, sensing trouble. She didn't know the girl's name, but she did know that the maid was one of the kitchen staff. There was no reason for her to be here. She looked nervous, like she would flee at any moment. Arian didn't like it. She watched, wary, as the maid bowed to Hosner.

"Your—your pardon, Lord Chancellor," she said, stumbling over the words. "The servants are being summoned to the kitchen."

Dread coiled in Arian's gut. She kept her face smooth through long practice, letting only confusion show.

"Who will clean my office, then?" Hosner asked, annoyed.

"Your pardon, my lord," the servant said again. "Someone will come to clean as soon as possible."

Hosner muttered something under his breath about irregularities, looking back at his paperwork. Arian breathed out and wiped her hands off on her apron, following the girl out the door. The girl didn't look at her as she walked, her face growing deathly pale as they neared the kitchens.

Arian reached out and grabbed her arm.

"What's happening?" she asked, but the girl only shook her head, lips pressed tightly together. Arian prepared for the worst.

The kitchen was packed with servants of all kinds, chambermaids and kitchen staff and butlers and stable hands all crowded into the cavernous room. Arian and the kitchen girl squeezed their way through the press, and Arian was not reassured when she noticed the armed guards standing by the door. Her feeling of dread only grew when she saw who else was standing there, in the only open patch of floor in the room. He stood flanked by two guards, the head maid and head butler, and it was hard to see him through the crowd, but Arian needed only a glimpse to know who he was.

Emeric Roth.

She hadn't taken anything from his rooms, and she had been careful—so careful—not to leave any trace behind. But there was that time she had lost hold of his protection spells. Only a moment, but . . . was a moment enough?

Inwardly, she cursed herself. She should have known better than to go around using magic. She wasn't even fully trained. And now her overconfidence was going to cost them all.

They waited in silence, none of them daring to so much as whisper. There were more shuffling sounds as servants filled the hall, and then, following some signal that even Arian couldn't decipher, the guards shut the kitchen doors, trapping them all in the room.

Roth turned toward the head maid. "Is this everyone?"

The head glanced at her subordinates, and Arian saw supervisors moving through the crowd, checking everyone off lists and rosters. She nodded to Roth. "Yes, lord."

Roth faced the crowd. He looked out at the servants as if they weren't people, as if he was studying the scenery. His lip curled in distaste. Arian shivered. She wanted to disappear into the crowd.

He knows.

Roth concluded his slow sweep of the room. When he spoke, his voice was soft, but in the silence, it carried.

"I have reason to believe that someone entered my rooms without authorization," he said. "This person used illegal magic to gain entry into my chambers, a crime that is punishable by death. I will begin to search for this person among you. If you have done nothing wrong, you have nothing to fear. Do not move. This will go quickly."

He held his arms out, palms facing the group. Roth's eyes drifted closed. All around her, servants muttered fearfully and shifted in place, but none of them tried to leave the room. Arian felt the power Roth was summoning as a prickle at the base of her spine. Her heart started beating faster, her eyes drifting from left to right as she tried to find an exit.

He was going to find her out. Panic closed her throat. She looked around, gauging the distance to the door. How many people would she have to fight through to get to it? And once she got there, there would be the guards to deal with. Could she break through them before Roth caught her in a spell?

And if she did, what then? Everyone here knew Riana was the personal servant of Lord Nasirri Rezavi. They'd be able to trace her back to Cavar, and Cavar's cover would be blown. Would Cavar and Linna be able to escape before the Empire tracked them down and killed them?

She wished she had the bracelet, something she could use to warn them. If she got out of this, she told herself, she was going to wear that damn bracelet every hour of every day, and screw Cavar and Linna if they protested.

If she got out of this . . .

Roth's spell went out, searching, questing, winding its way through the assembly. The spell felt like a question, one that moved through the line, asking each servant in turn if they were the one. She could almost hear the answer, a sensation rippling through the air.

No.

No. No. No.

The spell neared her, and Arian held her breath, fighting off a wave of panic. She could lie with the best of them, could fool just about anyone, but how was she supposed to lie to a spell? She *had* used magic, and he was going to find her. She tried to keep her face smooth, but her mind was racing, her heart pounding. She must have looked guilty, to anyone who glanced her way.

Not me. It wasn't me. I didn't do it. It wasn't me.

The spell touched the servant next to her. She felt the question, heard the answer. No.

It wasn't me. I'm not here. It wasn't me.

The spell passed over her without touching her, moving to the servant beside her. Arian heard its answer.

No.

It moved on again.

Relief ran through her, and Arian nearly sagged at the force of it. She didn't know if the spell had simply missed her, or if it hadn't found whatever trace it was looking for, but whatever it was, she was grateful for it. It meant she still had a chance.

The whole process had taken a minute, maybe two, but it felt to Arian like an age. When it was done, she felt the spell return to Roth, saw him open his eyes, his expression one of confusion and frustration. He didn't look into the crowd.

"Dismiss them," he snapped to the head maid and head butler, walking out through the back doors.

Arian filed out with the rest of the servants, glad that Riana's skirt was so long. It hid the way her legs were shaking.

Sloppy, she thought. She'd taken too much of a risk, using magic on that day. She had to stop making mistakes.

This could *not* happen again.

CHAPTER 45

LIAM

FROM ABOVE, IT WAS DIFFICULT TO MAKE OUT ANY DISTINCTIVE features of the building, a narrow structure that looked like it had been wedged into a space too small for it, but its long-dead architect had stubbornly decided to go on with construction anyway. If it hadn't been for the violet banners hanging above the entranceway, or the marks scratched into the stone of the rooftop paths that warned travelers not to approach, Liam would never have thought it was an Imperial guard station.

Although, when he thought about it, that was probably the point.

This particular station was hidden deep in the heart of Old Leithon, tucked into a rarely used side street and surrounded by the abandoned, hollowed-out shells of buildings that had not been particularly prosperous even in the days prior to the occupation. It had been placed here only as a formality, and to discourage Leithonians from using the abandoned buildings for criminal or seditious ends. Liam had heard that the Imperial military saw this station as a convenient dumping ground, a place to put useless soldiers or too-proud officers who could not be dismissed from service for one reason or another, but who needed to be kept out of the way until they could be sent back to Aelria.

Which also, Liam thought, made it the perfect place to hide something if the Imperial military was keeping secrets from other members of the Empire, or even from itself.

There were lights shining in the windows, but only a few. This outpost was famously understaffed, and it was late enough now that most of the guardsmen stationed here would be getting ready to sleep, with only the night crew awake. Still, its position in the center of the city and the presence of those guards meant that Liam couldn't risk anything like the flashy show of magic he had used to get into Blackstone Deep. No, if they were going to break in and confirm what their scouts had told them, this was going to require a softer hand.

Thankfully, he didn't think this place was magically protected. That hadn't stopped him from bringing the staff. He was starting to feel uncomfortable with leaving it behind, and with Roth in the city, he couldn't be too careful.

Liam turned to look at Lyndon and Reid. Just the three of them today, a quick in and out. It was the sort of job that Liam was most familiar with, the sort he and Arian often worked together.

"You're sure we'll find something in there?" he asked.

Reid shrugged. "Can't be sure of anything these days. But that's what people are saying. That when it's time, weapons'll be distributed from here."

Lyndon snorted. "Would be a good way to round all the rebels up. Get them to come down here and start asking for weapons. The Empire wouldn't have to lift a finger; we'd have practically arrested ourselves."

"Maybe, boss," Reid said, with another shrug. "Is that what you think is happening here?"

"I have no clue what's happening here, and I won't until we get in there and see for ourselves," Lyndon said. "What do we know about the building?"

"Used to be cheap apartments, way back in the old days," Reid said. "Empire picked it as a base because it's one of the only buildings around here that has a basement, and because it's small and easy to defend. But they've only taken up the first four floors. The higher floors are empty."

Liam nodded. It was a common story, and probably the only reason why the underground had survived the occupation. Unlike

Leithonians, Imperials just weren't used to climbing stairs. Aelria rarely had buildings as tall as Leithon's, and if they didn't have to, they didn't like climbing to the upper floors. It was a dangerous position for them, all the way up there. They didn't know the rooftop paths, so it would be easy to cut off their retreat from below.

"You think they're keeping the weapons in the basement?" Reid asked.

Lyndon shrugged. "Could be. But they've also got a bunch of floors they aren't using—could be in any one of those. Heck, could be in their sleeping quarters—in which case we're never going to be able to check. Maybe there aren't even any weapons at all. This is why we brought the mage."

He leveled his gaze on Liam, who swallowed, but nodded.

"I'll need a few minutes," he said. "Keep watch to make sure I'm not disturbed."

Wordlessly, the two of them turned their backs to him, standing lookout. Liam sat down cross-legged, keeping his gaze on the building across the street. He was always surprised how quickly ordinary Leithonians obeyed when a mage told them to do something, even hardened rebels like Lyndon and Reid. As if he knew everything in the world, just because he knew a few tricks for channeling power. It made him nervous, because he didn't think that he knew much at all. But with them counting on him, now was hardly the time for self-doubt, so he reached into his pocket and pulled out a lump of iron, setting it on the ground in front of him. And then he placed his hand on the staff and channeled power into it, just a little.

The staff came to life instantly. He felt it grab at him, sinking its teeth into him and draining magic from him like blood from his veins. He bit back a gasp at the cold sensation and touched the lump of iron with his other hand. He had nothing else to feed the staff but his own life force, and it was hungry. He had to move quickly, before it drained him down to a husk.

Liam channeled his awareness through the lump of iron briefly, letting his magic get a feel for it. Then he cast his awareness out, using the staff's power to help him propel it through the building, a searching net unlike any he had made. Instead of detecting magic, this detected *metal*, anything similar to the iron in his other hand. He took stock of the building as he moved the net through it, top to bottom.

Nothing on the top floors but the pipes and a handful of gutted remnants of a life lived. The first four floors lit up in his mind. They were full of metal, Imperial weapons, Imperial badges, Imperial coin—but nothing that looked like a stockpile. When he reached the basement, though, he paused, feeling out the space there. Crates, stacked into the corner. Each full of weapons. Swords—mostly. More than the outpost would ever need. Enough for a small army. He couldn't tell if they were Imperial made—he could only feel the shape of them. But they were in an Imperial outpost, and surely that was evidence enough.

He pulled back, gasping for breath, and not a moment too soon. The fingers of his free hand were already going numb. He shook out his hand and flexed the digits, trying to work some life back into them as Reid and Lyndon hurried over to him.

"What did you find?" Lyndon asked.

"Weapons—basement," Liam said, still too shaken to put more than a few words together. He swallowed, worked some will back into his throat. "More than this one outpost needs."

The two of them exchanged glances.

"Back entrance," Reid said, in answer to an unspoken question. "We can probably get in through a window."

Lyndon turned to Liam. "We're going in. Are you coming with?"

Liam nodded, getting shakily to his feet. His arm was coming back to life, and he clenched his jaw against the feeling of pins and needles, spreading from fingertip to elbow. With his other hand, he held the staff, now dull.

"I'm coming. I think you might need me."

Because there was a thought lingering in his mind, something he couldn't quite let go of. He couldn't be sure, because he had been searching for metal and not magic, but he thought he had felt a hint of magical protections too. Nothing too powerful, nothing he wouldn't be able to break, but if he was right, that meant that Imperial magebreakers were involved. And that was a problem, because the Imperial military might be fractured, but the magebreakers would answer to only one man. And that man was currently in residence in the Bastion. That man had killed Liam's mother.

"Are you coming?" Reid asked from the stairs that led down from the roof.

Liam shook himself, realizing that he had been lost in thought again. "Yes, sorry!" he said, hurrying to follow them. Down the roof and into the dark.

CHAPTER 46

ARIAN

SLIPPING OUT OF THEIR SUITE UNDER THE COVER OF DARKNESS was surprisingly easy. She piled her pillows up on the bed, then waited for Cavar to fall asleep before heading out of the room. She didn't try to leave through the front door. It was too close to Linna's room, and sneaking around two Weavers in one night felt like pushing her luck. Instead, she went out through the window, dropping down into the courtyard below and slipping back through the maze of hallways until she stood right outside Nathaniel Hosner's office.

The night had given Arian a fresh perspective, and it was hard to believe that she had been so scared of Emeric Roth just a few hours ago. It felt like she had thrown off a disguise. She wasn't a scared serving girl anymore. So what if she couldn't use magic to sneak around the keep anymore? When had she ever needed magic to get her way? She was Arian Athensor, the finest thief in Leithon, and that was magic enough.

Slipping into Hosner's office was laughably easy. The office was far enough away from the treasury that the bookkeeper probably kept no valuables here, and as such, saw no need to protect it from thieves. The lock was fancy, but it opened easily beneath her fingertips. Once she was inside, she paused to check for traps, but compared to Roth's chambers, this was a walk in the park.

She gave the room a cursory scan to make sure she hadn't set anything off, then made her way to the desk. A quick examination revealed a safe hidden behind a false panel, a Leithonian classic. Arian thought she even knew the artisan who had created it. The safe had a trap built into it, but it was a common one, a blast of indelible dye that would mark the thief for hours on end. Arian skirted her way around it, then picked the lock and pulled the safe open.

Inside were a handful of official documents, which she ignored, and a key. It wasn't a traditional key, instead a heavy pendant that hung at the end of a substantial chain, but Arian had seen enough magical locks in her time to know it for what it was. She reached for it carefully, feeling for wards.

Here, at least, the chancellor had been diligent. The air hummed with power around the key, loaded with protection spells.

Okay, so maybe she would need *some* magic after all. But it would take only a second.

She activated the small windup cube she had used on the night of the ball to pretend that she was still in bed. Instead of copying herself, she had it copy the key, creating a fake key that she quickly transferred the original wards onto. It wouldn't hold up to close inspection, but it would last the night.

And the night was all she needed.

She held her breath as she slid the key from the safe. When no alarms sounded and the network of magical protections over the safe remained unchanged, she grinned in triumph, standing with the key in hand.

A hand grabbed her arm, pulling her back.

Arian moved without thinking, twisting her body around her trapped arm. With a deft twist, she brought her captor in close to her, pinning the offending hand into a wrist lock and reaching for her knife with her free hand. It stopped an inch from her captor's neck as Arian realized who he was.

Cavar, damn him, was laughing. It was a soft laugh, muffled out of necessity, but Arian could hear the echoes of it in his breath, see it in the way his shoulders rippled with the motion. This was, Arian thought, exactly the opposite of a situation in which one should laugh, and she made her point by applying more pressure to his trapped wrist. He gasped in pain and the laughter ceased.

"All right, all right," Cavar wheezed, touching his hand to his thigh in a muted version of a martial artist's tap. "I give. You've made your point."

Arian scowled, but released her hold, sheathing her knife. "What the hell is wrong with you?" she whispered. "You have a death wish?"

Cavar rubbed at his sore wrist, still grinning. Arian watched him with the dizzying realization that he had lost his mind. The Weaver wasn't wearing Lord Nasirri's bedclothes, which was what he had been wearing when she saw him last. Instead, he was dressed in black leather armor that let him blend into the shadows, a hood pulled over his head and a mask on his face to hide his features. The mask exposed lips and chin, but Arian thought that even if he had covered his face fully, she still would have recognized him.

No one else would be foolish enough to sneak up on her in the middle of the night and skillful enough to accomplish it.

"I wondered where you went," Cavar said, giving his hand one last shake before turning toward Arian. "Is that the key to the treasury?"

"Yes, it is," said Arian, holding the key just out of his reach. "And before you get any ideas, it's *mine*. I won the wager fair and square, Weaver boy."

"Hmm, I wonder," said Cavar. "I seem to remember the terms of our wager being that whoever *entered* the treasury first won. We're nowhere near the treasury, Arian."

"Yet," said Arian. "And the terms were that whoever *figured out* a way to get in won." She waved the hand holding the key for good measure. "Way found. Ergo, I win."

"Did you just use the word *ergo*?"

"Yes, Cavar. I've picked up a book at least once in my life. Get over it."

"Well, you still haven't found a way into the treasury," Cavar said. "We're nowhere near there." He smiled. "Anything can happen between now and then."

Arian took a step back. She opened her mouth to dare him to try it, but Cavar moved before she could get the first word out. He moved like shadow and mist, one of his hands trapping her free arm against Hosner's desk while the other reached for the key in her outstretched hand.

The move pinned her between him and the desk, their bodies pressed together as she stretched her arm over her head, keeping the key out of his reach. It wasn't exactly a comfortable position, but there *were* certain merits to it, Arian thought, feeling a low heat flare up in her belly. Still, she'd *much* rather have their positions reversed.

Her foot slid between his, hooking around his ankle and sweeping him off balance. At the same time, Arian turned, sliding her arm out of his grip. Her free hand shot up to his shoulder, pushing him back against the desk as she flipped them and held him there with her weight.

The key was still clutched in her hand, high in the air where he couldn't reach it. She flashed him a wicked smile.

"You were saying?"

Cavar smiled back, and while his hand was stretched toward the key, his eyes were fixed on hers, and they had gone enticingly dark. "If you're asking me to complain about this, Arian, you're going to be very disappointed."

The sound of footsteps outside the office door made them both freeze, Cavar's breath stilling on a laugh. Arian went tense, her eyes drifting from the door to the space beneath the desk. There was no time to hide anywhere else. The two of them released each other, scrambling under the desk just as the door opened.

Arian held her breath at the sliver of light that entered the room. She hadn't replaced the cover over the safe. A rookie mistake. If they were caught because of this—

But no one stepped into the room just yet. Instead, Arian caught the first questing touches of a searching spell.

Roth.

Warmth ran out of her with her breath, that same whisper-quiet sensation of invisibility that had saved her in the kitchen settling onto her skin. She felt it spread over her like a blanket, hiding her and Cavar, hiding the open safe. The spell pulled back, startled. A second later, she heard footsteps enter the room.

Cavar went rigid beside her, and she felt his hand going to his knife. Not daring to breathe, Arian reached back, grabbing his wrist and squeezing tightly to stop him. The figure came around the table, ignoring the safe entirely, and peered down into the space beneath at the two of them. Arian found herself staring up into Roth's blue eyes, at the red glow of a talisman in his hand.

She waited. A second later, Roth frowned, walking away.

When the door of the office closed, Arian drew a shaky breath, sagging against Cavar's side.

CHAPTER 47

LIAM

ARIAN WAS IN THE OSSUARY WHEN LIAM RETURNED FROM THE guard outpost, which was unexpected. He was already exhausted from the night, still thinking of the crates they had found in the outpost basement—three of them, all full of gleaming swords—and of the man he had seen on their way out, an Imperial lieutenant coming to call on a deserted guard station in the dead of night when there should have been no reason for him to be there. Lieutenant Leon Albrent, he remembered, one of four Imperial lieutenants stationed at the Bastion, besides Zephyr. He, Lyndon, and Reid had managed to avoid detection as they raced back up the stairs and onto the rooftop paths, but his arrival had stopped them from taking any of the swords as evidence.

The night had revealed two things—that this was an Imperial plot, and that there were likely more weapon caches in the city that they hadn't discovered.

Once they were clear of the building, Liam set the basement on fire. The expenditure of power had nearly knocked him out completely, and he'd had to lean against Reid for a time to catch his breath, gulping down air. But he'd made it look like an accident, and the outpost was swarming with yelling Imperials by the time the three of them made their escape. Reckless, but he knew fire could dull a blade's edge—Arian had yelled at him about it enough times. With any luck, the weapons had been damaged beyond repair. What followed was a hasty meeting at the Spinning Wheel, with Lyndon and Reid recounting what they had seen while Liam gave them Albrent's name and tried to keep from falling out of his seat.

By the time he made it back to the ossuary, all he wanted was to crawl into his bed, but from the look on Arian's face, that wasn't going to happen. Cavar was with her too, arms folded and expression strangely thoughtful as he leaned against the ossuary wall. He wasn't dressed as Lord Nasirri, but instead wore simple dockworker's garb. Arian wore her Riana disguise, although it was incongruous with the way she held a knife in her hand, casually gouging slivers out of the ossuary's wooden table.

"You're out late, little brother," Arian said as he approached. "Where have you been?"

If Arian didn't know about the weapon cache, he wasn't going to tell her. Maybe it was petty, but he was too exhausted to get into the details, and he still hadn't forgiven her for hiding Roth's presence from him. Besides, he still smelled of smoke. If she knew anything about what was happening in the city, she could figure it out.

He pulled out the seat opposite her and sat.

"I was just out running errands. I thought it was too dangerous to make contact directly?"

A look passed between Arian and Cavar that Liam couldn't decipher. It made him uneasy; there had once been very few things that Arian had been able to hide from him. Cavar tilted his head forward, a barely perceptible nod, and Arian reached into her pocket, drawing out a heavy metal pendant on the end of a chain. She set it on the table between her and Liam.

Liam looked at it, then back up at Arian. "What's this?"

"The key to the treasury," Arian said. "We managed to steal it."

The treasury. The Star. Liam felt excitement, followed by sudden disappointment. If they succeeded in their mission, they would have to leave the Bastion, and he wouldn't get another chance at Roth.

He studied the key, using it as an excuse to avoid her eyes.

"I'm assuming you have a plan?"

"We're planning on hitting the treasury soon," Arian said. "The whole city will be on us when that's done. We'll need a place to run to. Can you help?"

Help. Right, that was his role here. To be their *support*.

"We've been fortunate that the key's theft hasn't been discovered yet," Cavar went on. "But our luck won't last for very long. I'm assuming we have a day at most, maybe two, before Chancellor Hosner feels the need to access the treasury. If possible, I'd like to get in there sooner rather than later. Tomorrow night." He pulled out a pocket watch, one of Nasirri's and entirely too fine for the humble clothing he was wearing now, glanced at it, and winced. "Er, tonight."

Arian nodded, leaning back in her chair. "The big shot over here has a dinner with Hosner," she said, jerking her thumb at Cavar. "He can keep him busy. I can get into the treasury, but after that, we'll need to clear out."

"I have contacts waiting at the nearest friendly port to take Linna and me back to the Wastes," Cavar said. "That part shouldn't be a problem. But we need your help to get out of this city."

Tonight. Liam wasn't ready for that. He still didn't have a way to get close to Roth, a way to get into the Bastion.

The idea came to him all at once, so brilliant in its simplicity that he was amazed he hadn't thought of it before. His fingers pressed into the wood of the table as he looked up, meeting Arian's eyes.

"We can get you out of the city," he said. "But if you're going to go after the Star, I'd urge caution. It might be dangerous to touch it if you aren't trained. Who knows what energies it's been exposed to since the fall of the Arcanum?"

Arian frowned. "What are you saying?"

"I'm saying I'd like to come with you."

"You want to walk into the heart of the Bastion? You can't be serious."

"You're doing it," Liam pointed out.

"We're not talking about *me*." Arian slammed her hand on the tabletop. "In case you've forgotten, you're a wanted criminal."

Liam's brows arched. "And you're not?"

"They don't know my *face*. If they did, I'd be dead by now."

"I'll disguise myself as someone else, then," said Liam, holding Arian's gaze. "The Star was our mother's, and I'm—" *Her heir. Her legacy.* Liam choked on the words. "—I'm the only one who can contain its power. If it's been tampered with, it'll be dangerous for you."

"I'm *not* going to let you get yourself killed—"

"But it's okay for you to risk *your* life? I've been doing this since the city fell, Arian. I'm not an amateur, but thank you for your concern. Do you think I *like* sitting at home while you put yourself in danger time and time again?"

Arian opened her mouth to argue and promptly closed it. Beside her, Cavar let out a long sigh.

"Just let him come," he said. "This isn't going anywhere, and Nasirri has places to be."

"How are we going to get him in?" Arian asked, twisting around in her seat to face Cavar. Cavar simply looked at her.

Arian swore. "Whatever I did back there was an *accident*. I don't know if I can do it on purpose."

"Can you try?" Cavar asked. "You have a little bit of time to experiment, and if you can't do it, we'll just go without him."

"What are you talking about?" Liam asked, breaking in.

Arian scowled, saying nothing, but Cavar said, "Arian can make herself and others invisible. She managed to do it when we stole the key."

Liam stared at Arian, his mind racing too fast for him to come up with words. A thousand thoughts flooded his mind, one after another, but he kept landing on one: that there were many kinds of magic in the world, but there was only a handful of people who could do what Cavar said Arian could do. A very select group of people. He felt a chill wash over him, his mind taking every memory from his childhood and putting it in a new context. Arian dropping out of the Arcanum, Arian leaving home, Arian refusing to speak about magic at all.

He looked at her and willed her to deny it, but Arian only lifted her head and said, "*Fine*. Fine. You want to get killed chasing after Mommy's legacy, it's your funeral. I'll figure something out so you can follow us in. We'll go after the Star tonight while Nasirri and Hosner have dinner."

She tipped her chair back, folding her arms and glaring as if daring him to challenge her. Liam didn't take the bait. He needed her to leave, to walk away so that he could be alone with his thoughts, so that he could figure out what it meant that this whole time, *this whole time*, his sister had what he'd always wanted and had never said *anything*.

"When do you want to meet?"

Cavar and Arian exchanged glances.

"Sunset?" Cavar suggested. Arian nodded.

"Sunset, then," Liam said. "I'll meet you at the Spinning Wheel."

Cavar started to leave, but Arian didn't follow. She waited until Cavar's footsteps had faded down the hallway before speaking.

"All right," she said. "What's this really about?"

Liam carefully avoided meeting her eyes. "I don't know what you mean."

"You've been content to stay in the background for over a year, and now that we're getting ready to do our most dangerous heist, you suddenly want to play phantom thief?" Arian snorted, rolling her eyes. "You may be getting better at sneaking around, but you're still a terrible liar, *little brother*. So tell me. What's this really about?"

Liam didn't answer immediately. The word *Roth* hung between the two of them, like a weight in the air. There was no way that

Arian would have been able to live in the Bastion without being aware of Roth's presence. The fact that she hadn't told him about it meant that she didn't want him to know.

That hurt. It hurt deep in a way that he didn't know how to process—it was so tied up in his feelings about his sister and this city and their mother and everything that she had left behind. It hurt because it told him that again, Arian was trying to protect him.

From the truth. And what she had never understood was that nothing that was true could ever hurt him as much as a lie.

He breathed deep and said, "Don't you trust me?"

"Trust goes both ways," Arian said.

"Then tell me what you're hiding."

"What?" she asked.

"You think I haven't noticed that whenever we talk about magic or Mother, you won't look at me? And now you can create *veils*? Do you know what that means?"

"It doesn't *mean* anything," Arian said, her voice suddenly harsh and sharp. "It doesn't mean anything, Liam, so just *let it go*. The Arcanum's dead. It's gone. We can't bring it back, so can we just *drop it*?"

"The Arcanum can't be *gone*," Liam said. "It's the center of the world's magic. If you stayed in lessons longer, you would know that."

"Well, I didn't stay in lessons. And I'm *not* a member of the Arcanum. I just want to get this job done!"

Liam stared at her helplessly, but Arian's expression had closed off, her gaze fixed on the floor instead of on him. He knew, because he still knew his sister, that no matter what he said now, he wasn't going to be able to get through to her. They would be repeating the same argument they had worn out in the days before the occupation, the days before the world changed.

Well, the same argument with one painful twist. But what was the point of it now?

"Fine," he said, with a defeated sigh. "Fine, let's just get this job done. And after—" If there was an after. If Arian still wanted to talk to him after he revealed his plans for Emeric Roth, or if Roth didn't blow him to smithereens. "—after, maybe we can talk about it."

Arian nodded jerkily, her arms folded tight across her chest. It wasn't a promise, but it wasn't a refusal, and before Liam could even think about asking her any more questions, she was already leaving the room.

CHAPTER 48

CAVAR

CAVAR WAITED FOR ARIAN IN THE TUNNELS OUTSIDE THE OSSU-
ary, thinking. He'd seen the look in her eye when she waved him
on, quietly asking him to give her some time to speak with her
brother. This meeting had been the first time either of them had
spoken to Liam since entering the Bastion, and he understood
Arian's concern.

There was a . . . change in him. It was subtle, difficult to place.
He looked like someone who had found his purpose, and now that
he knew what he was supposed to do, he wouldn't let anything
stand in his way. Those were the sort of people who changed the
world, who unraveled the threads of fate and rewove history. But
those were also the sort of people who died, who burned themselves out hot and fast on nothing but a dream.

The sound of soft footsteps, nothing more than a whisper
against stone, made Cavar look up. Arian was walking back toward
him, a pensive frown on her face. He straightened up from his place
against the wall.

"How did it go?" he asked, conscious of the way his voice
echoed in the tunnels. It felt odd hearing his own voice come back
to him, but here, at least, they could talk freely.

Arian didn't answer immediately. She had her arms wrapped
tight around herself as if she were cold. The posture was strangely
vulnerable, and Cavar was possessed by the urge to hold her. He
stopped himself, only because he knew that the gesture wouldn't
be well received. Not now, not like this.

"Arian . . . ?" he said instead, his voice gentle.

Arian looked up sharply, staring at him as if she had only just noticed him there. It took her a moment to register his question, and when his words struck home, she shook her head, lips pressed tightly together. "I don't think I want to talk about it."

Cavar inclined his head back toward the ossuary, toward Liam. "He's changed."

"We all have," said Arian. "But the way he is now . . ." Cavar watched her arms slowly unwind from around her chest, hands balling into fists as they fell to her sides. He half turned, expecting her to say that it was time to leave, but she continued to speak. "I'm scared."

It was only the second time Cavar had heard her say those words. The first time had been the morning before they entered the Bastion. Then, she'd been afraid of losing herself. Now, he had a feeling that that was no longer true.

"Are you scared of your brother?"

Arian shook her head, snorting softly. "Liam could become a monster, burn down an entire city, slaughter orphans and drink their blood, and he would still be my little brother. I'm not afraid of him."

Her voice went soft, her gaze dropping to the ground.

"But?" he asked.

"I'm afraid of this. Of what's about to happen. I'm scared that when all's said and done . . ." Her voice caught. "He's my only family, Cavar."

"You're afraid of losing him."

Arian said nothing.

"Is there something you're not telling me?" Cavar asked, as gently as he was able.

Arian scoffed. "There's a lot of things I'm not telling you, Weaver boy."

"I'm not going to pry."

"I appreciate it," said Arian. "Really, I do."

He shot her a glance, and Arian lowered her gaze to the ground beneath her feet.

"I'm not good at all of this," she said. "This . . . trust thing. I've got secrets down so deep that even I forget they exist. And it's not that I don't want to tell you."

"Arian, it's fine," Cavar said. "Tell me someday, whenever you're ready."

"Do we have someday?"

Arian said the words so quietly that Cavar almost couldn't hear them. He looked back at her and saw her shaking her head, her hands held in loose fists at her sides.

"I . . . I'm not naive . . . ," she said. "I'm not exactly *skilled* in the romance department, but—I've noticed the way you look at me. But I'm not going to be a game for you, or a *conquest*." She spat the word out like it hurt her. He took a step toward her and froze, because he realized he was doing exactly what she didn't want him to do. "If everything goes well tonight, we'll get the Star and you'll leave the city. What happens then?"

Cavar swallowed. Thoughts were swirling in his mind, the same thoughts that had been nagging at him every time he paused to catch his breath. That the Weavers hadn't gone after Aelria when they should have, that there had to be a *reason* Rinu eth'Akari had not come back to Leithon, that there was so much he didn't know about his mother and her plans. That there were too many questions, even for him, and that maybe he didn't want to be a Weaver at all.

He opened his mouth to say all that but realized it would be pointless. Even if he told Arian that he wanted to leave the Weavers, she wouldn't believe him. She would just think that he was offering her false hope.

Besides, he still wasn't sure what he wanted to do.

He took a step forward, hesitant, and said, "It's not a game to me." When Arian didn't respond, he took a chance and placed his hand on her shoulder. She sucked in a breath and he felt her shiver, but she leaned into the touch and didn't pull away.

"*You're* not a game to me," Cavar said. "And if I could, I'd—"

"You'd what?"

Arian raised her head. Her eyes gleamed in the light of their lamp, glistened with unshed tears. It surprised him—he'd never seen Arian cry. He made to let go of her, to pull his hand back, but she raised her hand to cover his and gently but firmly held it there.

"You'd what, Cavar?" she asked again.

There was no point in denying. "I'd take you to the Wastes. Or I'd stay with you in this city. If I could."

Arian was silent for a long time, and then she let out a breath, releasing his hand. His skin felt cold without her touch. "Yeah, well . . . That's the problem, isn't it? If you *could*."

She bit her lip, looking at war with herself. And then, slowly, reluctantly, she pulled his hand off her shoulder. She held it for a little while before letting it drop, a second longer than necessary, and Cavar wanted to—

He didn't know what he wanted. Lately, his wants had begun to scare him.

He wanted to hold her, to kiss her, to tell her that he would never let her go, but that wasn't his promise to make. And from the look she gave him as she backed away, she knew it too.

More and more, though, he was starting to wonder why not. He wasn't a child anymore. He could make his own decisions. And if he wanted to stay with her . . .

Linna would have fits. But he'd been a Weaver his whole life. Arian was the first person to make him want to be someone else. He certainly wouldn't be the first Weaver to take a . . . leave of absence, to explore an alternate path. To find a path in life that *he* wanted, not the one that had been chosen for him.

That was probably why he felt so drawn to Arian.

She made him want to be *free*.

"We have a job," she said, her voice laced with regret. "We need to focus on that. And I need time, if I'm going to figure out how to do my invisibility trick on purpose. So, we should head back."

A thousand words, a thousand empty promises, all jostling for space in the back of his mind. But she was right. There was never enough time. Whatever the case, he would see this mission for the Weavers through.

Even if it ended up being his last, he would see the Star returned where it belonged.

CHAPTER 49

ARIAN

IT ENDED UP BEING SURPRISINGLY EASY ONCE SHE PUT HER MIND to it. The magic was just there, golden and shimmering, making up the fabric of the world. After a restless two hours of sleep on her cot in the dressing room, it hadn't been hard to close her eyes and lift those shimmering threads up from where they lay, to weave them into whatever she wanted them to be. They almost seemed to *sing* as she reached for them, as if they had been awaiting her touch for a very long time.

She practiced with a few objects lying around the room, ate something, slept a bit more, and then started trying to hide herself. Once she had Cavar's confirmation that she was, in fact, invisible, she started working on making him invisible with her.

It should have been harder, but it wasn't. The magic felt like an old friend, and Arian, numb with a sense of guilt and loss, guided it where it needed to go.

By sunset, she was ready. She left the Bastion on one of Lord Nasirri's errands and returned with Liam, hidden underneath her veil. She led him, a shimmer of light beside her, past the gates and through the corridors into Lord Nasirri's suite, where she could safely drop the veil. Then they started preparing in earnest.

Cavar would be going to dinner with Nathaniel Hosner, which gave them some time and a distraction. Hosner wouldn't be checking the contents of the treasury at dinner, after all. But Arian couldn't keep Liam hidden forever, and sooner or later, their deception would come to light.

It was now or never. They were going to take the Star home tonight, or never at all.

When Cavar started getting ready for dinner, Arian took Liam into the dressing room to make preparations of their own. He hardly looked at her. She knew from the dark look on his face, the way he kept pacing, tapping that odd staff on the wall at intervals, that he knew what her being able to use this magic meant.

He knew, and resented her for it, and everything Arian had ever done—quitting her studies, leaving home, hiding her talents— everything she had done to keep Liam from resenting her had been for nothing.

She swallowed and said, "You should probably know. Emeric Roth is here."

"I know."

That surprised her. "You know?"

He nodded. "He couldn't come into this city and hide from me for long. Are you worried he'll see through your illusion?"

Arian shook her head. "I've hidden from him before. I think I can hide from him again."

Liam frowned. "Roth is . . . tricky. He's a monster, but his skill in magic is almost unparalleled. We should stay away from him if we can."

Arian drummed her fingers on her knee. The conversation was making her think about the near miss with Roth. How she had hidden not only herself, but also Cavar and the safe. She had done it without thinking. Had she always been able to cast a veil without thought? Had she done it before?

Her mind took her through each of her previous jobs, each impossible escape. She'd gained a reputation for being able to move like a shadow, for going where no one else could. How much of that was her own skill, and how much was magic?

If she thought about it, she'd started gaining that reputation shortly after *that day*, ages ago.

The day that she'd quit magic for good.

Arian thought that she had put this behind her, that she'd left everything behind when she left their mother's house to go live in her little attic room above the Spinning Wheel. But she could feel its hooks in her even now, digging into her skin, drawing her deeper into a web. It was like cords binding her, pulling her into a future she couldn't escape.

She clenched her hand into a fist. No, that wasn't true. She could walk away. After tonight, she could take the Star and leave this city. She could go with Cavar to the Wastes, and then from there, she could go wherever she wanted. She was still master of her own destiny.

There was nothing tying her to this city. Nothing.

"Arian?" Liam asked.

He said her name so softly, startling her. When she looked up at him, he was her little brother again, not the stranger he had become. Liam watched her with concern, the same crease in his brow that formed whenever he encountered a problem he couldn't solve. A wave of nostalgia washed over her, nearly breaking her resolve. There was so much in this city, so much of her life in its stones and its paths and its harbors, and so much of the city buried inside her. She would give almost anything to go back to the past.

But she couldn't. That past was gone. And it would never come back.

"I'm fine," she said, in answer to her twin's unspoken question. "Just thinking."

Liam hesitated, and for a second, Arian was horribly afraid that he would ask her if she wanted to *talk about it*. She was never more relieved to hear a knock at the door. Arian raised her arms up over her head in a stretch, feigning calm as she got lazily to her feet.

"Well," she said, striding over to let Cavar in. "Showtime."

THEY LET CAVAR LEAVE FIRST. ARIAN WENT OUT DRESSED AS
Riana to see him and Linna off, while Liam watched from the safety
of the dressing room. Cavar wore Lord Nasirri's best, and Linna
the ornamented armor of a lord's attendant. They went over their
signals one last time, using the bracelets that Arian had given them
for the ball. She watched them disappear down the hallway, then
she slipped back into the room.

She and Liam waited in the dressing room until Cavar sent the
signal that he had met with Chancellor Hosner. Arian got herself
ready while she waited for the second signal that would say they
had sat down to dinner. There was no point in a disguise—if all
went well, it wouldn't be needed for much longer—so she hid her
weapons and the rest of her gear around a close-fitting suit beneath
Riana's dress. The second signal came, informing her that Lord
Nasirri had sat down to eat and that it was safe to begin. She made
sure there was nothing important left in the dressing room, aware
that they might not be coming back. Then she and Liam left Lord
Nasirri's quarters for what was hopefully the last time.

She put up her veil as soon as they left the dressing room,
concealing herself and Liam both. They took a circuitous route
through the Bastion, dropping off the supplies they had prepared
for their distraction. At the mouth of the stairs that led to the treasury, Arian paused. The treasury hall's wards would find them,
veiled or not, and Arian didn't dare get too close. Instead, the two
of them waited, Arian counting down the seconds until the distraction started. She estimated that she had about a minute left before
things went completely to hell.

Liam breathed in sharply, drawing her attention. Arian turned
her head to see Zephyr and Lord Kaolin moving through the
hall ahead of them, Zephyr dressed in plain clothes and deep in

conversation with the young lord. Arian scowled in impatience, thrusting her elbow where she thought Liam was. She felt it impact something soft, and Liam gasped in pain.

"Leave her," Arian hissed. "Focus now."

"Right," Liam said, his words sounding pinched. "Sorry."

An explosion rang out of a nearby hallway, and then everything began.

CHAPTER 50

LIAM

THE EXPLOSION WAS DEAFENING, EVEN AT THIS DISTANCE, THE force behind it enough to set the walls and floor trembling. Next to him, Arian went completely still, but despite the shock, she kept the veil up over them both, hiding them from sight. It was as if magic was effortless for her, as if the costs of power didn't apply.

He bit back his resentment and jealousy. Now wasn't the time. People were running, screaming, most of them moving away from the explosion. Zephyr shoved Lord Kaolin away from the initial blast before hiking up her skirts and running toward the noise. Lord Kaolin, Liam noted, picked himself up off the ground and followed her, one hand on his sword.

The explosion had done its job. All but two of the treasury guards charged out into the hallway. They ran down the corridor toward the explosion's source, missing Liam and Arian completely. That left two guards in place, but he and Arian had expected that. Given the treasury's importance, it was unlikely that they would leave it completely unguarded.

"The protection spells," Arian whispered when the guards had gone past them. "They're bigger than anything I've dealt with before. Do you have something to counter that?"

Liam nodded, then realized she wouldn't be able to see him.

"Yes," he whispered back.

Arian linked arms with him, and together, they made their way across the packed hallway, pausing to dodge frightened servants. A maid, running across the hall, slammed into Arian's shoulder and nearly took her off her feet. The two of them stopped, holding their breaths, as the maid jerked upright and glanced around herself with wide eyes. But whatever explanation she came up with must have worked for her, because she kept running.

They made it to the mouth of the treasury corridor. Here, there was nothing but two frightened guards at the end of the long hallway and a network of protection spells across the entrance. The spells were some of the most complex in the Bastion, layer after layer of wards to keep the treasury from coming to harm. There were spells against fire and flood, spells to protect it from earthquakes, and even spells to make it a safe shelter, should the rest of the castle fall. And of course, there were spells against intruders. He could do what he had done at Blackstone Deep and use his staff to redirect their energies, but he didn't dare. The staff was just as likely to sap the power from Arian and her veil as it was to take it from the spells, and unlike at the Deep, he didn't have anywhere he could safely send the energy. Instead, he relied on something else. An assumption, an application of logic.

The spells had been created and renewed by the Speaker of the Arcanum herself, and they likely held a loophole, one that no Imperial mage would ever predict. The Speaker of the Arcanum would always ensure that the spells could be accessed by the next Speaker, in case anything happened before it was time to renew them.

If he was right, they would have no problem getting through.

As much as it made his stomach twist to admit it.

"Lend me your hand," he told Arian.

Arian gripped his hand tightly. "What—?" she began, but she didn't get very far, because Liam started drawing on her power.

He didn't attempt to alter the wards. Instead, he laid Arian's hand gently against the opening of the hallway, feeling the energy of the spell at his fingertips. Liam summoned his will with a thought, letting it course through his body, down his arm, through his fingertips and into Arian's, and from there into the net.

We are blood of this city, he thought. *We have come in great need. Let us through.*

Power swirled around him. He could feel the spell's interest, felt it rushing them both, searching. Beside him, Arian let out a gasp that she quickly stifled, sagging against his side. She sucked in a breath, and it sounded like it was coming through her teeth.

"It pricked me," she whispered, voice so low that Liam could barely hear it. "That fucking . . . whatever it was. It just attacked me."

Liam didn't have time to answer her. The spell parted around them. He felt it as a ripple through the net, like movement through a curtain, before the spell drew apart.

Confirmation, then. He should have felt something other than numb, other than empty, but it was all he could do to maneuver Arian through the gap, pausing against the nearest wall for her to catch her breath. All this time, her veil stayed up. A masterwork of illusion.

He looked at her in concern, not daring to speak because of the guards who were still staring out into the chaos of the hallway.

"What?" Arian asked, her voice soft.

Liam glanced at the guards and hoped Arian's masterwork could conceal sound as well. "What do we do about them?"

"I've got it," Arian whispered. "Let's get closer."

Liam nodded, keeping a hand on her arm as she moved toward the guards. As they neared, he felt Arian draw something out of her pocket. The next thing he knew, she was pressing something into his hand. A damp cloth. She pushed his hand up toward his face a few times, hitting him in the forehead and across the nose before he realized she meant for him to cover his face with it. He did so, squeezing her hand to show that he understood, and she threw something out from under the veil.

It was a disk with shutters built into the sides, crafted in metal, without the aura of magic that most of Liam's creations possessed.

It skittered almost noiselessly across the stone floor. The disk hissed and sputtered as gas flooded out of it, and even from this distance, Liam tasted something acrid on his tongue. One of the guards opened his mouth to let out a shout of alarm, but whatever he was about to say was cut off as he swayed, slumping forward. Arian pulled them both forward so she could catch him, keeping him propped upright. Liam did the same with the other guard, and then froze them both to the wall to hold them there. It wouldn't hold up to close inspection, but the hallway that led into the treasury was long enough that anyone who looked in at the mouth of it would see the two guards doing their duty.

"What was that?" he asked, his voice slurred. His tongue felt numb.

"Sleeping gas," Arian said. "One of Lyndon's old tricks. In."

She pulled him toward the treasury door. Liam went, watching as the key appeared from beneath her veil. She slid the key into the lock, and Liam heard things whirring and clicking into place.

The door slid open. Liam checked for wards, holding his breath. The tang of magic was heavy in the air, and he could practically taste the life force that came from the Star. The room was laced with it from the Star's years of storage. It was his mother's magic, her signature, and he knew the feel of her like he knew his own name.

There were no other dangers. He squeezed Arian's hand to show that it was safe, and together, the two of them stepped into the treasury.

Liam had, in his more childish fantasies, imagined a vault piled high with gold and treasure. This was nothing like that. It was more like a library than a treasure trove, although the gleam of gold did shine from some of the boxes arranged around the room.

Once they were inside and Arian had closed the door behind them, she dropped the veil, letting them see each other. Liam held out his hand, summoning a soft light into his palm. The two of them moved, searching the shelves. Each one had an inventory list mounted on it, cataloging the items inside, but while Arian hung back to read the listings, Liam kept walking. He was drawn to one shelf in particular, in the back where the feeling of magic was strongest.

This shelf was largely ignored, and dust hung thick on its contents. Liam scanned the listing as Arian trailed after him. Kuthil's Star was the third item, and the date recorded next to it was only a day after the invasion of Leithon. He found the indicated place easily, but quickly ran into a problem.

The Star was gone. There was nothing but the taste of his mother's magic in the air to show where it had been, and a clear circle in the dust.

PART THREE
EQUILIBRIUM

CHAPTER 51

ARIAN

"WHAT THE FUCK?" ARIAN DEMANDED, STARING AT THE PLACE where the Star had once rested. "What the actual fuck?"

"I heard you the first time, Arian," Liam said. He pinched the bridge of his nose, holding the light in his hand higher as if he could somehow make the Star materialize out of thin air. Arian chose to ignore that remark.

"How can it not be here?"

"They must have moved it."

"To where?! This is the only treasury in Leithon—you would have noticed if they'd taken it out of the Bastion, and there isn't a mage around here strong enough to move it any—" Arian broke off suddenly, her eyes widening. "*—fuck!*"

"What?" asked Liam, glancing over at her. He looked worn out, and sounded like someone had squeezed the life out of him, but Arian could barely spare her brother a thought right now.

"Roth. Roth has the Star." She checked her watch. Cavar might still be at dinner. She didn't know where Roth was, and hadn't seen the Star the first time she broke into his suite, so he might not have been keeping it there, but just because she hadn't found it, it didn't mean that he hadn't *taken it*. Her breath came in rapid pants, and her vision swam. She knew she was panicking, losing control, but she couldn't get it back. "All right, so—we need to get this key back before our cover's blown—but the explosion—I can't get into Roth's suite again—shit, we are *so* screwed, *gods-dammit!*"

"Arian, calm down!" Liam said, reaching for her arm. His fingers closed around her wrist and she nearly yanked her arm out of his grasp. Something in his words registered, and she sucked in a breath through her teeth, lowering her arms to her sides. She drew in deep breaths to calm her racing heart. As the panic receded, Arian felt a flush of shame. She was supposed to be a professional, not someone who went to pieces at the first sign of difficulty.

She pressed her lips tightly together and nodded, looking back at her brother.

"That's better," he said. "Now, *please*, can you tell me what's going on? What do you mean Roth has the Star?"

"I saw Roth walk toward the treasury one day, not long after Lord Kaolin's arrival. So I followed him."

"All right," Liam said, carefully releasing her arm. "Go on."

"He came this way."

"To the treasury?"

Arian shook her head. "Yes, but . . . but not through the entrance. He came along the side, somewhere—"

Arian paused, looking around the room. She reconstructed the map of the Bastion in her head, then started walking. Her feet carried her to a wall just opposite the shelf where the Star had been. Arian pressed her fingertips to the stone, thinking. The stone felt solid beneath her gloved hands. Cold. She couldn't imagine anyone entering the treasury this way.

"Arian?" Liam asked, walking up behind her.

"He came through here," Arian said, indicating the expanse of wall in front of her. "Somehow. Straight through the wall."

"That's impossible," Liam said. "It must have been an illusion."

Arian shook her head, frustrated. "I know what I saw, Liam."

"But magic can't do that. It works *around* matter. It destroys or manipulates it. But it doesn't make matter cease to exist. I can't think of a spell that would let you walk through a wall without destroying it, let alone take something as powerful as the Star back out that way."

Arian scowled in frustration. "Who cares if you think it's impossible? I'm telling you, I saw him do it, and he has the Star now."

Liam frowned, resting his hand on the wall. His brow furrowed in concentration. "This wall doesn't show any signs of tampering. So unless Roth turned himself into a ghost—"

"Could he have done that?" Arian asked, interrupting.

Liam broke off, "Done what?"

"Turned himself into a spirit." The thought nagged at her, and she paced back and forth in front of the wall, her hands at her sides. "I mean—aren't there, like, different planes of existence or something? Magic draws power from a different plane, right? Couldn't he have just—gone there?"

Liam's eyebrows nearly shot up into his hair. He gaped at Arian. "I—*yes*, that is how magic works. But you can't just enter the astral plane, Arian. It would kill you instantly; you would never be able to rejoin your body. The only way Roth could enter and exit the astral plane at will would be—"

This time it was Liam's turn to stop talking, his eyes going wide. Arian glanced over at him and saw that he was staring at nothing in particular, lips moving quickly as if he was reading off something in his mind.

"Liam?" she prompted. "The only way?"

"The only way to survive would be . . . if you were a spirit yourself," Liam said. "A wight—a ghost summoned and bound to its master. But that—that would mean—"

"That would mean what?" Arian asked, staring at him. Liam had started shaking, his eyes wide. "What, Liam? You're scaring me."

"That would mean that Roth was already dead," Liam said. "When he came into the Arcanum—when he killed our mother. That sword of his—it must be his focus, the thing holding him to this world. But if that were true, then Roth—Roth can't touch anyone.

He's not really part of this plane; he's not a solid being. The only person he can truly touch would be his master, the necromancer who summoned him."

Arian's mind was already racing, trying to fit what Liam was saying to what she had observed of Roth over the weeks. "He's a recluse. He stays in his chambers most of the time and doesn't allow anyone to enter. He stays an arm's length from people and barely eats. I've never seen him touch anyone, except—"

A feeling came over her like cold water, a rush of fear that shot straight down her spine. She was thinking back to that evening when she had gone into Roth's chambers, when Roth had gone to the ball with Cavar and Linna. Something Cavar had said to her when she came back.

The only time I saw him interact with someone was when he nearly knocked Kaolin over by accident...

"Kaolin," Arian said.

"What?" Liam asked.

"Cavar said something to me after the ball. Roth bumped into Kaolin before he left. He helped him up, apologized. They talked for a bit. Then he left."

Liam went pale. In the dimness of the treasury room, the unnatural light gave his features a ghastly pallor. "Zephyr."

"What?"

Liam looked at her, eyes wide with fear. "Zephyr," he repeated. "She asked to meet me. She told me that she thought Kaolin had changed and I—reacted badly." His face flushed and he shook his head. "She's with him now. I have to go to her, Arian."

"Slow down," Arian said, placing both of her hands on Liam's shoulders. Liam tensed. Arian held fast, her fingertips pressing into his skin beneath his coat. "Liam, slow down. Look at me. We can't go find Zephyr now. We need to get the Star away from Roth before we lose any more time."

Liam shook his head. He spoke quickly, not looking at her. "It's my fault. She warned me, and I didn't listen. If anything happens to her, Arian—" He broke off, pressing his lips tightly together. "I need to find her. Please. She doesn't know. I need to get her away from him."

Arian stared at her brother, feeling helpless and frustrated all at once. She wanted to rage at him, to scream that they weren't here to be heroes, they were here to be thieves, and proper thieves needed to *leave* before everything went up in smoke. But the desperation in Liam's eyes stopped her. She found herself thinking of Lyndon, for some odd reason. Of Reid. Of Cavar telling her he knew how much she cared about this city.

She pulled away from Liam. The day of the invasion, she had tried to go to the Arcanum. But when she saw that its doors had been broken, that mages were being killed where they stood, she fled. Her mother had died, her brother had barely escaped, and she hadn't done anything to help them. She'd run away.

Damn it, she was so *tired* of running.

"*Fine*," she said. "Fine. Let's go find Zephyr. And then let's get Cavar and Linna, find Roth, and get the hell out of this death trap of a castle."

CHAPTER 52

LIAM

LIAM FOLLOWED ARIAN OUT THE DOOR, DUCKING BACK UNDER-neath her hastily constructed veil. Around them, people screamed and ran, while guards herded frightened nobles through the corridors, yelling at people to get out of their way. No one had noticed the unconscious guards at the end of the treasury hallway. Liam checked his pocket watch and found that only fifteen minutes had passed.

Fifteen minutes, but it felt like so much longer. He followed Arian as she led him through the maze of corridors, dodging guards, soldiers, and servants until they reached the site of the explosion.

The hallway was a hive of activity. Guards had set up a perimeter around the nearest explosion site, stopping anyone from approaching, but most civilians had been cleared out of the area. Commander Selwald, an imposing man in Imperial violet, had come to the blast site himself, but no mages had set up protections around the area, so it was easy for them to slip through the knot of soldiers. The commander came within an inch of them, close enough that his voice rang in Liam's ears as he and Arian stopped.

"This is a distraction!" Selwald shouted. "Secure the treasury and the armory. Where the hell is Venari?!"

"With Lord Eismor, I'd expect," a young officer in violet drawled. "Where else would she be?"

Liam jumped, turning to face the voice. Leon Albrent, the man he had seen at the guard outpost. Arian squeezed his hand in warning, and it was only then that Liam realized he had started to step forward, closer to them. He held his breath, forcing himself to stand still and wait.

Selwald scowled, but whatever the commander thought of Zephyr being with Kaolin, he clearly had more important things to worry about.

"Then leave the lordling to Venari!" he barked. "Albrent!"

Lieutenant Albrent snapped to attention. "Sir!"

"Find Roth and bring him here. Orden, take two squads and keep the blast site secure. The rest of you, to the treasury and the armory. Now!"

Arian tugged on Liam's hand, pulling him against the wall as the soldiers scrambled to obey. Neither of them spoke until Selwald had left, then Arian whispered in Liam's ear.

"He's going to find the treasury guards. Once that happens, security's going to get pretty tight. Where the hell is Zephyr?"

Liam looked around at the wreckage, his mind racing. She had been running toward the site of the explosion with Kaolin the last time he'd seen her.

If Zephyr saw an explosion like this, she would assume that the Bastion was under attack. And if she had Kaolin with her and there was tension between the young lord and Selwald, she wouldn't have gone to the commander. She would have found somewhere where she could keep him safe.

The only question was *where*. Liam tugged Arian away from the explosion site, the two of them walking quietly until they reached a deserted hallway. There, Arian pulled them to a halt.

"Well?"

"You know this place better than I do," Liam said. "Try to think like a soldier. What's a safe, easily defendable location not far from here? Somewhere no one would expect Lord Kaolin to be?"

Arian paused, then began walking, pulling him with her.

"Come with me."

She led him to a storage closet farther down the hallway, a nondescript wooden door barely noticeable amid the ornamentation and finery. Liam reached for the doorknob and tried it, but the door was locked from the inside. He raised his hand, about to knock, then stopped, thinking. If Zephyr really was in there, he didn't want to startle her.

Arian cleared her throat impatiently, telling him that he had been standing still too long. He stepped away from the door and out from under Arian's veil, pulling a sheet of paper out of the inside pocket of his coat. Liam touched his finger to the corner of the sheet, drawing fire to his fingertip. A design burned itself into the paper, a replica of the bird he had given Zephyr once, the bird she had used to contact him. Before Arian could stop him, he rapped on the door and slid the sheet beneath it.

He waited.

After a moment of tense silence, the door opened. Liam caught sight of gleaming steel in Zephyr's hand as she poked her head out into the hallway, but then she saw him. Arian dropped her veil before he could say anything, shoving him into the room.

The closet was large as far as storage closets went, but it was packed with cleaning supplies, and with the four of them in there, it was feeling quite crowded. While Arian shut and locked the door, Liam studied Kaolin.

The young lord was sitting on an upturned bucket, watching him curiously. He had a hand on his sword, but didn't seem about to strike, and the quiet caution he exuded was not unusual for a man of his station. Liam wouldn't have thought there was anything strange about him at all, but if he extended his senses toward him, he could feel it. The faintest touch of compulsion, so subtle that he might not have noticed it if he hadn't known exactly what to look for.

Something flashed in Kaolin's eyes. It was like two people were watching him where Lord Kaolin stood—the young lord and another. Liam kept his eyes on Lord Kaolin even as Zephyr turned toward him.

"Liam, what—?"

Liam extended a hand toward her, cutting her off. In his other hand, he was already beginning to work a spell. "I'm sorry I didn't listen to you, Zephyr." To Lord Kaolin, he added, "Kaolin Eismor, I presume? This might come as a surprise to you, but you're being possessed."

"What are you talking about?" Arian asked.

Liam didn't take his eyes off Kaolin.

Kaolin's mouth opened to disprove the claim, and Liam saw the instant the other presence took over. It was like a curtain was drawn over Kaolin's eyes, the light in them guttering as a malicious gleam replaced it. In an instant, fire erupted from the young lord, bright flames rushing toward the three of them. As Arian swore and Zephyr leaped back, Liam channeled power into his staff, raising it in the air. He grabbed at the flow of magic, redirecting it around the three of them, pressing them back against the wall. In the narrow confines, the heat was intense, and he struggled to maintain his shield. Flames scorched the walls and burned through the door, but left the three of them untouched.

Laughter rang out from the flames, high and cold. The laugh made the hair on the back of Liam's neck stand up. A bright blue light pierced through the fire, and Liam felt something wash over him that nearly made him drop his shield.

His mother's magic, like water, like rain. He would know it anywhere.

Kaolin—or whoever was inside him—had *the Star*.

Somehow, he had gotten hold of it, and somehow, he was using it against them.

The flames struggled against Liam's hold, pressing down on him like a physical weight. The staff in his hand grew hot to the touch. Liam felt his knees buckle, their circle of protection shrinking into a dome just large enough for him, Zephyr, and Arian. The flames erupted out into the corridor, scorching the stone. His vision went black, but he fed the staff more of his power, holding the flames at bay until the terrible pressure eased.

When the flames faded, Kaolin was gone. Liam had only a moment to process that before Arian cursed. He looked at her to see her holding up her wrist, eyes on the silver chain bound around it.

It was jerking against her skin in a repetitive pattern, a distress call.

CHAPTER 53

CAVAR

THINGS STARTED GOING WRONG FROM THE MOMENT CHANCELLOR
Hosner led Cavar and Linna into his sitting room, where Emeric
Roth waited at a table set for three. Cavar hesitated, but Roth rose
smoothly to his feet, offering him a bow that was only slightly less
formal than one he might use for his own lord.

"Lord Nasirri Rezavi, I presume?" Roth asked. "I don't believe
we've ever had the chance to speak."

Cavar gave Roth a quick bow, a Parani aristocrat's greeting to a
commoner of renown.

"You honor me, magus. But you must forgive my surprise. I
wasn't aware that you would be present today. I'd hoped to interest
the chancellor in a business deal, and I'm afraid such talk makes for
poor dinner conversation."

"Ah, well," said Roth. "I'm afraid you aren't the only one who
has business to discuss with the good chancellor. I suppose we'll
simply have to take turns."

"I've become quite popular of late, it seems," said the chancellor, offering them both a wry smile as he walked around to his
own seat.

"The result of access to the treasury, no doubt," said Roth. He
smiled, giving Cavar a knowing glance. Cavar reminded himself to
breathe. Chancellor Hosner didn't seem to have noticed.

"Yes, I suppose that's true," he said with a laugh. "But come, gen-
tlemen, take your seats. There will be plenty of time to talk business after we eat."

Cavar offered the chancellor a short bow, the three of them taking their seats at the table. Linna took up her position against the

wall, and he felt the bracelet on his arm shift as she adjusted it. It wasn't one of the signals they'd agreed upon, but Cavar knew that she was trying to get his attention. The question was clear.

What do we do now?

Cavar didn't know. But as he sat down, he reached for the bracelet under the guise of adjusting his cuff and gave it a quick press. It was the signal the four of them had agreed upon to tell Arian to begin. He felt Linna's eyes boring into the back of his head as he faced Roth and Hosner, thinking.

If Roth was here, he wouldn't be searching for Arian and Liam, and Cavar could keep an eye on him. They would never have a better time to go after the Star. At this point, it was all or nothing.

The chancellor offered them wine before the first course arrived. Cavar accepted, but drank only sparingly. Roth did the same. The chancellor was less cautious, imbibing a little more deeply. Cavar noted a flush spreading across the older man's cheeks.

At first, the conversation stayed strictly away from business. They spoke of the weather and of Nasirri's family in Paran. Linna's presence was hardly remarked on—neither of them saw anything odd in a bodyguard accompanying a young lord.

Chancellor Hosner, Cavar thought, was remarkably easy to read. He was happy to be entertaining two such personages, excited about Lord Nasirri's supposed offer. He was doing his best to play the gracious host, keeping them happy until it became appropriate to speak of other things.

Roth was harder. His manners were impeccable, and he treated Cavar exactly like the young lord he pretended to be, but there was a look in his eye that Cavar caught at times, when Roth thought he wasn't looking. Something predatory. Roth reminded him of a snake waiting for its moment to strike.

Cavar was often in the company of predators. He didn't often feel like prey. The longer dinner went on, the more he thought that he should signal Arian to abandon the plan. But he held fast, waiting.

They were halfway through the fish course when Roth struck.

"Tell me again, Lord Nasirri," he said. "Is this your first visit to Leithon?"

Cavar could feel the trap's jaws, closing in on him. He offered Roth a quick smile. "Officially," he said, in a way that made Chancellor Hosner chortle. Roth's smile widened a fraction.

"Of course. Officially. The young have their diversions, after all."

"I will admit to coming to Leithon in search of more . . . worldly pursuits," Cavar said. "It's a fascinating city."

"It has always been." Roth glanced at Hosner, who was wiping his mouth with a napkin after taking another drink of wine. "We must remember, dear chancellor, that our Lord Nasirri is still a boy, and has a boy's vices. I would think on that if I were planning to treat with him."

"Oh, I think you're being a little harsh on the lad," said the chancellor, smiling. "After all, he's the same age as your own young charge, isn't he?"

"Ah, yes," said Roth, and Cavar felt the jaws of the trap pull tighter. "Young Lord Kaolin. The two of you have become good friends lately, have you not?"

The first rule of adopting a disguise was to never break character. Cavar wasn't simply a Weaver *pretending* to be Lord Nasirri, he *was* Lord Nasirri. And Nasirri would respond to that question. He wouldn't react to what was likely a trap because he would have no reason to fear a trap in the first place.

"Kaolin is good company," Cavar said. "He'll be good for this city, if he manages to take hold of it."

"That's true enough," Roth said, leaning forward. "And do you intend to see that happen, Lord Nasirri?"

"I wouldn't go that far," Cavar said, letting his expression—*Nasirri's* expression—go grave. "I have no ties to this country. If there's to be trouble, I'm off to Paran."

A rumble passed through the floor, rattling the dishes on the table. Chancellor Hosner yelped as he spilled his wine. In the distance, Cavar heard alarm bells ringing. He started to rise from his seat, turning toward the sound.

"What on earth—?!" the chancellor began.

Roth smiled, his fingertips tracing the rim of his glass. He seemed supremely unconcerned. "I wouldn't worry too much about it, dear chancellor. I'm sure we're quite safe here." He turned his gaze toward Cavar, and Cavar felt a jolt somewhere in his belly, a flash of warning. *Danger.* "After all, we have a Weaver to protect us, don't we?"

The bottom dropped out of Cavar's stomach. He managed, somehow, to keep his face smooth.

"I'm afraid I don't know what you mean, Master Roth."

"Don't you?" asked Roth, picking up his wineglass. "Tell me, boy, which clan are you from? Estani? You look like an Estani—although of course, it's impossible to tell, given your people's proclivity for mixing bloodlines."

"I'm afraid you're mistaken," Cavar said, his face hardening. "I am a lord of Paran."

"So it is Nivear, isn't it?" asked Roth, lowering his cup. "I thought you reminded me a bit of Reiva. But your coloring is a little different. Parani father?"

Danger, Cavar thought. *Danger, danger.*

His hand moved, fingers coiling around the bracelet at his wrist. He had just managed to get the distress signal off before Roth raised his hand, fire filling the room.

CHAPTER 54

ARIAN

"WHAT WAS THAT?" ZEPHYR ASKED AS THEY TOOK OFF RUNNING down the hallway. "What's going on here? What happened to Kaolin?"

Arian ignored her, picking up speed. Zephyr followed, keeping pace with her easily despite the dress she was wearing. Out of the corner of her eye, she saw Liam start to fall behind. She didn't slow down. She didn't have *time*, not with the echoes of the distress signal still tingling against her skin.

Riana's dress had a wide skirt, making it easy for her to move, and she was dressed for battle underneath it. At the nearest opportunity, she slipped the dress over her head and tossed it away, leaving her standing in tight-fitting dark clothing, her weapons strapped around her waist and thighs. Zephyr glanced at her, then bent down and ripped the side of her dress, giving her more room to move. Arian nodded in approval, but whatever grudging respect she had for the other girl faded when Zephyr looked up, green eyes hardened in a glare.

"You aren't taking another step until I get some answers," she said, and even unarmed, she managed to make it sound intimidating.

Arian scowled. "Fine. Where do you want us to start? The fact that your lordling is apparently being possessed by a ghost that has access to a magical artifact capable of taking down the entire city, or the fact that half of our team is in trouble right-fucking-now and you're delaying us with pointless questions?"

Zephyr flinched, but she recovered, eyes on Arian. "By the other half of your team, do you mean Lord Nasirri?"

"Yeah, sure," Arian said. "Whatever."

"You think that Lord Nasirri's . . . distress might have anything to do with what just happened to Kaolin?"

"Who the hell knows? And who the hell *cares*?"

Zephyr held out a hand toward Arian. Arian stared down at it, scowling.

"What?"

"Knife," Zephyr said.

"Are you serious?" Arian asked. "I'm not arming you."

"Then you're wasting time," said Zephyr, resting her hands on her hips. "I'm useless to you unarmed."

Arian's eyes narrowed in suspicion. "And armed? How do I know you aren't going to stab us in the back? No offense, Zeph, but your track record has been, uh, less than perfect on that score."

A look of pain crossed Zephyr's face, and Arian had to fight the urge to take the knife she had formed with her words and twist it deeper. That would only cost them more time. Liam opened his mouth to speak, probably to say something along those same lines, but before he could, Zephyr looked up.

"Yes, all right," she said. "I admit it. There's no forgiving what I did. But I was trying to save my family, Arian. On some level, you have to understand that."

Arian's eyes narrowed. "And now?"

"Now I'm not making excuses. Something is happening here that will destroy Leithon if we let it. And I'm not going to stand back and let that happen again. Give me a blade."

"What will you do with it?" Arian asked, her hand drifting to the long knife at her waist.

"Fight," Zephyr said. "I'll fight the way I wasn't able to four years ago. I swear it."

Arian looked past Zephyr at Liam, her fingers curling around

the hilt. From behind Zephyr, Liam looked grim, but he nodded.
She drew the blade and handed it to Zephyr hilt first.

"Don't do anything reckless with it," she said. "Let's move."

⚜⚜⚜

BEFORE LEAVING FOR THEIR DINNER, CAVAR AND LINNA HAD MADE
certain that Arian knew exactly where they were and how to find
them, a fact that Arian was grateful for as she led Zephyr and Liam
through the corridors. Stealth was useless now—the entire Bastion
was in an uproar after the explosion, both the inner and outer keeps
crawling with soldiers. Arian ran like her life depended on it, paying no heed to the way her lungs burned, the way Liam and Zephyr
trailed behind as she pushed herself harder.

She imagined kicking down Chancellor Hosner's door when
she arrived, but when they reached the scene, she was forced to
reconsider. For one, there was no door. It had been torn apart,
splinters littering the tiled floor of the hallway.

Arian drew her two remaining knives as she skidded to a stop,
peering into the room. She had to duck to the side as another blast
rippled through the air where she had been standing, narrowly
missing her. It struck the opposite wall, knocking paintings from its
frames. From inside, Arian heard a male voice, crying out in pain.

Cavar.

She leaped into the room, barely pausing for breath. The floor
was slick, and it took Arian a moment to realize that it was wet with
blood. A figure was lying on the ground amid the wreckage of the
dinner table, sword in hand and blood seeping out through the rent
in her gray armor. Another man, the chancellor, was curled up in a
corner of the room, weeping.

Cavar knelt in the middle of the slowly spreading pool of blood,
head thrown back and jaw clenched as if he was trying to stop

himself from crying out again. Faint white lines surrounded him, binding him in place, and standing ahead of him, looking down at him with malicious glee, was Roth, arm outstretched. He curled his fingers, and Cavar let out another choked-off gasp, muscles growing taut.

Arian saw red. She ran toward Cavar and Roth. She didn't think, only swiped her dagger upward, the blade cutting through the threads of light that bound Cavar to the mage. Cavar sagged as the bindings were cut, taking in a ragged breath of relief, and Arian launched herself forward, using the blade in her other hand to stab at Roth's gut.

Roth jumped back, inhumanly fast, and Arian's blade cut through empty air. She felt like her blood was on fire, power and rage crackling in her veins, and it was only when she glanced down at the knives in her hand that she realized they were glowing.

Behind her, Cavar struggled to sit up, his breath coming in short pants. Arian put herself between him and Roth. She sank down, taking a defensive stance.

Roth watched her. Power crackled in the air around him, sparking at his fingertips as he recalled the remnants of the threads that had bound him to Cavar. He tilted his head to the side, considering.

"I knew there was something strange about you," he said. "The witch had two children, after all."

"Shut up," Arian said, tightening her grip on her knives. Roth raised his hand, power flooding the space between his fingertips. Arian braced herself.

"Arian!" Cavar gasped from behind her.

Arian's eyes widened and she looked down. Veins of light had spread themselves across the floor, crisscrossing beneath her feet. She moved on instinct, not thinking as she stabbed the point of one dagger down into the ground, throwing the other at Roth. Light flared up in a circle around the knife in the ground, shattering the veins. The second dagger struck a barrier and powered through it. It broke apart with a sound like breaking glass.

Roth vanished like a shadow before the light. Out of the corner of her eye, she saw something dark retreating down the hallway. She fell to her knees.

"Arian!" Liam shouted, bursting into the room after her. Zephyr was behind him—Arian could hear her footsteps—but her vision was blurring, her mouth dry. She heaved and barely managed to not be sick all over the floor. Roth's parting words stuck with her as she tried to rein in her spinning mind.

. . . *the witch had two children, after all.*

CHAPTER 55

LIAM

LIAM STOOD IN THE ROOM AFTER ROTH'S EXIT, TRYING NOT TO gag on the smell of blood. His hands opened and closed uselessly at his sides, grasping at nothing, but his mind was racing, trying to understand what had just happened. It was too much all at once, and the feel of Roth's magic on his skin reminded him of the Arcanum, the day when all he had been able to do was hide.

He wasn't the same person anymore. He had to do—*something*.

But there was nothing he could do. Roth had been here, right in front of him, and Liam hadn't been able to do anything. Hadn't been able to save anyone.

Linna was dead. There was nothing any of them could do for her but arrange her in some sort of repose, closing her eyes. He left her there and walked back to Arian and Cavar. The two of them were seated on the ground, leaning against the wall. Cavar's face was pale, his head in his hands, but physically, he seemed unharmed. Arian was in much the same state, dazed but unhurt.

He exchanged a glance with Zephyr. She was standing guard, one hand on her sword. Chancellor Hosner lay beside Cavar and Arian, his wrists bound behind his back and a gag over his mouth. They didn't want to hurt him, but neither did they want him to call the guards.

The tight look Zephyr gave Liam reminded him of what he already knew. They needed to leave.

He turned to Cavar first. The Weaver looked up at him, a question in his eyes that died the second he saw Liam's face. He turned away.

"She was protecting me," Cavar said. "She threw herself in front of a blow meant for me."

"You must have meant a lot to her," Zephyr said cautiously.

"We grew up together," Cavar said, pushing himself to his feet. "She deserved better than this."

"We have to leave," Liam said. "We can't stay here."

"I know," Cavar said, but he gave Linna's body one last regretful look.

"Are there any rites?" Liam asked. "Anything I can do for her?"

Cavar shook his head. "The best thing we can do for her is to see this through. But burn it all."

Liam nodded gravely, stepping aside to let Cavar go past him and inclining his head toward Zephyr so she would follow.

That left him alone with Arian. Arian and the weight of all his suspicions, all the things that lay unsaid.

She was sitting with her knees curled up close to her chest, her fingers drumming out a nervous rhythm on her leg. Liam stared at her, aware that he didn't have much time. He held out the knife she had thrown at Roth. Arian took it, sliding it back into its sheath.

"Your spell worked," she said, her voice hollow. "You made my knives proof against magic. Good for you."

"You and I both know I didn't do that, Arian," Liam said. He had enchanted her daggers, true, but those enchantments had been meant to guard against minor spells. Nothing like the power that Roth had brought to bear.

Arian shook her head, pressing her lips tightly together. For a moment, Liam wanted her to deny it, to tell him it wasn't true. That his sister hadn't suddenly rendered him irrelevant.

The thoughts passed through his mind one after another, but behind them all, there was an ever-increasing urgency. There wasn't enough *time*.

"You can't keep hiding it," he said. "If you're—who I think you are."

Arian refused to look at him. But as he extended a hand to help her up, she took it, letting him pull her to her feet.

They walked to the door, pausing only to haul Chancellor Hosner to his feet and drag him out of the room. In the hallway, they found Cavar and Zephyr waiting for them. Before they left, Liam stopped in the doorway, holding out a hand and setting fire to the room. No one stopped to watch the place burn.

Their first priority was to get away before someone called the guards. They deposited the chancellor in an empty sitting room not far from his own chambers, then moved back down the hallway, taking refuge in a storage closet similar to the one in which they had found Zephyr and Kaolin. Arian ushered them inside and pulled the door shut. Liam felt magic rush over his skin as she created another illusion, covering the door from the outside.

"We can't hide in here forever," Arian said, looking around at the others. "We need a plan."

"Agreed," Cavar said, his tone sharper than usual. "What do we know?"

"Emeric Roth is a wight," Liam said. "A necromantic creature bound to his master. At the moment, that seems to be whoever is possessing Kaolin Eismor."

"Kaolin?" Cavar asked, looking between Liam, Arian, and Zephyr. "What about Kaolin?"

"Kaolin is being controlled by something," Liam said. "A spirit, I suppose, something otherworldly. I think that spirit might be Roth's master. I don't know when he would have taken control, though. Zephyr mentioned noticing a change in him recently, but it could have happened before he even came to this city."

Cavar shook his head, his expression grim. "Do we know who or what is controlling him?"

Liam and Arian exchanged a glance.

Arian said, "Well, whoever he was, he had the Star. Could that have anything to do with it?"

"You said the Star can steal souls," said Cavar. "Could the source of possession have come from *inside* the Star, somehow?"

Silence fell. Liam stared at the others, thinking. He hadn't considered that, but if it was possible, then that would mean that a soul could retain some sort of presence inside the Star. And that would mean—

Arian reached the conclusion first. She stared down at the floor for a few moments, then looked up, straight at Cavar.

"That man," she said. "The one our parents fought. The Weaver who stole the Star."

Cavar exhaled, muttering something under his breath that sounded a lot like a curse. "Kesi. Kesi eth'Akari."

"Kesi eth'Akari. The Weaver who had stolen the Star in the first place. The reason their parents had met.

What was it Cavar had said, in the ossuary that first night?

His mother had turned the Star on Kesi, absorbing his soul. Everything suddenly snapped into place.

"We thought Kesi was dead," Cavar said, "But if his soul survived . . . if it's been lurking in the Star this whole time, waiting for its chance . . ."

"A soul can't do much without a body," said Liam. "If Kesi wanted to act independently from the Star, he would need one. But what I don't understand is *when* he had the chance to summon Roth. If we're talking about the same person Mother fought—this happened before we were born."

Arian shrugged. "Roth isn't exactly young," she said. "And I found a clan symbol in his room. Eth'Akari's. Maybe he'd been in contact with Kesi before—before Kesi even came here."

"The point is, he's possessing Kaolin now," said Zephyr. "That's it, isn't it? This Kesi acted through Roth to get the Star back, and he's in Kaolin now. Using Kaolin's body."

"But why?" Liam asked.

"It can't be anything good," said Cavar grimly. "We have to stop him and reclaim the Star. And we need to do it tonight. Roth is clearly not concerned with hiding his true intentions anymore. I assume the same can be said of his master."

Liam remembered the charred remnants of the corridor. A shiver ran down his spine, and he nodded. "I'd say that's accurate."

"So there are two things we need to do," Cavar said. "We need to track down Lord Kaolin and remove the Star from him, and we need to deal with Emeric Roth. He's too dangerous to be left to his own devices."

"Roth is easy," Liam said, although even saying the words left a bitter taste in his mouth. He glanced at Arian. "He's technically already dead. If you can break his connection to his master, there will be nothing tying him to this world anymore. You could do it. You've disrupted his magic before."

"I don't even know how I managed that, though," said Arian. "I don't know if I can do it again."

"There's . . ." He hesitated, looking away. Admitting this *hurt*, more than he would have expected it to. It felt like the words were knives, cutting into him from the inside on their way out. "There's somewhere you could go, that would make you stronger. But you already know that, don't you?"

Arian didn't answer, but she did look away. That was confirmation enough for him.

"I can't go there with you," Liam said. "You have to do this without me."

"Why *not*?" Arian asked. "Where the hell are you going?"

"To do my duty," Liam said. "As the . . . as the last mage of the Arcanum. For now." He turned away from Arian and faced Zephyr instead. "Zeph, does your family still have your ceremonial gear? The ones proof against magic?"

Zephyr nodded. "In House Venari."

"All right," said Liam. "Let's go get it. We'll need it if we want a chance at defeating Kesi."

CHAPTER 56

ARIAN

THEY LEFT THE CLEANING CLOSET IN PAIRS, FIRST LIAM AND Zephyr and then her and Cavar. Between the two of them and Arian's veil, they managed to dodge the guards, avoiding the steady stream of armed men heading toward the explosion site.

The nice thing, Arian thought, about having such a clear center of activity was that everywhere else was pretty much deserted. There was no point in sending security guards to cover the area outside the laundry rooms, for instance, when there were explosions in more important parts of the keep. So it was only when she and Cavar reached those deserted parts of the Bastion that she slowed to a stop, looking back at him.

Cavar stopped running when she did, but he was looking past her, his eyes fixed on something she couldn't see. It took him a moment to realize that she was waiting to speak with him, and when he did notice, it took him a moment longer to shift his gaze up to her eyes. He looked like a swimmer coming up for air, trying desperately not to drown, and Arian would have been sympathetic if they had any gods-damned *time* left for that.

"Do you trust me?" Arian asked.

Cavar frowned at the question, but he nodded. "Of course."

"Good," Arian said. "We need to leave the Bastion. Now. I need to get into the city."

Cavar blinked at her, and she saw the moment when her words sank in. His expression shifted from dazed to clear, but it was a sharp, clinical sort of clarity. She'd take it, for now.

"What about Roth? I thought we were supposed to deal with him."

Arian let her hand drift down to the knives at her waist, the ones Liam had enchanted. Liam was right; what she had accomplished with Roth wasn't purely because of his enchantments, but they'd helped. She wasn't sure what she had done, only that she wanted to get Cavar away from him, and that something—some power, or some awareness—had traveled through the channels Liam had already created. She didn't know if she could do the same thing on purpose.

She sucked in a breath. "I don't know how I did what I did. And I'm not going to go up against Roth hoping for a miracle."

Cavar's brow furrowed. "So we're . . . running away?"

"*No*," said Arian. The word came out sharp, sharper than she'd intended. The memory of the occupation came back to her, of the Arcanum from the outside, its gates smashed open and its courtyards laid bare. The memory of the fire. She gritted her teeth, clenching her hand into a fist. "I'm never running away again."

"Then why are we leaving the Bastion?" Cavar asked.

"Because there's something I need to do. And it's about time I stopped avoiding it."

Feelings churned in her gut. Guilt, fear, *inadequacy*. Arian pushed them all away.

Cavar looked at her, holding her gaze. When he spoke, his voice was oddly gentle. "What are you going to do, Arian?"

Arian opened her mouth, and she was surprised by how steady her voice sounded when she spoke.

"I'm going to open a door."

🐾🐾🐾

A DOOR, LIAM HAD SAID. A DOOR THAT COULD ONLY BE OPENED BY the Speaker. She could feel its touch against her skin, a steady tug in the right direction as she led Cavar down, down past the dungeons, down beneath the courtyard, down into the farthest reaches of the fortress.

They moved through the halls like ghosts, following a call only Arian could hear.

Cavar didn't speak. She was grateful for that. She didn't know how she would answer him if he decided to ask questions now. Instead, she concentrated on the task ahead, on putting one foot in front of the other.

The walk was longer and shorter than she expected. Short enough that when she checked her watch, she saw that not much time had passed since she and Cavar had first started walking. Long enough that she could feel memory weighing her down with each step, as if she wasn't walking simply along the Bastion's hidden corridors but along the hidden paths of the life she had lived.

Everywhere she looked, she saw glimpses of the life she had denied. It stuck with her, thwarting her best attempts to escape it. She saw it in her childhood, in her and Liam studying magic together. She saw it when she was six years old and managed to make light for the first time, and while Liam had already moved on into making fire and moving earth, her light was the brightest in the room. She saw it in the look in her brother's eye, in the pride he took at being a skilled mage. She saw it in the guilt she felt when he looked at her, eleven years old and starry-eyed, and told her that he would be the next Speaker someday. She saw it in the day she stopped studying magic, twelve years old and full of fire, saw it in her life afterward, running with Lyndon's crew, staying at home as little as possible, saw it in the constant arguments with her mother.

But more than that, she saw it in the moment her mother had taken her, ten years old and afraid, to a stone door in the depths of a very cold place where dust wouldn't settle.

I want you to do something for me, Arian. Place your hand on the door.

Why? Arian remembered asking. Catherina Athensor had looked at her daughter and shaken her head, lips pressed close together.

I have a thought, she said. *Just . . . humor me for a little, please.*

The memories faded in a rush as she found herself standing in front of the door, Cavar waiting behind her.

It was a stone door set into the wall, unmarked, without any handle or hinges, almost identical to the door Arian had stood in front of so many years ago. Cavar moved aside as Arian stepped up to it. She could feel his eyes on her as she drew up in front of the door, hesitating.

"I don't know if you can follow me in," she said. "I've never opened it from this side before."

"That's fine," Cavar said. "I'll keep watch out here."

Arian nodded, then, before she could have second thoughts, pressed her hand to the stone. It was cold. She could feel the cold even through her gloves, along with something sharp and intense, the rush of power. It washed over her, searching, and this time, she gave herself over to it. She let the power fill her, running through her body, mind, and soul. It passed over her and through her.

Slowly, the door opened.

CHAPTER 57

CAVAR

ARIAN STOOD AT THE MOUTH OF THE PASSAGE FOR SEVERAL LONG
moments, unmoving. Her hands were clenched tight at her sides,
her eyes on the passage ahead. She was shaking. He cleared his
throat, and she jolted, her eyes widening as she looked back at him.

"I've been denying that I could do this for years," Arian said.
"For so long that I almost believed the lie."

She sucked in a breath, slowly unclenching her fists. He pretended not to see her blink tears out of her eyes.

Arian stepped over the threshold and walked forward a few
steps, then paused, breathing out. Some of the tension left her as
she looked back over her shoulder at him. All along the walls to
either side of her, lights flared up, filling the corridor with a soft
white glow.

"I think . . . it's safe for you to follow," she said. "Come on."

Cavar nodded. The second he stepped over the threshold, the
door slid back into place behind him, leaving him alone with Arian,
the magic, and her ghosts.

THE PASSAGE WENT ON FOREVER, LONG ENOUGH THAT CAVAR LOST
all concept of time and direction. He felt that they were somewhere
under the city, but he wasn't sure, and he didn't dare break Arian's
concentration to ask. Arian walked just ahead of him, her eyes fixed
on the distance, their way lit by the white lights that winked into
existence ahead of them and extinguished themselves once they
had passed.

As they walked, the path grew colder, until eventually, Cavar could see his breath in front of his face. Frost crystals formed on the walls and ceiling ahead of them. He shivered but kept moving.

Arian seemed wholly unaffected by the cold. He looked at her feet and saw ice melting beneath her as she walked.

At the end of the corridor was another door, this one with symbols carved into its frame. Some instinct made Cavar give it a wide berth, stopping as soon as it came into sight.

"Is this where I leave you?" Cavar asked, when Arian didn't speak.

"Maybe," Arian said. "I think you can come right up to the edge of the door, but no farther."

Cavar nodded, and Arian reluctantly rested her fingers against the door.

There was a low, groaning sound, stone grating against stone. A cold blue light spread from Arian's fingertips, settling in the runes and carvings along the outside of the door. The light flared, and the door began to groan and shudder, stone sliding away beneath Arian's touch.

On the other side—

—on the other side was light, bright and blinding. It was an all-consuming sort of light, and for an instant, terror like Cavar had never known washed over him. When Arian stepped forward, he moved before he could think, grabbing her arm.

"Arian, wait—!"

Arian turned back to face him, looking resigned. He could feel something in her when he touched her, a power thrumming beneath her skin. It chased the cold away from inside him, leaving him with a sense of warmth and wholeness. And fear.

"I'm sorry," Arian said. She gave him a sad smile. "I have to go, Cavar. I'm the Speaker of the Arcanum. I told you before, didn't I? There's never been a door I couldn't open."

Her eyes met his, and Cavar stopped himself from saying what she already knew. That the Speaker was bound to this island, body and soul, for the rest of their lives. That until someone else could be found to bear the weight of this power, they could never leave. That she would never be able to leave Leithon with him.

What would be the point? The choice had been made a long time ago.

He let go. It was the hardest thing he had ever done, but he uncurled his fingers from around Arian's arm. She nodded and took a step back, crossing the threshold into that blinding light.

The second she did, the quality of the light changed. It flared brighter, so bright that Cavar had to cover his eyes with his arm to avoid being blinded. Then, as the brightness receded, Cavar caught a glimpse of a figure moving toward the center of the light.

Arian.

The power rose and twisted around her, turning her into a shadowed silhouette in the center of the light. She held out her hand to it, and the power flowed into her palm like a stream. In that light, Cavar saw promise and hope, power and honor and glory and everything intangible in the world. The power of creation shrinking smaller and smaller until Arian held the entirety of it in her hand.

Bathed in that light, she looked different. Like something other, something more than human. She was still wearing the clothes she had worn earlier today, still wore her hair the same way and her weapons at her side, but there was something about her that made her greater than the sum of her parts. It was as if the power had become one with her and she one with it, as if all those things he had glimpsed and more were inside her now.

He understood, for the first time, what his mother meant when she called the Arcanum the linchpin that bound the fabric of their reality together. When she called the Speaker the hand bridging the gap between seen and unseen.

Arian held the power of the world in her hand. And then, as he watched, she released it.

Power swelled from her, expanding until it flooded the stones around her, the ground beneath her feet, the corridor that Cavar was standing in. The power brought with it warmth and fire, chasing away the cold. Above Arian, stones groaned and moved, snapping back into place. That power, that restorative force, shot ever upward, and the ground beneath him shook so hard that he had to rest his hand on the wall to keep steady.

Then it was quiet again. The light in the chamber was gone, and Arian stood alone in that cavernous room, her eyes fixed on the world above her as the last rumbles of power traveled onward and upward. One of her hands was curled close to her chest, her expression strangely thoughtful as she stared into the distance. Cavar held his breath.

The last sound faded away. Arian bowed her head, letting her hand fall back to her side.

"What did you do?" Cavar asked, the sound strangely loud in the new stillness.

She turned toward him then, a satisfied smile on her face, the gleam of triumph in her eyes. Cavar felt a thrill. She was beautiful in that moment. Beautiful, powerful, deadly, and so very *Arian*.

"I sent a message," she said. "Now the whole world knows Leithon has its fight back."

CHAPTER 58

ZEPHYR

THE FIRST THING ZEPHYR NOTICED WHEN SHE APPROACHED House Venari's estate were the guards. Imperial soldiers stood outside the gates, more numerous than usual despite the chaos in the Bastion. She guessed that Kallan Venari was still considered a threat to the Empire after all this time, that Selwald was worried he might see the current difficulty as an opportunity to cause trouble. And knowing her father, Zephyr wasn't too sure that Selwald was wrong.

The manor looked as it always had. Her home, the place where she had grown up. She could feel memory tugging at her with each step she took toward it, weaving its hooks into her heart and her bones and her soul.

Home.

The thought was so powerful that she had to stop for a moment, hesitating on the path that led up to the main gates.

It had been so long since she had allowed herself to think of this place as home.

But this house was her home. This *city* was her home.

She'd been fooling herself for years trying to pretend that it was any different.

"Zephyr?" Liam asked from beside her. "Are you okay?"

Was she okay? Her hands were shaking, the tremor spreading from her fingertips up her arms and into her whole body. She opened and closed her fists, breathed deep. No, she was not okay. But she was ready.

She nodded. Liam's attention shifted from her to the guards.

"How are we going to get in there?" he asked. "I could come up with a spell to distract them?"

"No," Zephyr said, straightening up. Her eyes drifted past the guards, toward the high walls of her family estate. She had no doubt that one way or another, her father would be watching what was happening outside the gates. And if she was going to come home after all this time, she needed more than magic. She needed to send a message.

She shifted her grip on the long knife that Arian had left her, glancing at Liam. "Can you craft me a shield?"

Liam looked uncertain. "It won't last very long."

"That doesn't matter," said Zephyr, eyeing the four guards standing outside the estate. "I only need a minute."

Liam drew in a deep breath and nodded, holding out his hands so that his palms were facing each other. He called power into them, droplets of water shimmering and coalescing in the air between his hands. They stretched out and solidified, forming a shield made of ice. Zephyr plucked it out of the air, gripping tight to the handle on the back. The shock of cold sent shivers across her skin, and she sucked in a breath through her teeth. The shield felt uncommonly light, although when she rapped on it with her knuckles, it felt solid enough.

"Your conjuration's improved," she said, glancing at Liam.

Liam looked away. "You always wanted me to practice. After everything that happened, I finally had the time."

A pang wormed its way into Zephyr's chest, the same sense of loss that she always felt when she thought about their past together. But now wasn't the time for reminiscing. She shook her head, turning away from him.

"Thank you," she said, facing the guards. "Please stay back."

For a moment, Zephyr was worried that Liam would argue. But he didn't. He simply nodded, retreating into the shadows as she approached the guards. It was like he understood that this was her fight and hers alone.

She made no attempt to hide, knife and shield in hand as she walked up to the gates. The Imperial guards went rigid as they saw her, closing ranks in front of the gateway.

"Halt!" one of them said, holding a hand up. "Who goes there?"

Zephyr stopped walking.

"You know who I am," she said. "I want to enter my family estate."

A wave of uncertainty passed through the guards. They exchanged glances, watching her warily. Their commander, the one who had spoken, recovered first.

"Where did you get that shield, Lieutenant?" he asked. "Leithonians are forbidden to use magic."

"It doesn't matter," Zephyr said, holding her knife out to her side. "Let me through."

That caused another murmur of discontent through the group. One of them, the guard standing farthest back, drew steel.

The group's commanding officer glared at her. "You would commit treason?"

"I've already committed treason," said Zephyr, shifting her stance. "This is something I should have done long ago."

They charged at her, all four of them, but Zephyr was ready. She raised her shield, light flashing across its surface as she caught the first soldier's sword. Zephyr let the force behind the blow pass through her and into the ground, ducking down beneath a second strike. She swung her knife out to the side, feeling the tip of the blade slash one of the guards across the torso. He grunted, stumbling, and Zephyr used the opening to shove the guard whose sword rested on her shield, knocking him away from her.

She spun, blocking a blow coming at her from behind. Zephyr caught the sword on her shield and swept it out to the side, stepping into the space left behind to slam her knee into her attacker's gut. As he rocked back, gasping for breath, she hit him around the head with her shield, knocking him unconscious.

The fourth guard thrust his sword at her throat. Zephyr parried the attack with the flat of her knife. She placed her shield between them and charged in, slamming into the guard's chest. The blow pushed him back throwing him into the wounded guard. The two of them crashed onto the cobbles, and she turned to face the commander.

She raised her shield to cover her torso as he charged, catching his sword on it, and slammed her knife's pommel down onto his wrist, feeling something crunch underneath the blow. He screamed in pain and fury, and she shoved him back, incapacitating him with a blow to the head.

The wounded guard dropped his sword, holding up his hands in surrender. The remaining guard rushed at her, but it was a sloppy attack. She spun to deal with him, slamming her shield into his head. She let the surrendering guard flee.

It was over in a matter of seconds. The shield on her arm shattered into motes of falling ice. Zephyr swept her knife through the air in a duelist's flourish before lowering it to her side. She stepped forward, walking calmly past the unconscious guards, and came to stand in front of the gate.

There, she drew herself up to her full height.

"I am Zephyr Venari," she called. "Daughter of the master of this house, Knight of the Blood, Keeper of the Trust. I request entry."

There was a long pause, one that set Zephyr's nerves on edge. It forced her into stillness, eyes on the gate, counting down the seconds.

Slowly, the great gate slid open.

✧✧✧

LORD KALLAN VENARI WAS WAITING FOR HER IN THE MAIN HALL. Word of the chaos at the Bastion must have spread, because he was wearing armor. It had been months since the last time Zephyr had seen her father, but she noted that he was wearing his sword, something that had been forbidden him under the terms of their surrender. His expression was solemn as she stepped into the hall, Liam in tow.

"I thought you said you were never coming back," he said.

"Circumstances have changed," Zephyr said, dipping into a deep bow. "I hope you can forgive me, Father."

Kallan left her bowing there for a long moment, and in his silence, Zephyr felt the years she had spent working with the Empire, felt the rift that had opened between them on the day Zephyr decided to open the gates. She held her breath, waiting for her father to scream at her, to rage, to throw her out of the house.

What she wasn't expecting was for him to place a gauntleted hand on her shoulder.

She looked up, and the face she saw in front of her was older than the last time she had seen it, lined with grief and pain, but with a fire somewhere deep in his eyes that nothing could ever fully quench.

"So you're a Knight of the Blood?" he asked, repeating her words from the gate back to her. Zephyr nodded, and Kallan let his hand fall away. "Then welcome back," he said. He offered Liam a nod of respect, inclining his head back toward the stairway behind him, the one that led down into the basement. "We have work to do."

Zephyr nodded, following him.

CHAPTER 59

ZEPHYR

ON THE DAY OF THE OCCUPATION, IMPERIAL TROOPS HAD searched her ancestral home, making records of everything they found there. According to those records, her family had an armory on the first floor, and all its contents had been carefully cataloged. But every member of House Venari knew that that wasn't the real armory. The *real* armory, the room entrusted to the Knights of the Blood, was hidden two floors underground, where no one, not even Roth's magebreakers, had been able to find it. It was protected by a magic as deep and as sacred as the power that kept the Arcanum whole, a magic that Zephyr was still not sure she understood.

She did understand one thing: The things contained in the armor room had been given to her ancestors under trust, to be used only when Leithon's existence was at stake. The last time any armor had left that room had been during the invasion. It hadn't turned the tide of the war, but then again, her father had been fighting alone.

This time, he wouldn't be.

She stood at a respectful distance, watching as her father approached the door. He placed a hand on it, pushing it open. The lamps on the other side were already lit, the room beckoning her with a warm, welcoming glow. She knew better than to approach uninvited, keeping her eyes on her father.

Kallan's expression was grim as he looked back at her. She had explained the situation to him on the walk, and while he seemed reluctant to even consider aiding an Imperial noble, she thought she had managed to convince him that what was happening had important implications for the security of Leithon.

"It won't be like last time," she had promised. "We'll rescue Kaolin. But we'll keep Leithon."

She knew that he had been weighing her words, trying to decide whether he believed them.

"I don't know if the armor room will admit you," he said.

The doubt in his voice stung, but she understood. She nodded.

"I'll take that chance."

Kallan watched her, his gaze piercing. Then, without another word, he stepped through the door.

The room admitted him easily. When Zephyr approached the entryway, however, she felt the door's scrutiny, a prickle of energy against her skin. She took another step closer, holding her breath while she waited for it to repel her. When nothing happened, she pressed her lips tightly together, stepping all the way through.

On the other side, she exhaled in relief. Kallan watched her, and there was something in his gaze that hadn't been present for a very long time, something that warmed her heart to see.

Approval.

He almost smiled as she came to stand next to him.

Zephyr looked back at door, searching for Liam.

Liam stood in the entryway, his hand pressed against an invisible wall that had formed over the front of the door. The smile fell from Zephyr's face.

"Liam?"

Liam shook his head. "I . . . don't think I'm welcome," he said. His expression became regretful, almost sad, and he took a step back. "I'll wait for you here."

Zephyr nodded numbly, everything she wanted to say catching in her throat. There was a world between her and Liam now, a world of separate experiences and memories that she knew nothing about. She wanted to say something to him, something to show that she understood, but her father was waiting for her, and they were running out of time.

She bowed her head and turned to face the stands.

All in all, there were seven sets of House Venari armor. Though they varied in style and in application, all were immune to magic and could dispel even the most intricately woven spells. With Venari armor, a warrior could take down the Arcanum, which was why only a true Knight of the Blood could touch the armor, why only those deemed incorruptible could enter the armory.

Kallan had already walked toward a stand displaying his favored armor, a set of heavy, jade-tinted plate with a design on the shield that looked like a tree with large, curling branches, spreading across the entire surface. Zephyr's eyes lingered on the smaller, lighter set that she had once favored—red-lacquered armor with embellishments like fire. She had trained in it, grown up in it, once known it like she knew her own breath. She took a half step toward it before she changed her mind, looking away.

She was different now. That Zephyr Venari, that girl who had once trained with her father, who had dreams of being the commander of the Royal Guard—that girl was gone. And she knew that that armor would no longer accept her. She wasn't the warrior of fire that she had once been. She had become something else, a remnant, a wraith. A warrior of ash and bone.

Zephyr made her way to the last of the seven sets in the room, the one that stood in the back, apart from all the others. Kallan noticed her trajectory and paused, but whatever he was going to say died in his throat.

The seventh armor, the exile's set, waited for her. In all their history, that set had never left this chamber. It was nothing but simple leather armor stained black, nearly weightless. Hanging on the rack beside it was a slender black sword in a sheath, a circular black shield. She slipped the armor on over her clothes, tightening the straps, tied up her hair and arranged it inside her helmet. She picked the blade up off the shelf, drawing it and running it through a few practice strikes, strapping the shield to her arm. Zephyr touched the charred patches in the leather, the remnants of a battle long passed, then looked up at her father.

"It fits," she said.

Kallan Venari gave her a solemn nod in return. "Help me with my armor."

Zephyr nodded, hurrying to his side.

⬇⬇⬇

LIAM WAITED FOR THEM OUTSIDE AS THEY LEFT THE ARMORY, leaning against the wall of the hallway. He had a small book in one hand and was steadily paging through it. The whole scene was calculated to give off an air of nonchalance, but Zephyr knew him well enough—still—to see through the lie. He snapped the book shut, tucking it into his pocket, and nodded at her.

"Ready to go?" he asked.

Zephyr nodded. "We need a plan before we charge in there. Do you have any ideas?"

"A few," Liam said. "Kesi probably knows we're coming for him. Drawing him out will be difficult. We'll need to find him first."

"That would be a lot easier if we knew what he was intending to do," said Zephyr.

"He's planning on using the Star as a containment unit," Kallan said, making the two of them stop and turn toward him. Noticing their surprised looks, he shrugged. "Leopards don't change their spots. If this truly is Kesi eth'Akari, he's going to try to do the same thing he did back then."

"Back then?" Zephyr asked.

"When Kit, when your mother, got hold of the Star in the first place," said Kallan. He turned toward Liam. "Kesi kidnapped her to draw your father out. He was trying to get Rinu to give up his soul—to complete some sort of ritual. That's when Kit absorbed him into the Star."

"If he was trying to take my father's soul, then it's probably one of the older forms of dark magic," Liam said. "Likely, it's the sort of ritual that involves bloodlines. Which means that either Arian or I would do."

"Do?" Zephyr asked, brows raising. "Do for what?"

"For bait, of course," Liam said. "What else?"

THEY WERE ON THEIR WAY BACK UP THE STAIRS WHEN A SERVANT caught them, bowing quickly at Zephyr and Kallan. "My lord, my lady. News from the Bastion."

"What is it?" Kallan asked.

The servant hesitated. "A—a soldier came to the gates," she said, glancing at Zephyr. "In gray clothes. He said to tell you both that the revolution's begun."

"Revolution?" Kallan asked. "What—?"

A tremor cut him off, a shaking deep beneath the city streets like the foundations of the earth had pulled free.

Liam broke into a run, pushing past the servant and taking the stairs two at a time. Zephyr turned to follow him, and that was when she noticed it. It was subtle, the sort of thing she might not have felt had she not been wearing her family's armor. But the air was laced with a charge, an undeniable power.

She took off after Liam.

Zephyr found him just outside the manor, his eyes on the horizon. She followed his line of sight. In the distance, a pillar of light had risen from the Arcanum. It burned a sharp white, cutting through the night. As Zephyr watched, stone rose around the pillar, snapping into place and forming the Spire that had once dominated Leithon's skyline. The sight took her breath away.

She turned to Liam and saw his expression, awe and jealousy and resentment all competing for space on his face. She understood.

Arian.

The earth shook a second time, a pillar of light erupting from the center of the Bastion, the inner keep's highest tower. As Zephyr watched, a second Spire rose to meet the first, climbing higher and higher. Zephyr stared at it for a long moment, then turned to face the servant who had followed them up.

"Go find the soldier who came here," she said. "Tell him to gather everyone who can be trusted and wait for my orders. I'm heading back to the Bastion."

CHAPTER 60

ARIAN

ARIAN RACED UP THE STAIRWAY OF THE NEW SPIRE, CAVAR behind her. It felt like running through a dream. The restorative magic she had unleashed had re-created the shape of the Spire, but individual rooms weren't where they had once been, and the carvings that Arian remembered had changed and shifted, growing in the wrong places. It was like the Spire had some intrinsic memory of what it was supposed to be, but it didn't care about the details. The result was a building that looked like the one Arian remembered from her childhood but wasn't the same. It reminded her that this was not her mother's Spire, not the Spire of the Speakers and Candidates who had come before her.

It was hers. A construct entirely her own.

She tried not to think about how that made her feel, tried to focus on what lay ahead.

The carvings on the walls glowed faintly, suffused with the same power and energy that permeated the Spire. That, Arian thought, was new and probably temporary. Before all this power ran out, she had to see what she could do with it.

The spiral staircase ended in the Office of the Speaker, the room at the top of the Spire that had once belonged to her mother. She stopped to think, looking around the room.

"Arian?" Cavar asked from behind her.

"We need to get to the roof."

Arian swept her hand out to the side. A delicate spiral staircase wrought itself out of the air, drawing from the magic that infused the tower. Arian leaped onto the stairs before they had finished forming, bursting out through a door that appeared ahead of her.

Stones parted and reshaped themselves to form a balcony at her feet. She stepped up to the edge, stretched out her hand, and a metal guardrail formed for her fingers to close around.

Cavar followed her up to the railing, looking down at the courtyard below. The light had moved outward from the Spire, restoring stones and benches, bringing overgrown gardens back into order. It hadn't yet reached the walls, and that was a problem, because another Spire had erupted from the Bastion, answering her.

To the naked eye, it looked like her own Spire, but to Arian's senses, it felt completely different. The power that formed that light came unwillingly, from a place of deep despair. It hadn't chosen its wielder. It was bound to it.

The Star.

Cavar stood next to Arian, watching the second tower form, an imposing obelisk of black stone. Arian noticed his hands were hovering over his daggers, as if that would help him at all in this situation.

"What is that?" he asked.

"Kesi's answer," said Arian. "A counter-Spire. He's trying to start another Arcanum."

He would succeed too, if the spell he was casting was ever allowed to come to completion. But as it was, Arian felt that it was still incomplete. They still had time.

But time to do what?

Kesi's power swelled, a bolt of lightning forming at the top of his tower and rocketing toward her. Cavar shouted an entirely unnecessary warning. Arian ignored him, reaching into the power that surrounded her. She swept her arm upward in an arc. Light pulsed from the courtyard, crackling up the broken walls and forming a translucent dome around the tower.

The attack struck the shield, rippling across its surface and dissipating. Arian felt the blow like a pressure on the inside of her mind, but as far as blows went, that one had been light, a glancing strike during a training exercise.

She swept her arm across herself, clenching her fist.

Blades rose up from her own shield, seven of them. They rushed toward the Bastion's tower in a dazzling display, searing through the clouds that hung low in the sky and causing thunder to boom in their wake. Her counterattack slammed into the nascent tower, colliding with shields that were even more rushed in construction than her own. She thought she could hear the snaps and booms even here, on the outskirts of the city.

The light faded, power rising up around Kesi's tower and filling the gaps she had created in its defenses. She felt the energy that surrounded that tower withdraw and understood that Kesi wouldn't attack again for a while yet. At least not across that distance. She lowered her arms to her sides but kept the shield up, just in case.

A tremor passed through the ground, and Arian felt connections shatter, the link between her and the Bastion breaking. She cursed. Kesi was sharper than she'd expected.

"What?" Cavar asked.

"He closed the passage," Arian said. She turned on her heel, jerking her head toward the door that led into the Spire. "Come on."

Cavar followed, the two of them descending the delicate metal staircase until they were standing in the Speaker's office once more. Arian leaned against the desk, folding her arms.

"We need to get back there. I can't stop him from here."

"We'll have to go through the city," Cavar said.

"I know."

Cavar looked out the window. Inside the Arcanum's domed barrier, it was quiet, but outside, rain had begun to fall, set loose by Arian's attack. The distance between the Arcanum and the Bastion wasn't small underground, but with the city of Leithon between them, it was daunting.

"He'll be expecting that," said Cavar.

"I know he will, but what choice do we have?" Arian asked.

"Your power is tied to this place?"

Arian clenched her hand into a fist, feeling the energy gathered there. "The Arcanum's power should cover the whole island. I don't know how strong I'll be outside, but it doesn't matter. I'm no good to anyone in here, and we need to go now."

Cavar nodded reluctantly. That was good, because if he didn't start moving, Arian would have grabbed him by the collar and forced him down the steps. The two of them burst out through the Arcanum's repaired archway and into the courtyard. The cobblestone path repaired itself for her as she ran across it, stones snapping into place. The gates swung open without her even having to think about them, leaving a narrow gap that allowed her to run out onto the road that led to Leithon proper. Outside the barrier, the rain was coming down in sheets, soaking her to the skin.

They had almost reached the city when Arian drew up short. There was a sound in the air, funneled through the Road of Shadows. It was distinct from the pounding of the rain, the rush of water in her ears. The sound of shouting. Of revolution.

Cavar skidded to a stop behind her.

"No," Arian said, shaking her head as she started running again. "No, come on, not now."

The two of them reached the first of the city streets, clambering up onto the rooftop paths. From the roof, Arian could see that the roads were clogged with people, a veritable army of Leithonian citizens marching on the Bastion with whatever weapons they could find in their hands. She could only guess what having that many willing souls throwing themselves onto the Bastion's power would do for Kesi and the Star. Arian gritted her teeth, letting out a volley of curses vile enough to make even Cavar recoil. Then she took a step back away from the edge of the roof.

"Change of plans," she said. "I need to talk to Lyndon."

CHAPTER 61

CAVAR

"LYNDON!"

Arian burst into the Spinning Wheel like a storm, kicking the door in and letting the rain and wind swirl into the bar in her wake. Patrons jumped out of their seats. Cavar kept a hand close to his weapons in case anyone decided to start trouble, but the Wheel's crowd took one look at Arian and wisely chose to ignore her. There were less of them around tonight than usual, and those who were here seemed keener on getting drunk as fast as possible than doing anything else.

Arian's eyes swept over the assembled crowd before she raised her voice again.

"Lyndon, where the hell are you?!"

"Upstairs!" a voice shouted from the Wheel's upper story. "Where the hell else did you think I'd be?"

Arian ground out a curse under her breath, stomping toward the staircase. Cavar followed her as she took the steps two at a time, practically hauling herself up by the banister.

Upstairs, the place was more crowded. A map of Leithon had been spread out on one of the tables, a dagger sticking straight out of the place where the Bastion stood. The smell of smoke hung in the air.

Arian marched up to the table. She grabbed Lyndon by the front of his shirt, pressing him back against it. She was probably about half his size, and yet she still managed to look intimidating as she pulled him down to face her, glaring.

"What the *fuck* is going on outside?" she snarled.

Lyndon was unamused. He returned the glare, radiating a quiet danger that Cavar hadn't felt from him before. It made Cavar reach for a weapon. Reid, who was nearest him, saw the motion and edged away.

"You better let go of me, girl," Lyndon warned.

"I'm not letting go of shit until you answer my question," said Arian. "I've had a long night and we're in a hurry. What the hell is going on?"

"What's going on is that I've lost control of my people, is that what you want to hear?" Lyndon asked. "They're fed up and not going to let the Empire take what they want anymore. I'd be proud of them if they weren't playing right into their hands."

Arian released him, surprised. "You know?"

"Of course I know," Lyndon said, rubbing at his neck with a scowl. "I know everything that goes on in this city." He paused, giving her an odd look. "Liam didn't say anything?"

"Liam?" Arian asked. "Why would he—?" She broke off suddenly, cursing. "You've got to get them away from the gates. There's magic going on out there. No one needs to get caught up in it."

"I noticed," Lyndon said dryly. He frowned at her. "The Arcanum. That was you, wasn't it?"

"It was always me," said Arian. "It was *always* me, and you knew that when you took me in. Didn't you? All those *daring escapes* I made, I was disappearing into thin air and you never said a thing."

An unapologetic grin spread over Lyndon's face. Arian rolled her eyes, turning away from him and facing the room.

"Listen up! I don't know what any of you are thinking, but if you're thinking that this is the time to rush the Bastion, let me correct you—this is *not* the fucking time. There's an evil bastard holed up in there just waiting for people like you to come rushing in so he can take your souls and use them to power some seriously bad magic—and another evil bastard hoping to use this 'revolution' for political gain. At this point, you tell me which one's worse. We've gotta stop those people from breaching the Bastion walls."

"How?" Reid asked.

"I don't know, you tell me!" said Arian. "When the hell did we become so useless? Aren't we the Leithonian underground? There used to be no vault we couldn't open, no prize we couldn't steal. And now you're telling me we can't even stop a revolution *we* started? Fuck that. Figure it out. I've got bigger fish to fry."

"The lady's right," said Lyndon, straightening up. He gave Arian an appraising look, then turned back toward the others. "Head out see how many folks you can round up. If we can get enough support, we can slow this march down."

He turned to Arian as people around him scrambled to obey, racing down the steps and out into the street. "It's not going to stop them completely, but it'll buy you some time. That's what you really wanted, isn't it?"

Arian nodded.

"What are you going to do?" Lyndon asked.

"What do you think? I'm gonna head to the Bastion, beat that evil bastard, and take my home back. I'll sort out all this Arcanum shit when it's done."

Lyndon gave her a wry smile. "Good to have you back, kid. But"—he slid his hands into his pockets, giving her a calculating frown—"this is the end of our association, isn't it?"

Arian faltered, dropping her gaze. It was a moment before she answered.

"After is after," she said. "Save those people now. Let me worry about that later."

"Aye," Lyndon said. "Happy hunting."

"Same to you."

She jerked her head at Cavar and started walking down the steps out of the bar. Cavar followed her. Arian was silent until they had left the Spinning Wheel behind, until they were crossing the rooftop paths toward the Road of Law, the sound of revolution heavy in the air.

"I never wanted this," Arian said, gesturing at the newly healed Spire, at the glow that still surrounded it, protecting and repairing. "I left home because of this. When I got chosen. I didn't want the responsibility. The Speaker is bound to the Arcanum, to Leithon. I wanted to be free."

They picked their way across slick rooftop stones, drenched in the rain. He looked at her and couldn't help but think of the future. Of freedom. Of staying in Leithon, of leaving the Weavers behind. There was a hole in his heart when he thought about Linna, a numbness and a grief that he couldn't acknowledge yet, but for the rest of it—

What was it she had told Lyndon? After was after?

"And now?" Cavar asked her instead.

"Now?" Arian lifted her gaze, focusing on the Bastion. On the false Spire that protruded from the top of the inner keep, gathering energy. "Now, I still don't know what I feel. But I don't think it matters. Because I'm not gonna be free until we all are. This whole damn city. They stole it from us, and I'm going to steal it back. Not bad for my last heist, huh?"

She was grinning, but with rain coming down, he would never know if she cried. He looked from her to the Bastion in the distance and said, "We'll do it together. It would be my honor."

CHAPTER 62

LIAM

ON THE OUTSIDE, THE BASTION WAS TRANSFORMING, BECOMING a Spire to echo the Arcanum's in height and glory. On the inside, Liam thought, the changes were rather anticlimactic. Kesi's magic hadn't restructured the maze of passages and hallways that marked the inner keep. It had simply expanded them, adding stairs where stairs had not been and making ceilings grander and higher. The result was a series of identical floors, stacked haphazardly on each other, with the same paintings and ornamentations on each floor as if some divine hand had created copies of the Bastion's interior and rearranged it to its liking.

It was a surreal experience, climbing the stairs, seeing the same painting four different times. It made Liam question his sense of direction, made him wonder if he was moving forward at all or walking in circles.

There had been a barrier surrounding the new tower, cutting it off from the rest of the world. It had been a barrier created from the Star itself, capturing the energy of anything it touched. Liam thought it unlikely that he would have been able to breach it had it not been for Zephyr. House Venari's sword had cut through, and Zephyr had stayed on the Bastion's first floor with her father.

Liam would draw out Kesi and the Star and would summon the Venaris when he had Kesi's full attention. That was the plan, at least.

He came to a stop in an empty room, feeling the churn of Kesi's energy in the air around him. From the feel of it, he had Kesi's attention. Liam drew in a breath, planting his metal staff at his side.

He waited.

The intruder was a dark stain on the surface of his mind, a spreading pool of malice and hate. Liam tightened his grip on the staff as he turned to face him, forming a shield of ice in the air. A bolt of energy struck the shield almost as soon as it had formed, the construct quivering underneath the impact. As the last of the energies died down, Liam saw a figure standing in the doorway, watching him.

It wasn't Kesi, but this would do just as well.

Emeric Roth stood there, right hand crackling with power. In his other hand, he held a silver sword, the blade he had used to raid the Arcanum. To Liam's eye, he looked solid, concrete, but Liam understood now what he couldn't have understood before: that the real Roth had died long ago.

"How long?" Liam asked.

Roth raised his brows in question, lowering neither his hand nor his sword.

"How long have you been in that state?"

"Ah," said Roth. "Have you considered that I might not be at liberty to say?"

"I just want to know who I should blame," Liam said. He leveled the point of the metal staff at Roth, mentally running through his list of spells. His mind touched on the pattern for the circle of unmaking and he drew power from that image, cold blue light tracing runes onto the steel. The air around Liam went cold, frost crystals beading at the staff's ends.

Roth watched the display with an impassive eye, not moving.

"It was my hand that felled the Arcanum," he said.

"But was it your will?"

"If I said no, would that change anything?"

"If you said no," Liam said, "I would tell you to get out of the way. My fight is with your master, not with you."

"Then the answer is irrelevant. I will not let you leave this room."

Liam shuddered, feeling the staff draw more power out of him, gathering it into itself. "Your master's orders?"

"In a manner of speaking. He wants you out of the way. You aren't the one he is interested in."

Arian.

Liam couldn't sense what was happening outside the Bastion, but he knew his sister. She was his twin, a part of him. As different as they were, he understood her as well as he understood himself.

If she saw what was happening at the Bastion, she wouldn't be able to stop herself from coming. She'd run away from the fall of the Arcanum, but he'd seen the change in her over the past year. She would come. Which only made it imperative that he finish with Roth and leave. Quickly.

"Last chance," Liam said. "Get out of my way."

"I have no particular attachment to this existence," Roth said, his eyes flicking to Liam's staff. "Although I do feel the need to warn you. If *this* is the path you choose to walk down, there will be no turning back. That magic is a taint on your soul. Shadow will consume you."

"Speaking from personal experience?"

"Perhaps," said Roth. "I tire of this. Come, if you will."

Liam didn't wait for another chance. He thrust the staff forward, releasing the energy he had been storing. The wind howled, rushing toward Roth in a single concerted blast.

Roth became a shadow, vanishing from sight. The wind ripped stone from the walls and tore into the door frame, missing him completely. Liam whirled to the side as he felt Roth's power coalesce, sweeping his staff through the air. The staff hit Roth in the ribs with a resounding crack, and Liam threw his weight behind it, shoving him aside.

Roth's eyes widened with surprise at the impact. The blow pulled him off his feet, throwing him to the ground. Liam grinned, raising his other hand to the staff. He summoned power, throwing a bolt of lightning at Roth. Thunder boomed in the wake of the blast, echoing in the room. Roth raised his sword. Lightning struck the blade and dissipated, grounded by the spells worked into the steel. He pushed himself up to his feet, one arm wrapped around his waist.

Liam gripped the staff in both hands, holding it like a spear with the tip pointed at Roth. He felt triumphant. It had been a gamble. The staff absorbed power. It was made to channel magic, to siphon and store it. And what could be a greater source of magic than a ghost, a being made entirely of energy?

"So," he said. "You can be touched after all."

Roth shot the staff in Liam's hand a malignant look. "That power won't protect you."

Liam gathered more energy into the staff. "We'll see about that."

"Liam!"

Zephyr's voice cut through the air, breaking his concentration. Liam looked over his shoulder and saw her standing in the doorway. The tip of her sword was pointed at Roth, her shield up and her eyes on him.

"Go on, Zeph," Liam said. "I can handle things here."

Zephyr looked conflicted. "But—"

"Kesi's still out there. I need you to protect Arian. Besides"—he looked back at Roth—"this is my fight."

Still, Zephyr hesitated, keeping her blade pointed into the room. Liam let out a hiss of frustration, summoning a wall of light between him and Roth. He looked back over his shoulder at her.

"Zeph," he said, meeting her eyes. "*Please.*"

Zephyr looked at him, all their history written in her eyes. Then she bowed her head, turning away.

"Be safe," she said, taking off at a run.

Roth had stayed still throughout the exchange. He turned toward Liam when Zephyr left.

"That was foolish," he said. "Had she stayed, she may have saved you the risk of losing yourself."

"I don't care," Liam said. "This is our fight, and this is where it ends."

"Very well," said Roth, sinking into a stance and raising his sword. "We'll see about that."

CHAPTER 63

ZEPHYR

THE SOUND OF BATTLE FOLLOWED ZEPHYR AS SHE RAN BACK through the halls, a silent accusation. She gritted her teeth against the sound of the clash, making her way back to the first floor.

She was alone. After getting the gist of the situation from her contingent when she arrived, she'd sent them below to guard the Bastion and attempt to stall the revolutionaries. Her father had already gone on, searching the upper stories. Selwald was in the tower somewhere, and Leon Albrent was nowhere to be found.

Albrent being missing worried her. Liam had warned her that he had been sighted in the city, near one of the outposts where the military had been inciting revolution. That alone told Zephyr that he was likely involved. Albrent had made his disdain for all things Leithonian very clear, and never went farther into the city than the Imperial Quarter if he could help it. But she couldn't worry about him now. Her father had told her to be the rear guard, to protect against any unexpected interferences.

Liam had told her to protect his sister.

Zephyr took the steps two at a time, her armor clanking as she ran back toward the entrance. Arian would be arriving soon, revolution be damned. Zephyr had to be there when she came.

Selwald stopped her on the second floor, his saber drawn. Zephyr raised her shield, facing him. There was a storm in his eyes. He didn't seem at all surprised to see her there, wearing her family's armor.

"There better be a good reason why you're here out of uniform, Venari."

Zephyr had spent the last year obeying him. The thought of doing so now made her want to choke. She sank into a stance, raising sword and shield.

"I won't let you destroy this city. *Sir*."

Selwald's brow furrowed in confusion. "What are you talking about, Lieutenant?"

For a moment, Zephyr faltered. But no, no. *Someone* had started the revolution. It had to be Selwald. She couldn't be wrong.

"Your revolution. You think I didn't know what you were doing? I knew that you were sending your men out into the streets, that you were inciting rebellion. You've been after Kaolin's position from the beginning."

"Is *that* what he told you?" Selwald asked. "Once again, Venari, your inability to think things through astounds me. What could I possibly gain from starting a revolution?"

Zephyr hesitated. Selwald sounded genuine—but no, she was sure, wasn't she? She understood what was happening here? It had all made sense at one point.

"You . . . you want to destabilize the transfer of power," she said. "To keep Leithon under martial law. That's what you want, isn't it?"

"You think I want to rule this city?" Selwald asked. "I've been trying to *save* this city. Contrary to what you may think, I don't wish Leithon any more harm. Would I put you in command of an entire contingent if I did? *You?*"

Zephyr hesitated, lowering her shield a fraction. She kept her sword pointed at Selwald, but with less conviction. "But *someone* from the Imperial army has been starting this revolution. If it wasn't you . . . then who?"

Selwald paused. "To be honest, I thought it was you."

"Me? I wouldn't . . ."

Selwald looked around the room, his eyes finally landing on

her. He spoke slowly, weighing each word. "Where is Lieutenant Albrent right now?"

Albrent.

Zephyr's gaze drifted to the endless staircase behind her. "Missing," she said. "He's—missing."

"Damn it," Selwald swore.

In the end, it was the vehemence in his voice that convinced her. Zephyr sheathed her sword, lowering her shield.

"What . . . makes you think it was Al—Lieutenant Albrent, sir?" she asked.

"You weren't the only one sneaking around behind my back, Venari," Selwald said, running a tired hand over his face. "It had to be you or Albrent. I knew you weren't working together—oil and water get along better than the two of you. I had you both watched, but that didn't clear anything up. You were running off to see Kaolin Eismor every second you had, and *he* was spending all his free time with Emeric Roth."

Emeric Roth. Kaolin would never have suspected someone so close to home, but in the end—

In the end, everything had come down to him. To Kesi.

Zephyr turned, offering a hand toward Selwald.

"It appears as though I owe you an apology, Commander."

Selwald glanced at the offered hand, then shook his head. "Save your apologies for later. Tell me what's happening now."

"There's some sort of spirit possessing Lord Kaolin. We—my associates and I—think that it's behind this whole thing. As near as we can figure, Emeric Roth is its creature. Leon Albrent too, I suppose."

Selwald listened with a soldier's stoicism, waiting until she reached the end.

"So, what you're telling me," he said, "is that unless we stop this— this demon, his plans endanger both Leithon and the Empire."

"Yes. That's the gist of it."

"Then I suggest we call a temporary truce."

Zephyr nodded. "My father is somewhere in the tower, search-ing for a way to stop its rise. He might need help."

"I'll join him, then," Selwald said. "I've heard of Lord Venari's skill. But after this, Lieutenant, you and I will be having words."

"Fair enough, Commander," Zephyr said. She hesitated, then raised her right hand in salute. "Good luck."

Selwald nodded, turning to leave. Zephyr drew in a deep breath, watching him disappear up the staircase. Her mind was spinning. Selwald was on her side. Liam and Roth were still dueling, and the city had turned itself completely on its head.

And she still had to find Arian. One step at a time.

CHAPTER 64

CAVAR

ZEPHYR MET THEM AT THE BASE OF THE STAIRS LEADING UP THE tower. Arian wasn't happy to learn that they would be working with Commander Selwald and was even less happy that Liam had run off on his own, but she gestured for them to follow her up the stairs, leading the way.

Arian followed a trail that only she could see. Occasionally, she would stop, look from left to right before making a decision, and then lead them down another blank, empty hallway up a different set of stairs. Cavar followed, keeping pace with Zephyr, who had her shield and sword ready in case of trouble.

He lost count of how many floors they climbed. The scenery was confusing, an endless repetition of the same elements, and the only clue he had that they were climbing higher was the view from the windows. But he got the sense that this tower was close in height to the Spire, and that they were nearing the top.

Arian stopped in the center of a wide hallway near the top floor, drawing her knives. Cavar did the same with his weapons, watching as Arian circled, looking for the source of whatever she was feeling.

"Arian?" Zephyr asked.

"We're close," Arian said. "Very close. He's here somewhere, on this floor."

"Which way?"

Arian closed her eyes, then gestured down a nearby hallway. "That way. Get ready."

Zephyr nodded, raising her shield. "I'll lead the way."

They moved down the hallway in that new configuration, Zephyr first, Arian in the middle, Cavar bringing up the rear. Cavar expected an attack to come at any time, was ready for it, but nothing happened. The three of them made their way down the hall without incident, stopping where the hallway widened into yet another stairwell.

Arian turned to the stairs, considering them, then shook her head. Her eyes landed instead on a small door just past them, practically hidden in the shadows of the hall.

"He's in there," she said. "I'm sure of it."

Zephyr nodded, approaching the door. Without preamble, she kicked it in. It splintered beneath her boot, and Cavar heard the snap of something breaking behind it. The three of them entered the room.

Kaolin was waiting.

The room was circular, and unlike the spartan, repetitious design of the hallway, it looked comfortable. The carpet was soft beneath Cavar's shoes, and there were bookshelves stacked against the wall, full almost to bursting. Beside him, he heard Zephyr take in a breath, as if she recognized the room. But they didn't have time to dwell on it, because Kaolin was moving.

He turned to face them the second they walked in through the door, wearing an expression that Cavar had never seen on the young lord's face. His eyes shone with power, the Star hanging from a chain at his throat as he launched himself at Arian.

Arian was ready for him. An answering wave of power rose up around her, a shield against his sword. Their powers clashed, the air crackling with electricity as Arian dropped her weight low, moving one of her knives in a slicing motion across Kaolin's chest, the other stabbing just beneath the first, aimed at his gut.

Kaolin avoided both of the strikes with a Weaver's easy grace. When Zephyr stepped in, bringing her sword down overhead, Kaolin stepped to the side, sweeping an armored hand along the flat of the blade and knocking it away.

Cavar darted in just as Kaolin pulled away from Zephyr. He tried for a feint, making as though he was going to slash at Kaolin's torso. At the last moment, he flipped the knives over in his hand, bringing the hilt of one down from overhead. He brought the other knife in from the side, aiming for a pressure point just below Kaolin's neck.

Kaolin stepped back, moving sinuously out of the way. Cavar had seen the young lord spar before, but he had never moved like this. He drew his sword from its scabbard in one smooth motion, balancing the rapier in one hand, and swept the sword in an arc in front of him, forcing the three of them back. Kaolin danced backward, leveling the point at Cavar.

"Nonlethal attacks, Weaver?" he asked, his voice dripping with scorn in a way that Kaolin's never had. "You betray your heritage. Have you actually grown attached to this young lord?"

"Possibly," Cavar said. "But I'm not the one you need to worry about."

Zephyr rushed in, slashing at him from above. Kaolin stepped neatly away from her, deflecting her incoming slash with a flick of his wrist. He ducked away, aiming a powerful kick at her left side where her armor was weakest. The blow connected and Zephyr gasped, turning away from the force. Kaolin's hand swept up, a shield of magical energy rising with it and catching Arian's blades in midair.

Arian glared at Kaolin from over her crossed blades, seething. He met her gaze, smirking.

"You're a pup snapping at your master's heels. A pity you've gone so long untrained. Such a waste of potential. But my cousin isn't exactly the paternal sort, is he?"

Cavar circled around before Arian could respond, searching for an opening. It was difficult. The three of them were looking for ways to incapacitate him without hurting him seriously, and Kaolin had no such qualms about hurting them. In some ways, the creature inside him was right. Cavar *should* have been trying to kill him. Every second they held back against him made Kesi stronger, and made them weaker. They would only grow wearier as the fight dragged on.

But if Kaolin died here, the Empire would retaliate with fire and fury. And Leithon's path to freedom would become that much harder.

He wasn't supposed to care about Leithon being free. He was a neutral observer until he was ordered to be otherwise. That was the path he walked, the story he'd woven for himself. But with every second that he fought, he knew that wasn't his real truth. That was the story his mother had told him, but it wasn't *his story*.

What he wanted for himself was—

He didn't have time to think. Kaolin held up his other hand, pointing the sword at Cavar. A bolt of power erupted from the blade, forcing Cavar to abandon his attack and leap away. Kaolin kept his eyes on Arian, who glowered at him.

"Don't talk about my father that way."

"The pup has teeth," he said. "But tell me this, child." He pushed Arian back, energy crackling behind his hand. Power swept her off her feet, slamming her into the wall. It held her there, encircling her throat when she struggled to break free. "If my cousin is so worthy of your defense, why isn't he here?"

Zephyr charged at him, yelling a battle cry. Kaolin swept his sword through the air, keeping his other hand stretched toward Arian. A barrier spread outward from him, halting Zephyr's charge.

Cavar used that as his opening. He ran toward Kaolin, pulling a glass flask from his pouch and tossing it at the ground between them. It exploded, letting out a puff of smoke that blanketed the area. At the same time, he slashed at Kaolin's outstretched arm.

Kaolin hissed in annoyance, leaping back. The spell restraining Arian fell apart, and she dropped onto all fours on the ground, gasping for breath. Cavar slashed one more time at Kaolin's midsection, forcing him back, then ran to Arian's side. He grabbed hold of her forearm, helping her to her feet.

"Are you all right?"

"Fine," said Arian, coughing. "Watch out, he's coming again."

A searing blast tore through the smokescreen, barreling toward them like a battering ram. Behind it, Cavar caught a flash of blue light, a glimpse of Kaolin's face contorted in rage. It was too fast, too powerful to dodge. He glanced at Arian, and in the split second before the attack hit, he made his decision.

He dropped his weight and grabbed her by the shoulder, using all his strength to throw her to the side. He saw her eyes widen in surprise, heard her gasp as she was thrown out of the way. He heard Arian scream his name.

And then the blast struck him head-on, tearing into him with all the force and fury of a storm, and the world went black.

CHAPTER 65

LIAM

ROTH OPENED WITH A POWERFUL STRIKE, A MELDING OF AIR AND lightning that shot toward Liam like a sword forged from the ether itself. Expecting this, Liam slammed the end of his staff onto the ground. A sound like a ringing bell erupted from the contact, a domed shield forming in the air over his head. The bolt slammed into it, the shield hissing and sparking across its surface at the contact. Liam clenched his jaw against the force of the attack, pouring all he had into his defense.

It would be easy to say that the attack had been a show of brute force, but Liam was too skilled a mage to assume that. He'd felt the delicacy woven into the spell, the artistry involved in tying together so many distinct energies into a single blade. It was a reminder that the person he was fighting, dead or alive, was a master of his craft, a true worker of the arcane arts.

It should have terrified him. Instead, Liam was surprised to find something inside him reveling in the challenge.

How long had it been since he had had a real mage to test his skills against? Too long. Roth was right. In some ways, the will that had led him to the Arcanum was irrelevant. The Arcanum had fallen by Roth's hand. And Liam was finally, *finally* avenging it.

It was a glorious feeling.

He held up his shield, pouring his will and power into it. In his other hand, Liam gathered up energy. He studied Roth, waiting for his opening.

The chance came when Roth's attack began to die down, in the instant before the assault let up completely.

Liam closed his hand into a fist, releasing the power he had gathered. The shield exploded, pushing the last remnants of Roth's attack away from him, then shattered, revealing Liam's counterattack. Blades of air rushed toward Roth, points leveled at him. Roth blocked two of the shards with his sword, then turned to deal with Liam, who stepped forward, thrusting his staff at Roth's gut.

Runes flared along the side of the staff as Roth stepped to the side, parrying the blow. As he did, a third shard struck him in the back. Roth let out a soft gasp, the blow knocking him off his feet. Liam pivoted in place, about to bring the staff down over Roth's head, but Roth held his hand out as he fell, a ribbon of fire streaming from his fingertips and rushing toward Liam.

Liam threw up his hands, channeling his power into the formation of another shield. The fire struck the shield, and he felt the heat of it cutting through the staff's ever-present cold. He sucked in a breath as he was thrown back, sliding across the stone floor.

The end of his staff dragged across the ground, a line of white fire springing up between him and Roth. Roth stepped nimbly around it as he moved toward Liam, his sword still upraised and his free hand crackling with power. Liam traced a circle into the ground around himself, energy flaring up like a wall and shielding him from magic. He raised his other hand, calling the last two shards that had broken off from the shield to rush toward Roth, their edges sharpening into thin blades.

Roth shot the shards an annoyed glare and raised his hand, firing off the power that he had stored in it. The blast slammed into the shards and tore them apart, blades shattering like fine glass. Shadows surged up around him and he vanished, disappearing from sight.

At first, Liam thought that Roth had run away, but he could still sense him there, somewhere in the room, hidden from view. He scowled in frustration and raised his hand, channeling power into his fingertips. The air above him crackled with static, electricity arcing from one corner of the room to another. Lightning bolts crashed down from overhead, searing every portion of the room apart from the single circle that Liam had marked for himself. In the barrage, he thought he caught sight of a figure darting from one spot to another, avoiding the lightning. He stretched his arm out toward the leaping figure, and light and power coalesced into a single blast, a line of energy fired not at Roth but at the space he was leaping into.

The blast sliced through the shadow, boring a hole into the stone of the far wall. And Liam sensed a presence behind him.

A silver sword sliced through Liam's shield just as he began to turn. The sword flashed, blood splattering onto the stone floor.

Pain erupted from Liam's forearm down to his side. He leaped back out of the circle, gritting his teeth. The onslaught of lightning stopped. Liam landed crouched on the ground, his free hand gripping his wounded arm, his eyes narrowed in anger and pain. Roth stared at him, expression impassive, his eyes moving from Liam to the blood on his sword.

Liam wondered if Roth was thinking the same thing he was, if he recognized that this was exactly the position Catherina Athensor had been in when he murdered her.

When he killed her, and Liam watched.

When Liam hadn't been in a position to do anything other than watch.

He felt that anger rush through him now, that helplessness and despair that had come over him as he watched the Arcanum fall. He remembered the rage he'd felt when he learned what Zephyr had done at the Bastion, the hatred that burned inside him, festering, with each sight of an Imperial banner. The pain.

He poured all those emotions into his staff, feeling the runes flare to life across the staff's surface. As Roth stared him down, Liam stabbed the staff down onto the ground, onto the blood on the floor.

A sacrifice.

Power flared, lines of light flowing through the pattern that had been etched into the surface by the lightning strikes.

The circle of unmaking rose around them, filling the whole room except for the circle around Liam's feet. The light held Roth in place, and for the first time since they had begun this duel, Liam thought he saw a flicker of fear in the wight's eyes.

"Where did you learn to do this?" he asked, staring at Liam. "How?"

"How doesn't matter," Liam said, breathing hard as he used the staff to help him push himself upright. "It's over."

"It will destroy you," Roth said. "This will break you. You don't understand what you're doing."

Liam paused, his hand upraised. There was truth in Roth's words. He knew that. But he had other truths.

He had been broken long ago.

Liam reached out, swiping his hand through the air. The circle flared up, a blaze of light, and Roth screamed. Energy consumed him, a light so bright it was blinding. There was a sharp crack like shattering glass, and then Roth *unraveled*.

It was beautiful and terrifying at the same time. The circle's power washed over him, and before he could scream, he came apart into motes of light, a steady stream of power that swirled and raged in the circle, angry at its confinement. And when Liam touched his bloodied hand to the edge of the circle and broke it, all that power and light flowed into him. Everything that Emeric Roth had been.

He sucked in a breath at the force and fury of it, pressing his hand back to his wound. Energy flowed through his fingertips, life in the face of death, and he felt skin and sinew knit itself back together. There was so much of it—it was hard to contain. He had never been filled with so much power before—power without a purpose. It was raging inside him, jostling for space with the parts of himself that made him who he was, and it felt like he was being ripped apart from the inside out.

The staff fell from his hand, clattering to the floor. Liam dropped to a knee, taking in sharp breaths.

He couldn't stop here, he thought, looking around at the room. He had to find Arian.

Slowly, laboriously, he pulled himself to his feet.

CHAPTER 66

ARIAN

CAVAR WENT DOWN.

Arian saw it as if it were happening in a dream. One moment she was being thrown into the air, and years of training were moving her body for her, turning her fall into a controlled roll. The next, she was rising from the ground, looking back to see all of Kesi's energies pouring into Cavar. He jerked in place like a puppet on strings, then fell to the ground, silent and still. She didn't know if he was alive.

Time stopped. In that moment, Arian was on the rooftop paths again, watching the Arcanum collapse. She sucked in a breath, looking up at Kaolin. She was so tired, so *tired* of seeing people get hurt for her. Of seeing people die for her.

She drew herself steadily to her feet.

All the power that she had been gathering rippled outward from her, a flare of bright light that emanated from her skin. Kaolin turned toward her as the power erupted.

"I see you've awakened, Speaker," he said.

Arian didn't know if she had awakened or not. But she did know this: She wasn't going to be running this time. This time, she let out a shout of rage, raising her hand. The blast of light that poured from her cut through the air, the resulting gale tearing books from their shelves and throwing them to the ground. Kaolin raised a hand to block it, but whatever paltry shield he was forming wasn't enough. The power struck him, sweeping him off his feet and slamming him into the far wall hard enough to crack stone. She kept her hand raised toward him, holding him there, then ran to check on Cavar.

Cavar was lying on his stomach, head pressed down onto the

carpet. She rolled him over onto his back, checking for a pulse. It was there. Weak, but there. When she held her hand in front of his face, she could feel his breath. He was in bad shape, but alive. She fought off a dizzying wave of relief. With her other hand, Arian peeled off a portion of her power, weaving it into a shield around him. Then she stepped out from behind that shield, walking toward Kaolin.

Zephyr was standing as well, ready for more. Arian watched as Kaolin struggled against the forces that pinned him to the wall, felt the strain against her mind. She looked over at Zephyr.

"Hey, Zeph."

Zephyr looked over, head cocked to the side.

"You still want to save your lordling?"

"What do you have in mind?" Zephyr asked.

"Deal with the Star," Arian said, tilting her head toward Kaolin. "I'll deal with him."

Zephyr nodded, sinking down into an attacker's stance. As she charged at Kaolin, sword flashing, Arian summoned power into her hand, waiting for her opening. She didn't have the same finesse that Liam had, the same ability to weave magic into the air, the stones, to turn power into fire or water or lightning. But the basics, the ability to call power into her hand, to take it into herself?

Well, she could do that just fine.

She breathed the power in, letting it flow beneath her skin until it filled her. When she launched herself toward Kaolin again, it was with inhuman speed, catching him off guard as he threw off the remnants of her shield, rolling out of the way of Zephyr's attack.

Kaolin raised his free hand, pointing it at the ground and firing off a concussive blast. The blast threw both Arian and Zephyr back. Zephyr slid across the ground, her shield raised over her head to protect her from debris as Arian rolled, landing neatly on her feet.

She poured power into one of her knives, infusing it with strength before flinging it underhand at Kaolin. A rope of white light connected the hilt to her hand as it shot toward him like an arrow. Kaolin jerked his head to the side to avoid the blow, the blade embedding itself in the wall and cracking the stone around it as it released its contained force. Arian tugged on the cord, bringing it back into her hand.

In the end, it had been fear that had driven her away from the Arcanum.

Fear of herself, of the power she had been chosen to bear. She thought that by running away, by joining the underground, she was giving it up. That the power would see that she wasn't worthy and choose someone else. Someone like Liam, someone who wanted it.

But it didn't work that way. The Arcanum had chosen her for a reason, and though Arian didn't understand what that was, she wasn't going to run away anymore.

It was time.

As Kaolin dodged the first blow, she flung her second hand out toward him, her knife pointed at his chest. Kaolin's eyes narrowed, and he raised his sword hand, the jewel at his throat gleaming as he called upon the power stored inside it. A shield formed in the air between him and Arian, catching the blade and holding it there.

Zephyr pressed the attack, coming at him from the side, sword arm extended over her head. She brought it down in one swift movement, and though Kaolin tried to call up a second shield to protect his unguarded side, it wasn't enough. The sword sliced through the thin barrier like paper, the backlash from the spell throwing Kaolin back.

Blood stained Kaolin's fine clothes, a shallow cut, not lethal but undoubtedly painful. He winced as he stepped away from Zephyr, the shield between him and Arian faltering. The dagger pierced it, but Kaolin dodged with ease as it rushed at him, bringing his sword up to bear and deflecting Zephyr's next cut with a quick movement.

Zephyr's sword and shield were in perfect harmony as she tore through his defenses, moving closer to him. She was *good*. Zephyr fought like artistry in motion. But he was good too. Arian could see in him not only Kaolin's training, but the training of the Weavers, the same movements that she had seen in Linna, in Cavar. In her father.

Zephyr stepped inside Kaolin's guard, knocking his sword away from her. The tip of her sword sliced the Star from its chain. Arian leaped forward, grabbing the falling jewel out of the air with both hands.

The Star in her hands flared.

Arian's world faded into light.

CHAPTER 67

ARIAN

LIGHT CONSUMED HER THE SECOND HER FINGERS CLOSED AROUND the Star, pulling her in. One moment she was making a flying leap for the jewel. The next, she was standing alone in a brightly lit void, on a crystal floor. Light refracted off the patterns beneath her feet, hurting her eyes. She averted her gaze, trying to make sense of the rest of the world.

There was no ceiling, no sky, no walls, only power, eddies and currents that brushed against her skin and her consciousness.

And she wasn't alone.

Kesi stood in front of her—not Kesi-in-Kaolin, but the man himself.

Looking at him, she could see the resemblance to her father. It was faint but there, hidden in the shape of his jaw, the look in his eyes, the way he carried himself.

It was an uncomfortable realization. In many ways, Kesi was responsible for the destruction of her family. For everything that had happened to her mother, and for what he had done to relatives unknown.

He smirked, standing across from her in the void.

"After all of that trouble I went through to find you, you've come to me willingly," he said. The corner of his mouth quirked. "Do you know where we are?"

Arian didn't need to look around to answer the question. She could feel the truth inside her, the steady pulse of power in her veins. It tugged at her, trying to unravel everything she was, trying to consume her.

"We're inside the Star."

"The seat of my power," said Kesi. "I'm sorry to say this, but you can never leave."

"Why not?" Arian asked. "What do you want with me?"

"You specifically? Not much. But I need the power in your bloodline. I *am* sorry it had to be this way. It's for the greater good."

"The *greater good*? You killed your whole clan and attacked my city, and you're telling me it was for the *greater good*?"

"There are things in the world that are more powerful than you can ever imagine. To stand against them, the world needs to be *united*. But I don't expect you to understand. You're just a child, after all, with a child's powers. I don't need to explain myself to you. This will all be over soon."

"We'll see about that," Arian said.

She let the magic she had borrowed from the Arcanum fly free, its power forming a shield around her that pushed the questing forces of the Star back. Without that power prodding at her, looking for an opening, Arian found that she was able to breathe, to turn her attention onto Kesi. He watched her, unconcerned.

"You've come into power you are in no way ready for," he said. "I have the experience of decades. That power rightfully belongs to me."

"It chose me," Arian said.

"It chose *wrong*. This isn't the time for children's games. I'm the one—the *only* one strong enough to do what has to be done. And once I finish with you, I'll deal with your brother."

There was a flash, and then he was gone. Arian had only a moment to process his disappearance. Before she could even begin to look for him, he was there, in front of her, his hand crackling with power. An invisible force slammed into her jaw, hard as any punch she had ever taken, and knocked her off her feet. She hit the ground hard, slapping at it to disperse some of the energy, and pushed herself up to her feet, jaw throbbing in pain.

"You stay *away* from my brother," she said.

Kesi's brows arched. "Or what?"

He held both his hands out, sending a wave of power at her. Arian called up the energies of the Arcanum, a shield falling into place between her and him. Kesi's attack struck the shield and shattered it, slamming into her chest. The blow knocked the wind out of her, and Arian let out a strangled cry as she was thrown back.

Kesi appeared in front of her before she could fall, casually shifting his weight. He kicked her across the face before she could defend herself and Arian coughed as she fell onto the ground, tasting blood in her mouth.

He stepped forward, hand threading through her hair. Kesi gripped it tightly and pulled, raising her head to meet his eyes. In his gaze, Arian saw a lust for power that could not be quelled. All resemblance to her father vanished. She glared at him, a gesture made significantly less effective by the trickle of blood coming from her split lip.

"You have spirit," Kesi said. "I'll grant you that. But this is *my* domain. You can't win against me here."

A void opened behind him, a swirling vortex of shadow. Inside it, Arian heard whispers, voices. A hundred voices, a thousand. She felt a chill as the sound washed over her, her eyes widening in fear.

Energy crackled into her hand, and she thrust it at him, trying to force him to let her go. Kesi swatted the blow aside with his free hand, supremely unconcerned, and tilted her head back farther, baring her throat to him.

Arian bit down on the gasp of pain that threatened to escape her, glaring at Kesi. He ignored her.

"Oh, Rinu doesn't know the prize that he brought me," Kesi said, smiling at her. "The Speaker of the Arcanum, with eth'Akari blood. With you, I could do anything. I wouldn't even need your father, or that brother of yours. I could have the world."

A snarl bubbled up in Arian's throat, the floor around her erupting in white light. Kesi slammed his foot down onto the ground and the light guttered, darkness strangling it until it was gone. He reached down and grabbed her arm, using it and his hold on her hair to haul her to her feet.

"Come," he said, turning her toward the void. "It's time to meet the rest of the family."

Arian struggled, tears prickling at her eyes as she pulled a few strands of hair free, but Kesi held fast. He shoved her forward, urging her toward the portal. She tried to fight back but found that she wasn't strong enough to resist him.

Was this the limit of her strength?

Was this all the power she had? Was this as far as she would ever go?

Was this the end?

No.

She clenched her hands into fists and dug her heels into the ground, fighting against his power. Light flared to life on her arms, on her legs, tracing patterns onto her skin.

Kesi pushed on her arm, trying to shove her into the portal. Arian rallied all her strength to bear against him, holding her ground. She threw back her head, letting out a loud cry.

Power surged toward her, energy flooding her veins. The sudden force of it was immense, threatening to overwhelm her. She didn't know where it had come from, but the power flooded through her now, bringing with it a renewed sense of purpose. And in that power, she felt a presence.

It was someone she knew very well. Someone dear to her heart. Someone precious and familiar.

Her mother's energy, stored in the Star for so many years, flowed through her. She felt it wrap around her like an embrace, felt its power drive Kesi's influence back from her and lift her off the ground. Kesi stumbled away from her, arm upraised against the light. She turned to face him and for the first time, Kesi looked uncertain. Afraid.

"No," he said. "That power is mine. How did you—?"

Arian felt her mother's power sink into her skin, into her veins. Her mother's will. She understood. Kesi had thought that the magic in the Star was just that, power for the taking, but it *wasn't*. Magic had a will, a mind, a heart. And that heart had chosen her.

Power erupted from her skin like fire. She stretched her other hand out, holding it toward the portal, and felt something else. The pull of her blood, the blood that flowed through her veins. The power and will of eth'Akari.

Her family, calling her home.

She breathed deep, inhaling that power into herself. The portal began to break down into black smoke, winding its way up her arm and into the center of her power. Arian breathed it in and felt, for the first time, complete. Alive.

She looked into Kesi's eyes.

"You don't know what you're doing," Kesi said. "Leithon *needs* the Empire's guidance, or the whole world will fall. You'll doom us all."

Arian clenched her left hand into a fist, so tight that she could feel the impression of her fingernails in her palm. Any thought she might have had of listening to him vanished with those words, replaced by a storm and fury inside her that she couldn't ignore. She was tired, so tired of *other people* telling her what was best for her, but she was also tired of people telling her what was best for her city.

Her city deserved to be free.

And so did she.

"I think we can guide ourselves just fine," Arian said.

She raised her other hand.

CHAPTER 68

LIAM

IT TOOK LIAM A WHILE TO FIND ARIAN AND THE OTHERS, MOSTLY because his head wouldn't stop spinning. He'd never tried the unmaking circle with anything more powerful than an inanimate object. The spell had worked as intended, supplementing Liam's stores of energy with Roth's and healing his injuries, but the mental toll was an entirely different story.

He was assaulted by emotions. Sentiments, memories, and *thoughts* that had never once belonged to him. Roth was gone, but whatever was left of Roth was inside him now, and as he made his way from the room where he had fought Roth and up the never-ending flight of stairs, he had to stop to remind himself where Emeric Roth ended and Liam Athensor began.

He had never been a child in the Empire's far reaches, never an awkward adolescent in Imperial mage training. There had never been a lover in his life with hair like fire, or a dark-haired man in the starlit wilderness who had brought him back from darkness and promised him the world. And he had never wanted to destroy the Arcanum. Not once.

He'd never felt fear like this, weighing down on his heart, surrounding him from all sides, making it hard to breathe. He didn't know if that was Roth's fear or just a side effect from the spell, but he felt like he was drowning in it. If it was Roth's, he wondered what Roth had been so afraid of, but the memories flew through his mind so fast that he could only see fragments of them. Something in the Wastes—something dark and terrible. Something hidden, something *hungry*.

He shuddered, coming to a stop and resting his hand on the wall.

The memory was so strong that he was nearly sick. He brushed his hand over the rough stone to calm himself—once, twice, three times. He let out a breath and opened his eyes.

Part of him wished that he had never completed the spell, that he had dealt with Roth some other way. The other part of him wondered what would happen if he turned that same power onto Kesi. If absorbing Roth had healed his wounds, had made his body and his magic feel this strong and powerful, what would it be like to consume a being that had been gorging itself on power for more than two decades? It was tempting, so very tempting to find out.

That told him a lot about the kind of person he was.

Never again, he told himself. Never again.

He breathed deep, pushing back the fear and Roth's memories, centering himself. When he felt collected enough, he started moving.

He didn't have any difficulty finding Arian. It would almost be impossible not to find her, with all the power she was expending. He followed the trail of that power, stopping in the doorway to a room.

The room looked as though it must have once been a comfortable study, but books had been thrown from the walls, paintings knocked to the ground and glass smashed and broken. Two figures lay sprawled out on the carpet. One of them, a magical barrier still crackling around him, was Cavar. The other was Lord Kaolin.

Zephyr turned to face him, still dressed in her armor. From the stiff way she was moving, he guessed that she had been injured. There was no sign of Arian.

"What happened?" Zephyr asked. "You're covered in blood."

Liam hesitated, touching two fingers to the tear in his clothes. The skin beneath was pale and new, as if the injury had never happened. He shook his head. "It's a long story. What happened here? Where's your father and Arian?"

"Father is with Selwald," Zephyr said. "They're trying to evacuate the tower. We separated the Star from Kesi, but the tower hasn't stopped growing, and Kaolin hasn't woken up."

Liam stared at her, confused. He understood all those words, but the order she had placed them in didn't make sense. He drew in a breath.

"I think you need to start from the beginning."

CHAPTER 69

ARIAN

THERE WAS SOMETHING TO BE SAID FOR POWER.

The feel of it in her hands, in her being, was intoxicating. She'd never held so much power in her life, and standing there, winding light and darkness into herself, melding Arcanum and eth'Akari together, she felt as though she had transcended humanity.

She understood, in that moment, how power could corrupt.

But it had never been in Arian's nature to seek power. She'd never wanted to be *powerful*, only to be *strong*. Strong enough that she would never have to lose anyone again. Strong enough that she would never have to feel hurt or scared or broken again.

She didn't want power. She had, in her childhood, been offered power that most people could only dream of and had run away.

She'd spent so much of her life running.

She'd never wanted power, but maybe that was why the power was so insistent on giving itself to her. Maybe that was why she was the person who had been chosen to bear it.

She focused on Kesi. As the former Weaver shrank back, scrambling across the crystal surface of the Star, she advanced, bringing all the power in her to bear. Eth'Akari voices screaming for revenge merged with the raw elemental force of the Arcanum, tempered into one stream. She let that power flow from her, the warm light expanding to fill the space. With it, her awareness also expanded, weaving itself into the fabric of the world around her.

She could feel Kesi there, a stubborn thorn in the fabric of reality, a relic that refused to be erased. And she could feel all Kesi's pain, his desire, everything that he had ever done that had led him to this point. She could feel the child he had been, alone and unwanted, dreaming of the day when he would do something great. And she could see something else in his memories, a dark heart in the center of the Wastes, trembling and pulsing with power. In his memories, she saw clearly what it was. A counterpoint to the Arcanum, the energies of destruction instead of creation, a thing that should not have existed, and it was breaking free. Even the echo of memory sent chills up her spine, and she understood what Kesi had done. He had taken the power he'd stolen from eth'Akari and had used it to keep that darkness at bay.

But it was still stolen power. Stolen lives.

That didn't excuse anything.

Arian saw all that in an instant, a life encapsulated into a handful of moments.

And in that moment, she chose to bring things to an end.

She gathered the full weight of her power into her hands, weaving the borrowed power from eth'Akari and the fire that belonged to the Arcanum together. Arian wrapped both of those energies around Kesi and held tight, increasing the pressure against his presence. She felt him struggle, felt him writhe and stand against the tide, but he was powerless to stand against her. And as she pushed against him, Arian thought she could feel a multitude rising up on her left side, the side that faced eth'Akari. A multitude of souls crying out for rest, for vengeance.

On her right side, she felt a gentle touch, a hand resting lightly on her shoulder. Out of the corner of her eye, she thought she could make out the figure of a woman, robed and wreathed in light.

Arian leaned into that touch and pressed harder. She heard Kesi scream.

And then his presence contracted, invaded by light and life and power. It came apart at the seams, and Arian pulled at it until it unraveled. She took the threads of Kesi's life and tore them apart, reducing them down into their smallest pieces, atoms and air and dust, until all that was Kesi was flung headlong past the barrier of the mortal plane and into whatever lay after, a stain removed forever from the earth.

↓↓↓

AFTER KESI'S DEATH, THE STAR WAS QUIET. THE FLOOR WAS STILL crystalline, the white void still extending on into infinity. Without Kesi there, it was almost peaceful. Time stretched on, a handful of seconds becoming an eternity. Arian sat in the center of that void, feeling the power that Kesi had stolen slowly trickle away, everything settling back into place.

She'd done it. She'd won. She'd taken the Star back, defeated an evil that had plagued her family for years.

She'd avenged her mother.

But even as she sat there, she knew that it wasn't over. The Empire still held control of Leithon, and what Arian had done wouldn't change that. If she wanted to reclaim the Arcanum, if she wanted to take her home back, there was more to do.

And there was that thing that Kesi had feared, that dark power. As much as she hated to admit it, by taking his life, she had taken on his responsibility to do something about that destructive force. The thought made her head ache.

Arms wrapped around her shoulders, a familiar warmth. Arian leaned back into it, closing her eyes. She could feel the comfort that the embrace gave her. Could feel the peace it promised.

It would be so peaceful to remain. To stay inside the Star with the shadow of her mother. To let the Arcanum choose another Speaker—Liam, perhaps, finally. To let Leithon sort its problems out on its own.

But she knew she couldn't do that. And she knew that whatever was left of her mother didn't want her to do that either.

As if responding to her thoughts, a gate opened in front of her.

Arian opened her eyes, studying it. She raised her hand to touch it, and warmth wrapped around her. Her fingers brushed something that felt like the skin of an arm before they passed straight through, power humming and crackling around them.

The presence held tighter. Arian sucked in a breath.

"We're doing okay, Mom," she said, speaking into the void. "Liam and me. We don't always get along, but what can you do?" Her voice sounded thick to her. Arian blinked, willing tears not to fall. "I have some things I need to finish. But I'll come back sometime. Maybe I'll bring him with me."

One last touch from the presence, one last embrace. And then it withdrew, leaving Arian alone again.

She rose to her feet, squaring off against the portal. Arian braced herself and took a step forward.

Light swallowed her again.

CHAPTER 70

ZEPHYR

ZEPHYR MISSED THE EXACT MOMENT OF ARIAN'S RETURN.
Her eyes were on Kaolin, watching to see if he would wake first, to see who would be looking out from behind his eyes when he did. If it was Kesi, she would kill him. She decided that, and kept her sword at the ready, all her focus on him.

When Arian returned, the air filled with a blinding light. Zephyr turned toward it, watching as a figure formed out of the light, hovering in the air for a few moments before settling on the ground.

Arian, holding the Star. For a moment, she looked transformed. Then the light faded, its brilliance retreating into the depths of the Star, and she was just Arian again. Zephyr watched as she looked around, sighed, and extended a hand toward Cavar.

The barrier lifted, dissipating into fine mist. He didn't wake, but his chest rose and fell. Zephyr let out a breath of relief. He was still alive.

Arian checked his pulse, his breathing, and brushed his hair out of his face with a tenderness that Zephyr was sure she didn't mean for them to see. What she found there must have satisfied her, because she left him and walked over to the window, picking her way carefully across the wreckage of the room. As she reached it, a great shudder wracked the tower and the sense of motion Zephyr had been feeling since she stepped into the place stopped. Arian looked out the window and let out a sigh of relief.

"The tower's stopped growing," she said, looking back at them. "Whatever Kesi did is still leaking power, though. It will take a while to disperse."

"Can you fix it?" Liam asked, and Zephyr didn't miss the strain in his voice, the hint of jealousy. She refrained from pointing it out.

Arian shrugged. "Sure. Maybe. But we'll need to get everyone out of here before I try, unless you all *want* to be trapped under tons of falling rock. Fixing it isn't the problem, though. We've got a bigger issue on our hands."

"What?" Liam asked.

"That," said Arian, pointing at something out the window.

Zephyr frowned, exchanging a glance with Liam. She rose, approaching Arian. As soon as she reached the window, she understood what Arian meant. The revolution happening outside the city walls hadn't stopped. Instead, they had all gathered outside the barrier, waiting. Now that the barrier was down, they were flooding in, attacking the Bastion soldiers with whatever weapons they could get their hands on.

It was breathtaking to see. Terrifying, but breathtaking.

Arian swore under her breath.

"I told Lyndon to stop them. Not to organize them."

"We should be grateful they weren't throwing themselves against the barrier," Liam said. "They were going to revolt no matter what."

Arian sighed, running a hand through her hair. "Yeah. I was just kind of hoping they'd give me a little warning. It's been a long night." She gave the window one last dirty look before turning to Zephyr. "All right, so the citizenry is revolting. You planning on telling the Leithonian contingent to stand down?"

Zephyr hesitated, looking out the window. She couldn't see her father or Commander Selwald out there, but she knew they had been busy evacuating the Bastion. There was no way they couldn't know what was happening. And while their truce might have been enough to stop Kesi, it didn't extend to revolution. She could feel

Arian's and Liam's eyes on her, could feel the tension in the room mount with every second that passed without an answer.

And then a small cough broke the silence, all of them turning to face Kaolin. He had opened his eyes, his head turned toward Zephyr.

"Tell the contingent to stand down, Lieutenant," he said. "And bring Commander Selwald to me."

Kaolin started to rise.

"Stop," Liam said, holding out a hand toward him. Power crackled around his fingertips. Kaolin stopped, watching Liam carefully. "Kaolin or Kesi? Until I know which one you are, you're not moving."

"It's the lordling," Arian said, without looking back. "Kesi's gone. I'm sure of it."

Liam hesitated, his eyes on Kaolin. Slowly, reluctantly, he lowered his hand. Kaolin nodded, starting to stand. He stumbled once when his feet gave out from under him, but righted himself before Zephyr could catch him, waving her off. She stepped back, embarrassed and fully aware that Arian and Liam were watching her closely. The hurt in Liam's eyes made her stomach churn, but Zephyr tried not to think about it.

"Selwald?" she asked instead.

Kaolin nodded.

"I'm not entirely sure what happened while I was ... indisposed. But if the people have gotten to the point of revolution, that changes things." His eyes moved across the room, landing on Arian. "Does the Arcanum stand with Leithon?"

Arian snorted, resting her hands on her hips. "If you want the *traditional* answer, the Arcanum doesn't stand with anyone. But if you want my answer, screw tradition. The Arcanum stands with the city."

"Then we can't hope to win," said Kaolin. "Not as we are now. Aelria sealed its fate when it attacked the Arcanum. I'm not going to sacrifice good people in a losing battle. I'm surrendering the Bastion." He looked back at Zephyr. "Get me Selwald, Lieutenant. We'll finish this tonight."

Arian cocked her head to the side, frowning at him. "And you're okay with that?" she asked. "You're just . . . giving it all up?"

Kaolin sighed. He looked paler than Zephyr had ever seen him, and moved stiffly, as if his whole body hurt. But he raised his head and looked Arian in the eye regardless. "It was never mine. I've been trying to make the best of a bad situation, but . . ." He winced. "It has recently been made clear to me that I've not been myself. And I'm tired of dancing on someone else's strings."

He took a step, and then dropped to his knees, coughing. Blood flecked his lips, spilling onto his hands where he tried to cover his mouth. Zephyr dropped with him, alarmed, and placed a hand on his shoulder.

"Kaolin!" she said. "What's wrong?"

Arian took a step toward them, but before she could get there, Liam moved in. He pushed Zephyr's hand aside, hesitating for a second before pressing both his hands to Kaolin's back. Pale blue light washed over him, and Kaolin gasped, coughing harder.

"What are you doing?" Zephyr demanded, rounding on Liam.

"It's an aftereffect of the possession," Liam said, brow furrowed in concentration. "Kesi's been feeding off him, like a parasite. His life force is distorted. I'm trying to—to reset the balance—"

He stopped talking, turning away from her. His expression contorted with the effort—whatever was happening couldn't be good. The light of his power flickered alarmingly, and Kaolin took in a sharp breath.

Arian ran toward them, placing her hands over Liam's. The glow of Liam's magic stabilized, suffusing Kaolin's body with light. Kaolin's eyes fluttered closed, some of the tension leaving him.

"Get him on the ground," Arian told her brother. "It'll be easier to work from there." She turned to look at Zephyr, her lip twisting into a snarl. "Don't just stand there gawping like a fish! Get Selwald!"

Zephyr leaped to her feet, startled into action. The revolution, the city aflame. She tore her eyes from Arian and Liam and ran for the door.

CHAPTER 71

LIAM

HEALING WAS NOT LIAM'S STRENGTH.

In fact, that might have been an understatement. It would have been more accurate to say that healing was the one discipline of magic in which he had no ability at all. Before the collapse of the Arcanum, he'd barely been able to heal a paper cut. And that wasn't odd. Healing was a very specialized discipline of magic and even his mother, the Speaker of the Arcanum, hadn't been able to do much more than keep someone stable until the real healers came.

But Roth, surprisingly, had been a good healer. And the knowledge that Liam had absorbed from him allowed him to do what he never could have done before.

Keep Kaolin Eismor alive.

He wove that knowledge together with Arian's power, directing the flow of her magic into Kaolin's body, and prayed that it would be enough.

The irony struck him that he was pouring all this effort into saving the single largest threat to Leithon's independence. But with Kaolin dead, there was nothing stopping this from ending in slaughter. The Empire would retaliate, and Liam wasn't fool enough to think they could stand against Aelria, not the way they were now. They *needed* Kaolin to survive, if only so he could be a hostage. If only to buy them a little more time.

They needed him.

But Kaolin's body seemed determined to die. He was losing his grip on consciousness. Kesi's power had torn through him, tapping on reserves of life force that would have been too dangerous for

Kaolin—had he been a mage—to use on his own. Magic required fuel, and while Kesi had taken a lot of power from the Star, he'd not been shy about drawing from his host. Without the twins taking what was left of his life force, augmenting it with their own, and spreading it over his entire body, Kaolin would already be dead.

Liam and Arian were keeping him stable, but it took effort to hold him there, and he was still flirting with mortal danger when Zephyr returned, Commander Selwald and Lord Venari in tow.

Selwald surveyed the room, his eyes narrowed in rage as they took in the sight of Kaolin convulsing on the ground.

"What the hell is this, Lieutenant?" he asked.

"It's what I described, sir," Zephyr said. Her voice was admirably calm. Liam didn't think his would be under these circumstances. "Lord Kaolin expressed his desire to surrender the Bastion to prevent further bloodshed. Before any of us could act on his commands, he collapsed."

"And you expect me to believe that?" Selwald asked. "You expect me to order my troops to stand down and hand over the Bastion to that rabble on the word of a tr—"

"On the word of a lieutenant of your army, yes," said Zephyr. "We can't win. You can order them to, and you can order *me* to order them to, but the Leithonian contingent will not fight against their own. Not willingly, and not well."

"I don't think the Leithonian contingent is necessary in this case," Selwald said. "My soldiers are well trained. They can handle a band of rebels."

"Half the city is out there," Zephyr said. "How many Leithonians are you going to kill to keep your hold on this city?"

"You aren't among friends here, Commander," Kallan Venari added, quietly drawing his sword from his sheath.

Selwald glanced at the blade, unconcerned. "Kill me, Lord Venari, and you lose all hope of ending this struggle before it starts. Even if the citizenry takes the Bastion, the Empire won't be forgiving."

"You're forgetting something," said Arian softly.

All conversation stopped. Arian wasn't looking at Selwald, keeping her eyes on Kaolin, but even without looking, she commanded the attention of the room.

"The Arcanum isn't going to sit by and let Leithon be taken by the Empire a second time," she said.

Selwald stared at Arian like a man assessing a creature he had never seen before. It took him a moment before he spoke. "I mean no offense by this, Speaker," he said, his voice level. "But as far as I can tell, the Arcanum consists of only yourself."

"There's two of us here," said Arian, with a glance at Liam. "And we're the only ones keeping Lord Kaolin alive. You can put up a fight, but it won't be easy. You'll kill some rebels, but you'll lose more of your own. Is that what you want? Because that's exactly what Lord Kaolin wants to stop, and if you're going to go against his wishes, let me know now. I'm wasting a lot of time and energy keeping him alive."

Selwald's eyes moved to the fallen lord. His shoulders slumped in resignation. Liam held his breath, hardly daring to hope, but he thought they had him.

"What assurance do I have that your people won't simply slaughter mine once they get into the castle?" Selwald asked. "By this point, it would be expected."

"Because that's what the Empire would do?" Arian scoffed. "We aren't like you, Commander. Order all your people into the barracks and lock the door. Then strike the Imperial banner from the Bastion and have Zephyr's contingent open the gates. I'll keep your people safe. Well," she added, with a glance at Kaolin, "assuming Liam can take this from here."

Liam nodded. "I think I can. I'll go with him into the barracks. He might still need medical attention when I'm done." He frowned, glancing at Cavar. "Cavar too. Send someone who's used to dealing with injuries caused by magic."

"I can send a surgeon for Lord Kaolin," Selwald said. "But the success of this venture depends on me trusting your word. And I believe I'm justified in asking for a little more than that."

"My brother's going with you," said Arian. "That's proof enough. I give you my word as Speaker of the Arcanum that no one will get in through the barracks door until all this is settled."

"And then we'll be prisoners." Selwald frowned. "That's not exactly a tempting offer."

"What you'll be when this is settled depends entirely on how you behave now," said Arian. "We're running out of time to argue. Do we have a deal or not?"

Liam glanced at Arian, surprised by the change in his sister. It had been a while since he had seen her so confident, so sure of herself. And in that moment, he was certain that there was more to it than just the Speaker's power.

Arian didn't carry herself like a mage. She carried herself like a *leader*.

Selwald must have seen it too. He nodded, his hand falling away from his sword. "We have a deal. Before anything, I'll send someone for Lord Kaolin, and—" His mouth twisted with wry chagrin. "—the erstwhile Lord Nasirri. Once I have the two of them and your brother with us, I'll give the order. Venari, I trust you can handle yourself?"

Zephyr nodded. "I'll go round up the contingent. Once you give the order, I'll have them open the gates." Her lips contorted into an echo of the commander's expression. "The irony isn't lost on me."

"Let this be the last time you turn your coat," Selwald said. "I grow weary of trying to understand your allegiance."

"Yes, Commander," Zephyr said, nodding. She paused, then turned toward him, snapping off a smart Imperial salute. "I'll do what I can to make sure that none of you are harmed."

"Your concern is much appreciated," said Selwald dryly. "But I believe the good Speaker was right in this case. We don't have much time."

He turned on his heel, leaving the room. Liam resisted the urge to watch him go, focusing on Kaolin. He could sort through his feelings on the matter later. Everything would collapse if he couldn't keep Kaolin alive.

CHAPTER 72

LIAM

THE REVOLUTION LASTED THROUGHOUT THE NIGHT, CITIZENS
flooding the Bastion, burning every Imperial banner or painting
that they could get their hands on, all while cheering and singing
old Leithonian songs. It was a loud, crowded, messy affair, and
Liam was almost happy to be out of the way of it. True to Arian's
word, no one entered the barracks, and he stayed there with the
remnants of the Imperial military long after Kaolin had stabilized
and the young lord had been removed from his care. Cavar woke
sometime after midnight, and Liam used what was left of his energy
to strengthen him before falling into an uneasy sleep.

By the time someone came to let him and Cavar out of the
barracks, it was almost dawn. The light bathed the outer keep in
shades of violet and blue and gold, and Liam had to shade his eyes
with his hand. The brightness was such a stark contrast to the darkness and gloom of the barracks, the sudden wide view frightening
and all-consuming in comparison to the narrow focus he had had
for the past several hours.

But it was glorious.

The Imperial banners were now a smoldering pile of ash and
embers in a corner of the keep. The gates had been thrown wide
open, and Leithonians from all walks of life were now moving
through the Bastion, laughing and cheering. Someone had broken into the kitchens and rolled out a few barrels of Aelrian wine,
which no one seemed at all shy about tapping into. There was not
an Imperial uniform in sight, and some of the Leithonian contingent had dug up their old blue-and-gold uniforms, wearing
them proudly as they paced the Bastion. He didn't spot any of the

Resistance members he knew, but he had a feeling they were out there somewhere, leading celebrations of their own or otherwise keeping the peace.

It was beautiful, but looking at it all, Liam felt uneasy. It was like he was looking at something hopelessly fragile, like a sculpture made of stained glass. They had beaten the Empire today, but it couldn't last. The Empire would come back.

Leon Albrent and his contingent had been conspicuously missing from the group at the barracks, and Liam had the feeling that they weren't the only ones. And there were guards in the city, in the outposts and even in their homes in the Imperial Quarter. If any of them, even one, had made it to the docks before the Resistance could catch them, if any of them had gotten on a ship and escaped, they would be in Aelria in weeks. And once the news was out, the Empire would come.

They were living on borrowed time. This city, maybe even the whole world. His memories from Roth had settled into dull impressions, fragments of the past that were already fading rapidly, as if he had just woken up from a dream. But it was hard to forget the memory of that thing in the Wastes, that ravenous void. He didn't know what role the Empire and the Weavers played in all that—Roth's memories had not been entirely clear—but the vague impressions he had were enough to turn his stomach. There was something happening here, something bigger than Leithon, something bigger than all of them.

"It's amazing, isn't it?" Cavar asked from beside him.

Liam jumped—he had almost forgotten that Cavar was there. The Weaver looked a little worse for wear, but the injury Kesi had dealt him hadn't been as damaging as Kesi's drawing on Kaolin's life force. Cavar was up and walking again, and although he looked like he could sleep for a week, there was a faint smile on his face as he looked at the scenes unfolding around him. Liam felt again that touch of unease, of discomfort—couldn't everyone else see what was happening? But Cavar was smiling as if the city's victory was his own, and Liam felt a little ashamed of himself. A foreigner could celebrate his city's victory, but all his thoughts were bleak, focused on the future.

He tried to smile and thought that he succeeded, that same smile that he had spent hours practicing in front of the mirror.

"It is," he said. "How are you feeling?"

"I'm alive. That's the important part," Cavar said. He looked out at the scenes around them one more time, and the smile faded from his face, replaced by something darker and more thoughtful. He shook his head, like he was coming up from underwater, and said, "I need to start thinking about what I'm going to do next, though. That won't be easy."

You and me both, Liam thought, but on the outside, he said, "Do you have any ideas?"

"I'll have to head back to the Wastes eventually," Cavar said. "Mother will need my report, and Linna—" He hesitated. "Linna should have her rites. But I have to admit, I'm interested in how this will turn out." He lifted his gaze, looking at the Spire. The renewed Spire, taking up its place in Leithon's skyline. The other Spire, Kesi's Spire, had been brought down by Arian at some point in the night. The smile was back, and Liam realized at that moment that Cavar was not seeing the present celebration, but the future, and the future he saw was so much warmer and brighter than any Liam could bring himself to imagine.

He felt cold, on the inside as well as out. But Cavar would never be able to see that, of course. Liam had learned very early on that people never understood what was happening inside his head, unless he made a special effort to communicate in a way that they could comprehend. And he hadn't dropped his smile.

"Can you make it to the ossuary on your own?" he asked. "I need to take care of a few things here."

He didn't, truly, but Liam didn't think he could carry on this conversation for much longer. But even as he spoke, Zephyr's face popped into his mind, and Liam realized that he hadn't had a chance to speak to her since the revolution began. The moment in the tower while they waited for Arian to return and Kaolin to wake didn't count. They had both been waiting to see whether the spirit that woke in Kaolin's body would be him or Kesi, and whether they would need to kill him.

There were so many things between them that were left unsaid.

He said goodbye to Cavar, who promised that he would be able to make it back to the ossuary by himself, and walked back into the Bastion.

Finding Zephyr wasn't difficult. He asked for directions from members of the Leithonian contingent, and they led him eventually to Selwald's office. In contrast to the mess in the courtyard, the room looked untouched. A pile of papers on the desk looked gently rummaged through, as if Selwald had been reviewing files before he was called away. The Aelrian banners on the walls had yet to be taken down. Entering this room made the scene in the courtyard seem like a dream, a product of an overactive imagination. Even the sounds of celebration were deadened, coming in through the keep's thick stone walls.

He found Zephyr standing alone in the middle of the room, her eyes on a landscape painting on the wall. A pastoral scene of fields and distant mountains—a common representation, Liam knew, of the Aelrian countryside. She was still dressed in her armor, but she had taken off her shield. It rested on the ground beside her.

"Zeph," Liam said softly to get her attention.

Zephyr jumped, and her eyes went wide as she turned to face him. "Liam!" she said. "Is Kaolin okay? I mean—are you—?"

She trailed off, looking embarrassed, but the damage had been done. He was thankful that he had spoken to Cavar before this. He had no problem returning to his fake smile. But that didn't seem to put her at ease, and Liam remembered that Zephyr had always been very skilled at separating his fake smiles from his real ones. The ones that didn't reach his eyes—whatever that was supposed to mean.

"Lord Kaolin will survive," he said. "He was still asleep when I left the barracks, but the surgeon thinks he will wake soon."

"I—" Zephyr looked away, wrapping her arms tight around herself. Her shoulders heaved as she took a breath, and when she turned back toward him, her expression was steadier. "That's good. We'll need him to negotiate with the Empire."

She wasn't fooling anyone, least of all him. Liam looked at her, framed in the center of that crowded office, and for the first time in a long time, he allowed himself to think of the future. Not the future of the world and the fate of empires, but his own future. A future where Arian was the Speaker of the Arcanum, and Zephyr defended Leithon against the Empire, and everything moved along just fine without him.

What could he do if he wasn't tied to this city? To them? Who could he become?

He realized, standing in that doorway, that he had already made his decision. That all of this had been him trying to reconcile that to himself, to accept what he had chosen to do.

He smiled, a real smile this time, and said, "You'll have your work cut out for you, then."

Zephyr heard what he was saying, the truth he had hidden in his words. She turned to look at him, her eyes wide, and for a second she looked lost, forlorn. He was surprised how little that made him want to change his mind.

"What do you mean?" Zephyr asked. "You won't be here with us?"

"Arian will be here," he said. "And you." And Cavar too, Liam thought, if he had his way. "The two of you are more than capable of seeing this through."

"And you? Where will you go?"

Where? That was an interesting question. He had an idea, but it was one that was still so new, so fragile in his mind that he was afraid to speak it in case he accidentally destroyed it. So instead, he spoke another truth, one that felt firmer, safer and more real.

"I think . . . I'm going to go see the world."

CHAPTER 73

ZEPHYR

WHEN THE SUN DAWNED, BRIGHT AND SCORCHING, THE ROYAL standard was flying from the top of the Bastion's highest tower. That, coupled with the white form of the Spire in the distance, made it almost possible to believe that the last four years had been a dream, that the Empire had never visited Leithon's shores.

Looking out the window of Commander Selwald's former office, Zephyr almost believed it.

But then she remembered the city's scars, remembered the murder of the king and queen and the exile of the royal family. Remembered the dead.

The parties in the courtyard continued long after Liam left, until at last, exhausted revelers started to make their way home. Zephyr watched them go, numb with weariness. The city was still smoking from the fires of war, the streets muddy with soot and other filth from the rain, and the Bastion's courtyards filled with the rubble that Arian had pulled down from Kesi's tower.

It could have been so much worse. If Kesi had had his way, the streets would have been empty, its residents either absorbed into the Star or cowering in fear for their lives from an unimaginable magical power.

But in the end, Leithon had taken back her independence in a "peaceful" uprising, and those who were left had to deal with the consequences—the barracks full to bursting with Imperial prisoners and the shadow of the Empire hanging over them.

Those who were left had to pull themselves together and rebuild.

Zephyr's first step had been to check on the Leithonian contingent. While the members of her group hadn't been imprisoned the same way their Imperial counterparts had been, they were still reviled by the populace. She knew that many people thought they were even worse than Imperials, because they were from Leithon.

She left the Leithonian contingent with orders to protect the Bastion and guard the prisoners, and then went to speak with the leaders of the Resistance to discuss the prisoners' fate. Lyndon, Arian's former mentor, was there, but he wasn't the only one. While the Resistance was an underground movement, it had several legitimate backers, many of whom had occupied positions of power in Leithon before the fall.

Those people were considerably less welcoming than she would have liked, but all of them had made compromises during the occupation, and none of them were innocent. They had given her a seat at the table. That meeting revealed several grim facts. Leithon was simply not ready to stand up against Imperial retribution. There was talk of leveraging the Arcanum against the Empire, now that they had control of that again, but Zephyr hadn't been the only one to notice that Arian had absented herself from the meeting. She had retreated to the Spire at some point in the night, saying that she had a lot of things to think about.

The next year looked bleak, but for the moment, they were free. The problem was what they would do with their prisoners. A handful suggested killing them all, making an example out of them. Cooler heads prevailed. Commander Selwald and Lord Kaolin had surrendered, and to break that faith would make them worse criminals than the Empire. But at the same time, Leithon could scarcely afford to house all of them.

In the end, they decided to release quite a few. Except those who were too valuable, those who needed to stay behind.

Zephyr left the meeting pensive. Her body felt sore, weighed down by her armor. She'd have to take it off soon, return it to the armory until the next time it was needed. She glanced down at herself, wondering if she, like the other members of her contingent, should change into Leithonian blue. But Leithon's colors didn't fit on her either. She'd lost the right to wear them, somehow. She still didn't know what she stood for, *who* she stood for.

She wasn't sure she would ever know.

Her feet carried her to the Imperial barracks before she knew what she was doing, walking past the sentries stationed outside. People called to her when they saw her, many of them shouting insults, some of them trying to curry favor. She ignored them all, walking past until she reached the infirmary.

Kaolin was there, awake now, lying in bed and staring at the ceiling. He still looked weak, but some of the color had returned to his face. He turned toward her as she took the empty chair beside him.

"Well?" he asked.

Zephyr blinked at him. "Well, what?"

"You look like the bearer of bad news," said Kaolin. "I'm assuming the provisional government has decided what it wants to do with us. Am I to be executed or exiled?"

"Neither. You're to be a 'guest of state.'"

"A hostage, then," said Kaolin, nodding. "To keep the Empire at bay. Not as bad as I expected. Selwald as well?"

"And a few other elites."

Kaolin considered that for a moment, lying in bed, head tilted toward the ceiling. "If you like," he said, "I could give you names. There are certain families the Empire values more than others. An outsider is hardly likely to know."

Zephyr stared at him, taken aback. "Why would you do that for us?"

Kaolin shrugged. "Who knows?" he asked. "Maybe I *have* developed some attachment to this city. Or maybe I've known for a long time that being sent here wasn't a gift from my father, but a curse. He couldn't have planned the way things would turn out, but he knew full well that the situation in Leithon wasn't stable. He wanted me in the center of whatever would happen here, and I bet he wanted Roth to help make it happen. He wanted me to die, or at least to be lost to him forever."

"Why would your father want you dead?" Zephyr asked, surprised.

"Because I'm a very troublesome heir," said Kaolin, offering her a smile. "I wanted to make something of Leithon, to spite him. But it seems Leithon is quite intent on making something out of itself. I'm willing to help where I can, but given all of that, I'm afraid I'd make a poor hostage. So, names."

"You're going to betray your nation to spite your father?" Zephyr asked.

Kaolin's expression grew grave. "I've seen who we are. I've seen what we can do. That's reason enough. Do you have a sheet of paper?"

"Yes," said Zephyr, fumbling for the small notepad and pencil that she kept in the pouch at her waist.

"If I were you," said Kaolin, "I'd start with Lord Valkmir. He's a minor member of his own house, but his family is closely connected to the Emperor. Then I would consider Lady Aubries. After that . . ."

CHAPTER 74

CAVAR

CAVAR FOUND ARIAN ON THE NEW SPIRE'S BALCONY, LOOKING out at the city. In the light of day, Leithon looked transformed, sunlight glinting off the sea in the distance, the royal standard hanging proud from the Bastion. From this height, there was almost no sign of the previous night's revolution. But the scars of Imperial occupation were there, in the broken-down buildings and the sections of the city given over to decay. In the fortifications around the ports and the dejected shuffle of people in the streets. It would take a long time for Leithon to forget the past four years, assuming the Empire gave them the chance.

Arian stood with her back to Cavar, her fingers closed around the balcony's railing and the wind blowing through her hair as she looked out over the city. She was dressed in a loose-fitting white blouse, a pair of dark trousers, and soft leather boots, knives strapped to her sides. More warrior than mage. But there was a subtle presence about her, a shift of power in the air. A reminder that it would be unwise to underestimate her.

She knew that he was here. It would be impossible for her not to. But he cleared his throat anyway, alerting her to his presence before he stepped out on the balcony. Arian didn't look back, but she did shift over, opening up the space beside her. He took the offered space, resting his arms on the railing and looking out over the city.

"Nice day, isn't it?" he said.

Arian didn't respond immediately. He watched her face, seeing the emotions play out behind her eyes, her fingers flexing and curling around the railing. She opened her mouth, letting out a long sigh.

"I never thought I'd see this view again," she said.

"Leithon?"

Arian shook her head. "Leithon from the Spire," she said. "When my mother died, I was devastated. We had our differences, but nobody wants that to happen."

"But?" Cavar prompted.

"But when the Spire was destroyed . . . I was . . . a little relieved. I thought I was free. And then I hated myself for it."

"You never wanted this power."

"I never wanted this *responsibility*," Arian countered, looking down at her hands. "Or any responsibility."

"We can't spend our lives running from responsibility. It'll catch up to us sooner or later."

"I know," Arian said. "Believe me, I know. But I could have done without this one."

Cavar didn't say anything to that for a few long moments, looking out at the horizon. The two of them stood there in silence, watching the fishing boats in the distance.

"So," Cavar said. "What happens now?"

Arian let out a long sigh. "A few mages popped up here and there. People in hiding like Liam. They saw the Arcanum coming back and figured they'd share in the fun. They know more magic than me, so I'm going to put them in charge of training novices. Maybe I'll take a few classes of my own. Feels like something I should know."

"And is Liam coming back?"

Arian shrugged. "Who knows? He's an adult. He can do whatever he wants."

There was an edge to her voice that suggested there might be more to the story, some meaning that could only be deciphered by a sibling. Cavar decided against pressing the issue. It wasn't his place.

And he didn't have time to ask, because Arian had turned the question back onto him.

"What about you?" she asked. "What's next for you?"

"I . . ."

Cavar took a breath, wondering how to phrase his answer. Arian's face fell. She hid it well, but he noticed it in the way her eyes dropped, pulling away from his to focus somewhere on the ground between them.

"You can say it. You're going back to the Wastes."

"Only for a little while," said Cavar. "I have to report in. And . . . there are rites. For Linna."

The name hung in the air between them, and Cavar saw a flash of pain in Arian's eyes before she turned away.

"I'm sorry about her," Arian said. "I know the two of you were close."

"Linna . . ." There was a heaviness in Cavar's voice that he couldn't shake, a tightness in his throat. "Linna knew what she was doing. She knew there was a chance she wouldn't make it out alive."

"Doesn't make it hurt less."

"No," Cavar agreed. "It doesn't."

"So . . ." Arian said, shoulders tensing like she was bracing herself for bad news. "You go back home. Tell your mother what happened, bury Linna. And then what?"

"I imagine they'll want someone to monitor the situation in Leithon," said Cavar. "And they'll want to make sure the Star is in good hands. You're keeping it, right?"

Arian touched the jewel at her throat with one gloved hand. "It's mine. It's doubly mine, on both sides of my family. I have that right."

"You do," said Cavar. "So, when the council decides they want to send one or two Weavers to check on what's happening in Leithon, I intend to volunteer."

"How long will you be gone?" Arian asked.

"I don't know," Cavar said honestly. "Months, probably. I intend to come back within the year, with or without the council's approval."

Arian exhaled, letting out a long breath. "Well," she said. "We'll make sure the city's still standing when you get back."

"Yes," Cavar said, his eyes alighting on the Bastion, on the Leithonian banner that flew from its standard. "I imagine you will."

"While you're in the Wastes," said Arian, "can you do me a favor?"

"Your father?"

Arian nodded.

"Let the old man know what happened, and give him a smack upside the head for me," said Arian. "Tell him that, you know, if it isn't too much trouble, his kids would like him to visit." She paused. "Well, his daughter anyway. I can't speak for the other one."

"I was thinking," Cavar said, "that if he consents, I'll drag him back with me."

"If he doesn't consent," Arian said, "I know a few potent sleeping poisons."

Cavar smiled. "Weavers are immune to most poisons. Part of our training."

"Of course," said Arian, rolling her eyes. "Fine, then. When are you leaving?"

"I'll stay to see how things shake out," Cavar said. "Maybe another day or two. But I'd like to leave before the end of the week."

"Probably for the best," said Arian. "Get out of here before the Empire decides we're too much trouble and they want to burn the whole thing down."

Cavar offered her a wry smile. "I'd like to think it would be more difficult than that."

"I'll make it more difficult," Arian promised.

Cavar glanced at her, brows raised, and wondered if he should ask about the city's future plans. But the look on Arian's face stopped him. Now wasn't the time. He said nothing, waiting for her to speak.

Eventually, she did.

"And after you come back? What will you do then?"

The silence stretched on between them. Cavar looked out at the blue sea in the distance, the sunlight reflecting off the surface of the water. He sighed.

"I don't know."

Arian let out the breath she was holding, her shoulders slumping with the motion. Cavar braced himself for whatever she was about to say next.

"I remember when my dad would come to visit," she said. "When Liam and I were kids. He'd stay for a couple of weeks, maybe three or four times a year. A couple of times, he managed to stay for months. But he always left again. And I saw how much that hurt my mom. I don't want that kind of life. Not even with you."

"I understand," Cavar said. "You can't leave Leithon."

"And you can't leave the Weavers."

"*Can't* is a strong word."

Arian stared at him.

"Don't," she said, eyes narrowing.

"Don't what?"

"Don't make promises you can't keep. Don't go saying you'll leave the Weavers for me. You barely even know me."

Cavar looked back out over the city. "I'm not saying that I will. Only that I can. I . . . have a lot of thinking to do. And I can't really work through all this right now. Let me go home. Let me bury my friend and talk to my mother. When I come back, I'll know more about what I will and won't do."

"*When* you come back."

"Yes," said Cavar. "*When.*"

She sighed, looking out at the sea. "I guess I can live with that."

Cavar turned his head toward her, a smile tugging at the corner of his mouth. He was about to say something more when he caught sight of something moving, glinting in the sunlight. A metal bird flew toward Arian, perching on the hand she stretched out toward it.

It was a kingfisher, exquisitely crafted. In its beak, it carried a piece of paper. Arian plucked the paper from it with the fingers of her other hand, her expression resigned. The bird spread its wings and leaped, taking off from her finger, and Arian tucked the paper away into her pocket without reading it.

"What was that?" Cavar asked, watching as the bird shrank to a point and vanished.

"Liam," said Arian. "Being a pain in my side. As usual."

"What do you mean?"

"What do you think I mean?" asked Arian. "He's gone. Just when we needed him around the most." She turned on her heel, walking back into the Spire. "Well, whatever. He can do what he wants. The rest of us have work to do."

CHAPTER 75

LIAM

THERE WERE A SURPRISING NUMBER OF BOATS LEAVING LEITHON in the wake of the revolution. Liam supposed that if you had a boat, leaving the island before the Empire came back to reclaim it was probably the sensible choice. It seemed cowardly to him, but considering that he was leaving as well, he didn't have much room to talk.

He stood on the deck of a merchant ship leaving Leithon at speed, hand outstretched toward a metal bird, flying back to him. Its beak was empty, which meant that Arian had received his message.

It also meant that she hadn't sent anything back.

Liam sighed, withdrawing some of the magic from the bird so that it became an ordinary figurine once more. He placed it in his pocket, watching the city fade into the distance.

The message had been coded in the cipher the two of them used to send messages to each other, when such messages were necessary. It had been short. He hadn't found the words to explain himself, to tell her why he had chosen this.

He had always hated goodbyes. It was cowardly, doing it this way. But he knew that if he saw Arian now, seated in the Spire, they would fight. He wouldn't be able to hold himself back, his jealousy and his anger and all those restless feelings inside him that he had always pushed away.

He would hurt her if he stayed. And so, he had to go.

He'd known it was true from the moment he stood in that office with Zephyr and considered the fact that he didn't belong in this city anymore. Not with everything he had learned, everything he had done. In the end, Arian and Zephyr and Cavar had faced down Kesi, rescued Lord Kaolin, and paved the way for the revolution.

All Liam had done was kill someone. Someone who was already dead, true, but he'd done it not to rid the world of a wight, but for revenge.

"It's something, isn't it?" someone next to him asked.

Liam jumped, startled. A man stood next to him, eyes on the Bastion where Leithon's blue standard hung proud. He was one of the senior merchants of the company that owned the ship, a grizzled man in his middle years.

"I never thought I'd see it again," the man said, indicating the flag. "When the Empire came calling, we jumped ship and set off for neutral waters. I always thought this city was done for. Maybe I was wrong." He sighed, eyeing Liam. "If I had my way, I wouldn't run off again, but—" He gestured at the ship behind him. "—the boss says the market's too volatile to stay. What he really means is that we don't want to get caught between the rebels and the Empire. Maybe if things settle down, we'll come back."

Liam didn't respond immediately, turning his head to study the whole of the city. The pennant streaming from the tower, the white stone of the Spire. From this distance, it looked whole and complete. It looked like *home*.

He felt it inside him, a longing. Suddenly, more than anything, he wanted to *be* there. He wanted to jump off this ship and swim to shore. Anything to make sure that he was there in the streets of Leithon, watching the city come alive.

But there was no place for him there. Not anymore.

The merchant caught Liam looking at the Spire and gave the staff in his hand a cool, appraising look. "Now that's telling. You wouldn't see anyone walking around carrying a staff in the Empire's day."

There was something more than curiosity in the statement. Something probing. Liam saw the man's narrowed eyes and held his staff closer.

"It was hard after the Arcanum was destroyed," Liam said. "The few of us who remained didn't want to get caught, so we hid. Or fled."

"So why leave now?"

The words cut him. Liam's mouth twisted and his grip tightened on his staff. The city faded farther into the distance.

"Maybe I'm just waiting to see which way the wind blows. Same as you."

"Maybe," the merchant said. "Guess I can't really blame you." He let out a long sigh. "So, where are we taking you?"

"Paran," Liam said. "If it's not too much trouble, drop me off in Paran."

And from Paran westward, into the wilderness. Into the unknown territory in the center of the map, the long stretch of land ruled by no one where the Weavers schemed and plotted the fate of the world. A mysterious society with its own agenda, the details of which had only vaguely been revealed to him. Where something waited, hungry in the dark, something terrifying enough scare a man who had already come back from the dead.

He looked up, watching the city fade away, feeling the cold weight of the staff in his hand. He didn't know what his plans were, where he was going to go from here.

But the Wastes would be a good place to start.

END

ACKNOWLEDGMENTS

This book wouldn't have come to print without the help of a lot of people, especially my editor, Rachel, who helped me sort through four POVs and streamline the original draft into this final version. Thank you to everyone at Swoon Reads and Feiwel and Friends who worked on this book, including Jean Feiwel, Lauren Scobell, Celeste Cass, Arik Hardin, and Dawn Ryan. Thank you also to Sarah Gonzales, who illustrated the cover and brought the world of Leithon to life, and to all the Swoon readers who read the initial manuscript and decided that this needed to be on shelves.

Stolen City's story began a long time ago, when two girls came up with four characters and decided to spend most of their high school years dreaming up stories about them. Arian, Liam, Zephyr, Cavar, and many of their friends have come mostly unaltered from this time of my life, and would not have come into existence without Benjie Girl "Tweety" Martinez. Thank you for still being my best friend, and for trusting me with these characters and their adventures.

When I first wrote Stolen City, I submitted it to Pitch Wars. Although I ultimately didn't get selected as a mentee, Ian Barnes and Laura Lashley gave me great feedback that helped me revise the manuscript. Their belief that Stolen City would be on shelves someday helped me believe in this project too. Thanks also go to the Post-PW Writers' Group of 2018. While I wasn't as active in the group as I would have liked to be, I really appreciate your encouragement and support. Parts of Stolen City were originally drafted during National Novel Writing Month, and so special thanks also go to Chris Baty and the NaNoWriMo team.

As a writer, I am part of a community, and I couldn't have gotten through the challenges of the past few years without the help and support of my peers. Thank you to the Swoon Squad, 22Debuts, and the Class of 2k22. Many of these people helped me with both *Dauntless* and *Stolen City* and I can't thank them enough. I would especially like to thank Caris Avendaño Cruz and Sam Taylor for reaching out to me during a very difficult time. You are a ray of sunshine, Caris; thank you so much. Sam, I really appreciated the check-in. Thank you for taking the time to talk to me. Special thanks also to Laura Rueckert, for all the information about how to be an author in Germany while publishing books in the United States. Thank you for sharing your research with me.

Thank you also to my family for continuing to support me. To Mom, Tata, and Isa, and to everyone who believed in me. And thank you, Rob, for all your help. I couldn't have gotten through it alone.

To Mamá, I'm sorry that you never got to see these books come out. Thank you for always believing in me and my dreams, and for never doubting that this day would come. Rest in peace. I love you.

21982320475159